Praise for Rebecca

'Rebecca Chance is a fabulous storyteller. These novels will keep you reading long after you should have turned off your light'   Charlaine Harris, author of the
'True Blood' series of Sookie Stackhouse novels

'Edgy, cheeky, knowing . . . Rebecca Chance sparkles'
Adele Parks

'This is a pacy read, dripping in diamonds, stuffed full of sex and most definitely not for prudes. It's occasionally outrageous and always entertaining'   *Daily Mail*

'If you're a fan of Jilly Cooper, you'll LOVE Rebecca Chance'
Vina Jackson

'Family secrets, revenge, diamonds and lots and lots of saucy scenes. What's not to love?'   *Sun*

'Sizzles with glamour, romance and revenge. Unputdownable. A glittering page-turner . . . had me hooked from the first page'   Louise Bagshawe

'With lies, theft and even murder, *Killer Diamonds* sizzles with glamour, romance and revenge!'   *OK!*

'If you're looking for a beach read, this saucy satire on reality-TV culture is perfect'   *Sunday Mirror*

'This one will have you glued to the sun-lounger'
Cosmopolitan

Bad Twins

Rebecca Chance is the pseudonym under which Lauren Henderson writes bonkbusters. Under her own name, she has written seven detective novels in her Sam Jones mystery series and three romantic comedies. Her non-fiction book *Jane Austen's Guide to Dating* has been optioned as a feature film, and her four-book young adult mystery series, published in the US, is Anthony-nominated. As Rebecca Chance, she has written the *Sunday Times* bestselling bonkbusters *Divas*, *Bad Girls*, *Bad Sisters*, *Killer Heels*, *Bad Angels*, *Killer Queens*, *Bad Brides*, *Mile High*, *Killer Diamonds*, *Killer Affair* and now *Bad Twins*, which feature her signature mix of social satire, racy sex and rollercoaster thriller plots. Rebecca also writes for many major publications, including the *Telegraph*, the *Guardian*, *Cosmopolitan* and *Grazia*.

Born in London, she has lived in Tuscany and New York, and she travels extensively to research glamorous locations for the books. She is now settled in London, where she lives with her husband. Her website is www.rebeccachanceauthor.com. She has a devoted following on social media: you can find her on Facebook as Rebecca.Chance.Author, and on Twitter and Instagram as @MsRebeccaChance. Her interests include cocktail-drinking, men's gymnastics and the *Real Housewives* series.

By Rebecca Chance

Divas
Bad Girls
Bad Sisters
Killer Heels
Bad Angels
Killer Queens
Bad Brides
Mile High
Killer Diamonds
Killer Affair
Bad Twins

Bad Twins

REBECCA CHANCE

PAN BOOKS

First published 2018 by Pan Books
an imprint of Pan Macmillan
20 New Wharf Road, London N1 9RR
Associated companies throughout the world
www.panmacmillan.com

ISBN 978-1-5098-5799-9

1 3 5 7 9 8 6 4 2

A CIP catalogue record for this book is available from the British Library.

Typeset in Minion Pro by Palimpsest Book Production Limited, Falkirk, Stirlingshire
Printed and bound by CPI Group (UK) Ltd, Croydon, CR0 4YY

Visit www.panmacmillan.com to read more about all our books
and to buy them. You will also find features, author interviews and
news of any author events, and you can sign up for e-newsletters
so that you're always first to hear about our new releases.

For the brains trust who polished the outline for me:
Randon Burns, who kindly informed me who the
heroine of the book actually was, and Michael Devine,
who brainstormed a crucial plot point with me.
Minds like steel traps, both of them!

And for Michael Coggin-Carr,
a dear friend and truly lovely person.

PART ONE

Chapter One

Jeffrey Sachs was neither a politician nor a ruling monarch, but when he issued an urgent summons to his presence, you obeyed. You jumped up from your Michelin three-star restaurant table, off the cross-trainer, out of bed with your lover; you told your chauffeur to turn around your limo, your pilot to alter the route your private plane was currently taking, your assistant to charter a helicopter. Whether you were a media tycoon, a Saudi prince, a Russian oligarch or a prime minister, you came when he called.

And if you were an underling, working for one of the many companies he owned, as you rushed to your meeting with him you were in a cold sweat of fear, scrambling desperately to work out why you had been ordered to his presence. Because this unprecedented command meant that the meeting was bound to be life-changing. All you could do was pray as hard as possible that it would be positive.

The four employees who were converging on Jeffrey Sachs's mansion in Maida Vale for the appointed time of three in the afternoon were his ultimate underlings: his children. They had been trained from birth to anticipate what he wanted from them even before he voiced the words, four little von Trapps who didn't need the whistle to get in line.

So when an Aston Martin DB11 bounced over the bridge that spanned the Regent's Canal, screeched around the corner of Warwick Avenue, hit the brakes, and reversed almost as fast into an achingly tight parking space, its driver was perfectly well aware that his other three siblings would already be sitting in their own cars, watching their phones tick the seconds away until a few minutes to three, at which point they would converge on the electric gates between two huge white colonnaded pillars set in the perfectly main-tained hedge that ran around the mansion. The four of them had not convened previously to discuss why they thought their father had called this very unusual family meeting. Jeffrey Sachs had played the game of divide and conquer with his children so successfully that sibling solidarity was non-existent.

'For fuck's sake, Bart!'

The driver of the vehicle parked directly behind the Aston Martin, a Jaguar SUV, leapt out and slammed the door furi-ously.

'You're practically up my exhaust pipe!' he shouted at the Aston Martin's driver. 'Do you *know* how much this cost?'

'God, Con, be cool,' drawled his brother Bart, sliding out of the seat of his sports car with snake-hipped ease. 'Don't be all . . . uncool.'

'You're a centimetre away from my bumper, you careless fuckwit! You nearly hit me!'

'But I didn't, did I? You know, years ago in St Moritz, I accidentally shunted this German chappie in a top-of-the-range Audi,' Bart informed his brother, his tone relaxed as he recounted the anecdote. 'Not a big shunt, but I definitely shoved him through the snow a bit. I was terribly sorry, of course – jumped out and told him I'd pay for any damage. D'you know what he did?'

'I hope he called you a twat and punched you in the face!' his brother Conway snapped. 'I'm close to doing that myself!'

'He got out,' Bart continued cheerfully, not a whit intimidated, 'walked around his car and had a squint at the back of it. Then he looked at me – huge chappie, good head taller than me, they breed them really big in Deutschland – and said, completely stone-faced: "Zis is not a problem. Zis is vot bumpers are for." Never forgot that. You need to take that attitude yourself, Con. Bit of Germanic calm'd do you the world of good.'

Visibly struggling to control himself, his jaw muscles clenching as he ground his teeth, Conway turned away from his brother, dragging his key fob from his jacket pocket to lock the SUV.

'You two! You never change, do you?' commented a woman's voice behind them, her high heels clicking onto the pavement as she swung both legs out of the back seat of her Range Rover, her knees pressed together as if she were an actress or a model surrounded by crouching paparazzi keen to direct their lenses up her skirt. She gave a nod of thanks to the driver, who had come around to open the door for her, and shook out her wonderfully thick mane of streaked blonde hair with a swift, practised move that settled her curls into the perfect shape into which they had been tonged by her hairdresser half an hour ago.

'Honestly,' Charlotte Sachs said dismissively to her brothers, 'you'll be in your nineties and still going at each other as if you were fighting about who gets to play with the Scalextric limited-edition Bentley, or whatever it was back then. When *actually*, we should all be worrying about what the hell Daddy's playing at, sending for all four of us on such short notice! He never does this!'

Unnoticed across the street, Jeffrey Sachs's other daughter, Bella, climbed out of her own car, a sensible Audi saloon which was quite overshadowed by the Aston Martin, the Jaguar SUV, and the Range Rover. Glancing over at Charlotte, Bella realized that her sister was clearly fresh from the Nicky Clarke salon on Carlos Place.

The way the two daughters had reacted to their father's summons, a call from his personal assistant which had come in a couple of hours ago, had been entirely typical of their respective characters. Bella had spent the time holed up in her office, frantically passing in review as many of her current and recent projects as she could, while Charlotte had rung up Nicky Clarke and insisted he shoehorn her in for an emergency appointment. To Bella's extreme frustration, Charlotte appeared not just perfectly groomed but superbly confident, much more prepared than her sister for a crucial, once-in-a-lifetime meeting with their father.

Because Charlotte was carrying herself with the assurance of a woman who had enough sway for Nicky Clarke himself to do her hair on such short notice, and who knew that the two-hundred-pound blow-dry made her look like a million dollars. By contrast, Bella was the sturdy workhorse to her sister's show pony. Bella reached a hand up to hook her shoulder-length hair behind her ear, gloomily aware that the best she could hope for was that it be neat and tidy. Meanwhile, Bart exclaimed wistfully, quite ignoring the last part of Charlotte's comment:

'That Scalextric! God, I was obsessed with it for years!'

His eyes were misty with memory. For a moment, he looked exactly like the small boy who had adored his racing cars. In many ways, he still was that small boy: impulse-driven, greedy, and highly skilled at coaxing others to give him what he wanted.

'Remember my 1970s McLaren Formula Ones, Con?' he continued, oblivious to his brother's scowl. 'I practically took them to bed with me every night.'

It would have been instantly obvious to any observer that the four of them were siblings. The family resemblance was extremely strong. They were all blond and fair, colouring they inherited from their mother who, though American, had entirely German family origins. Christie had been a model for years, famous for her extraordinary cornflower-blue eyes; like hers, her children's irises were unusually large, which made their eyes seem almost otherworldly, flooded with intense colour.

As children they had all been angelically flaxen-haired, which had added to the unearthly impression. Bart's tousled locks, more like a surfer's than a businessman's, were still sun-kissed, though their bright gold, like Charlotte's, owed more to art than to nature. Charlotte's exquisite layers of pale caramel to gilt were hand-painted every two months using a technique called balayage; Bella never seemed to have time for the colourist, and her hair was the exact shade that Charlotte's would have looked had she left it untouched, a soft, light golden brown. Since Bella's husband preferred the natural look, however, she was perfectly fine leaving it as it was.

That decision, however, always weakened when she saw Charlotte again. It wasn't just the hair. Since the sisters were identical twins, Bella was the living example of how Charlotte would have looked had she never gone to the gym, hired a dietician and nutritionist, seen her personal trainer three times a week, taken Yogalates classes or had both a breast and a nose job. Even when the twins were small, Bella had felt that she was a distorting mirror version of Charlotte: plumper, dowdier, less toned, half a step behind, her demeanour anxious where Charlotte's was coolly confident.

As soon as they could toddle, Jeffrey had joked that he could tell that Charlotte had been born first. Charlotte was quicker-witted, with a tremendous need for attention and an instinct for grabbing the spotlight. As the girls grew up, Charlotte was the one with the innate sense of style, spending a great deal of time choosing her outfits every morning. Bella had swiftly given up any attempt to compete. Better to be different than a weaker copy of her five-minutes-older sister. At least this way she had her own identity, even if it meant being cast as the shy, retiring, quiet one.

So Bella was the overlooked child, the one who could be absent from a room without anyone noticing, the one who put her head down and got on with work. She was the only one of the four to take a first-class degree at university, though that was attributed by her father to her being a plodder, rather than her having superior brainpower. Even now, she noticed, her siblings had formed into a triangle, albeit a grumpy one. Conway was telling Bart to shut up about his bloody Formula One Scalextric cars, Charlotte was mocking Bart's childishness, but none of them were looking around for Bella, the least important, the second violin in the quartet.

She was used to it. But it never stopped hurting.

'It's two minutes to three, everyone,' she said as she crossed the street, and then wondered why she had bothered. Why she was acting as a sort of personal assistant to her more glamorous siblings, rounding them up, when they were all in their thirties and perfectly well able to check the time on their extremely expensive watches?

The trio turned to look at her, almost surprised at hearing a fourth voice. The men could have been Ralph Lauren models in designer business wear, dark suits of which they knew Jeffrey would approve. Bart, in a form-fitted purple shirt intended to be worn without a tie, was dashing and rakish, but Conway, with his smoothed-back hair, immaculate suit and crisp white shirt, was the picture of a handsome but conventional executive, the sexy, buttoned-up boss who starred in a thousand soft-porn fantasies.

'Hey, sis!' Bart bounded over to hug Bella. 'Looking good! This is bloody weird, eh? What the hell's going on, d'you think?'

He had an easy compliment for every woman he met, and every recipient blossomed into a delighted smile at the words: whether they were sister, administrative assistant, CEO or prime minister, no female was immune to his boyish charm and the sincerity in his periwinkle-blue eyes. Because Bart meant every word of every compliment he paid. He adored women, and they returned that emotion even more fervently.

'Hi, Bart,' Bella said, glowing happily at the embrace. He smelt wonderful, as always, his body hard and muscled under the expensive suit.

She pressed the gate bell, heard Maria the housekeeper respond. It was a voice as familiar to the children as that of their mother and father, possibly even more. Maria had been working for Jeffrey Sachs for over thirty years, but her accent was still as strong as ever; she barely spoke English apart from at work, as she lived in the Portuguese stronghold along the Golborne Road, twenty minutes away on the borders of Notting Hill. So many of her fellow immigrants had opened businesses there that it was quite possible to speak Portuguese the entire time.

'It's us, Maria,' Bella said, the door buzzing and clicking open even before she had finished.

It was September, and the garden was at peak beauty. It wasn't large by general standards, but for central London it was generous, made to look even more so by the clever, architectural use of perspective, low topiary contrasting with high narrow cypresses and carefully placed statuary. A fountain tinkled gently behind a sculpted wave of lavender and rosemary bushes in which bumblebees were busily buzzing; the lawn was as perfectly manicured as the topiary, a smooth sheet of green which looked as if every single stalk had been measured with a ruler and cut to the same length. The only colours were the soft mauve of the lavender and the textured greens of the foliage. Jeffrey Sachs did not like flowers.

He did not particularly like nature, either. One might have expected to find the owner of this flourishing, immaculately maintained garden to be sitting on the terrace in the sunshine, listening to the softly flowing water and the bees in the rosemary, the lawn flooded with golden light that made the grass glow a deep emerald. His children, however, knew better. They walked up the wide pathway to the white-stuccoed Georgian mansion without even a glance sideways to the sprawling lawn beyond.

'Miss Bella! Miss Charlotte! Mr Conway, Mr Bart! I'm so happy to see you all!'

Maria, short, stout, greying hair pulled back, not a scrap of make-up on her round beaming face, was at the door to greet them. She hugged her employer's children as they came in, not letting each one go until she had wrapped her arms around them for a good ten seconds.

'I never see you no more!' she complained. 'All my babies, and I never see you!'

Their task was to accept her reproaches without protesting, and they knew it. The reasons why Jeffrey Sachs's adult children rarely visited the house in which they had grown up were known to all, and could not be said aloud. Maria embraced Bart last and longest; he was her favourite, naturally, being the baby and the most adorable. She ruffled his hair fondly.

'Always a mess!' she said with a huge smile. 'Always so naughty! You have a girlfriend, Mr Bart?'

'Maria, it's just "Bart"!' he said as he always did, dropping a kiss on her forehead. 'Come on now!'

'He's got twenty girlfriends,' Charlotte said to her reflection in the huge silver-gilt mirror over the marble fireplace as she rearranged her tresses post-hug. 'They all know about the others, but they're all hoping they'll be The One.'

Bart threw his arms wide, grinning bashfully.

'It's Maria's fault!' he said. 'She didn't have a daughter for me to marry! That's the only woman who could make me settle down.'

'How's Ronaldo?' Bella asked, a touch of pink appearing on her cheeks. She had glanced into the mirror once Charlotte had turned away, not wanting to see the direct comparison between herself and her twin sister, and was annoyed now to notice the colour that had blossomed there, the sparkle in her eyes. This always happened when she mentioned Maria's ridiculously handsome son, with whom the children had, to some degree, grown up; Ronaldo had been her first crush, and was still her absolute physical ideal, though she had not seen him since she was a little girl.

'Oh, he is very good, very good! But you must go in,' Maria said nervously, looking up at the huge ebony grandfather clock, which had been chiming as the children walked in. It was already five minutes past the hour. 'Mr Jeffrey don't like to wait.'

Conway huffed out a sarcastic laugh.

'You don't need to tell us that, Maria,' he said, shooting a quick look in the mirror to reassure himself that his tie knot was perfectly centred. Careless, charming Bart, the spoilt playboy of the family, was the only child of Jeffrey Sachs's not to bother to check that his appearance was as immaculate as his father would demand; he strode across the black-and-white-chequered hallway, his heels ringing a tattoo on the marble. Setting his hands to the double doors at the far end, he slid them open simultaneously, pushing them into their recesses. The grooves in which they moved were polished and oiled, so the process was near-soundless, but the effect was undeniably dramatic.

Even more so, however, was Bart's reaction to the sight before him. He stood stock-still as, behind him, his siblings, eager to follow him into the living room and demonstrate to their father that they had been on time, cannoned into his back; they had naturally been expecting him to walk straight in.

'*Well!*' Bart said, unabashedly staring at the woman draped over his father's armchair as elegantly as a swatch of silk velvet in a fabric store which had been expertly thrown out from its roll by the salesperson to show the drape and shimmer of the material. 'This is quite the turn-up for the books! And who might *you* be?'

Chapter Two

The woman returned Bart's stare with an absolutely impassive expression in her long, greenish eyes. She was like a leopard at the zoo, idly regarding the human on the other side of the bars as if Bart were the exhibit, and one for which she could not summon up much interest.

Her perfectly shaped lips did not part to answer his question. He might as well have not uttered a word.

'Come in, come in!' Jeffrey Sachs said irritably. 'What are you doing piling up there in the doorway like the Keystone Cops?'

He was nearly eighty, and he looked it. His American contemporaries were permatanned, dermabraded, their liver spots faded with peels and retinol, their hair awkwardly dyed – it seemed impossible for men of a certain age to dye their hair with any plausibility – their cheeks plumped with fillers. It was an interesting phenomenon that these procedures made them seem barely any younger, just different. One would still have looked at them and evaluated their age more or less accurately.

But they were, perhaps, not aiming for the appearance of eternal youth so much as trying to look less like a memento mori, a reminder of inevitable death. Jeffrey's deep wrinkles, his skin, like thin tissue stretched over bone, the dark patches of sun damage on his face and hands, the sparse white hairs stretched over his scalp, the sagging body in the grey suit that seemed too large for him, all spoke eloquently of the ravages of time.

As did the contrast with the beautiful woman who had one hip propped on the arm of his chair, one arm lying along the back of it, whose skin was as firm and peachy and smooth as Jeffrey's was not. His children, filing into the living room and lining up in front of the armchair, stared at her in frank disbelief. Conway was the last in, and he had turned to pull the sliding doors closed; when he turned back, and got his first clear view of her, he swallowed, his hand going to the knot of his tie in automatic tribute.

None of the children were going to say a word. Why put your head above the parapet if you were likely to get it blown off? Jeffrey had always been scathing if they came out with a statement that he considered blindingly obvious; they had learned the hard way to think before they spoke. Even Bart, the least inhibited of the quartet, limited himself to staring silently at the tumbling chestnut mane, the flawless, tanned skin and the slender yet curvaceous body of the leopard, sheathed in a sleek snake-print silk dress.

'Well? Cat got your tongues?' Jeffrey barked eventually.

Bella knew better than to roll her eyes, or to glance sideways at how her siblings were reacting to this. However, from the restless shifting of their feet, the rustle of their clothing, she was aware that this question had irked her siblings as much as it had her. You were damned if you spoke up, but equally so if you didn't; with a father like Jeffrey, you couldn't win for losing.

'What do you want us to say, Daddy?' asked Charlotte eventually in crisp tones, arching one eyebrow. 'Clearly some major change is under way, and you've summoned us here to show, not tell.'

Jeffrey barked again, but this time it was more like a laugh.

'Well, sit down, sit down!' he commanded, waving one thin, liver-spotted hand. 'What are you all waiting for?'

As they dutifully sank into the long sofa that faced the armchair, the girls on the cushions, the boys on the arms, Bella noticed that the woman draped over Jeffrey's armchair had not moved one iota. It couldn't, she thought, be a particularly comfortable position; she was twisted at the waist, like a model posing for the cameras, not a woman actually reclining comfortably next to her . . . whatever Jeffrey was to her.

'I'm getting a divorce,' Jeffrey announced, a statement that by now came as no surprise to anyone.

'No shit, Sherlock,' muttered Bart irrepressibly.

'How's Jade reacting to this?' Charlotte asked, leaning forward.

'How d'you think?' Jeffrey said, a hint of amusement creeping into his voice now. This was as brusque and strong as ever, belying his frail stature, and it still intimidated Bella as if she were a small child. She wondered if it had the same effect on her siblings. Probably not Bart, she thought; Bart was fairly bulletproof, as he simply didn't have as much to lose. His trust fund was secure, and he had no career ambitions he needed his father to support.

Turning to look at her sister, Bella saw, just as she had expected, that a smile of pure pleasure was lighting up Charlotte's face. Out of the four children, Charlotte hated their stepmother Jade the most. Once Jade had grappled her hooks into Jeffrey, she had swiftly proceeded to alienate him from his children as much as possible. Jeffrey's children were banished from the house along with their mother, forbidden to show up without an invitation, not even to come in through the tradesman's entrance to sit in the kitchen with Maria and have a cup of tea and one of the *pastel de nata* pastries she brought to the house every day from the Lisboa Patisserie on the Golborne Road.

Naturally, those invitations had been very few and far between. Jade had got pregnant almost immediately, the classic gold-digger move to ensure not just alimony but child support and much better accommodation if a divorce should happen. Which, considering that Jeffrey had shown himself vulnerable to gold-diggers by leaving his wife for her, was by no means unlikely . . .

Jade had used the birth of baby Roman, and then baby Brutus, to effectively exclude Jeffrey's children by Christie from their father's life. Jeffrey had not raised a finger to stop Jade when she declared that she would no longer be hosting the extended family in Warwick Avenue for Christmas and birthdays. Jeffrey's children, Jade said, were much too loud and boisterous, and upset hers; they interfered with the new family that Jeffrey was building with her.

Even as the four children grew to adulthood, as Conway and Charlotte had children of their own, there was almost always a problem when they tried to arrange events with their father and his new wife, some fresh roadblock that was thrown up. Like many fathers in this situation, depressingly enough, Jeffrey seemed oblivious every time this happened.

Charlotte was significantly incensed by this treatment, more than any of the others. Having been her father's favourite daughter, Daddy's little girl, she felt that it was not just her mother, but herself who had been supplanted by another woman. It was insult added to injury when her precious children were banned from seeing her father, from playing happily in the house in which she had grown up.

For Conway, it had not seemed that important. He was not particularly invested in his children, who were being brought up principally by his stay-at-home wife Samantha, and he had always been encouraged by his father to see himself as the favoured son, the presumed heir-apparent to Jeffrey's empire. Family gatherings were not his priority. Bella had always been overlooked anyway, so expected nothing else, and Bart flitted through life so lightly that very little bothered him.

So it was Charlotte who was positively beaming now.

'Where *is* Jade?' she asked. 'And the kids?'

'Oh, she's renting a house in Mayfair,' Jeffrey said with a little shrug. 'We're working out the details now.'

'I imagine the prenup will have been pretty much ironclad,' Conway said, his focus on the finances rather than personal revenge.

'That's what my lawyers say,' Jeffrey agreed blithely. 'Hopefully we'll get it sorted out as soon as possible. It should be fairly straightforward.'

Charlotte's lips pursed together as she remembered the

brutality of the previous divorce negotiations. At least Christie had emerged from them with a considerable chunk of money, and had negotiated even more fiercely for her children than herself. Jeffrey and Christie had not had a prenup, and Christie had helped to build up a considerable part of his hotel empire; she had been furious at being ousted by a woman twenty-five years younger than her who had made the running while Christie was struggling with early-onset menopause. The delicate process of balancing her hormones, adding testosterone to combat lack of sexual desire, then booking in lipo for the pot belly which had grown inexorably despite her iron discipline with diet and exercise, had fatally distracted Christie while Jade, the consultant hired to curate the Sachses' expanding art collection, had moved in for the kill.

What Jade's weakness had been, Charlotte had no idea. But as Jeffrey reached up his liver-spotted hand to take that of the young woman lounging on his armchair, it was eminently clear that, in turn, there had been a chink in Jade's armour. And it made Charlotte's heart sing like Callas and Caruso's voices soaring in a glorious duet.

'And it won't come as any surprise,' Jeffrey continued, 'that as soon as the divorce is finalized, I'll be marrying Adrianna.'

As if she had been under an enchantment till this point, only stirring to life at the mention of her name, Jeffrey Sachs's future wife uncoiled herself. Sitting up straight on the arm of the chair, she gazed directly at her future stepchildren, giving a little nod to acknowledge their presence. She did not, however, feel the need to utter a word.

'She's making this old man very happy,' Jeffrey announced unnecessarily.

'I *bet* she is,' Bart agreed enthusiastically.

'Hah! There's life in the old dog yet, eh?' Jeffrey said, grinning at Adrianna, who smiled back at him, her face so devastatingly beautiful in movement that everyone but Charlotte caught their breath.

'I look forward to many years with my Jeffrey,' she said, her voice husky, her accent Eastern European. 'I feel very lucky to have found my soulmate.'

'Dad, what's going to happen with the family trust?' asked Conway, and at this question every single one of the children stirred eagerly.

Typical of Conway, Bella thought, to go straight to the finances. He was the most selfish person she had ever known. He hadn't cared about his mother being set aside for Jade; even when Jade had had sons, he had calculated that they were simply too young to be a threat to him at the Sachs Organization. Should they want to challenge him for the position of CEO, they would need to graduate and attend business school first, and by that time he was confident that he would have consolidated power over his father's entire business empire.

However, the family trust was something to take very seriously. Currently, only Jeffrey and the four children by Christie had an interest in it; he had five votes, his children one each, so that he would always have the majority. There had been no suggestion up till now that Roman and Brutus should be given voting rights, but none of the adult children knew the terms of the prenup, or what Jeffrey might be pre-pared to concede in a divorce settlement.

The Sachs family trust was as safe as Fort Knox, estab-lished by the best trust lawyers in the country at Christie's insistence during the divorce. Conway, Charlotte, Bella and Bart could be sidelined from power, but they could never be disinherited. They could, however, conceivably have to share that inheritance, to a minor degree, with Roman and Brutus.

Jeffrey looked levelly at his older son.

'Might've known you'd be the one to cut to the chase, Conway,' he said, without any expression in his voice.

His son shrugged.

'It was bound to come up,' he said. 'I know I speak for my siblings when I say we'd all strongly object to the little boys being put on an equal footing with us after we've devoted our lives to the family business.'

Even Bart nodded along with his sisters. He wasn't com-pletely oblivious; he could see that there was no benefit to him of voting rights being extended to his two younger half-brothers.

'Nice to see you four agreeing on something for a change,' Jeffrey said, cracking a smile that made Bella, very attuned to his moods, instantly wary. She was suddenly acutely aware of the hairs on the back of her neck, prickling with sweat. 'Enjoy the moment. I doubt you'll all be singing from the same song book when I tell you why I've got you here.'

Bella darted glances at her siblings and saw that they were all staring at their father, on high alert. Moments before, they had been as relaxed as they could be in his presence. Jade, the interloper, had been pushed out by a younger version. Jeffrey's tastes in women were clearly catholic: he had progressed from Christie's Germanic blonde beauty to Jade's striking Chinese-American good looks, and now this statuesque Eastern European dazzler. Jade having been discarded meant that her sons were much less of a danger to Jeffrey's older children than they had been up till now: with the mother rejected, the children's value automatically decreased. Adrianna would certainly have children, but no matter how much Jeffrey might dote on them, they would be much too young to pose a challenge to their elder siblings' careers at the Sachs Organization.

The ground had just fallen away from beneath their feet, however. Because surely Jeffrey had summoned them here to tell them that he was divorcing Jade and had a new, younger wife already lined up? How could *that* not be the key piece of information he wanted to divulge?

'I'm retiring,' Jeffrey announced. 'On the day Adrianna and I get married. And one of you is going to take over my job.'

His pale-blue eyes, as keen and sharp as ever, scanned his children's faces, his amusement at their reaction very obvious.

'Nothing's set in stone,' he said, to make his point absolutely clear. 'I haven't made any decisions yet. But in six months, one of you four will be running the entire company.'

Chapter Three

Up till that moment, Adrianna's physical control of her body had been extraordinary. Bella guessed that as well as the modelling Adrianna had doubtless done, she had taken extensive yoga classes, enabling her to hold positions for a considerable length of time. This brought images to Bella's mind that she would much rather not contemplate, and she pushed them firmly aside, noticing instead that, for the first time, Adrianna had made a spontaneous movement. Instead of staring serenely out into the room over the heads of her lover's children, as she had been doing, she was now looking straight at Jeffrey. Her sculpted features were clearly Botoxed into immaculate smoothness, but her heavy brows were struggling to meet in a frown.

'This old guy wants to spend the rest of his life with his beautiful new bride,' Jeffrey said, squeezing Adrianna's hand. 'I never thought I'd say this – I've always been such a workaholic! But she's a gem, and I want to enjoy every minute I have with her. We've got so much in common.'

'*Really*,' Charlotte was unable to resist muttering.

'Chess!' Jeffrey said surprisingly. 'We play a lot of chess.'

Adrianna nodded automatically, but her brows were still

quivering in an attempt to move close together. Also, her nostrils were twitching slightly, a sign that the twitcher has had so much Botox that the normal muscles that show emotion are entirely paralysed.

'I've got plenty of time left,' Jeffrey said cheerfully. 'I might even go to LA and get all those treatments the tech guys have. Blood transfusions, cryogenic chambers, the works. Hire myself a personal trainer. I used to scoff at 'em, but now I get it. You want to stay active as long as possible when you've got a beautiful young wife to keep up with. I don't think Adrianna much fancies pushing me around in a wheelchair for twenty years! She'd much rather have a husband with a bit of vim and vigour, wouldn't you, darling?'

He winked at his fiancée, who made no sign of agreement. Instead, her face stopped struggling to express itself, reverting to the perfect impassive mask it had been for most of the conversation. Bella concluded that this meant that Adrianna would infinitely prefer a husband she had to push around in a wheelchair to one who was submitting himself to a range of probably humiliating and invasive treatments in order to keep himself sprightly enough to . . .

'Yikes, Dad, TMI alert,' Bart said frankly as Conway, unable to restrain himself a moment longer, exploded with:

'*What did you mean, one of us is going to take over the company? Who is it?*'

'That's up to you!' Jeffrey said, with the peculiarly crocodile-like smile that he used as a challenge. 'I've been told by my lawyers that I can get this divorce done and dusted in six months. I'll be marrying Adrianna pretty much the day after it goes through, and on my wedding day, I'll announce which one of you takes over from me as CEO of the Sachs Organization.'

On hearing this confirmation that Conway was in fact not the designated heir after all, Bella's heart pounded in her chest so violently that it was all she could do to keep still. She felt as if she were being resuscitated with the metal plates doctors applied to patients *in extremis* to shock their heart back into beating. Heat flooded her body. Her hairline prickled again with sweat. She did not look at her siblings; she didn't dare, as she knew her facial expression would be much too revealing.

'It's a competition, then,' Charlotte said, her voice crystal clear, each word dripping ice. 'But what are we being judged by?'

Their father emitted what could only be described as a cackle. Bella thought he looked like a wicked old elf from a fable as he rubbed his brown-spotted hands together glee-fully.

'Everything!' he said briskly. 'Absolutely everything! I'm not setting any targets for any of you. That would be much too easy, wouldn't it? You'll have to challenge yourselves. Pull out rabbits from hats I didn't even know existed. Go an extra hundred miles. I've got no favourites here, despite what some of you might think.'

Charlotte, Bart and Bella promptly turned to look at Conway, whose jaw was set.

'Hah, yes! I know you all thought Conway was set to take over from me!' Jeffrey chuckled. 'And maybe he was, once upon a time.'

This fairy-tale reference made Bella start in surprise, having just made that comparison herself.

Though there should be three of us, not four, for it to be a proper fairy tale, she thought. *Three sons sent off on a quest to see who gets to rule the kingdom. It's always the youngest who wins, but the likelihood of Bart pulling it off is practically nil . . .*

'But everything's up for grabs now, as the Americans say!' Jeffrey continued. 'Exciting, isn't it? Go forth and conquer! Knock my socks off! I'm going to have my hands full negotiating with Jade and organizing my new life with my lovely bride-to-be – I won't be overseeing you much for the next six months. There'll still be my board, of course. You'll have to answer to them. Take risks, but don't fuck up. Impress me.'

'Whoa,' Bart said slowly, pushing back his blond-streaked hair with both hands. 'I must admit, Dad, I did *not* see this coming—'

'You bastard! You fucking bastard!' screeched a woman's voice. It was strangely muffled, but instantly familiar to almost everyone present.

Everyone jumped and looked across the wide living room. At the far side were three big double French windows, running the length of the room, which opened onto a stone terrace bordered by a balustrade elaborately decorated with finials, decorative balls, and cypresses in pots. A dark blur of movement streaked past one set of doors and smacked into the central French windows, resolving itself into a woman's body, the face pressed up against the glass, glaring into the room: everyone jumped again.

'You bastard!' shrieked the woman, grabbing the handle

of the door and rattling it madly in an attempt to open it. Having no success, she dashed over to the next set of doors and tried them too. She was dressed entirely in black, a long-sleeved zipped top over exercise tights; with her equally black hair falling over her face, she looked like a deranged ninja.

The second set of doors failed to yield. She doubled back the way she had come, attempting to enter by the French windows she had passed. Everyone's head turned from side to side, watching her like spectators at a tennis match. It was all so fast; she moved with the speed of a woman who regularly entered competitive triathlons. Which she was.

'Well, don't just sit there!' Jeffrey said sharply to his two sons. 'Do something!'

The third door was also locked, a tribute to the general security levels necessary when you lived in central London. The woman shrieked again in frustration, slammed her fist against the glass, and disappeared from sight around the side of the house.

'Shall I ring the police?' Bart asked, which made his father grind his teeth in frustration.

'No, you *fool*!' Jeffrey yelled; if he had had a cane he would have banged it on the floor. 'Think I want this story getting in the papers? Go outside and shoo her out!'

'*Shoo* her?' Conway repeated, getting to his feet. 'Honestly, Dad, the way she looks she'll take my face off! I'm inclined to agree with Bart – we should ring the police. They have all that gear—'

'Tell 'em to bring riot shields,' Bart quipped.

Charlotte huffed out a laugh.

'She won't get in,' Jeffrey said. 'Maria's under strict instructions not to let her in the door, no matter what she says.'

'Lovely,' Charlotte muttered to Bella. 'Quite a familiar scenario, isn't it?'

Bella nodded, vivid memories rushing back. The twins were not close, but at that moment, as their eyes met, they exchanged a look of such absolute understanding and sadness that their resemblance was even more marked than usual.

Because, as Jeffrey's estranged wife Jade had been screaming and rattling the French windows of the house which had once been hers, Christie's daughters had been vividly reminded of what Jeffrey had done to them, although their mother had behaved with infinitely more dignity. From one day to the next, their lives had been utterly upended. Christie, too, had been evicted from the house to which she brought back her children as newborns from the St John & St Elizabeth hospital in St John's Wood; in which she had raised them; from which she had taken them every morning to the Stepping Stones kindergarten on Fitzjohn's Avenue, then driven the twins to the Francis Holland School in Regent's Park, while the boys caught the bus to Westminster School.

Christie had been the perfect wife to Jeffrey, faithfully following the routines and rituals of the affluent, society-conscious one per cent who lived in St John's Wood and Maida Vale. She had produced four attractive and well-bred children, organized their admissions into suitable schools, thrown intimate dinner parties, hosted gala balls, all while sitting on the board of the Sachs Organization and overseeing the decor of the five-star hotels in their portfolio. Jeffrey had been neither the perfect husband nor father, either taking his family for granted or browbeating them for the tiniest of faults, but he had never shown any signs of being likely to stray.

So it had been an utter surprise when, one Tuesday, Christie had picked up Charlotte and Bella from an after-school activity and returned home to find an enormous pantechnicon outside already full of wardrobe rails, suit-cases packed with clothes, boxes of her children's toys, books, musical instruments, the move overseen by a sobbing Maria, whose swollen, puffy face clearly indicated that she had been crying for most of the day. And Christie realized with cold, bitter clarity that Jeffrey had chosen that Tuesday because he knew she had appointments from nine onwards and would be far too busy to pop home before the after-school pickup, so that the coast would be clear for a good eight hours . . .

Bella and Charlotte, lost in memory of their mother's tears that long-ago Tuesday, were the last to realize that silence had finally fallen in the living room. Jade had stopped screaming. Everyone was frozen in place, wonder-ing if she had given up and gone away.

'It's too quiet,' Bart said suddenly.

As if on cue, the double doors slid open so violently that they smashed into their recesses and a slender black figure stumbled through the gap, her eyes wild.

'Fuck you, you bastard!' she screamed. 'You can't do this to me and the boys! You can't just throw us away like we were nothing! I won't let you, I *won't*! Where is she? I'll tear her to pieces! *Where is she?*'

The mansion was entirely surrounded by a high hedge which Jade would have had to scale, or push through, in order to gain access to the garden; the entrance gates were specifically designed to be climb-proof. It was clear that she had come by the hedge route from the leaves and small twigs in her dishevelled hair and sticking to the fleece of her fitted, zipped jacket, and from the nasty graze on her cheek. In contrast to her previous swift-as-lightning pace, she was now limping slightly.

Behind her Maria appeared, wringing her hands.

'The toilet window!' she said miserably. 'I hear Mrs Jade and check the side door is locked, but I was wanting to make the air in the guest toilet to be fresh, as we have guests – I forget I leave the window open—'

She looked unhappily at the children, hating to call them 'guests'.

'I had to scramble through the hedge and bang my leg climbing in through the guest toilet in my own fucking *house*!' Jade shrilled. 'Look!'

She dragged up one leg of her exercise tights to show a large bruise rapidly forming on her shin.

'Nasty,' Bart said sympathetically. 'You want to get some arnica on that. Shall I—'

But Jade totally ignored him. Since she had always done her best to pretend Jeffrey's children by Christie didn't exist, this came as no surprise to anyone.

'*You!*' she said, her eyes lighting on Adrianna, whom she had not spotted when she had peered frantically through the window, as Adrianna had been sitting on the far side of the large, high-backed armchair. 'I *knew* you'd be here, you bitch! What's he doing, introducing you to the fucking family? They should see the pictures of you on his phone, you dirty slut! *That'd* be the real introduction!'

'*Nooo!*' Bart exclaimed. 'Dad! I don't know whether to be shocked or impressed.'

'Oh, *yuck*,' Charlotte muttered.

The leg of her tights still pulled up, Jade launched herself towards Adrianna, who jumped up, strategically putting the armchair between her and her assailant. Jade tore round the chair, and Adrianna shot away, moving at a good rate of speed, but hampered by her tight-fitting dress and five-inch strappy heels; even limping, Jade was much faster. Adrianna was sensibly making for the sofa, which would be a much more effective barrier than the armchair, but Jade lunged forward and grabbed at her hair, managing to clasp a full handful.

Adrianna gasped and staggered on her heels, trying to get her balance. Jade tumbled towards her, jerking Adrianna's head back. Adrianna reached behind her, grabbed Jade's fingers, and dragged open their grip, bending the fingers back painfully to force Jade to release her hair. Jade screamed in pain.

With Jade's hands now clutched in each of her own, her arms behind her, Adrianna raised one knee high, the sound of her dress ripping audible as she did so, and kicked back, a donkey kick that hit her assailant in the stomach and sent her flying back through the air. The wind knocked out of her, Jade landed on the carpet, bottom plopping down, hands over her stomach, mouth open in shock. Adrianna drew a long, deep breath, stabilized herself on her high heels and shook out her hair.

'Bloody *hell*,' Bart said admiringly. 'Were you in the secret service back wherever you come from? Nice moves!'

Adrianna shot him a sideways glance from those long green eyes, clear and cool, acknowledging nothing.

'Darling, are you all right?' Jeffrey, who had sat out the scuffle to protect his ageing bones, stood up now and walked towards his girlfriend. 'That was very fast of you! All that dance training, eh?'

Unnoticed by him, Charlotte looked at her twin and hissed, '"*Dance training*"!' sarcastically, adding, 'Catfights at the pole-dancing club, more like!'

Adrianna was rubbing her scalp ruefully. The act of lifting her arms had the effect of raising her perfect round breasts and pushing them against the snakeprint fabric of her dress. Conway, Bart and Jeffrey were so hypnotized by this that even when she assured them, her voice as low and husky as ever, 'I am okay. It was not so bad,' they continued to stare in silent worship at her bosom. With Charlotte bitching to Bella, this left only Maria to notice that Jade, having got her second wind, was climbing to her feet. Maria yelled an incoherent warning, pointing at Jade, who was coming forward to tackle Adrianna.

Bella had only a split second to react. She had never been involved in a physical altercation in her life, and lacked fast reactions. Charlotte had been the sporty one, playing lacrosse and hockey at school; if Bella was unlucky enough to be assigned to a team, it had always been as a defender on the stronger one to limit her access to the ball as much as possible.

But her heart was racing, and she was fired up with anger and resentment at her memories of being locked out of this very house by the woman who was now running towards her. Snatching up a bolster from the sofa, Bella swivelled at the waist and smashed it into Jade's face. Jade staggered back; the bolster was firmly stuffed, and it landed a significant buffet.

Adrianna, seeing Jade advance on her, had started forward, a martial look in her eyes, her fists clenching. Bart, seeing his opportunity, stepped behind his stepmother-to-be and grabbed her by the elbows, pulling her back against him.

'Steady on, tiger,' he said in her ear. 'No need to break one of those pretty nails. Con, grab Jade, will you?'

But there was no need. Bella was dealing with Jade all by herself. Advancing on her stepmother, she whacked her with the bolster over and over again, the action incredibly satisfying. Sheer rage flooded out of her, rage she had pent up ever since her childhood, since the day she had come home with her mother and sister to find their belongings being loaded onto a moving van, and they had looked up to see, at the landing window, a strange dark-haired woman standing there, gazing down at the scene with a smile on her face . . .

Now Bella had that woman at her mercy, and nothing had ever been so satisfying. An impulse buried deep inside her, one she had repressed so profoundly that she hadn't even known it existed, had burst forth, and she was relishing it with every fibre of her being. Jade was reeling under the repeated buffets, retreating under the assault, driven back against an armchair, screeching in pain as she banged her bruised leg against its solid frame.

But Bella kept on going, gripping the bolster with both hands spaced wide. She might have been a contestant on a TV show she and her siblings had loved when they were young, called *Gladiators*. One of the challenges had been for the contestant, dressed in padded clothes, to battle a gladiator, the pair trying to knock each other down with big padded cylinders.

This was how they had held those weapons for maximum effectiveness, and they had known what they were doing. The bolster was fearsomely effective. Bella forced Jade so far back she stumbled and fell into the armchair, legs flying into the air, doubling up once again.

And then it was over. Bella couldn't whack her any more, because it would look bad to keep hitting Jade once she had her down, but she wanted to, she wanted to *really badly*, she wanted, honestly, to beat the shit out of her . . .

She stopped, the bolster clasped tightly in her sweaty hands. She was sweaty all over, her breath coming fast, her scalp prickling. The impulse to keep going was so powerful that she was wrestling it with all the willpower she possessed, a silent struggle: she knew if she hit Jade again that her siblings and father would consider that she had crossed the line.

'Well done, Bella!' Conway exclaimed, starting to clap. 'Really well done! I didn't know you had it in you!'

'I didn't either,' she mumbled.

She realized that her fingers were cramped from digging

into the bolster so tightly, and started to release them. Someone else was clapping: as she turned away from Jade, to stop herself being tempted to keep hitting her, Bella saw, to her great surprise, that it was her father.

'Very efficiently done,' Jeffrey said, smiling at her.

Bella felt like a little girl again, blossoming under rare praise from her father. Cheeks pinkening, she busied herself tucking the bolster back into place on the sofa.

'You can let me go now,' Adrianna said over her shoulder to Bart.

'Whatever the lady wants,' Bart said, releasing his grip on her elbows and stepping back. Adrianna glided across the carpet to Jeffrey, sliding her arm through his.

'Jeffrey will be tired now,' she said. 'He should rest.'

'She's quite right,' Jeffrey agreed, smiling up at his statuesque girlfriend, beside whom he looked even more like a wrinkled, aged elf. 'But I could do with a cup of tea first. Maria?'

'I make it now,' Maria said, bustling away to suit the action to the words.

'Oh, and take your stepmother out with you when you go,' Jeffrey said to his sons. 'She shouldn't cause you any trouble. Bella seems to have delivered the *coup de grâce*.'

Gingerly, Conway and Bart approached Jade, who was struggling in the armchair like an upended turtle trying to right itself.

'Best to grab the elbows,' Bart said to his brother. 'Then they can't hit you with 'em.'

'I wonder how you know *that*, Bart,' Charlotte said dryly. 'Have you had to restrain lots of women in your time?'

Bart flashed her a cheeky smile.

'Just occasionally I've had a girlfriend kick off a bit when she found out she wasn't the only one,' he said. 'Things tend to get a bit – well, breaky.'

Approaching Jade from behind, Conway and Bart leant down and grabbed her under the arms, taking hold of an elbow each, hoisting her up and out of the chair. They were both well-built young men, and Jade was very slight. It was easy enough to lift her up and set her on her feet, pushing her shoulders gently to start her walking in front of them as they crossed the living room. Charlotte and Bella fell in behind their brothers.

'Uh, goodbye, Dad,' Charlotte said as they passed Jeffrey, the other siblings swiftly chiming in.

'Goodbye!' their father said cheerfully. 'Remember what I said, eh? Six months, no more. Then I walk into the sunset with my lovely bride and one of you takes over. May the best man win!'

Charlotte rolled her eyes at the word 'man', but kept her face averted from her father. The group crossed the entrance hall in silence, Jade wriggling now in Conway and Bart's grip; Bella went ahead to open the front door, and stood back on the terrace as Conway and Bart half-carried their stepmother down the steps and along the garden path. Bella opened the high garden gate. Once through, the brothers looked at each other and, as one, let go of Jade while giving her a firm push away down the pavement, as if she might turn and bite them if she were too close.

Jade righted herself, and bent over to finally pull down the leg of her exercise tights. Her thick, straight black bob was tangled, hair plastered to her face, her breathing sharp and angry.

'Fuck you all!' she spat.

'It doesn't feel good, does it?' Charlotte hissed. 'Being thrown out of the house you used to live in, that you saw your kids grow up in? All your stuff chucked out as well? Your life totally turned around from morning to evening? I hope you're enjoying it, because I am!'

Jade pushed her hair back from her sweaty face, looked as if she were about to say something, then didn't.

'You know what my mother used to say when we cried about what had happened to her?' Charlotte pursued inexorably. '*You lose them how you get them.* And she was right. Our father would never have left our mother if it weren't for you. You got him to trade her in for a younger model and then you got hoist with your own petard. I literally could not be happier right now. Think it's hard being kicked out of your house and seeing another woman in there? Try being a *kid* going through that!'

'I know!' Jade retorted. 'How do you think my boys are feeling right now?'

'Boo fucking hoo,' Charlotte snapped. 'My heart's breaking for your brats. And don't think for a *moment* they're getting a vote in the family trust. You just pissed all over any chance they had of that. Dad'll never give voting rights to the kids of someone who just behaved like you did. Our mother was *dignified*. She acted like a lady the entire time and my father respected her for that, all through the divorce where I'm sure you tried to get him to cut us off without a penny!'

She took a deep breath, staring narrowly at Jade, positively daring her to contradict this. Jade was still silent.

'Now fuck off or I'll call the police,' Charlotte finished, folding her arms.

Jade favoured her with a black stare before turning on her heel and limping off down Warwick Avenue.

'Bit harsh there with the kid thing, Lottie?' Bart suggested, but both Conway and Bella shook their heads in vigorous disagreement, Conway saying that he thought Charlotte had nailed it, frankly. Bart subsided.

'D'you think the old man was actually serious about the whole winner-takes-all thing?' he asked instead.

'No, Bart,' Charlotte said, putting a hand on his arm and smiling up at him sweetly. 'Not at all. He was just teasing.'

'Really?' Bart's handsome brow furrowed under his fall of blond-streaked hair.

'No! Of course not! Of course he meant it!'

Charlotte, much more in touch with her emotions than Bella, had run the gamut that day. Having just unloaded her fury on Jade, she now flipped from sarcasm to intense irritation with her feckless younger brother.

'What, you think he called us all over, which he *never* does? Just to have a fun family joke while we meet the Slovenian hooker who's going to be our new Mommie Dearest?' Charlotte continued.

'Looked more Estonian to me, actually,' Bart said, with the professional air of a man speaking on a subject in which he is an expert.

'*You're* the family joke!' Charlotte said impatiently.

'Look, enough of this,' Conway said. 'I'm going back to work. I've got stuff I need to finish today.'

The siblings paused, looking at each other for a moment at the mention of work. It was no shock that their father had set them against each other like this; they had always been in competition. Not only did all four of them work for the Sachs Organization, but they always had. Taking a job anywhere else would have meant immediate disinheritance. Conway, as CFO, was the most senior, but both Charlotte, in charge of the boutique hotel division, and Bella, who ran the main hotel chain, from which the majority of the Sachs income was derived, could legitimately be considered in the running to take over when their father retired.

In the minds of Bart's siblings, it was definitely a three-way race. They were sure he presented no competition to them. No one quite understood what his role at Sachs was: he was some sort of celebrity figurehead, a staple in the gossip columns, bringing glamour and sex to the brand, arranging cross-promotions with his racing car driver and footballer friends, the models and actresses he dated; a fixture at charity balls. He had an office in the building, his title Executive Director for Charity Initiatives. He went on star-studded fundraising expeditions with Prince Toby and Tor Ahlssen, the celebrity explorer; raced in the Dakar Rally, lamenting that it was not, as in the old days, from Paris to Senegal, but across South America; and attended the Pitti Uomo menswear show every year, staggering out of Florentine nightclubs and parties at the Gucci Museum in the small hours of the morning, as draped in beautiful women as the male models on the catwalk were in fashionable scarves.

So surely, Conway, Charlotte and Bella felt, no one in their right mind would give Bart a company, or indeed anything, to run. Though Jeffrey Sachs might be nearly in his eighth decade, he unquestionably still had the full complement of marbles with which he had been born. It was impossible to know if Bart was aware of his siblings' opinion as, saying something about having to see a man about a dog, he waved them an amiable goodbye and ambled towards his Aston Martin.

'Oh,' he said, turning on his heel, having gone a few steps. 'I've been seeing this Italian girl recently. Bit of a cracker, but a brainiac too. She watches a lot of those very slow films in black and white. Ones where nothing much happens, as far as I can see, but apparently they're hugely significant or something.'

'Oh my *God*, Bart, I have a *life*,' Charlotte said impatiently, sounding like a tween snapping at her brother rather than a grown woman.

'*Padre Padrone*,' Bart said.

'What?' Conway asked, even more impatiently than Charlotte.

'It's an Italian film about a father who bosses his son around and runs his entire life,' Bart said. 'Dad's a shepherd, so son's got to be a shepherd too, that sort of thing. The title means "Dad the Boss". Caterina was watching it the other day and I thought "I must remember that and tell everyone." So now I have. *Padre Padrone*. Says it all, really, doesn't it?'

With another wave, he unlocked the Aston Martin with a click and levered himself gracefully into the low-slung seat.

'He won't even remember Caterina's name next month,' Conway said, sounding rather jealous. 'Well! Back to work indeed!'

He looked from sister to sister, a little smirk briefly playing across his well-shaped mouth, indicating very clearly that he did not see either of them as much more competition to his chances of becoming CEO of Sachs than he did Bart.

'Absolutely,' Charlotte said briskly, and Bella nodded. With no further words exchanged between them, the three of them separated, heading for their cars. Bart was manoeuvring the Aston Martin out of the tight space, and Conway stood there watching this anxiously, Bart teasing him by almost kissing the cars' bumpers before spinning the wheel and sending the DB11 zooming out onto Warwick Avenue and away over the canal bridge.

Muttering swearwords, Conway climbed into his Jaguar and headed off too. He did not notice that his sisters were not following suit; as Bella reached her Audi, turning on the phone which had been silenced during the meeting with their father, she saw a text ping in from Charlotte.

Hang on till boys go.

Conway passed Bella, looking ahead, his lips moving; too occupied, presumably, with cursing his younger brother to raise a hand to salute his sister. Bella watched the car turn towards Paddington Basin and disappear around the corner of another exquisite white stucco villa surrounded by high, perfectly maintained hedges. Then she looked over the street at Charlotte, who was leaning against her Range Rover.

With a tilt of her head, Charlotte indicated that Bella come to her, and though a small voice inside Bella asked her, quite unexpectedly, why, when Charlotte wanted to talk, she should not cross the street to meet her twin rather than summoning her imperiously, old habits are very hard to break. For as long as she could remember, when Charlotte had commanded, Bella had fallen in line.

'What is it?' Bella asked as she reached her sister, the slimmer, blonder, chicer version of herself, so elegant in her belted greige suede coat dress and matching high heels.

'We need a battle plan,' Charlotte said intently. 'Con doesn't deserve it, but unless we do something drastic, Daddy's bound to give the company to him. You heard what he said – "Let the best man win"!'

'It's just an expression—' Bella started to say. But Charlotte rode right over her.

'It should be one of us!' she said. 'One of us twins, I mean. Con's always so bloody entitled and smug! Did you see that snarky little smile he gave us? He doesn't think either of us have a chance!'

She set her jaw resolutely.

'You were going back to the office, weren't you?'

Bella nodded.

'I knew it! You're such a workhorse. Well, don't. Come back to mine. Whatever you had scheduled this afternoon can't *possibly* be as important as having a war council! It's Friday afternoon. No one has crucial meetings on a Friday.'

Charlotte stared hard at her twin, compelling her to obey.

'We have to take Conway down,' she said, 'and it has to be in a way that he can't come back from. We need to salt the earth so he can't get up again. And we don't have much time, so we'd better get cracking!'

Chapter Four

Charlotte lived very near to Maida Vale, just the other side of the Edgware Road, in a small development of modern houses built off-street in a gated private close. Bella followed her on what was barely a five-minute drive from one house to the other. Charlotte was the only child who had chosen to stay so close to the area in which they had spent the first years of their lives, the house from which they had effectively been banned.

Lovely though St John's Wood was, child-friendly and close to Charlotte's children's private school, Bella had always considered it strange of her sister to want to live surrounded by unavoidable memories of a happy childhood turned so sour. But Bella's attempt to discuss Charlotte's decision – because it had been entirely hers; Charlotte made all the decisions for her family – had been shut down as soon as Bella raised the question.

Instead of answering, Charlotte had smiled that bright, beautiful ice-queen smile of hers, which conveyed 'this subject is not up for discussion' more effectively than words could have done, and started talking about how much she missed Pang's Chinese restaurant, to which they had gone very regularly as small children. It had been an iconic place for them all, with its ceiling-high entrance fountain into which they had loved to push their fingers, squealing happily. Children adore repetition and ritual, and all the little Sachses had been addicted to ordering the duck pancakes and lemon chicken, until, out of the blue, one evening over dinner, Jeffrey had laid down the edict that they must try something new: when they protested, he banged the table in fury, sending cutlery flying.

Of course, in retrospect, it had been nothing to do with their food order. Jeffrey had been in a foul mood and was taking it out on his children. But you never realized that when you were young. All Bella had heard was that her father was angry, and she had dissolved in floods of tears at the thought of never being able to eat lemon chicken again. Jeffrey, hating weakness, had turned his fury on his younger daughter and she had fled to cry by the fountain. The sibling who had followed to comfort her was not her twin, but lovely Bart, who hated anyone to be unhappy. Charlotte had stayed at the table and dutifully picked something else from the huge menu, happy to demonstrate her superiority over her sobbing sister.

So Bella could not be unhappy that Charlotte was unable to take her son and daughter to Pang's, following in the old family tradition, introducing a new generation to the lemon chicken, the sweet and sour pork and the sea spice aubergine they had loved so much. For Bella, the family traditions had been entirely corrupted by the contemptuous way in which her father had discarded his first family in favour of the one he had had with Jade.

Strangely, resentful though Charlotte was of her father's abandonment, she still seemed to want to recreate their childhood for her own little boy and girl. Pang's old premises had been turned into an Everyman cinema, and Charlotte's children were regularly taken there to see live screenings from the Royal Ballet and Royal Opera, curling up on the cinema sofas while eating halloumi burgers and jelly retro candy, washed down with Fentiman's rose lemonade, brought to them by the ushers who had been summoned by the discreet bell push beside their seats.

The gates were sliding open. Charlotte's chauffeur drove the Range Rover into the courtyard. Bella followed, thinking, as she always did, how ugly these new-build houses were, basic square blocks built with jaundiced Imperial London yellow stock bricks. The houses were designed for people who wanted to own a house in this area but could not afford the exorbitant sum they would have to pay for one. St John's Wood was the first area in London to be built with a preponderance of villa-style housing, rather than terraces, so that rich men could house their mistresses there and be able to visit them discreetly. The elegant, detached villas meant that NW8 was one of the most expensive postcodes in the city.

Charlotte had not married a financier but a male model, and though she had a trust fund and an extremely well-paid job, their combined incomes were nowhere near those of the Russian, Singaporean and Chinese non-dom bankers who had bought up half of St John's Wood. Nonetheless, Charlotte had had her heart set on living in NW8, and the modern house was the price she had had to pay. It had cost in the high seven figures, but a villa with the comparable space was easily into the eights.

Bella got out of her car, watching Charlotte's chauffeur jump down from the high seat of the Range Rover and open the back door to help his employer down, extending an arm so that she could balance as one high heel after the other touched down to the concrete of the courtyard. Charlotte took it for granted that she would be waited on. Bella didn't know where she had got it from. Or, Bella reflected, it would be more accurate to say that she didn't know why she didn't have it too.

'Come on, don't just stand there!' Charlotte called, and turned towards her front door.

Although the house was boxy and ugly – the outside was very rarely photographed – its modern internal layout was ideal for Charlotte's needs, enabling her to make it a show-place that regularly featured in architecture and lifestyle magazines. She redecorated very often to keep the design cutting-edge, documenting everything on her Instagram account, which was eagerly followed by hordes of women aspiring to what appeared to be her effortless style.

A photograph posted yesterday documenting an addition to a shelf in her son's bedroom, a witty little vase shaped like a toy soldier who was holding a single flower, a bright yellow gerbera which popped with colour against the pale-green wall, had drawn thousands of likes already. Charlotte was well aware of her value not just as a style icon but a wife and mother. Her husband Paul might not be a high earner, but his ridiculously photogenic looks meant that their Insta-grams were breathtaking, and Posy and Quant were equally stunning. Charlotte had given them those names because the initials would look so good in her posts; she could cutesily say that she was 'minding her P&Q' when looking after the kids.

With the aid of her young, hip social media team, Charlotte blogged, Instagrammed, Pinterested and tweeted on a daily basis. She was determined to keep building her personal brand, entwining it with that of the 'Sash' boutique hotel chain which she had created and oversaw; the Sachs hotels were old and staid by comparison, and there was no question that the chicer, more intimate, hipper Sash brand had given a much-needed gloss to the reputation of the entire Sachs Organization.

'Wow,' Bella said, stepping inside. 'Your flowers are amazing.'

She was used to this by now, the way that her sister's house was always camera-ready. *Architectural Digest* or *Wallpaper** or *Good Housekeeping* might be due any minute to document another perfect slice of Charlotte's perfect life. The whole ground floor was open-plan, with gleaming white surfaces everywhere one looked, dazzling the eye: it was the kind of hyper-groomed interior decoration which made anyone less pulled-together than Charlotte feel instantly scruffy by comparison. The gigantic glass vases in the built-in embrasures were full of a striking white flower Bella didn't even recognize. They were not arranged in the conventional way, with their stems in water; instead, the flowers were entirely submerged, floating in some sort of pale greentinted liquid.

In the centre of the huge space, a glass-sided staircase

soared up to the first floor, a dramatic ascent, as the ground-floor ceiling was double-height. It helped to separate the various areas into which the ground floor was divided. A huge, sprawling, elegantly curved lemon velvet sofa, especially commissioned for the house, wrapped around an entire corner of the living area, facing a glass-fronted wood-burning fireplace. Built into the back of it, on the kitchen side, was a pizza oven. Charlotte never cooked, but Paul did, and their photos of him experimenting with gluten-free cauliflower and courgette pizza bases, topped with home-made tomato sauce and buffalo mozzarella, had recently been particularly popular. Especially the shots of ridiculously handsome Paul licking sauce off his fingers.

'I'm changing it all next month,' Charlotte said casually, dropping her butter-soft Gucci handbag onto the white lacquered console table by the door.

'Really?' Bella asked as she set her own, extremely sensible square-framed leather handbag down beside Charlotte's whimsical, light-as-a-feather, highly buckled suede bag whose pale blossom tint would pick up every stain. Not that it mattered, as Charlotte would carry it for only a few months, till there were knock-offs of the design everywhere, and then give it to her cleaning lady or housekeeper, who would promptly sell it on eBay.

Why, Bella wondered, did she have to be such a contrast to Charlotte? Why couldn't she go to Knightsbridge or Bond Street and snap up a whole raft of new handbags? But Thomas, her husband, had bought her this bag. He was always so thoughtful. It had a whole series of perfectly designed compartments which helped her keep meticulously organized.

And its dark camel leather went with everything, something their mother had taught them. Camel for blondes was like navy for brunettes, a perfect neutral.

'I'm so sick of that lemon,' Charlotte said. 'It's like a migraine in sofa form. I was thinking of rolling it out for the Sash sofas, as an accent pillow, but I think it'll make guests irritated without knowing why. I swear, the kids have been more argumentative since that sofa's been in the house. Colour is *so* key.'

'That reminds me – I've been asking your office for *ages* to coordinate with me about integrating some more design elements from Sash into my five-star portfolio,' Bella said. 'The last ones were a huge success – did you see the feedback? We did a survey of business travellers that showed—'

'Not now, Bell!' Charlotte said impatiently.

'I'm just saying, it's overdue,' Bella persisted. 'We need a real push towards integration across the entire hotel collection. Right now we're months behind on that schedule, which you agreed to, and—'

'Bell! Save it for the office!' Charlotte threw herself onto the despised lemon sofa. 'We've got half an hour before Paul brings the kids back from the park, and we need to strategize! Just imagine, if Conway takes over everything and he's our boss – can you *picture* how obnoxious he'll be? And micro-managing? Conway's perfectly capable of cockblocking me on something as tiny as . . . lemon scatter cushions, for God's sake, just to throw his weight around! And we'll be fucked, because we can't leave Sachs. If we leave, God knows what Dad'll do in the will, you know? Think about *that*!'

Bella sank onto the sofa, settling into one of the indentations that faced her twin; the sofa undulated, snake-like and ridiculously comfortable for something so cutting-edge in design. For a moment she toyed with the idea of asking Charlotte if she could have it when Charlotte replaced it. She had coveted this sofa from the moment she saw it, and could have it reupholstered so the lemon didn't make her irritable. But although it would fit in her unnecessarily gigantic mansion in Hampstead Garden Suburb, it would also stand out like the sorest of thumbs. Her style – she didn't really *have* a style, if she were honest – the generic, beige and mahogany decor of her over-furnished home, was the polar opposite of Charlotte's Italian-designed house, with its one-off, individual, audaciously coloured pieces. Bella would have to jettison every piece of furniture she owned if she took this sofa.

And, suddenly, she had an overwhelming impulse to do just that. But what on earth would Thomas say if he came home from his latest business trip to find a sofa curving like a big, fat, sexy yellow boa constrictor around the sitting room? The image of him reacting to the sight almost made her laugh. Thomas would not think the sofa was sensible at all, even re-covered: nothing could possibly be sensible if it meant you throwing out the rest of your furniture.

Since Thomas's practicality was one of the things that Bella loved most about him, this was an unusual conflict for her. Thomas grounded her, kept her safe where her family had not, valued everything about her they looked down on. Her brains, her ability to organize, her quiet focus and determination; he shared those qualities, and his pride in them had given her a different, much more flattering mirror in which to see herself, rather than her father and siblings' view of her as Boring Bella.

But maybe, just maybe, there was a middle ground? One that might involve a frivolous handbag every now and then, one that lacked a specially positioned elastic into which to clip your pen? Bella remembered Thomas showing her a handbag organizer he had found in the *Telegraph* Sunday offers supplement a few weeks ago. It was a large rectangular plastic case with different compartments into which you could slot wallet, glasses, make-up, phone, etc. so that you could move it from tote bag to tote bag and never leave the house without your essentials.

The entire supplement had been full of useful ideas for affluent retirees. Booster cushions for older people who couldn't sit all the way down in armchairs any more, or get out of them once they had. Grabbers, so you could reach out for something without getting out of the armchair, even with the help of the booster cushion. Padded gilets with extra pockets so that you didn't even need your tote bag with movable plastic organizer; you could just load it all into the gilet instead.

It had been disconcerting, however, for Bella to realize that her husband thought that she, at thirty-two, could benefit from a product targeted at the over-sixties. And now she could vividly picture what would happen if she asked Charlotte to give her that light-as-a-feather handbag when she tired of it: Bella would come home with it dangling prettily from her wrist, only for Thomas to frown at it and ask her how she was going to fit all her essentials into it, let alone find them easily. What if she needed a pen in a hurry? And what if that pen leaked all over the suede, ruining it? That would be considerably less likely to happen if it were held vertically in its own neat little elastic loop . . .

Today had started out so normally, and yet it was proving full of unexpected revelations. Bella, who had never hit any-one in her life, had pummelled her hated stepmother with a bolster so violently that she'd knocked her into an armchair and had to use all her willpower to ensure she didn't keep going. And now she was fighting a wave of resentment towards her beloved husband, because if she came home with the Gucci suede frivolity, without even paying the thousands it must have cost Charlotte, his disapproval would ensure that she ended up returning to her eminently utilitarian, hard-framed leather handbag.

The disapproval would not be explicitly voiced. Thomas had quite a range of effective pointed stares and quiet sighs. But he might also explain to her at length why he didn't think the Gucci would be a good idea, and his explanations were something Bella tried very hard to avoid. He was always right, of course. They just went on so very long.

'So here's what I think,' Charlotte said, quite oblivious to her sister's distraction. She kicked off her heels and folded her perfect slim legs beneath her with the ease of a woman who practises yoga. 'We have to take Con down, like I said. And we won't be able to do that because of any business fuck-ups. He's solid there. Boring, but solid. Though—'

She paused for a second, her eyes sliding to the side as something occurred to her.

'Well, leave that for now,' she continued. 'The thing is, I've heard some rumours about him. He's been seen at the bar in Novikov and the Playboy Club having what don't look like business meetings with a mystery blonde.'

'Oh *no*! Poor Samantha!' Bella exclaimed, her eyes round with shock.

Samantha, Conway's wife, was elegant perfection. She was actually the Honourable Samantha, being the daughter of a viscount. To his father's considerable approval, Conway had married not only into the landed gentry, but to a woman who seemed to be linked to every single influential, old-money family in Britain. Her relatives were politicians, judges, Lord Lieutenants of their county; she knew everyone worth knowing and was ensuring that their children were being successfully woven into the web of intergenerational family connections. They went to the right kindergartens and schools, socialized with the right friends, engaged in the right after-school activities. Over it all presided the Honourable Samantha, immaculately dressed, immaculately groomed, wearing clothes from British designers, carrying Smythson bags, the perfect wife for the son of a hotel tycoon who needed to attend endless galas and work events, her brown hair worn in a chic modern style, her rather horsey, aristocratic smile polite but never over-enthusiastic. Obvious enthusiasm would be much too lower-middle-class.

'I've never liked her,' Charlotte said frankly. 'She's a bloody snob. We'll never be good enough for her. You know that, Bell.'

'She can't help being posh,' Bella protested.

'She *can* help looking down her nose at us, though,' Charlotte said. 'With that patronizing gummy smile of hers, as if being so inbred you look like a Grand National winner was some kind of prize she won in the lottery.'

Bella was unable to prevent herself from sniggering at this vivid and accurate description of their sister-in-law's habitual expression.

'Say what you really mean, why don't you?' she said between giggles.

Charlotte shrugged one shoulder, a very elegant gesture she had copied from a Frenchwoman of her acquaintance.

'*I'd* be hanging out at Novikov with a slutty-looking blonde if I had Samantha at home,' she said. 'Wouldn't you? I bet she's a really cold fish in bed. Anyway, the point is that if Con's having an affair, and it gets into the press, that'll totally cancel out any advantage he has over us! Don't you see that?'

'But how would it get into the—'

'Hire a PI,' Charlotte said brutally. 'Get a ton of pics, sell them to the tabs, soon as possible.'

Bella stared at her sister, her jaw dropping.

'I don't think we should—'

'So you don't want to be CEO?' Charlotte leant forward, staring intently at her sister's face. 'You don't mind if Con takes charge and lords it over us for the rest of our lives with that patronizing smirk of his?'

Bella felt paralysed. This was all happening so fast. In the space of an hour, their father had issued a shocking challenge; she had not only seen her hated stepmother humiliated, but taken her own very satisfying personal revenge; her sister was suggesting they scheme together to expose their brother's affair; and Bella hadn't even had time to drill down on how she felt about the idea of being CEO of the Sachs Organization . . .

'I don't know!' she blurted out as Charlotte's blue eyes drilled into her. 'I don't know, okay? You know me, I always take ages to make decisions! But—' she drew a breath – 'okay, no. I don't want Con to be our boss! Of course I don't! I never thought Daddy would be so – all or nothing. I just assumed that, when he retired, we'd all keep running our divisions and the board would have a more supervisory function to ensure that we took majority decisions—'

'Oh my *God*, Bells, you really are *beyond* naive!'

Now that she had dragged from her sister the admission that she too would resent their brother ruling the roost, Charlotte sat back, wriggling her legs out from under her and disposing them elegantly to one side.

'As if Daddy would ever let us all run Sachs together in some kind of joint trust thing!' Charlotte continued, flicking back her perfect blonde hair. 'He'd see that as one step away from living in a commune! Way too hippy-dippy for him! You *know* what he's like. He's been sitting in the middle of his web like a big, fat spider for his entire life. He was always going to hand the reins ceremonially to one of us. Only one person can sit on the Iron Throne. I was amazed that Daddy didn't just give it to Con, but he's always loved to pit us against each other, so, knowing him, this makes even more sense.'

Bella nodded. Her sister was right on all counts. But Bella hadn't answered Charlotte's question: did she want to be CEO? Bella realized that she had done what she always did when there was a big decision to be made. She had put it on hold until her brain finished its processing and gave her the answer. Slow and steady, Bella was incapable of the lightning-fast leaps of deduction or inspiration that were so natural to her twin sister.

Still, once her brain – rather like an ancient super-computer you saw in old films – had completed its calculations and spat out the answer, it was always right. Unlike Charlotte, Bella never backtracked or revised her decisions. Waiting for a while was only what Bella was used to: but with great surprise, she took in the fact that her answer had not been an automatic 'no'.

'So you'll do it?' Charlotte finished, and Bella blinked: her sister had obviously been talking, and Bella hadn't even noticed.

'Sorry,' she said, grimacing. 'I was away with the fairies there.'

'Oh, *Bell*! Get it together – we don't have much time!' Charlotte said, frowning impatiently. 'I said, you call the PI and I'll deal with taking the info to the tabloids if he comes up with anything. Or she. Actually, a "she" would be better, wouldn't it? No one's suspicious of a woman – she could take photos of Con and his blonde while pretending she's just doing selfies.'

'I don't think I – how would I even *find* a PI?' Bella protested, feeling that things were moving much too fast for her. But then, she always did feel that with Charlotte.

'Ask your security team, for goodness' sake,' Charlotte said, sounding irritated. 'They'll know exactly the right person to use. I don't see why I should have to do it all myself. And look, if Con isn't cheating, if I've been told malicious gossip or there's some perfectly innocent explanation, then nothing'll come of it! So really, there's no harm either way.'

'But—'

'We don't have to use the pictures even if we get them,' Charlotte continued inexorably. 'We can decide then and there. Look, sort out the PI. I won't even know what they come up with unless you show it to me. It can be your decision. Just don't sit on it for months like a hen hatching eggs, like you usually do.'

This coaxed a reluctant smile from Bella. She digested Charlotte's words, seeing the good sense in them; Bella would be in control of the process. Even if the PI did come up with compromising information on Conway, Bella could bury it and never let Charlotte know. But the thought of paying a private detective to spy on her brother was so shocking, such a betrayal, that Bella's instincts were telling her very strongly that she would feel guilty for the rest of her life if she did anything like this . . .

'Let's Skype Mummy!' Charlotte was saying, jumping up lithely from the sofa and grabbing her laptop from the kitchen counter. 'She's going to be over the moon when she hears about Jade!'

Immediately, this brightened Bella's mood. She pushed the question of the PI to the back of her brain, where it could marinate in company with the issue of why she hadn't immediately said that, no, she had no interest in being named the CEO of Sachs, and got up too, though less balletically than the lean and lissom Charlotte. Bella went over to her handbag, pulled out her little make-up case and quickly fixed up her face, patting concealer onto areas that needed it, powdering over the top to set it, then applying lipstick and a fresh coat of mascara. She knew all too well that practically the first words out of Christie's mouth would be to comment on the appearance of her two daughters.

Which was ironic, considering that they had to bite their tongues till they nearly bled to avoid mentioning the subject of Christie's own physical appearance nowadays . . .

'Mummy? Mummy!' Charlotte was saying eagerly, looking at the screen.

Of course Charlotte hadn't needed to bother to touch up her own make-up; it was always perfect. How Charlotte managed it, Bella had no idea. By mid-afternoon Bella might as well have not applied her foundation and mascara that morning. She was often rubbing her eyes, or resting her chin or her cheek on her hand as she thought something over; business was highly absorbing to her. She could become utterly lost in thought, or consumed by a back and forth in an important meeting, and was famously unselfconscious about how she came across to her associates.

'Mummeee!' Charlotte carolled blissfully as the screen pipped and beeped and clarified into the face of the first Mrs Sachs. Sitting on one of the frighteningly slender-legged white leather-topped stools by the breakfast bar, Charlotte gestured at her sister, summoning her over. 'Mummy, I'm so glad you're around! You won't *believe* what happened today, you simply won't, not even when we tell you!'

With their mother, Charlotte reverted to the breathy, good-girl, wide-eyed persona that had been extremely successful for her while she was growing up. It made Bella feel even more stolid and dull by comparison, but that, she reminded herself, was her own fault, not Charlotte's.

'Hey, girls!' Christie Sachs exclaimed. 'How great to see you both together! Wow, that barely happens nowadays! This is a lovely surprise! Charlotte, your hair's just *darling*. Bella, honey, get the name of your sister's hairdresser and make an appointment! But it's nice to see you in lipstick. So, what's up?'

The twins stared back at their mother, momentarily speechless. They had braced themselves, as they always did, before they saw her. It was impossible to predict what new procedure she might have had since their last conversation. Over the years, they had been confronted with bright red, burnt-looking skin from a facial peel; two bruised eyes and a splint over her nose; lips blown up like pink rubber balloons; and eyebrows so much higher than normal on her forehead that they might have been held up by invisible tape.

And they had learnt, very quickly, that any attempt to mention their concerns about the near-constant plastic surgeries that Christie had started undergoing almost immediately after the divorce would be shut down with the force and speed of a steel trap dropping into place. So as Bella cautiously levered herself onto the high stool next to her sister's – it had a spring-loaded seat that made sitting on it feel very precarious – she found herself blinking madly. This was what she did when she needed to respond to something physically, but couldn't show any facial reaction for reasons of discretion. Something had radically altered with Christie, but Bella couldn't tell what.

Beside her, Charlotte shifted and raised her fingers to her

right eye, as if she were scratching the most fleeting of itches. Her twin decoded it instantly. Christie's eyes were now a completely different shape, even bigger, round for the first time ever, and frighteningly fixed and staring; she had undergone a blepharoplasty, an operation to remove excess skin and fat from above and below the eyes. It had utterly changed her face.

'You're looking good, Mummy,' Bella managed to stammer, transfixed by the headlamp stare of her mother's now-huge, bugging-out Bette Davis eyes. It was particularly distressing as they had been such an intrinsic part of her beauty; yes, the skin around them had been sagging a little, the eyelids becoming heavier, but those cornflower-blue headlights had always lit up a room. Now they had transformed into a horror show from which everyone would want to avert their own gaze.

Charlotte huffed irritably at her twin's pathetic attempt to suck up.

'Mummy, amazing news!' she cut in. 'You won't believe this! Daddy's actually kicked out Jade!'

Chapter Five

Christie was at her villa in the South of France, which was stunningly positioned on a promontory overlooking St-Jean-Cap-Ferrat. Even though she was inside, bright Mediterranean sunlight flooded the screen; behind her was visible blue sky without a hint of cloud. The glorious sunshine, however, was as nothing to the smile that lit up Christie's face on hearing this news.

'*Finally!*' she exclaimed, and watching the skin stretch tightly over her bones as she beamed widely was painful for both her daughters. She was slim, blonde and lissom, dressed in a translucent silk kaftan in bright shades of flame with a snug red swimsuit underneath, and draped in gold: earrings, a tangle of fine gold necklaces, multiple bangles tinkling lightly on her wrists.

From behind, from a distance, she might have been thirty, and if she had limited herself to discreet tweaks and a jowl lift or two, she would still be a beauty. But the divorce had sent Christie into a spiral of self-doubt, and although many plastic surgeons would categorically refuse to do unnecessary work, referring clients to psychologists specializing in body dysmorphic disorder if they had any doubts about whether to go ahead with a procedure, there were still plenty who were unscrupulous enough to keep taking a client's money even if they were doing more harm than good. The one who had stretched out her eyes like that, Bella thought, wincing, should be shot.

'I *knew* this would happen sooner or later!' Christie continued ecstatically. 'How did it happen? Tell me *everything*!'

Her daughters launched into a stream of description, their words tumbling over each other, blending together: Christie, very used to hearing the twins telling a story in sync, listened intently without needing to tell them to slow down or take it in turns. Her expression grew steadily more blissful as they went on, and by the time Bella was enthusiastically miming a dramatic yet accurate depiction of the way she had gone after Jade with the bolster, Christie was clasping her hands in front of her and resembling nothing so much as a saint transfixed by a revelation delivered to her directly from the mouth of God.

'Good girl!' she sighed ecstatically. 'Good *girl*!'

Charlotte, always competitive with her siblings, bridled at her mother's praise of Bella.

'So after Daddy said to throw Jade out,' she chimed in, 'oh, Mummy, that was *amazing*, I wish you could have seen it! Conway and Bart pulled her out of the chair and frog-marched her across the room, with Daddy and the new slut standing there watching – anyway, when we got onto the street I told her just what you always used to say, that you lose them how you get them! And I said you were a lady all the way through the divorce *and* that her brats would never get voting rights in the trust and then I told her to fuck off or I'd call the police!'

'I couldn't be prouder of both of you!' Christie sighed. 'Oh, how I wish I'd seen it! But all four of you did, and that's *wonderful*! Wonderful! My babies, all watching her get her comeuppance! She climbed in *through the toilet window*?'

'And over the hedge! Or through it, I'm not sure,' Bella said eagerly. 'She was cut up – she had a big bruise on her leg and she'd scraped her forehead . . .'

'I couldn't be happier! I *couldn't*!' Christie clapped her hands. 'Brice! *Du champagne, s'il te plaît! Vite, vite!*'

A young man ambled across the screen behind Christie; she was reclining in her living room, on a sofa upholstered in blue-and-white-striped linen, and it looked as if he had been outside by the swimming pool, as he was wearing only a small pair of red Speedos and a gold chain around his neck. Neither Bella nor Charlotte had seen him before, but his type was very familiar to them. Christie had been working her way through the twenty-something male population of the French Riviera since she moved there.

From St Tropez to Cannes to Nice to Monaco, the word had got out that any slim, relatively hairless, dark-haired young man with a winning smile and an accommodating nature could live the good life at the Villa Rosa in St-Jean-Cap-Ferrat for a year or so, until Christie's eyes started to stray once more to assess the new crop of bartenders, waiters, pool boys and lifeguards displayed in all their glory on beaches up and down the coast. She could afford to be very generous; each young man left with the very expensive gifts Christie had bought him during their residency – watches, clothes, a car – and, if he had played his cards well, he would have a raft of connections to other rich widows or divorcees who were also looking for a new plaything.

'*Des bonnes nouvelles?*' Brice asked, scratching his balls as he went.

'*Oui, oui, les meilleures du monde! Fantastique!*'

Christie beamed back at her daughters as Brice disappeared from view to get the champagne.

'I told him it's the best news in the world!' she informed them, unnecessarily, as she knew they both spoke French. 'You should toast too! Charlotte, go get some fizz, honey! If I can't be there with you and give you both a big hug for standing up for your mom today, we can at least raise a glass to that bitch getting her comeuppance!'

Charlotte jumped down from her stool and went over to the built-in drinks fridge. As she pulled out a bottle of Taittinger, Christie continued:

'You two must come over for a weekend real soon! It's so close, it's crazy you don't visit more . . .'

'Yikes, Mummy!' Charlotte called from the kitchen. 'We'd love to, of course, but I'm going to be working like a maniac for the next six months! Oh God, we need to tell you about that too—'

As Charlotte pulled champagne coupes out of the drawer in the freezer which was specifically designed to hold chilled glasses, Bella took over, relating to Christie their father's challenge to the four siblings, their six-month trial to present themselves as the best candidate for CEO of the entire Sachs organization. By the time Charlotte had filled the coupes and returned to the breakfast bar with the foaming, ice-dappled glasses, Christie was fully briefed and doing her best, despite her surgeries and Botox, to frown.

'But of course it'll be Conway!' she said, looking from one twin to the other. 'Come on now, you know that! You girls work too hard as it is. Charlotte, you need to spend more time with your family, not less. I love seeing you all on Instagram, but honey, that's staged for the cameras, with a bunch of people round you styling you and the kids, doing make-up and hair, taking the photos. You need to kick back with Paul and Posy and Quant when there's no one else around, make sure you get proper family time.'

'What about telling Conway to spend more time with his family?' Charlotte said indignantly. 'He's barely ever at home – Samantha's bringing up those kids pretty much by herself!'

'He's working *for* his family, honey,' Christie corrected her patiently. 'That's way different, can't you see? And Samantha's fine as she is – she's really happy being a stay-at-home mom.'

Charlotte's eyes bulged in frustration as her mother continued:

'And Bella, sweetie, you need to start your family with Thomas! What are you waiting for, honey? The clock's ticking – you don't want to be left behind!'

Once more, Bella's eyelashes fluttered in a nervous tic, the words she wanted to say bitten back. Luckily her mother was distracted by the arrival of a beaming Brice, who had donned a loose white linen shirt which hung open over his slender, slightly hollow tanned chest, a champagne glass in each hand.

'*Voici, Christie!*' he said, his French accent completely mangling her name but also turning it into a thing of beauty.

'*Merci, mon cher,*' Christie said, taking her glass as Brice slung one leg over the arm of the sofa and perched on it nonchalantly, the contents of his Speedos bulging through the shiny fabric, which was thin enough to outline every specific detail. They pouched even more as he leant forward to chink his glass with Christie's. Charlotte reached out and nudged the laptop, moving it just far enough to cut out Brice's package, though his lightly furred, suntan-oiled thigh was still in view.

'You girls think you can have it all, but you can't,' Christie said earnestly, pushing her hair back, her bracelets jingling as she did so. 'Listen to your mom, okay? Learn from my fuck-up! I thought I could sit on the board of Sachs and do design work and bring up four kids and keep my husband, all at the same time. And you know what happened! I got distracted and that slut took advantage!'

'Well, she got her comeuppance today!' Charlotte said quickly, trying to steer their mother away from one of her favourite subjects, young women today and how they should be focusing less on their careers and more on making sure their husbands had no time to look around at the even younger women making eyes at them. 'And we're toasting that! To losing them how you get them!'

'To losing them how you get them!' Bella and Christie chorused, raising their glasses.

The twins clinked their coupes together and then raised them to the screen, as Christie was doing. Mother and daughters flashed happy smiles at each other before taking sips of champagne.

'So you'll come visit?' Christie said hopefully. 'We'll have such a great family time. No business talk allowed! Posy and Quant can spend all day in the pool, they'll love that! They're such water babies—'

Just then, to the twins' relief, they heard a key in the door. It was Paul, Charlotte's husband, returning with the adorable pair of five-year-olds from a romp in the playground in Regent's Park. Twins, it had turned out, ran in the family. Christie's attention immediately switched to her grandchildren, and as Posy and Quant lisped greetings to her, Paul kissing his wife in greeting before unbuttoning the kids' coats and hanging them up, Charlotte and Bella took the opportunity to slip away.

'It's a red-letter day for Granny Christie!' the proud grandmother was saying blissfully. 'Paul, honey, get yourself a glass of champagne, and can the kids have a little too? Just a drop? Let 'em put their fingers in your glass. Today we're having a big celebration!'

Charlotte poured Paul a glass, as Posy piped up, reaching to point at the bit of Brice's leg which was visible on the screen:

'Who's that, Gwanny Cwistie?'

Leaning forward helpfully, Paul turned the laptop back to its original angle before either Charlotte or Bella could screech a warning to him. The subsequent kerfuffle ensured that Christie completely forgot about lecturing her daughters on being attentive wives: she was too busy apologizing to Paul and the kids, shouting at Brice to get off the sofa, button up his shirt and hide his *bijoux de famille*, and promising Paul and Charlotte that it would never happen again.

Quant's hands were clapped to his mouth in shock: Posy kept asking why the funny man was in his underpants. Meanwhile Paul was, in his most serious voice, explaining to Christie that while he was bringing the children up to be completely comfortable with their own and each other's bodies, he and Charlotte, as parents, wanted to be able to control the level of exposure the children had on their journey of self-discovery . . .

'Drink some and get a grip,' Charlotte said curtly, thrusting the champagne coupe at her husband. 'Honestly, he's in a swimsuit. It's not *that* big a deal!'

Bella turned away to hide a snigger at this inadvertent double entendre, especially because Brice, at least in a resting state, was more chipolata than Cumberland sausage. Charlotte, seeing this, realized what she had said and bit the inside of her cheeks to stop laughing too. The sisters moved away from the breakfast bar; on the screen behind them, Brice, climbing off the sofa to obey Christie's order, accidentally turned his red-clad bottom to the camera and made both Posy and Quant hoot with laughter, point and yell about the funny man's bum-bum.

'Oh my *God*!' Christie exclaimed, grabbing her laptop and leaning in so that the only thing visible was her face. 'Granny's sorry, kids! Brice, *fiche-moi le camp! Dépêche-toi!*'

'Hard to believe that's the first gigolo crotch we've seen on Skype, considering how many of them have been through Villa Rosa,' Charlotte said *sotto voce* to Bella. 'Christ, Paul's going to bang on about this for ages. He's so *serious*. The kids'll just think it's funny unless he hammers on so much he gives them some sort of complex.'

Glancing over at Paul, handsome as a Greek god with the black curls clustering densely over his scalp, his clear blue eyes and sculpted features, his striped V-neck Nigel Hall cashmere sweater clinging to his gym-toned torso, his slim-fit Tom Ford jeans performing the same service for his tight buttocks, and his jaw set as he tried to summon his patience while explaining his childcare philosophy to a fervently apologizing Christie, Bella found it as difficult as she always did when Charlotte said something negative about her husband.

She actually agreed with Charlotte this time: Paul was making it worse by emphasizing the brief glimpse of Brice in his Speedos, rather than laughing with Posy and Quant about Granny's silly friend's bum-bum and then distracting them with a dab of champagne on their tongues. But Paul was so good-looking, so perfect, such a great father! Charlotte was insanely lucky! Yes, Paul could be ponderous sometimes, but in Bella's view that tendency of his had intensified over the years to balance out Charlotte's carelessness with the children. She loved to play with them and dress them up like pretty dolls, but Paul and the nannies had the hard work of bringing them up to be civilized human beings. It was highly frustrating for Bella to watch Paul being an ideal husband and father while Charlotte criticized the one thing that she could dredge up about him.

'We're having courgette passgetti for dinner!' Posy was saying eagerly to her grandmother. 'Daddy makes it in the twirly machine!'

'That's the spiralizer,' Paul explained to Christie. 'We're working on getting a balance between proteins, carbs and vegetables in our daily diet, and courgette spaghetti is a fun way to—'

'Why are Gwanny's eyes all funny?' Quant piped up, pointing at the screen. 'They're all big now.'

'Oh yes!' Posy exclaimed, leaning forward to stare at the close-up of Christie on the screen, stabbing at it with a chubby finger. 'Gwanny looks funny!'

Christie hastily put the laptop down on the coffee table again. The wider shot showed Brice, re-entering the room with his shirt buttoned up and a pair of capri trousers covering the lower part of his body, pulling a very comical face in a swift, involuntary reaction to Quant's innocent question.

Luckily, Christie was entirely unaware of her current toy boy's amusement at the elephant in the room being mentioned. She struggled to come up with an answer as Paul said reprovingly to his son:

'Quant! You know it's rude to talk about people's appearances! Say sorry to Granny Christie at once.'

'*Naughty* Quant!' Posy said with great satisfaction.

Quant relieved his embarrassment by turning to punch his sister, and Paul grabbed the kids to separate them. Bella gathered up her bag.

'I should be going,' she said half-heartedly.

It was always difficult for Bella to drag herself away from the St John's Wood house. Though the gleaming white surfaces weren't exactly cosy, still, at this time of day, with Charlotte and Bella playing with the kids, a log burning in the glass-fronted fireplace, Paul in the kitchen starting to plan out one of his gourmet yet healthy meals, the warmth and happy chaos created a family atmosphere that was entirely missing from her own home.

'You can stay and have courgette spaghetti with Paul and the kids if you want,' Charlotte offered nonchalantly. 'I have business drinks later at Claridge's, but I'm sure they'd be happy for the company. Paul made this amazing chocolate avocado mousse last night, and there's some of that left over. Thomas is still away, right?'

'Yes, he's back tomorrow morning,' Bella said. 'He's getting the red-eye from Dubai.'

She was repressing a strong wish to stay, to play house with Paul and Posy and Quant. But she knew it would feel worse if she stayed and left later; it would be even harder to wrench herself away. After dinner came bathtime, and Paul would be more than happy to let Bella supervise the kids as they played with the bubbles in the whirlpool bath and built wobbly, towering wigs on each other's heads, screaming in excitement as the coloured lights under the water changed in sequence . . .

And then 'flying' them out of the bath, drying off their squirming little bodies, getting them into their pyjamas for Paul to take over and put them to bed while she quietly let herself out of the house, to go back to her own empty one on a Friday night, with her husband away . . . no, she had done that before and it was the most depressing moment she could imagine, when your hosts were ready for you to go, but you were not.

It wasn't just the kids. It was Paul, the house, the whole

package. Despite what Christie had said, Charlotte really did have it all. And when it was not merely your best friend, or even your sister, but your twin who had it all, that was a particularly bitter pill to have to swallow, not once, but on a near-daily basis.

Chapter Six

It was an easy drive home. A left turn out of Charlotte's private courtyard took Bella up to the Finchley Road, which led almost all the way to Hampstead Garden Suburb. It was, Bella's husband Thomas always said with amusement and pride, the only suburb in the world which boasted of its status to the point of incorporating it proudly in its name.

The Suburb, as it was known to its inhabitants, had been intended as a retreat from the noise and bustle of London. Built in the early twentieth century, specifically planned with widely spaced houses on gracious tree-lined avenues interspersed with public gardens, the Suburb had been entirely successful in achieving its goal: though it contained two churches, they were banned from ringing their bells, and the trust which governed the management scheme had recently cracked down on overly noisy lawnmowers and leaf blowers. Thomas was one of the four elected trustees and had been at the forefront of implementing this policy. The Suburb, which was the major freeholder, also required that homeowners get the trust's approval for felling trees, building garden sheds and even major changes to their gardens, and Thomas was equally enthusiastic about ensuring that it remained as pristine and unspoilt as possible.

When they first moved there, five years ago, Bella had loved the quiet, tranquil atmosphere. Thomas had grown up there and always planned to return when he got married, considering it the perfect place to settle down and raise a family. He had been the first man she had dated who had been ready to nest, and the relief when she realized that he felt the same way as she did had been overwhelming and unexpected.

Because Bella, at twenty-eight, had found that her peers still wanted to play the field. On business trips to America, women her own age had told her that in the US, you could talk on your first date about what you wanted in a partner, weed out the men who weren't able to say that they too were ready for a serious commitment leading to marriage. For an Englishwoman, however, this kind of frankness was anathema, and even if Bella could have summoned up the requisite bravery to try it, any Englishman would have run a mile. So she bounced unhappily from one boyfriend to another, men in her own social circle who had plenty of funds of their own and didn't need to marry a Sachs daughter for money and status. When she finally met forty-year-old Thomas at a dinner party, it had felt like the happiest of endings.

She pulled the Audi into the driveway, next to Thomas's. His car being home, however, did not mean that he was. As always, he had taken a cab to the airport. Thomas, a senior commodity trader, travelled a great deal for work. He had given Bella to understand that this would change once they were married, but it had not, and when she reproached him, he had acted surprised and pointed out that he had only been speculating on what his work would allow; he had never made any kind of definite promise.

It was true: he hadn't. He had said he would try to modify his travel schedule, but so far, it hadn't altered in the slightest. And as Bella locked her car and walked across the neatly maintained path to her front door, she looked across the street at the neighbours' perfectly maintained hedges, and considered bitterly that when Thomas *was* in London, he probably spent as much time at the Hampstead Garden Suburb Trust offices on the Finchley Road, sitting through endless meetings to debate hedge heights and the latest batch of applications to build garden sheds and conservatories, as he did at home.

The house was as quiet inside as the most demanding resident of the Suburb could possibly have wished. It was so full of soft furnishings that any noise would have been muffled by the curtains and pelmets and carpets and cushions and armchairs. Nothing if not comfortable, it was, however, distinctly old-fashioned. Bella had often thought that it was as if she had deliberately reproduced the very classic, dated style of the Sachs hotels in her own home, while Charlotte was the Sash brand, hip and cutting-edge.

But she was trying to update the Sachs hotels, she reminded herself now as she deposited her handbag on the console table in the hallway. Her design team was coordinating with Charlotte's on the hugely cumbersome project of shifting them into the twenty-first century, updating the rather tired, though imposing, fittings and furnishings into something fresher and more modern, closer to Charlotte's

Sash hotels, with their witty touches and sleeker lines. On the table sat a large china vase, a wedding present from Thomas's parents, which was filled with an elaborate arrangement of pink and white flowers, stiff and formal, a world away from Charlotte's magic white flowers submerged in tinted liquid.

The flower arrangements were delivered on a weekly basis from a local, very traditional florist in Temple Fortune. But Bella found herself wondering now if they might be able to manage something fresher, more modern, if she asked them. They wouldn't have floating flowers, of course, not in Temple Fortune. But maybe they could come up with something that looked as if it belonged in the house of a thirty-four-year-old, rather than an elderly dowager? After all, Bella was a grown woman, very successful in business, in the running to become CEO of a world-famous company: shouldn't she have flowers in her house that she liked?

The trouble was, this was exactly Thomas's taste: the formal flowers, the heavy dark-wood furniture, the beige and bottle-green colour scheme, the thermal-lined curtains that kept the house warm and peaceful. Everything within these walls was as traditional and conventional as possible. This Sunday, Bella would cook a roast lunch, as she always did when both of them were in London for the weekend. She had already ordered the ingredients, to be delivered Saturday morning by Ocado in their weekly pre-paid time slot, 10 to 11 a.m.: the sirloin of beef on the bone, the prepped vegetables, the Yorkshire puddings, the meat stock for gravy, the lemon syllabub, the redcurrants to decorate it. The wine cellar was stocked with expensive reds, most definitely not ordered from Ocado, to accompany the meal.

And after a few glasses of St Émilion, Thomas would doze off in the living room in front of whatever sport was on, while Bella would stack the dishwasher. It was almost parodic, but they enjoyed the cosiness of it all. They lived in the Suburb, and they had the most quintessential of suburban Sundays. Fresh from the family atmosphere of Charlotte and Paul's, Bella found herself suddenly craving Thomas's return. Yes, he would be jet-lagged on Saturday, needing to sleep till lunchtime, but then they would have the rest of the weekend to cuddle up together in marital happiness . . .

In his continuing quest for tranquillity, Thomas had deactivated the beep on the answering machine, so whenever Bella came home she automatically put her head into his study to glance at it. Seeing a red light flashing, she went over to click the 'play' button.

'Hey, darling,' came the voice of her husband. 'It's me. Sorry not to catch you on your mobile. Bad news, I'm afraid! I'm stuck here till at least Monday. The client's being unexpectedly tricksy and I've got to hang on until we've ironed out all the creases. Can we freeze the beef? I was so looking forward to my roast! I'll ring again when I've got things firmed up. Much love.'

Bella checked her handbag, extracting her mobile from its compartment. She had forgotten to turn on the ringer again after silencing it for the meeting with her father. However, that would have made no difference, as there were no missed incoming calls. This wasn't the first time Thomas had claimed to have tried her mobile, leaving a message on the home phone when he knew she would be out, and it was always with bad news involving his staying away longer than had been planned.

She sighed; she had half expected this. Even when she had told Charlotte that Thomas was due back on the red-eye Saturday morning, she had doubted whether he would actually be on the plane. It seemed to be happening more and more, and the worst part was that he denied that a pattern was forming of his business trips increasingly covering weekends. He would get irritated if she tried to point out the dates that they had been supposed to spend lazy Sundays together only for a last-minute message to arrive, telling her to put the meat in the freezer . . .

Put the meat in the freezer. The words rang in her head, taking on an extra meaning, as she walked into the kitchen. Because it wasn't just the sirloin she was putting on ice, but their Sunday morning sex. This was the only time they did it all week, the routine they had established once they had settled into married life. The excitement of courtship over, Thomas explained that he was generally too preoccupied by work to have sex on weekdays, and on Saturdays he was still distracted, so Sunday was the one day he could fully relax and get in the mood.

It was frustrating for Bella, who wanted sex more often than her husband, especially because she knew he had no difficulty getting an erection. If she grazed his crotch playfully with her hand, as she had used to do at the start of their relationship, before he had made it clear he didn't like her to touch him there spontaneously, his penis would instantly respond. Bella had said jokingly that maybe Thomas could stay out of it, letting her and his cock get on with things between themselves, and he had smiled politely and simply let the remark fall into the space between them.

The power of passive resistance in a marriage was extraordinary, she had discovered. Thomas was an immovable object, while Bella was no irresistible force. He got his way, and she adapted to it. She had stopped asking for sex any other time, stopped trying to seduce him, as the quiet continual rejection was intolerable to her. Besides, he made her feel thoughtless and unreasonable for not respecting his wishes. He had, effectively, trained her into expecting only what he wanted to give.

But what if he was now training her even more, getting her to stop expecting even the once-a-week sex? It had been difficult enough to accept the swift dwindling in frequency as soon as they had got married, but Bella shivered in fear at the idea that it would be cut down further . . . or a worse possibility, that she would lose not only the sex, but her husband's company at the weekends, because he wasn't able to address whatever issue he had and preferred to stay away as an avoidance tactic . . .

After all, you get married not only for regular sex, but to have someone to spend the weekends with, she thought as she opened the fridge and stared at the cheese compartment. It was packed with an enticing selection her housekeeper had purchased from the local French delicatessen: Cambozola, Gorgonzola and mascarpone layered with pesto and pine nuts, pecorino aged in chestnut leaves, ridiculously expensive pea shoots to garnish. Both Bella and Thomas loved good cheese, and Bella had also got the housekeeper to buy delicate seeded crackers and deliciously crusty bread from the deli. She had been planning to arrange a plate for Thomas. When he walked in the front door the next morning, jet-lagged and bleary-eyed, he would have been delighted to have something yummy to snack on before he took a long nap.

The cheese, the bread, the wonderfully crusty bread with its soft doughy centre, spread with slabs of unsalted butter . . . Bella's mouth watered. She needed comfort, and here it was, just sitting in her kitchen waiting for her to eat it up. But then she thought of the courgette spaghetti Paul was making for him and the kids, of Paul's perfect lean body, of Charlotte so slender in her belted suede dress, and she shut the fridge so smartly that the plumbed-in water dispenser rattled.

Before she could change her mind she left the kitchen, removing herself from temptation. She came to a halt in the hallway, though, asking herself what she could do to distract herself from thoughts of bread and cheese. They had a gym in the basement, with a treadmill, stair climber, exercise bike and free weights. Thomas worked out every weekday morning; Bella did not. She barely used the gym, as she absolutely hated exercising. But she could grab a magazine, climb on the bike, spend half an hour satisfying the demands of the stupid FitBit Thomas had bought her last year. Bicycling was sitting down, so it wasn't really exercising, looked at in a certain way . . .

And then you'll get off that bike, walk up to the kitchen and dive into the cheese, Bella acknowledged to herself. *You'll convince yourself you deserve it after putting yourself through that, and you'll end up eating way more calories than you've just burnt.*

There was no denying that Bella would almost certainly find herself back in front of the fridge some time that evening. She had never been good at being alone. To her, it had always been synonymous with loneliness. Charlotte, however, had seemed fine with it. Though, of course, the difference was that Charlotte had never *needed* to be alone. From their schooldays onwards, she had always been popular, surrounded by friends and admirers, with a string of boyfriends arriving in due course; when she was by herself, it was by choice, and that was entirely different.

Charlotte, for instance, had never had to watch Bella get ready for the evening, dateless herself. Before their marriages, when they lived together in the huge flat their parents had bought them in Notting Hill, it had inevitably been Bella buzzing in whoever was lucky enough to be Charlotte's date while her sister finished her hair and make-up and eventually emerged. Always at least half an hour late, she was so stunning that all the young man could do was gape at her in tribute.

While there was Bella, on the sofa, downloading episodes of *Charmed* and telling herself that she was very happy to have an evening in with her favourite show. Bella, who looked so very like Charlotte, but without Charlotte's sparkle and fizz. It wasn't the extra pounds that made Bella so comparatively undatable. She did at least know that. The twins had curvaceous friends who got plenty of attention, but those girls also had strong personalities; they weren't wallflowers. Any attempt Bella made to draw attention to herself made her feel like a weaker copy of Charlotte, and the men she attracted were, in their turn, weaker copies of Charlotte's boyfriends. She was lesser all the way around. It was easier just not to try at all.

So meeting Thomas at that dinner party had been a godsend. He had asked her, on their first date, if she'd had boyfriends of his age before, and on her responding in the negative he had looked genuinely taken aback. She had, he had told her, a quiet poise and gravity that was very unusual for a young woman in her mid twenties; he had thought she was older, would not have asked her out if he had realized how comparatively young she was. He hoped he was not too old for her, at forty. Was she all right with the age difference?

Bella blossomed with excitement. Of course she was! Finally she was perceived as different from Charlotte in a positive way! Not shy, not insipid and boring, but grown-up for her age: composed, attractive to a man who wanted to settle down. Thomas expressed surprise that she was not regularly asked out by older men who did not want to go out with frivolous, squealing twenty-somethings but preferred women who were sensible, dignified, serious professionals.

It had never occurred to Bella that she shouldn't be dating her peers, but as soon as Thomas had voiced this she realized that he was absolutely right. Who had been most interested in what she had to say at university? Her professors, who had singled her out, asked her to join inner-circle reading and debate groups, invited her to sherry parties. Older people, who valued her brains and, as Thomas had put it, her poise and gravity. Who had rewarded her with a first-class degree in due course, and suggested she continue in academia.

That had never been a possibility for Bella, however. She might be the only intellectual among the Sachs children, but that brainpower had been trained and developed entirely for use in the family firm.

Now, however, it occurred to her that for all Thomas's praise of her during their courtship, he was, for whatever reason, choosing to see less and less of the qualities that had so enchanted him back then. She remembered working her way through those episodes of *Charmed* in her single days, lying to herself that this was exactly how she wanted to spend her Friday nights. And here she was, married but still alone on too many Friday nights. On the drive home she had planned an early night so she could get up tomorrow, do her hair and make-up, make sure the house was perfect for Thomas's return, arrange the cheese plate, and, as he snacked, tell him the amazing news about her father leaving Jade for Adrianna, and setting the six-month deadline at the end of which she or one of her siblings would be made CEO of the Sachs Organization . . .

A flood of endorphins surged through her at the words 'made CEO'. It was the first time that the reality of it truly hit home. Her legs felt suddenly weak. There was a chair in the hallway next to the console table, one of those pointless hallway chairs that no one ever used. Until now. She sank down onto it as slowly and carefully as if she had arthritis, physically shaking. Only now, alone, was she able to absorb the fact that she was in with a genuine chance to take over from her father and run Sachs.

Bella could taste the rush of excitement in her mouth like iron. She had a first-class PPE degree from Oxford. She ran her department with superb efficiency. She wasn't creative, like Charlotte, but she had an excellent MBA, which Charlotte didn't. Conway had one too, but he hadn't graduated summa cum laude from Harvard Business School. First her studies, then her business career: this had always been the part of her life over which Bella had absolute control.

She knew that she could do it. And not only *could* she run Sachs, she *wanted* to. When Charlotte had asked her if she did, Bella had hemmed and hawed. Had she not been sure, or was it that she had not wanted to admit it in front of her sister, her rival? Perhaps she *had* been sure, and had already started to play the six-months-long game?

Bella realized in shock that the iron taste in her mouth was because she had bitten into her lip enough to draw blood. It was painful, but strangely, the pain felt good, a release for her pent-up feelings. The small red smudge of blood as she wiped her mouth on her hand looked hugely symbolic, as if she had made a pact with herself.

Bella could not bring Thomas home from Dubai tomorrow morning. She could not make him have sex with her when she wanted, only when he did. It was the first time she had fully admitted this to herself. She had tried and tried to think of ways to make him want her more, stay home more: welcome him home with hair and make-up done at nine in the morning, dress to be seductive, make the house perfect, spend a fortune on cheese and bread and *pea shoots*, for fuck's sake, to make a platter for his arrival, and it had been an utter and total waste of energy which she could have diverted somewhere much more productive.

No more trying to control her husband's actions. The release that rushed through her once she had made that resolution was so huge she was glad she was sitting down. Instinctively, she reached out and put her hand on the console table to brace herself. She still felt lonely, but it was different now. She was no longer fighting her loneliness; she could admit the truth.

Instead, with all that energy, Bella would throw herself into this quest for the next six months. She would create some extraordinary achievement that would convince her father she was the best candidate of the four, stand in a spotlight she had never realized that she wanted. It was a revelation. She pictured herself on a stage, the applause deafening, a bouquet in her arms, a smile irradiating her face. It felt wonderful. Even deserved.

The weakness had passed. Bella jumped to her feet, grabbed her handbag and keys, headed for the front door. She was going back to work. And the first thing she would do, once back at her desk, was to ring her security team and ask if they knew of a reliable PI they could recommend.

Charlotte was right. Conway had such a huge built-in advantage as the oldest child, the son and presumed heir, that she would never win this battle fighting clean. A couple of hours ago the thought of setting a PI to dig up dirt on her brother had been a profound shock to Bella. It was very telling that now she had admitted her ambition to herself, she was making it a priority.

Much more of a priority, in fact, than ringing her husband. Because it hadn't even occurred to her to call Thomas back.

Chapter Seven

Mummy doesn't know what she's talking about, Charlotte thought smugly as her driver dropped her off at Claridge's. *You can have it all. And I do – well, almost! When I'm made CEO of Sachs, then I'll really be able to say I do.*

She set her jaw in determination.

And that's a when, not an if.

The Range Rover pulled up not at the main entrance of the hotel, but the door on Davies Street which led to the bar. Charlotte was, after all, heading for a business meeting. Just before entering, she reached into the Birkin slung over her arm and extracted a pair of tinted Elizabeth and James sunglasses, slipping them on. They were fashionably oversized, large enough to conceal a considerable part of her face. She walked straight through the bar, slipping easily past the row of big red leather stools. Head ducked, glancing briefly from side to side behind the huge sunglasses, she did not spot anyone she knew. Nor, as far as she could tell, had she been recognized.

The bar was not large and she crossed it swiftly, heading for the main lobby, where, after a brief exchange with a concierge, she took a room key and went up to the third floor, sunglasses still on. Her hair was loose, still with the wonderful Nicky Clarke blow-dry; she had showered and changed before heading out, but been careful to keep the glossy waves dry, and they hung around her face, providing her with extra cover. She wore a beige belted Burberry raincoat, the most neutral outfit possible for these surroundings.

The room was a deluxe king, its decor instantly recognizable as Claridge's. It had a distinctive, signature blend of art deco furniture with a colour palette of beige, greys and browns, offset with the occasional touch of navy in the upholstery of the leather bench at the foot of the huge bed and the decorative throw across its base, trimmed with pale-gold satin. The colours were intended to convey tradition, luxury and calm, and were far from being Charlotte's taste. But then, her Sash hotels were a very different category of hotel to this one. It was classic: hers were boutique chic.

And frankly, Charlotte had no interest whatsoever in what the room looked like. She had chosen Claridge's primarily because it had a separate entrance to its bar, so that her driver could legitimately say, if questioned, that he had not left her at a hotel per se. This was far from being the only early evening 'business meeting' that she had had, and while one drop-off at a hotel might be perfectly reasonable, repeated ones, if they came to her husband's ears, would not.

She unbelted her raincoat and tossed it on one of the shell-curved, 1940s-reproduction beige suede chairs by the window. Pulling her phone out of her bag, she sent a swift text and then placed the phone on one of the bedside tables. Then there was nothing to do but to pace back and forth across the room, watching her reflection in the four huge glass wardrobe panels that comprised most of the wall on the far side of the room from the window embrasure.

Beige, blue, brown. Heavy sand-coloured curtains with a navy trim, a visual echo of the bed throw, the colours reversed. Pale greige carpet beneath the heels of her shoes, its design architectural, classic art deco, strong lines and circles in dark blue and dark grey. Three framed pictures above the dark wooden frame of the bed, specially commissioned deco motifs in more beige, blue and brown. The more she paced, the more the quiet elegance of the room annoyed her. Charlotte found it almost as muffled, as smothering, as her sad sack of a sister's Hampstead Garden Suburb house. No passion, no energy. It was enough to make you crave a lemon velvet sofa which would irritate you, yes, but at least it provoked some emotion—

A knock on the door broke into her increasingly irritable thoughts; she practically ran over to open it. An immaculately dressed room-service waiter wearing burgundy trousers, a white shirt and a neatly buttoned burgundy waistcoat stood there, a silver tray balanced on the palm of one gloved hand. On it was a bottle of white wine in a silver cooler, two chilled glasses and a plate of small, perfect hors d'oeuvres.

'May I come in, madam?' he asked deferentially.

'Of course,' she said, standing back, holding the door as he crossed the room and set the tray on the slender-legged table that served as a desk, letting the door swing shut behind her.

The waiter turned, but without producing the slim leather folder that he would customarily hand to the customer, waiting for her to sign for her order and add a tip. Instead, he advanced towards her.

'You want it, don't you?' he said in an accent which was much more London now, much less the RP which every British employee of a five-star hotel was required to use.

'*What?*'

Charlotte's beautiful features stretched into an expression of sheer disbelief. She backed away, moving in the direction of the door, darting a glance back over her shoulder to judge how far it was.

'You want it, I can tell,' he said, and now he edged around, mirroring her movements so that he was partially blocking her access to the door. 'I know just what you posh birds are like. Ordering some booze from room service so you can get a waiter up to your room for a nice dirty fuck behind your husband's back.'

He looked her up and down, his expression insolent. He was extremely handsome, very well built: it was entirely plausible that bored and horny clients of the hotel would regularly try to seduce him. His colouring was classic Mediterranean. With his smooth olive skin, dark hair and eyes, and his accent, he could have been North London born but Cypriot in origin, as so many are in that area of the city.

'I think there's been a huge misunderstanding—' Charlotte started, holding her hands up to ward him off.

'*Right*,' he said. 'Okay. If that's how you want it, love.'

He smirked, his full, well-shaped lips quirking at one corner. It was not a pretty smile.

'Not my fault,' he said, advancing on her again. 'The nasty

man fucked my brains out but I told him no, so I don't have to feel guilty. Don't worry, I got the message.'

Reaching out, he grabbed the neckline of the white blouse she was wearing, ripping it open. Buttons flew and scattered as Charlotte's white lace bra was revealed.

'No!'

She looked down in horror for a split second, then turned to run for the door. He grabbed her, swinging her back, tearing at her blouse more, dragging it out of the waistband of her pencil skirt. Frantically she brought up her hands, clawed, trying to scratch at his face. He grabbed her wrists, blocking her: as she opened her mouth to scream he wrenched her round and marched her across the room, shoving her down onto the bed, mashing her face into the coverlet.

'Don't you fucking scream. If you even try, I'll knock you out,' he hissed, bringing her hands into the small of her back, pinioning her down, straddling her. She writhed frantically as he dragged up her skirt, revealing thigh-high stockings with a wide lace band and white lacy hipster underwear that matched the bra.

'Pretty,' he grunted. 'Shame I've got to do this—'

The next second she felt his hands on her buttocks, grabbing at the lace. With a loud rip, he tore the hipsters open, baring her completely. She squealed into the coverlet, hardly able to breathe, imploring him, begging him to stop, not to do this; he told her to shut the fuck up and spread her legs. Instead she managed to get her elbows under her, dragging herself across the bed, away from him. His response was to sink a hand into her thick tresses and wrench her head back, making her scream involuntarily.

'I told you to fucking shut up!' he said, and flipped her over, grabbing one of the decorative pillows from the bed and shoving it into her mouth. 'Spit that out and I'll break your nose!'

She stared at him, wide-eyed above the pillow, as he shoved his knees between hers, her skirt around her waist, her underwear hanging in lace rags. Swiftly he ripped open his trousers, and she saw that he was wearing no underwear. The pillow dampened as she moaned, her head thrashing from side to side, her blouse hanging open, her screams getting louder as he raised a hand to his mouth, spat on it and rubbed his palm between her legs, his expression wolfish, predatory. He shoved her torso down with the heel of one hand, half-knocking the breath from her, and with the other he took hold of his big uncircumcised cock and shoved it between her legs, driving into her like a battering ram.

Charlotte screamed again, but this was an entirely different sound from before. Her arms flew out wide, gripping the coverlet, and her groin thrust up to meet him and take him in as deep as she could. Reaching down, he grabbed the pillow and pulled it from her mouth even as he drove into her again and again, a hard, fast fuck that was exactly as he had promised her, just what this scenario called for. She bounced again and again on the mattress, her hair rippling like a shampoo advertisement filmed for a porn channel. His hands braced, Charlotte's lover pumped away, watching her face flush in pleasure, her eyes roll back in her head, her slender body arch towards him.

'This what you wanted, rich bitch?' he said, still keeping

up the pretence that he was an anonymous assailant. 'You wanted to get the brains fucked out of you by a room-service waiter?'

'Yes,' Charlotte moaned, 'yes, Jesus, fuck me hard, you dirty bastard, fuck my brains out, make me take your big cock all the way, all the fucking way, up to the knot—'

He pulled out, making her moan in frustration, his cock huge and red and practically dripping, she was so wet.

'Get on your knees in front of the mirror, slut,' he ordered, grabbing her hair, pulling her up as she screeched in genuine agony, wincing. 'Watch yourself get fucked by a room-service waiter, come on—'

As she scrambled to obey, he pulled her knees as wide open as they would go; she gasped again in shock and pain as, having opened her up, he drove into her once again, twisting her hair into a rope, using it to force her to watch the sight in the huge mirror, him rearing behind her, his upper body still dressed in his shirt and waistcoat, his thick dark hair slicked back, the perfect image of the gorgeous waiter from an illicit fantasy.

Reaching down, plunging in and out of her, he grabbed at her bra, dragging the straps off her shoulders, baring her small breasts; hair roped round one hand, the other snaked down over her shoulder and pinched a nipple. She shrieked; this, as he knew, drove her crazy, and her pelvis danced against his frantically. The sight of her, eyes mad with lust, face red by now, practically sobbing with satisfied desire, drove him over the edge. His pounding became frenzied, a shuddering, out-of-control pile driver, and just in time he pulled out and shot over the pencil skirt that was wadded up around her waist, collapsing on top of her, pancaking her flat to the mattress.

'Fuck,' she sobbed against the coverlet, her face mashed into it, barely able even to move her lips. 'Fuck, fuck, *fuck . . .*'

Her hips still bucked against his, his cock juddering against her buttocks. They were both covered in sweat. He was dripping through his shirt and heavy wool waistcoat. Charlotte had showered just forty minutes ago, working her favourite body wash, Rose Silence by Miller Harris, into every crevice, and then scented herself with matching perfume and body cream, layering it to smell exquisite for him; his face was pressed against her neck, and he took in a long breath, sighing in pleasure.

'Fuck, you smell good,' he said, his voice now back to RP instead of the North London accent.

'It's the smell of rich bitch,' she mumbled. 'A rich bitch gagging for a good seeing-to from the dirty waiter.'

'You didn't come,' he said apologetically. 'I was going to do it, but then I thought that wouldn't be in character for the waiter – we didn't discuss that bit—'

'Oh God, no problem. It was *amazing*. So fucked up. You really went for it! Let me up.'

Charlotte started to squirm, and he eased off her, rolling to the side. She turned languorously to face him, smiling, reaching one hand between her legs, the other pinching at her nipple. It took barely a minute for her to start coming, and he watched her as she worked away at herself, one knee bent so that he could see exactly, explicitly where her fingers were moving.

'You dirty rich bitch,' he said, back into the waiter persona. 'I knew you fucking wanted my big cock, I knew you were getting wet for it . . . you wanted me to throw you on the bed and give it to you like the whore you are . . .'

'Oh!' Charlotte's face flushed a furious red again as she slipped back into the fantasy, surrendering to it completely. 'Yes, yes, *yes* . . .'

She shook all over, losing control as she came, thrusting hard against her hand. When she collapsed limply, bonelessly back onto the coverlet, he pulled her towards him, turning her so that they were spooning, sliding his own hand between her legs to keep going.

'No, no . . .' she protested, but she had no more strength to fight him off.

'Say the safe word if you want me to stop,' he whispered. 'If not, the dirty waiter's going to finger-fuck you no matter what you say, with his spunk all over your back. I'm going to give you the rich bitch seeing-to of a lifetime, you fucking slut! Come for me, come all over my dirty waiter hand . . .'

Charlotte moaned and writhed and grabbed at his wrist to pull him away, but feebly, and he easily wrested it away and held her hand captive as he kept on.

'No, stop, no, stop . . .' she sighed, even as everything about her body screamed a yes, the turn-on clearly intensified by the pleasure of the contradiction.

'I'm getting hard again,' he said. 'I've been saving myself for this. You want another waiter fuck?'

'No! No! Basingstoke! No! Please! Give me a moment!'

Charlotte was half giggling, half serious. She batted him away, and now that she had said her safe word, the name of a town she had never visited but which sounded like the least sexy place imaginable, she rolled onto her back.

Neither he nor Charlotte was to the slightest degree concerned about the bodily fluids they were smearing all over the coverlet and throw. Luxury hotels were their playground, and they were utterly careless about their surroundings. It was a very upper-class attitude, although neither of them were from that social stratum. Charlotte would check out of this room in an hour and a half, throwing a twenty-pound note on the bedside table without the slightest degree of embarrassment that the cleaner would have to bundle up a coverlet and throw smeared with their sweat and come.

'I need a break,' she said, gasping, still flushed right down to her breastbone. 'And my bra's killing me . . . ow . . .' She reached behind her, unfastening it. 'It's so hard to get sexy push-up bras that don't dig in! I do *not* wear this kind of thing to work, let me tell you.'

'Aww,' he said, grinning, as he sat up and unbuttoned his shirt and waistcoat, pulling them off. 'You're ruining my fantasy! You mean women don't wear thigh-highs to work?'

'About as often as we wear garter belts,' Charlotte said, wriggling off the bed, unfastening her skirt, shrugging off her blouse. Clad in only her thigh-highs, she walked with complete nonchalance over to the silver tray, extracting the bottle of Sancerre from the cooler and starting to open it. 'How did you manage this, by the way?'

'I ordered it an hour ago and carried it over when you texted,' he said, dropping the shirt and waistcoat to the floor and kicking off the trousers that were puddled around his ankles. Sitting up, he unlaced his shoes and peeled off his socks. He was a magnificent physical specimen, his chest thickly furred with tight dark curls of hair, which were now plastered to his dark-gold skin with sweat. An almost palpable energy emanated from him, and as he had told her, his cock was getting hard once more, heavy and half-distended in its nest of dense black curls.

Charlotte filled two glasses and brought them over to the bed.

'Get the snacks too,' he suggested. 'I could do with an *amuse-bouche* or three.'

'*Amuse-bouche*,' she echoed mockingly as she handed him the glass and went back for the plate, setting it on the navy leather bench at the foot of the bed. 'Listen to you! So where did you get the uniform?'

'Bought it online, of course,' he said, drinking some Sancerre. 'It was terrifying coming down the corridor and thinking I'd bump into an actual room-service waiter.'

'Hopefully it added an extra bit of spice,' Charlotte said. 'God, this wine is good! I should have had a glass at home to take the edge off. I was absolutely shaking with nerves waiting for you. I had to pace up and down, I couldn't sit still – I didn't know if I was going to go through with it—'

'It was okay, though?' he said. 'I was listening out really closely – if you'd even tried to say your safe word, I'd have stopped—'

'No, it was *amazing*!' she said, reaching over to touch his thigh reassuringly. 'I definitely want to do that one again. What about you?'

'Shit, yes.' He grinned, his teeth very white against his

glowing skin. 'I just have to be careful not to mark you, that's all.'

'Yes,' she said a little regretfully. 'It's actually more the kids than Paul – they notice everything. A bit of a mark here and there I can blame on my trainer, or doing boxercise, but nothing bigger than that.'

He nodded. 'Finish your wine.'

Once she had done so, he took the glass from her and set it down with his on the bench.

'I've had my dominance switch flicked on today,' he said, pushing her down to lie flat. 'And I can't turn it off. I'm going to do that slow thing we thought we invented back in the day, when I finally got some control of myself.'

'Oh God, I *love* that! Flashback!' She smiled up at him deliciously as he reached down and grabbed his trousers, pulling out a condom, tearing it open. 'Do we have time?'

'If we start right away, we do.'

She licked her lips, watching him roll the condom onto his cock, which had sprung to attention as soon as he had started talking about what he was going to do to her. It was big and veiny and had made her sore just now; she was still sore, and yet she couldn't wait for it to be inside her again. She stretched out, curling her fingers and toes, arching her back, knowing exactly how beautiful she looked, how much he wanted her; as he knelt between her legs, she tilted her hips up fractionally, and sighed in bliss as he slowly entered her.

His body lowered onto hers, almost flattening her. In this position she took almost all of his weight, their hips nearly fused together, just his forearms bracing on the bed to make sure he didn't crush her ribcage. His tongue slid into her mouth and she closed her eyes, sucking on it, as he began to rock infinitesimally back and forward, his cock barely leaving her, just an inch in and out, rubbing against her clit every time it returned, a rhythm that, if kept up steadily, would eventually bring her and then him to bone-shattering orgasms. He would come inside her this time, hence the condom.

His weight kept Charlotte from being able to do anything to speed him up, even as the frustration built and built; she couldn't writhe seductively, dig her heels into his buttocks, reach for his balls and tickle them, slide a finger up him. His legs pinned hers down, his chest her torso; her arms were wrapped around his strong neck, and all she could do was kiss and kiss him, darkness behind her eyelids, focusing entirely on the point he was working, stroke by stroke, slow and steady, breaking her into pieces.

It was almost an out-of-body experience. She knew by now that he could be trusted to get her where she needed to go, that the rhythm was exactly the right speed, the angle was perfect; all she could do was lie there and cling to his neck and kiss him. As he had said, it was utterly dominating for the male partner, and required huge self-control on his part. Thus ideal for a second bout of sex, where the first head of steam had burnt off and the fire could be stoked more slowly, with more control. She might as well have been tied hand and foot, blindfolded, as he worked on her; they were sweating hard again, his hips slipping against hers, lubricated with sweat, his pubic hairs grinding into her soft skin, the base of his cock stroking against her clit again and again . . .

She was moaning now, her mouth open, with not even enough self-control to keep kissing him. All she could do was breathe his name over and over, a kind of prayer, a kind of entreaty: 'Lee, Lee, Lee,' she whimpered on every stroke, half-singing it, and he looked down at her and gritted his teeth and refused to speed up, drawing this to the absolute maximum of their mutual endurance, until sweat was dripping from his forehead onto her face, until their bellies were running with it, the coverlet under her back outlining her entire body with moisture, her cries unintelligible now, not even his name any more, but birdlike, wispy.

Charlotte could have been flying, high above the man's body crushing her to the mattress, soaring away just as she gasped and throbbed and felt the first moment of inevitability, when she was tipping and nothing would be able to tip her back again, the waves driving her along the river to the start of the waterfall. Lee groaned deeply, a sound that seemed dragged up not from the pit of his stomach but his groin.

Until now he had made no noise apart from his even-spaced, ragged breathing; but now, finally, after what must have been twenty-five minutes of hard work, he allowed himself to let go. The groaning grew, and as Charlotte's cries became even more unearthly and birdlike, Lee was almost bellowing as he kept up the rhythm to the bitter end, fighting himself, his impulse just to pull back and ram into her for a last few frantic strokes. His sweat dripped into her open mouth, salty and hot, almost like come, and the taste made her whole body clutch and tighten around his cock and then unfold, fall apart, her eyes rolling back behind her still-closed eyelids, a faint thin scream with all the breath she had.

It was an extraordinary experience. With Lee's weight still pressing her down inexorably, her pelvis could only rock fractionally back and forth as the orgasm flooded through her. Lee, feeling her convulsing, finally let go and came in such a hot stream that she could feel it through the condom; she sobbed at that, sobbed aloud, covered now in a slick of their sweat as his orgasm roiled and his cock swelled and pulsed as it shot inside her.

Hers seemed to last forever. This was the benefit of this position; he swore his was intensified by the torture of the delay, but hers was not only stronger but very prolonged, his hips crushing her even as she kept spasming against them, on and on and on . . .

Red blotches bloomed over her face, her neck, her chest. Lee, finally recovering from the aftermath of his explosion, looked down at her thrown-back head, her open mouth, and greedily fixed the sight in his mind for future solo sessions where he would replay this image as he pulled at his oiled cock. He lowered his head and slid his tongue once more in her mouth, forcing a deep kiss on her, feeling the response as her hips jerked against him, knowing that she loved the extra penetration.

She struggled to breathe, which made her convulse more, which made her come even more, and he deliberately kept his weight on her as long as he thought she could bear, because the confinement of her body, they had found after prolonged experimentation, made her orgasm even more intense. Only when one of her hands balled up into a fist and hit his shoulder in desperation did he take his weight from her, reaching down, securing the condom and sliding out, flopping onto the coverlet beside her, drenching it with sweat.

They lay there for a good five minutes without saying a word. Eventually Charlotte's eyes fluttered open slowly, her pupils acclimatizing back to the light. Their chests were heaving as if they had just finished a triathlon. In fact, Lee eventually mumbled:

'This is why I work out . . . got to know my heart can cope with fucking you like this as I get older . . .'

'It's my turn next,' Charlotte managed in a half-whisper. 'You did all the work this time.'

'Hell yeah,' he agreed. 'I'm just going to lie there while you cowgirl me like you're riding a bull! You better take extra spin classes to get your thighs in prime condition.'

'They *are* in prime condition!' she said indignantly. 'How *dare* you!'

Lee laughed. 'Oh, I've always been daring, haven't I?'

He turned his head to look at her, and she mirrored the motion. They stared languorously at each other.

'Always,' she said, licking her lips, tasting his sweat again. 'Always. But I made the first move.'

'You'll never let me forget that, will you?'

'Never,' she said with a wicked smile. 'Oh my God, I'm going to have to text Paul to say I'll be late. I won't be able to walk for at least half an hour and I need some wine to help me pull myself together. Why did I leave the bottle so far away?'

'Give me five,' he said, his chest still heaving. 'Or ten. I've got nothing right now. I can't move a muscle.'

'I want to wiggle over and put my head on your chest,' she said, 'but I can't, because of my blow-dry! Paul's fairly oblivious, but he'll notice if I come back from a business meeting with my hair dripping like a fountain with your sweat.'

She sighed. 'I wish you could come inside me,' she added wistfully.

'We just can't risk it,' he said matter-of-factly. 'Yeah, I want to as well, but we've been over this. I get tested every so often, but I can't guarantee that you won't bring something back to Paul.'

'I know, I know,' she said, without any rancour at the clear indication that she was not his only lover. 'We're doing the right thing. It's just—'

'I know,' he echoed, grinning at her. 'You want it all.'

'I *do*!' she said, and that stirred up enough energy for her to twist onto her side, curl up her knees and push herself up as yoga students did at the end of a class, the easiest way to sit up after a full-body relaxation in Shavasana, corpse pose, her head coming up last.

'I have to talk to you about something. I'll get the wine,' she said, shaking back her hair. 'I'll text Paul and get the wine. You just lie there and listen.'

'Bring the nibbles too,' he said, teeth white as he smiled at her, his heels pushing him back to the head of the bed, his arms hoisting him up onto the stack of pillows at enough of an angle to sit sipping Sancerre and picking at the hors d'oeuvres. He looked down complacently at his still-big cock, dwindling gently inside the condom.

'They're going to have to wash this coverlet at ninety degrees,' he observed. 'We sweated like we ran a marathon in the tropics.'

'I wouldn't know,' she said over her shoulder with a knowing smile in return. 'And not about the marathon. I haven't used a washing machine in my entire life, unlike some.'

Lee grunted in amusement as he reached out for the tissue box on the side table and started to clean himself up. Charlotte bent down to remove her thigh-highs, which had worked themselves down to her ankles by now. The sight of her doing that made him moan happily even as she straightened up and brought a glass of wine to the bedside table for him, tapped out a quick message to her husband, then joined him on the bed, glass in hand, setting the plate of nibbles between them.

'You're so red still,' he said appreciatively, reaching out to touch her collarbone, where the skin was still mottled. 'Red and wet. You start off so blonde and elegant and pale and by the time we're done, you're raw and red and wet and thoroughly fucked up . . .'

'Ugh, you make me sound like a steak!' she said, drinking some more wine and contemplating herself in the big mirror. 'I *do* actually look like a steak. I'll need a long cold shower to cool down and fade it away. Paul knows exactly what it means when I get red like this.'

'Will your hair be okay?' he asked.

'Yes,' she said, with the confidence of a woman very used

to cheating on her husband and covering it up. 'I brought a really good shower cap, and I have dry shampoo and spray as well as a whole fresh set of the same clothes. You wouldn't think you could fit all that in a Birkin bag! But it was made for Jane Birkin because she complained to a guy at Hermès that she needed a travel bag she could fit everything in, so I suppose it's meant to be a weekender . . .'

She reached over, sank a finger into his belly button, drew it up the centre of his ribcage to the base of his neck, and licked off the sweat she had collected.

'I hate that I can't keep your smell on me,' she said, 'like I could in the old days.'

'How's Paul?' he asked, his tone just as easy as hers, not a shred of awkwardness or jealousy in it.

'Oh, just as always! He's at home making courgette spaghetti for the kids! The perfect father and husband.' She winked at him. 'Quite unlike you.'

'*Quite* unlike me,' he agreed. 'So? We haven't got all the time in the world. What did you want to talk to me about?'

'Having it all,' Charlotte said simply. 'You won't believe what Daddy's pulled! I'll give you a quick rundown, but basically I have an amazing idea about how to pull it off . . . and I don't think I can do it without you.'

His eyebrows shot up, but he said nothing, though his dark eyes were now intent, his beautifully shaped lips no longer smiling.

'I need you to do something pervy,' she said. 'Something you've never done before.'

'That's quite a short list,' he said, 'as you well know.'

'Trust me.' Charlotte's blue eyes gleamed in wicked relish.

'I *know*, a hundred per cent, that you've never done *this* before!'

And bending over him, her small pointed breasts hanging delightfully close to his face, she began to tell him the plan she had been hatching ever since Jeffrey Sachs pitted his four children against each other for a prize only one of them could win.

Chapter Eight

LIKE FATHER LIKE SON!

Two weeks after Jeffrey Sachs's shock announcement that he's divorcing trophy wife Jade for an Estonian nightclub hostess, golden-boy son Conway caught cheating with a Russian model!

NAUGHTY BOY!

Jeffrey Sachs's heir-apparent son Conway hauled over the coals by Daddy for following in his footsteps!

WHY SAMANTHA SHOULD
HAVE BEEN MORE CAREFUL:

by Marjorie Tucker for the Herald –
The Woman Who Tells It Like It Is!

They're called 'Natashas'. And every wife of a rich man should fear them like Ebola. Only wives of seriously rich men – ones worth at minimum in the high eight figures. You'll find the Natashas at Sunseeker yacht launches, at Mayfair bars like Novikov, and at certain private members' clubs – the ones that charge men much more for membership than women – the ones where you know not to ask the men what they do for a living, because they don't like answering 'arms dealer'.

In Eastern Europe and Russia, the women are much more beautiful than the men. Lucky for them, as it's their only currency in that brutal world. The Natashas were born in Kazakhstan, Estonia, Azerbaijan, the furthest reaches of Russia, in towns with names as unfamiliar as Ust-Kamenogorsk, Nizhny Novgorod and Arkangel. Literally weeks by train away from anything resembling civilization, they've grown up living on black bread and boiled broth. It's no wonder that when they manage to reach the First World, they're insatiable.

I know one businessman who openly boasts about being married to a Natasha. You know why? Because it shows that he's rich enough to afford to satisfy her every demanding whim: couture, a Sunseeker yacht, expensive jewellery. She's the ultimate financial status symbol.

I can even be sympathetic to them for using what they have to get ahead. Until what they're greedy for is other women's husbands.

Now Samantha Sachs is the latest wife to learn about the Natashas the hard way. What was she *thinking*? Not even her aristocratic status, her family connections, her calm elegance, could save her. And maybe she should have known that! Maybe she should have spent more time with her husband and less time with her children?

Stay-at-home mothers, harried multi-tasking wives

may rise up against me for this! They have before. But I'm going to continue to warn them that you have to nurse your marriage as well as your kids! Yes, we saw Samantha on the red carpet with her very handsome husband. Yes, she always looked ladylike, chic, fashion-forward in her high-necked pussycat-bow blouses, her demure midi skirts.

But where was she when Conway was at Morton's in Berkeley Square, meeting the Natashas, who are equally expensively dressed, but not exactly ladylike with their low-cut tops and miniskirts? Did Samantha never ask herself where Conway was when he stayed out so late? Because those damning photos of him canoodling in the bar at Novikov with a young woman showing more skin in one outfit than Samantha does in ten, were taken well after midnight.

Samantha's family and friends will rally round her, of course. She's the wronged wife, to whom sympathy and comfort is due. But next time – whether she decides to stay with Conway or move on – she'll have been warned about the Ebola in high society. The Natashas. And she'll be on high alert for signs of infection.

'Ugh,' Bella said, dropping the tabloid onto Charlotte's lacquered white desk, where it fell onto the pile of other newspapers Charlotte's PA had brought in. 'Those women who write nasty stuff about other women while pretending to be sweet and caring make me feel sick.'

'To be fair, this one's not so sweet and caring!' Charlotte said. 'And she's a hundred per cent right, you know.'

'Poor Samantha,' Bella said, grimacing.

'Oh, come on,' Charlotte said briskly. 'You saw those photos and you handed them over to me anyway. Remember what I said? Who *knows* how many girls Conway's cheated with? He could be bringing all sorts of diseases back home with him! I hope she goes and gets herself tested. Actually,' she added, pushing it now, 'if you look at it that way, we've done her a favour.'

'*Charlotte*,' Bella said reprovingly, sitting back in her chair; she was facing her sister across the desk.

'I'd want to know,' Charlotte said. 'Wouldn't you?'

'Yes, of course,' Bella admitted. 'But not like this!'

'God, Bell.' Charlotte was impatient now. 'You did it. We did it. Daddy's in Conway's office right now, ripping him to pieces. We got what we wanted. Enough with the buyer's remorse and fake guilt, please!'

Charlotte's PA tapped on her door, and, on hearing her boss call 'Come!', entered, carrying a tray on which sat a pitcher of filtered water and glasses, an exquisite Japanese bowl full of frozen grapes and strawberries, and two perfect cappuccinos, made in the bean-to-cup Magnifica S De'Longhi coffee machine that Charlotte possessed both at home and at work.

'Cashew milk for you, Charlotte,' the PA said, placing the oversized cup and saucer in front of her boss, very well aware that, despite etiquette, she was required to serve Charlotte first. 'And skim milk for you, Ms Sachs.'

'Oh, Bella, please,' Bella mumbled. 'Thanks.'

'You have to stop drinking that skim milk,' Charlotte said to her sister: she didn't even acknowledge her PA. 'I keep telling you, it's all sugar. This low-fat nonsense is so bad for you. They take the fat out, but they put in sugar instead, which is even worse.'

To Bella's mortification, the PA, who had just been comprehensively snubbed by her boss, nodded in agreement as she set down the frozen fruit bowl and turned to leave the room, tray under her arm. Both Charlotte and her employee were slim as wands, so could be presumed to know much more about nutrition than Bella did.

'I don't even like skim milk,' Bella confessed. 'It's so . . . thin.'

'Oh, for God's sake,' Charlotte said impatiently. 'Of course it is. There's nothing *in* it. Toyah! Make my sister a decent coffee, will you? Full fat, cashew or hemp milk, Bella?'

And at Bella's blank face – she had no idea which one to choose – Charlotte said:

'Make all three and bring them in. Quick now!'

Toyah shot from the room before Bella could protest that there was no need to bother. In any case, Bella told herself, it would have been a waste of time; Charlotte would overrule her.

'So!' Charlotte beamed at her twin sister. 'I'm dying to sneak up to Daddy's office and eavesdrop, aren't you? I bet he's yelling his head off at Con right now – maybe loud enough even to hear through that gigantic door!'

Bella actually trembled at the idea. She was much more frightened of their father than Charlotte, who had been highly skilled, even when young, at charming her way out of trouble. Bella couldn't even imagine being summoned to his office for a dressing-down without her legs going weak with fear.

To be fair, this was partly because Jeffrey had designed his twentieth-floor office at the Sachs Building to be as intimidating to the visitor as possible. With its heavy oaken panelling, massive Victorian leather-topped mahogany desk and matching oversized chairs, it could almost have been a nineteenth-century court of law. The impression was intensified by the fact that the desk, and Jeffrey's towering, almost throne-like carved wooden chair behind it, were on a small dais.

It was the ultimate businessman's power ploy, echoing the advice in management books to make your visitors sit in a chair that was lower than yours in order to establish dominance immediately. Typical of Jeffrey to have taken it one step further. All that the ambiance was missing was a horsehair wig and the black cap judges used to don when a defendant had been found guilty of a capital offence and was being sentenced to hang.

Although Jeffrey Sachs had unquestionably been successful in business, his approach would never have worked for Bella; her style was quite the opposite. She had worked very hard to make her own office as inviting as possible. It wasn't chic, like Charlotte's, which was as white and gleaming as her home, a pop of colour provided not by a lemon sofa but the huge vase of mauve agapanthus, two feet high, at the far end of the desk, the open ball shape of the flowers a stunning contrast to their slender stems, which were fixed underwater in small mauve glass balls clustered densely at the base of the vase. The arrangement was a work of art in itself.

Bella couldn't possibly rival this elegance, and, as with the rest of her decisions around her relationship with her twin, she hadn't tried. But in her office, free from Thomas's rather suffocating preference in interior design, she had created a cosy yet businesslike atmosphere, bright and welcoming, in which her team regularly gathered to brainstorm ideas to great effect. And unlike Charlotte, who went through PAs like a hayfever sufferer did tissues, Bella had had the same staff around her for many years. Some had been with her for the entire decade she had been working for Sachs, ever since she had graduated from Harvard with her MBA.

As a result, her connections throughout the entire firm ran very deep. Her PA, Nita, was a crucial part of the inner circle, the executive assistants' network which communicated through a complex network of subterranean messaging threads and had its finger pressed directly to the pulse of the Sachs Organization.

Bella opened her mouth to tell her sister that Nita would know what was going on with Jeffrey and Conway through Jeffrey's own PA, that Nita was probably getting a running brief right now on a secret WhatsApp group. Then she shut it again. Charlotte was Bella's rival, more than she had ever been. Why share that with her? It was Bella's ability to inspire loyalty in her staff that gave her a direct line into the web of connections which might prove crucially useful in her quest to become CEO of Sachs.

'What were you going to say?' asked her twin sister, who knew her very well indeed.

But Bella was spared having to make up a lie by the office door being thrown open. It was not Toyah, having miraculously managed to make three cappuccinos at high speed while painstakingly cleaning the milk-foaming jug each time; it was Conway himself, his angry face dark with blood, slamming the door against the wall with a dramatic crash.

'You bitches!' he yelled. 'I should have known! I went to Bella's office and her assistant said she was here—'

Noticing the little details much more acutely than she had ever done, Bella realized that Conway did not know Nita's name, even though her PA had been with her for ten years. Conversely, Bella knew what all Conway's staff were called. Of the four siblings, Bella truly was the one who knew everyone in the main divisions, how they worked, who pulled the strings in each one.

And if she didn't, Nita did.

' – and of *course* she is!' Conway was continuing. 'Of *course* you two're sitting here, gloating about having set me up! It's no coincidence this happened just after Dad's deadline, is it? You two are bloody getting together to take me down!'

Bella would have babbled a feeble denial which would only confirm her brother's suspicions. Luckily for her, however, Charlotte was much more skilled at dealing with direct accusations and knew that attack was the best defence.

'Con! Jesus, take a chill pill!' she said sharply. 'You can't barge into my office and start yelling at me! You'd be livid if I pulled something like this. Just because Daddy's given you a bloody hard time, that doesn't give you the right to take it out on me and Bell!'

Conway's handsome face was contorted, his blond brows lowered as if he was about to charge. The anger was very upsetting to Bella, as it reminded her so vividly of Jeffrey's rages. Charlotte, however, was not a whit intimidated.

'Who took those photos?' he demanded. 'I mean, who knew to go to Morton's?'

'How the fuck should I know? A member of the club, or one of your whore's friends trying to make some money?' his sister snapped. 'You can't think *Bell* had any idea what you were up to! She never goes anywhere cool or sexy!'

Humiliating as it was for Bella to be cast as the boring sister, she could only be grateful when, as Conway's forward-thrust head turned to her, he drew a long breath as he acknowledged the truth of Charlotte's last statement.

'You two are sticking together, though,' he said, but his tone was much less combative. 'You twins. I still think you were behind it – you, Charlotte! This is exactly the kind of thing you'd do! Why is Bella here, anyway?'

'Oh my *God*, Con, don't be so stupid,' Charlotte said with utter disdain. 'We just found out that you've been cheating on Samantha! It's a bit of a shock for your sisters, as you can imagine! Obviously we're going to talk about it with each other!'

Bella was deeply impressed by her sister for coming up with such an excellent explanation for her twin's presence in her office.

'What did Daddy say?' Charlotte asked, pressing her advantage.

Conway muttered:

'Oh, I'm sure you can imagine. It's terrible bloody timing,

just terrible. He didn't want any coverage about him and Adrianna, or at least any more than the bare minimum. He's been calling in favours from the press and media he knows, all the newspaper owners.'

'Mmn, yeah,' Charlotte murmured. 'I noticed that the gossip bitch in the *Herald* steered well clear of mentioning Daddy's new girlfriend.'

Conway heaved a sigh.

'He's told me to sort things out with Samantha so there won't be any more stories like this,' he said. 'Stage a big reconciliation. But frankly, I don't know if I want to.'

This was a genuine surprise: Bella looked at him with wide eyes.

'*Really?*' she said.

'Yeah. Ever since the kids were born, Sam's been ploughing all her energies into them, and I haven't got much of a look in. It happens sometimes, they say. It hasn't really been much of a marriage for years . . . I'm pretty sure she knew what was going on. I tried to talk to her about setting things right, but it was never a good time, so eventually I just—'

'Okay, enough pathetic male excuses for cheating with a bar slut,' Charlotte said, holding up one perfectly manicured hand. Not a French manicure, nor shellac; she had learned from observing Samantha that the upper classes did not consider either of these U, or upper-class, and Charlotte was always aspirational. 'We get it.'

'I'm glad to hear Samantha won't be upset,' Bella ventured.

'Of course she'll bloody be upset!' Conway bellowed at her, finding something onto which he could legitimately release his frustration. 'Don't be more ridiculous than you can help, you silly cow! She was quite happy to go along with all the perfect-wife-and-mother routine: I was always there for her family, we've got two lovely kids, all the money and status in the world, and me quietly getting myself sorted out when I needed to, nice and discreet – why *wouldn't* she be upset at losing all that?'

He loomed over Bella, and for a moment she shrank back. Then she thought how well Charlotte had just handled him, deflecting his direct accusation, and how Charlotte had refused to let him bully her, and how Bella would never make an effective CEO if she let men shout at her. So, much to everyone's surprise, she pushed back her chair and got to her feet.

'Don't *yell* at me!' she shouted. 'I'm sick and tired of people yelling at me!'

Conway's expression at the sight of his mild-mannered sister, arms folded across her chest, shouting angrily back at him, was a picture of disbelief. Charlotte huffed out a laugh.

'Well, well, well,' she commented. 'The mouse who roared.'

'Excuse me . . . Charlotte . . .'

Toyah, sounding and looking on the verge of panic, put her head around the door. She was young, pretty and highly fashionable, like all of Charlotte's staff; they helped keep her in touch with the latest apps and social media platforms. They were up to date with which non-dairy milk was currently in vogue, and they were attractive enough to be used to pose in shots for the latest Sash branded products. The choice of toiletries in the Sash boutique chain alone was endlessly debated, and Charlotte had her team test them out and take cheeky, sexy selfies of themselves in the smart office bathrooms for the Sash blog, holding the latest branded products.

However, choosing a young and pretty team meant you got neither experience nor the kind of common sense that is developed when a candidate cannot rely solely on good looks and charm. Twenty-seven-year-olds who were truly talented and photogenic were PR stars, highly paid influencers, not PAs to difficult bosses who seemed to have based their management style on the worst kind of fashion editor. Poor Toyah looked absolutely terrified as she said:

'Shall I bring in the coffee? I was going to, but then Mr Sachs came in, and I couldn't stop him, and I wasn't sure—'

'Well, you *should* have stopped him!' Charlotte said, very unfairly, as it would have taken three Toyahs working in unison to physically block Conway from entering her office. 'And yes, bring in the coffee, Bella must be desperate for it by now!'

Toyah carried in the tray, her hands shaking, the cups rattling a little as she set them down.

'This is full fat, and this one's—' she started. But before she could continue, Conway, naturally assuming that Toyah had made a round of cappuccinos for the three of them, picked up the one closest to him and took a long sip, without, Bella noted, thanking Toyah, let alone acknowledging her in any way.

'*Pffffft!*'

Milk foam spewed out of Conway's mouth.

'What the *fuck*?' he spluttered as the beige liquid splattered over Charlotte's desk. 'What *is* this shit?'

'Looks like Conway got the hemp milk,' Charlotte commented dryly. 'Well, don't just stand there gibbering like a maniac, Toyah! Get a cloth and clean up my desk! What are you waiting for?'

Chapter Nine

It would have taken her father jumping out from an open doorway, dressed in a clown costume and yelling 'Boo!', to make Bella react as she walked very slowly back to her office. She was as lost in thought as if she were making her way through thick white fog which blinded her to any noises or sights that weren't immediately within her narrow field of vision. Having worked in this building for ten years, she could navigate through it on autopilot. She was so clearly distracted when she reached her own suite of offices that Nita, stationed in the large anteroom to Bella's suite, took one look at her and stood up, following her boss into her office and closing the door behind them.

'What happened?' Nita asked intently. 'Sit down. How was it? I heard Conway got taken to the cleaners by your dad, then went to Charlotte's floor in a flaming temper . . .'

Bella flopped into her chair, her head still spinning.

'Yes,' she confirmed. 'He shouted at me. And I shouted back.'

'You shouted back?' Nita's big, black, heavily outlined eyes widened as she sat down opposite her boss. 'You shouted *back*?'

'Yes. It felt . . . okay. I didn't enjoy it, but I had to do it.'
She considered a moment.

'It felt better than okay, actually.'

Nita's face was a picture: she tended to say very little but express much, and this time was no exception. Usually Bella was very attuned to her assistant's reactions, but she was too busy staring ahead of her without seeming to focus on anything, let alone small, smooth-haired, carefully made-up Nita.

Nita had ensured that she, or rather her own assistant Tal, had refreshed the jug of ice water on Bella's desk since Bella left her office forty minutes ago; Nita was a detail-orientated caretaker. And now, as her PA reached out, poured a glass of cold water and slid it over to her, Bella took it with a grateful smile and a murmured 'thank you', more than Conway or Charlotte ever gave to their PAs.

'Nita,' Bella said eventually. 'I could totally run this company, couldn't I?'

'Of course! I've been telling you that ever since your father—'

'No. Wait. Stop.' Bella set down the glass. The icy water had been just what she needed to clear her brain: she'd never ended up drinking that promised cappuccino, not after watching her brother spit his out. 'That's not what I mean. I'm nice to everyone.'

Nita stared at her, frowning intently as she focused on what Bella was trying to say.

'I'm a good manager,' Bella continued. 'I know everyone's strengths and weaknesses. The Sash people, the financial people, the tech team. I know the *assistants*' names. I eat lunch in the canteen with everyone else, unlike my brother and sister. I'm not siloed. And you know everyone. *Everyone.* You're this close with HR.'

Bella held up index and middle fingers, pressed tightly together.

'You're so close with them that I don't even need to run anything by their office, because I can just check with you. You know what they're going to say before they say it. And they run a lot of things past you, even though they're not supposed to.'

'I can't confirm or deny anything,' Nita said, with the tiniest of smiles. 'But yes, I have a very good working relationship with HR.'

She leant forward, steepling her fingers on the desk.

'Look,' she began, 'Conway's actually fine as the CFO, but he's alienated a lot of people in his department because he's so entitled. Let alone the rest of us! He thinks we all work for him, and he makes that very clear. Meanwhile, your sister has never built what I'd call a team. She's very, very good at what she does, but it's all about her, which definitely wouldn't fly if she weren't working in a family company. Besides, that boutique brand is never going to be anything but a marketing leader for Sachs hotels overall. It's not our core business and it's not where the vast majority of the revenue stream is generated.'

Bella nodded. 'It only just occurred to me that neither of them has any *people*,' she said. 'While I have a machine, and all the goodwill they don't have.'

'I thought you knew that already,' Nita said, looking surprised.

'No. I've been so . . .' Bella still felt as if she were wrapped in white fog. 'I was distracted by how glamorous Conway and Charlotte are. They *seem* so popular, I only took in now how badly they treat everyone. I could go to Daddy after six months with pretty much the whole company behind me, not just my division. I could put an entire package together. I could cherry-pick people from finance and Sash to join my management team and build all the bridges that Daddy and Conway and Charlotte haven't bothered to do. We could transform how everyone communicates here—'

'But your dad won't give you the job just on that basis,' Nita said intently; it was a mark of Bella's management style that her staff knew they could interrupt her if necessary without consequences.

'No. Which is why we're going for the new points scheme as the huge pitch, plus the website rollout,' Bella said, like a robot computing everything slowly but surely.

This had been her priority for the last two weeks, ever since her father's announcement and her realization of how much she wanted to run the whole company. It was a project she had been developing for a while, but now she was living and breathing it, aware of how extremely complicated it was to slot together all the nuts and bolts, the tiny workings that would pull the scheme to fruition. It was an incredibly thankless task because, if it worked, it would seem like an effortless transition, while if there was the tiniest glitch the media would be ready to jump all over it.

And yet, if she pulled it off . . . if she launched a scheme which let the Sachs point-holders buy goods from major online travel retailers, upgrade on a partner airline and pool together with family or friends to book holiday packages; if they could combine their points with money on a sliding scale, as some airlines allowed, to make them go further, or buy and gift them to friends and relatives; if Sachs Plus members could digitally select their hotel rooms online, with 3D video of the layout of the room or suite – even the view – available to help them with their choice, and then be issued a digital 'key' sent to their smartphones, so that they no longer needed to check in at the front desk . . .

It would be revolutionary. Bella's name would pass into industry legend. The technology had been in existence for a while now, but other chains were baulking out of fear that the rollout would be so fraught with teething problems that any positive press and attention would be entirely overshadowed by the individual stories of family woes and stranded business travellers, on which the press could be guarantee to pounce gleefully, knowing that sad faces made catchy clickbait.

But if it worked, business travellers, dying to expedite their endless weary routine, would be able to choose their rooms in advance, check in from the Wi-Fi-enabled plane, walk in and out of a Sachs airport or conference hotel without having to wait in line for a receptionist, avoid making the same clichéd conversation as they waited for their room key . . . even see the charges being assigned to their room account updated every few hours, so they had no unpleasant shocks on checking out. If there were a minibar or bar tab query, for instance, so very frequent and so niggly, not to mention potentially embarrassing to dispute in public, the guest could dispute it immediately online, able to check the scanned receipts and the electronic records from the sensors in the minibar.

Not only would this process, if it worked, streamline the Sachs Organization's front-of-house wage bill, it would naturally roll out through Charlotte's Sash hotels too, demonstrating Bella's overarching authority as the organizer in chief, the ultimate manager.

'We're going to be working like dogs for the next six months,' Nita said, and her black eyes sparked with anticipation. 'But we're all up for it, Bella. We *want* to. We want to take on the other divisions and win. We're not glamorous. We're not Instagramming our fingernails in the loo every other minute. Because we're getting our heads down and getting on with our work, and we're bloody good at it.'

'We are,' Bella agreed, and despite the cold water she was drinking, she felt what was almost a burning sensation under her ribcage. This was such a risk, and such a tight timescale, considering the huge scope of the rollout. Every existing Sachs Rewards account would need to be upgraded, the guest points accumulated moved over. Those balances were watched like hawks by their owners; they were like alternative bank accounts for the frequent travellers. Any mistakes would be pounced upon, requiring a massive temporary hire of IT and customer service staff to mop up the mess.

'We'll do all of it,' she said, pushing back her chair. 'Even the Points Plus Money. We can keep that basic at first – use big chunks of points that can't be broken up, to simplify the calculations. Pull in extra IT staff as temporary contractors. We've got all that space on the fourth floor since the reshuffle and it's perfect for this. I honestly don't care how much it costs, though you're the only person I'd trust enough to say that to!'

Nita's face lit up.

'Oh, trust me, I *love* negotiating with staff agencies,' she said almost dreamily.

'And while you do that, I'll be on a whistle-stop tour of our major hub offices.' Bella counted them off on her fingers. 'Chicago, Dallas, LA, Tokyo, Sydney, Berlin, minimum. I don't want to town hall this and stream it for them. I want to be there on site, doing the presentation, making sure they know what we're shooting for, that this is a real deadline, getting any queries resolved—'

'Making sure you have designated tech people in place to drive this and managers to report directly back to you—' Nita chimed in.

'Bella!'

The door to the office flew open, and there, framed in the doorway, golden and glorious, was Bart, with Tal, Nita's assistant, hovering behind him, flapping her hands.

'I'm so sorry, Nita!' she babbled. 'I tried to stop him, but he's, you know, *Mr Sachs*, and—'

Nita held up a palm, both to tell Tal to back off and to reassure her that she was not in trouble.

'Bart, *please*!' he said to Tal with a dazzling smile. 'Hello, Nita! I was worried for a moment when I didn't see you out there. I should have known you and Bell would be in here putting your heads together.'

Nita hadn't even mentioned Bart to Bella; like everyone else, she had immediately dismissed him as a serious candidate for CEO. But she was more than happy to bask in the glowing radiance of his film-star handsomeness, and she smiled back with great pleasure.

'Everyone's screaming and throwing things around!' Bart complained, entering Bella's office and throwing himself into one of the oversized plaid-upholstered chairs by the window. 'Christ,' he added in parentheses, 'this chair is *comfy*. Conway's stormed out of the building yelling like a madman, apparently. Poor Samantha, eh? Bloody humiliating for her and the kids. I popped up to see Dad and he bit my head off. This is all so messy!'

Bella stared at him, frowning a little at his air of surprise. 'What did you *think* was going to happen, Bart?' she asked. 'Daddy's pitted us all against each other! It's going to be hell for the next six months. And then God knows how we'll all settle down when he picks a winner and everyone else has to work for them after trying to rip them apart!'

Bart looked as hangdog at this truth-telling as the little boy he had once been, playing with his Scalextric, when Conway and his friends had swept in and insisted on bagsying the McLaren Formula One set for their own use.

'Ugh, it's *awful*,' he said on a long sigh. 'And Conway being in the papers today! Such weird timing! I don't understand anything that's going on, really.'

He stretched his arms wide along the back of the armchair, staring out of the window at the bustling Holborn streets many storeys below.

'Bart,' Bella said, indicating to Tal that she should shut the office door. 'Do you *want* to be CEO of Sachs?'

Her brother turned to look at her, his eyes infused with

colour: of all of them, he perhaps had the largest irises, the most hypnotically blue eyes.

'Honestly, Bell, I don't know!' he said, and her heart sank, because she had been hoping for an unequivocal no, and then perhaps even an agreement to back her bid for the top job. 'I mean, two weeks ago I thought absolutely not. But now I'm thinking that maybe if I were the boss, I could be a peacemaker, stop everyone fighting like this . . .'

Bella and Nita's eyes met, briefly but eloquently, both of them rolling fractionally to signify their derision at this. The idea of Bart successfully intervening between a battling Conway and Charlotte was as likely as a golden retriever managing to break up a fight to the death between a pair of Rottweilers.

But then Bella thought: *Is that even true, though? Is Bart saying he wants to be a peacemaker to make me think he isn't competing with me for the job? Because there's no way Daddy would make Bart, or anyone, CEO with that pitch, and he must surely be aware of that. So is he playing stupid to lure me into a false sense of security, while still keeping his hat in the ring?*

She looked back at her brother, at those huge, winsome blue eyes, so wide, so apparently innocent of any secret motivation or double-dealing. So much was at stake in these coming months. Bella had agreed to sabotage Conway, and guilty as she had felt, she had handed over to Charlotte the photos to pass on to her media contact. She wasn't going to pretend that her hands weren't dirty. Bella had thought that Charlotte was her main rival now that Conway had tarnished himself in his father's eyes; Bart's refusal to rule himself out of the running, however, was making her nervous.

What if Jeffrey, softened by infatuation with Adrianna, ready to retire, tired of all the contention and fighting and politicking that had characterized his rise to the top of the hotel industry, decided that his youngest child would be the perfect candidate to unite all the warring factions? Could Bart actually persuade their father that a new, holistic approach was the way forward for the Sachs Organization, with Conway, Charlotte and Bella all working away under benevolent, sunny, easy-going Bart?

On the face of it, this seemed an entirely ludicrous speculation. But no one had predicted that Jeffrey, in his eighties, would divorce Jade, whom they had all assumed would cling to him like a limpet until he died so that she could scoop a huge pool as his legal widow. No one had predicted, either, that he would retire; his children had all pictured him dying with his hands still on the reins of power, delegating more and more as he aged, but absolutely refusing ever to give up the kingdom he had built on the twentieth floor.

So if they had been entirely wrong about both those predictions, could it be that they were wrong about this too? Bella knew that Charlotte and Conway were counting out Bart as competition, and strongly suspected that they were dismissing her too. But she too had discounted Bart, and now she was doubting even that calculation . . .

Once more, Bella met Nita's eyes, and saw that her right-hand woman, too, was narrow-eyed, tight-lipped, as she processed Bart's surprising refusal to rule himself out of the race. There were no certainties any more, no safe places. The bones of Bella's skull seemed to tighten as she realized she had a headache coming on.

The next six months were going to feel like an eternity.

Chapter Ten

'We're very excited about this, Bella,' the head of PR for the Chicago office said eagerly. 'It's so much to take in! I'm really psyched to craft a press release that'll hit all of our key target points and get the entire media buzzing—'

'Robin?' Bella interrupted. 'I love your enthusiasm, but I've been briefing people all day. Can we take a break from the reward scheme until tomorrow?'

And good luck, Robin, Bella thought wryly. Down the line, if anything went wrong with the points scheme – *which it won't*, she told herself firmly, repressing for the millionth time a cold stab of fear, *it absolutely won't* – Robin's team, like all the other Sachs PRs, would be on the front line trying to mop up a flooded dam with kitchen sponges, smiling brightly even as hordes of angry customers took to Twitter to share their complaints with the world—

Stop! Have a drink! Have two! Talk about something else, anything else!

'I totally get that,' Robin said earnestly, nodding to show how much she got it.

Every time Bella visited the States, she was reminded all over again about the very different energy levels that

Americans had in business compared to the Brits. Robin was bubbly, bright-eyed, unashamed to gush with enthusiasm, underline her statements with her gestures, make and hold plenty of direct eye contact. It would have been too much for most British companies, especially in the corporate world. If Robin wanted to work in London, she would find herself gently encouraged to tone herself down, cultivate irony rather than eagerness, and certainly lose the habit of clapping her hands and exclaiming 'Yay!' when agreement was reached on crucial points under debate.

However, though it might not be British culture, Bella liked it. She particularly liked it this visit, when the project she was here to brief on was so critical. Robin's American positivity was just what Bella needed as she started her world tour of Sachs offices. She could leave confident that this charismatic and popular woman, while not being directly responsible for the points scheme rollout, would work with the IT department and the CEO, motivating them to their absolute best efforts; she had seen Robin achieve excellent results before, though never on so large a scale.

They were having a much-needed drink before Bella retired to her suite at the Chicago Sachs for room-service dinner and a thorough review of the notes that had been taken at the various meetings throughout the day. Robin had picked the perfect bar, of course, which was an essential skill for someone in her profession. It was bustling, high-ceilinged, classic yet fashionable, with hugely comfortable armchairs and five-star service, offering the latest cocktails; but not so hip and trendy that it was over-packed, over-loud and staffed by pierced and bearded young people who acted as if they had invented Campari as they patronizingly explained its flavour to you without even being asked.

Sipping her cocktail – a martini with olives stuffed with blue cheese, whose calories Bella always convinced herself didn't count – she surveyed Robin, feeling wistful. Somehow, after an entire, punishing day of work, with a catered sushi lunch in the boardroom eaten on the fly, Robin was still sleek, her straightened black hair pinned into a chignon, not a single flyaway hair, her wide lips beautifully outlined and filled in with a caramel gloss that did not seem to have shifted in twelve hours, though Bella had not seen her re-apply it.

Not only did Robin have enviable energy levels, her grooming was, even by American women's standards, superb. And in Bella's extensive experience, American business-women were almost always more polished. She had seen both UK and US versions of reality shows and been struck by how the female US contestants were as camera-ready, hair and make-up perfectly done, as if they had their own professional team; some must have been up since the small hours putting rollers in their hair and contouring their features. By contrast, the British women were either plastered in make-up or wearing the minimum, and the few who had taken time to fully style their hair looked overdone by contrast with the others.

'It's the natural look,' she said out loud, realizing the difference.

'Excuse me?' Robin's perfectly threaded and pencilled brows rose a little.

Bella explained the theory she had just formed, that

American businesswomen were the reigning queens of achieving a maquillage that looked as if they were wearing practically nothing.

'The opposite is the French style,' she continued. 'That's where all you put on is mascara and red lipstick, and if you don't have dark circles under your eyes you draw them in to look moody, or as if you've been up all night with your new lover, having sex and arguing about philosophy.'

Robin burst out laughing, quite spontaneously, not the forced amusement of an employee feeling obliged to show amusement at her boss's jokes. Bella flushed in pleasure. She really did like spending time in America; their open and straightforward attitudes made her feel easier and more relaxed, and their all-consuming business ethos normalized her own workaholic tendencies.

'We're all MAC girls here,' Robin said. 'MAC and Bobbi Brown. You're right, it's the no-make-up make-up. Just tons and tons of neutral shades and you contour and blend for hours. It's all about the brushes. You should *see* how many brushes I have! You work the powder in and then it really does last all day. I mean, I touch up, of course.'

She glanced at Bella, and her large, dark, slightly up-tilted eyes were so warm and friendly that Bella didn't flinch under the scrutiny, despite knowing that she was considerably less powdered and brushed than Robin.

'Hey, why don't we go together while you're here?' she suggested. 'There's a great Bobbi Brown in Bloomies, only a couple of blocks from the Sachs. What about—'

But Bella was very regretfully shaking her head.

'I'd so love to,' she said, 'but I just don't have the time. I'm on such a whistle-stop tour.'

'I'm an idiot!' Robin mimed slapping her own head. 'What am I *saying*? I was talking to you like a girlfriend, and you're *Bella Sachs*! I'll get my PA to call 'em first thing tomorrow morning. We'll get a Bobbi Brown or a MAC make-up artist into the office tomorrow. They come to you – you don't go to them!'

'Oh! That's so nice of you, but—'

'Seriously, this kind of thing is real easy to set up,' Robin said with complete nonchalance. 'And then we can get them to send over whatever you want after they've worked their magic. Plus a full set of brushes. Honestly, they'll change your life. Like I said, it's *all* about the brushes. Blending, blending, blending. It takes way more time than the French chicks drawing in their dark circles, but it's worth the effort.'

Bella was still unsure whether she could spare the time, and was about to say so: but her breath caught in her throat, and the words never came out. Because just then, across the bar, a group of businessmen in suits moved and re-formed into a different configuration to welcome a new arrival. A waitress passed with a tray of drinks as they did so, and the man smiled at her and said something lightly as she went that made her pause for a moment and return his smile as she replied.

Bella stared at him with such shock and wonder that her jaw dropped open. She actually felt saliva forming on her tongue, as if she were a dog panting through its mouth to cool itself down.

'Uh, Bella, that okay?' Robin said a little nervously,

misinterpreting her boss's reaction. 'I didn't mean to be pushy – I just thought you might like me to set something up . . .'

'I'd love it,' Bella said without looking at her or even really listening; her gaze was still fixed on the dark-haired man in the slim-fitting navy suit.

Actually, if you could bring someone here right now to wave some sort of magical make-up wand over me, that would be perfect! she thought. *Could you do that? I'm at the end of a long working day, I'm jet-lagged and I don't have any of your magic brushes.*

I've imagined this scene so many times. Hundreds? Thousands? It's been well over twenty years – it could be in the tens of thousands by now! When I picture it, though, I'm dressed up for a gala, my hair and make-up done, walking down a red carpet for a charity fundraiser in a fabulous dress. He turns and recognizes me and stares in complete amazement.

Like Prince Charming seeing Cinderella across the ballroom and knowing straight away that she's The One. Not just that she's the most beautiful, breathtaking woman in the world, but also because he knows her already, because they were childhood playmates, and he's remembering all those happy times they had together. And his past and present are blending together, like the moment in a film where the hero walks through a doorway, a garden gate set in a high stone arch. It's dark under the arch, but as he moves through it he sees a rose garden flooded with sunlight beyond, and there she is, the love of his life, standing there dressed in white, and they reach out their hands to each other, and that's it – that's the happy ending, the one I always dreamed of . . .

Ridiculous, all of it. A childish, Disney fairytale fantasy from when Bella was a small child. For as long as she could remember she had had a crush on him, the older boy who was nice to her, listened to what she said, played with her, unlike awful Conway, who did nothing but pick on the weaker and less confident of his younger sisters. The crush had only been increased by his utterly unexpected disappearance from her life, that terrible day when they came back to the only home she had ever known to see her doll's house being packed into a huge moving van, Maria standing by the front door crying as if her heart would break, and Jade looking down on them in triumph from that upstairs window.

And before anything else, before her confusion about the strange woman standing at the landing window; before taking in that the entire family wasn't moving, that this was about Daddy not wanting them any more; before losing her beautiful room with her canopy bed and window seat with the view over the canal, Bella's first thought had been: 'Does this mean I can't play with Ronaldo any more?'

He had not been there that day, at some after-school activity or hanging out with his friends. She had begged Maria to say goodbye for her, but she had not then had the faintest idea that she would never see Ronaldo again, or she would have been a wreck. The family estrangement had been very pointed at the beginning, as Jade got pregnant twice in quick succession to ensure her status and inheritance, marking her territory by effectively banning Jeffrey's children with Christie from the house of which she was now the chatelaine.

Although Christie's new house was appropriately luxurious, the gardens of the Maida Vale house were to Bella a lost sunlit childhood paradise now occupied by Jade's brats, who had the golden prize: access to Ronaldo. To console herself, Bella had focused on the fact that he was thirteen when the first was born, would have no interest in a baby; her two little half-brothers would never have been Ronaldo's playmates. The visits paid to the house by Christie's children had been extremely formal and as brief as Jade could make them. Bella had been lucky to snatch a few words with Maria to ask her how Ronaldo was doing; there was no time for a quick trip to the kitchen to see him, let alone play together.

The news had been fantastic, Maria brimming with pride. At sixteen, Ronaldo had achieved extraordinarily good GCSE results, and on hearing this Jeffrey had stepped in, offering to take Ronaldo out of the Edgware Road comprehensive he had been attending and send him instead to a private boarding school at his own expense. From there, Ronaldo's A levels having proved equally stellar, Jeffrey had sent him to Harvard for his undergraduate degree.

Where, in due course, Bella also went. She would have taken her MBA at Harvard in any case; it was unquestionably where you went to business school if you were in the top echelon of academia. But oh, how she had hoped that she might cross paths with Ronaldo there! He would be long gone as an undergraduate, of course, but he could have stayed on, maybe, as a TA, working towards a master's degree or a PhD, attending business or law school?

But no. She had checked all the student directories and failed to find his name, though she couldn't help looking out for him anyway; maybe he would come back to visit a professor, catch a football game . . .

Eventually she heard from Maria that Ronaldo had got a green card, stayed on to work in America. Whenever Bella visited the States, she wondered if she would bump into him. She had pictured meet-cutes as they found themselves side by side in business-class seats on a flight, or sitting next to one another at a bar. Ronaldo would turn to smile politely at his seatmate as he settled in, then realize who she was. And she would see that expression on his face, the mesmerized look Prince Charming gave Cinderella at the ball, and her heart would feel like a snifter of brandy, rich and warm and intoxicating . . .

Now, she felt just as if she had drunk that glass of brandy. No, an entire bottle, filling her chest cavity, burning hot. She shook her head in disbelief, her eyes never leaving him. Ronaldo, in this Chicago bar! She had absolutely no doubt that it was him, despite more than two decades having passed. She would have known him anywhere.

The sheer intensity of her stare must have drawn his attention, because he was turning towards her, away from the group of men he had just joined, his dark eyes meeting hers. It looked as if colour was flooding into his cheeks, though she couldn't be sure of that, because of the diffused, golden glow from the great architectural copper light fixture, large as a Smart car, shaped into gigantic bubbles clustering below the domed ceiling. The bustling, well-dressed people, the chink of glasses and the hum of conversation: it wasn't completely unlike the ballroom of her childhood fantasies.

'Hey, do you know that guy?' Robin was saying. 'He's really staring at you. Maybe he recognizes you, d'you think?'

His lips moved to form the word '*Bella?*', his expression disbelieving. She couldn't hear him, of course, but it was very easy to lip-read the shape of her own name. She started to nod frantically like one of those gold-coloured crazy waving cats in the windows of old-fashioned Chinese restaurants, her hand coming up to complete the resemblance; she would have stood up but her legs were wobbling, and she was scared she might stumble awkwardly hoisting herself out of the big, soft leather sofa.

'Oh wow, he's coming over!' Robin exclaimed.

Bella paid her not the slightest attention. She was entirely fixated on Ronaldo as he strode gracefully through the crowd, his eyes fixed on Bella, managing somehow to deftly dodge and weave around anyone who crossed his path. He almost ran up the short flight of steps that led to the raised curving area in which Bella and Robin were ensconced, and she felt as if she were a princess and he her chosen prince, racing back to her side, up to the dais on which she sat. He held out his hands, just like the fantasy, taking hers, pulling her to her feet, looking down at her with a smile on his full, beautifully shaped lips.

'Bella,' he said, his mouth making the same shape again, her name. It was hypnotic. She wanted to see him saying 'Bella' over and over again.

'Ronnie!' she answered, all she was able to say with her heart in her throat, the hot brandy in her chest. He laughed out loud, shaking his head once more.

'After all these years!' he said in disbelief, 'in such a

random bar . . . but why not? It could be anywhere, couldn't it? Why not here?'

'Uh, guys,' Robin said, rising in her turn, picking up her bag and coat, her tone tactful in the extreme, 'I can see you have a lot of stuff to catch up on, and I could totally do with getting back home and running through what we need to do tomorrow, so I'll get going, okay? I'll settle our bar tab.'

Bella barely noticed Robin leaving. She nodded vaguely in her direction. Ronaldo's manners were much better than Bella's; he did give Robin a swift apology for being so rude. It was just, he explained, that Bella and he were childhood friends, had completely lost touch and were overcome by meeting each other so unexpectedly. But he barely looked at Robin as he spoke, could not tear his gaze from Bella's face. Robin was by any standards an extremely attractive woman, and to have Ronaldo hardly glance at her was Bella's fantasy doubled, tripled: Prince Charming unable even to appreciate another woman's beauty when Cinderella was present.

They sank down onto the sofa together, as if choreographed. A waiter appeared and Ronaldo ordered champagne: Ruinart, the best, he said; only Ruinart was good enough for a celebration like this, a crazy meeting in his home city with little Bella, all grown-up now and looking so wonderful.

'I recognized you straight away. Don't worry, it's not like you still look ten years old!' he said, and he reached out to ping her nose playfully with his finger, a teasing gesture he had made so many times when they were young. 'Of course I've seen photos of you kids over the years – I know what you look like all grown up. Bart's always in the gossip columns. And jeez, I saw about your dad getting divorced, and that story about Conway! How's the family doing? You guys are going through the wars right now!'

'Hah, Lottie's over the moon that Jade's been kicked out!' Bella said, and before she realized it she had kicked off her shoes and curled up on the sofa as familiarly as if she were with a member of her family, having a gossip. 'You should have heard her rip Jade to pieces outside the house – it was amazing! Maria must have told you about what happened, right? About Jade climbing the fence, and—'

'*Oh* yeah, Mum was so happy to tell me all about it! What a total bitch that woman was!'

He grinned, a beautiful smile, his teeth perfect as only American teeth can be; from that alone, Bella would have known that Ronaldo was now a resident of this country.

'I'd get hauled straight to HR if I used that word around anyone I work with,' he said cheerfully, 'but sometimes you just have to. You were never snobs to me, and your mum wasn't either. But the moment Jade moved in, she made it damn clear that I was the son of the help and needed to know my place, which meant barely visiting the house. You know how I'd come round to yours after school till Mum was finished for the day?'

Bella nodded. Ronaldo's father did shift work and wasn't home by the time school let out, so during the week Ronaldo had usually been at the Maida Vale house for a few hours in the early evening. That was when the children had gathered to play, though gradually the demands of homework had cut into the playtime somewhat.

'So the first time Jade saw me coming in – through the servants' entrance, of course! – she came downstairs and gave me and my mum the third degree,' Ronaldo continued. 'Who was I, why did I think it was okay to be here, she didn't want a strange kid round the house distracting my mum from her work, etc., etc. That was actually what made Mum angriest, I think – the suggestion that she might not be doing her job properly. It was okay for me – you guys were gone, and I was twelve, old enough to get the bus home and let myself in till Mum or Dad came back. But it really hurt Mum.'

'Oh, is *that* why Daddy paid your school fees and sent you to Harvard?' Bella asked. 'Because Jade was such a bitch to you?'

He shrugged.

'I guess. I mean, nothing was said about that outright, you know? But it might have helped. I know Mum went to your dad to boast about my GCSEs. She was royally pissed that I couldn't study at your house any more, so she was making the point that I had to do my homework on my own with no supervision. Motivate myself. And Harvard happened because my boarding school had all these international students, so it had plenty of affiliations with overseas universities. I got fed into the programme with the rest of the kids. I was really lucky to have the opportunity – it transformed my life. I got a scholarship, but your dad still helped a ton. I'm so grateful to him.'

'I'm so glad,' Bella said in heartfelt tones. 'Honestly, it's nice to hear of Daddy doing something good for once!'

They both laughed at this. They were so close; their bodies had rolled towards each other on the deep, squashy sofa. She reached out and touched the back of his hand, even that brief contact intensifying the fiery brandy sensation in her chest. He smiled at her. Bella was openly staring at him, seeing the child in the man's face. Dark almond eyes, thick dark hair, full lips; he had a shading of five o'clock shadow around his jawline, a dark bluish tint, and that was strange, as she had always known him as a smooth-skinned pre-pubescent boy.

'You've got the advantage of me,' she managed to say. 'You knew what I looked like as a grown-up. I'm still in shock.'

'But you recognized me straight away!' he marvelled. 'I can't believe it!'

'I know!' she said, quite as if she hadn't spent an infinite amount of time in her teens and twenties imagining what Ronaldo would look like.

'When I'd see those photos of you guys in the magazines, you know what I'd think?' he said.

'No!' Bella said over-eagerly, greedy for any possible compliment that might be coming. She heard her tone – too high, too excited – and sat back, grabbing at her glass of Ruinart to look at that instead; she was terrified of seeming as gushing and needy as she truly was, revealing the size of the crush she had been nursing all these years.

'I'd think,' Ronaldo said, picking up his own glass, 'that nowadays we'd all have phones! Kids nowadays have phones from the time they're in double digits. We'd have been texting constantly – we'd never have lost contact like we did. Back then, what were we going to do? We didn't even have each other's home phone numbers.'

This had never occurred to Bella before, and for some reason it hit her hard. She stared at him, the glass sweating in her hand. It was such a small thing, a mobile phone, a little rectangle of plastic and metal, but the difference it would have made was absolutely crucial. If he and the Sachs kids had had phones, they would never have lost touch. She would never have lost him.

And then a horrible thought struck her. She glanced at his left hand. There was no ring, but not all men wore them. And he had spoken so easily about kids nowadays . . .

'Do you have children? Are you married?' she blurted out, and then busied herself with putting down her glass of champagne on the table so she wouldn't see him answer yes.

'No. Never found the right woman,' he said lightly. 'Still looking! And you?'

It hadn't occurred to her that she herself was married. Her expression would have been comic if there had been any spectators to appreciate it.

'Married, but no kids,' she mumbled, and realized that she had wrapped her hands together and started to squeeze her wedding and engagement rings as if to minimize them. 'He's, uh, he's a lot older than me.'

Ronaldo nodded politely, as if he understood why she had chosen to phrase it this way, and reached out to refill her glass.

'So you stayed on in the States?' Bella said quickly. 'I mean, obviously.'

'Yes!' He beamed. 'I love it. It's so can-do here. That's a total cliché, of course, but it's true. Sure, there's a class system, though they like to pretend there isn't. But as a Brit, I skip all that. Back home I'd always have been the son of a housekeeper. Coming here was the best thing that ever happened to me.'

'And you live here? I mean, in Chicago?'

Ronaldo was an advertising agency executive; he lived in Lake Shore East, in a condo with spectacular views, he told her. He'd bounced around the States like an eager puppy, trying out different cities to settle down in as soon as his green card came through: New York was too crammed, LA's highways insane, San Francisco lovely but too laid-back for him. Chicago had everything he wanted – great buzz and nightlife, with amazing summers during which he made the most of the thirty miles of beach that bordered the city. Did Bella know that Chicago's motto was *Urbs in Horto*, or 'City In A Garden'? Despite the fact that Bella's family ran one of the biggest hotels in the city, she had to admit that she did not.

Yes, Ronaldo acknowledged, the winters were harsh, but coming from Britain, he couldn't settle down on the West Coast. He needed to live through full seasons: it was great to have snow in winter and the glorious Chicago summers, watch the changing of the foliage that was so famous in America. He'd been learning to paddleboard, he said, patting his completely flat stomach, as he was really starting to have to take his exercise seriously if he wanted to keep eating the local deep-pan pizza . . .

Deep-pan pizza! Had Bella ever tried it? She hadn't? He supposed whenever she was here on business they took her to fancy restaurants. She said that actually, she mostly ordered from room service when travelling, to wind down after a long day's work, and that was what she had been planning to do that evening . . .

From then on, events moved so swiftly they seemed to

blur together, a TV show on fast-forward. Ronaldo whisked her away in a cab to a branch of what he said was the most famous pizza place in Chicago, Lou Malnati's. There were practically no choices, he explained, because these toppings were just the best: plain cheese; spinach, mushroom and tomato; sausage or pepperoni; that was pretty much it. They ordered three, so Bella could try the full range, and Ronaldo would not allow any of them to be thin crust. Her first time at Lou's had to be all deep dish, he said, because she was finally eating out properly in his adopted city.

Curled into their red leather booth, her stockinged feet once more under her, drinking cheap red wine, Bella could not remember when she had been happier. This was totally spontaneous, down-to-earth, like a date, like being normal, not someone who lived such a five-star life that she had no idea of the last time she had gone out to a chain restaurant, sat in a diner booth, kicked off her shoes.

When they finally admitted defeat, pushed the still-brimming pizza plates fractionally away to signify that they were finished, laughing at their crazy ambition, they didn't sit back in the booth. They stayed leaning forward, elbows propped on the table, their faces close. Ronaldo apologized for bringing Bella Sachs, of all people, to such a destination; Bella promptly fell over herself to tell him that she had enjoyed it more than anywhere she had eaten out in months. He asked how long she was staying: could he make amends by taking her somewhere seriously chic and smart tomorrow night?

Bella's schedule was tightly planned, every section of her world tour fitted together as perfectly as the workings of an antique grandfather clock. Tomorrow was another full day in the office: the next morning was an early flight to Dallas and then an equally full day of meetings there. It was unthinkable that she could go out after work twice in a row, drink this much – God knew what state she would be in tomorrow morning, they were well into their second bottle of Chianti! – and get on a plane in any decent state to send her bags to the Sachs Dallas on landing, so that she could head for the Texas office and the team who were waiting to be briefed by her.

Even tonight had been insane. She ought to get an Uber or a Lyft straight away, head back to her suite, take a sleeping pill, hope that tomorrow's hangover wouldn't be too painful. She opened her mouth to tell him this and heard herself say instead:

'That sounds lovely! I'm here for quite a few days, I think. We have lots to get through and I haven't visited this branch in a while. But can you spare the time? Two nights in a row? I know people in the States book themselves up really far ahead—'

She was fishing pathetically to see if he had a date planned for tomorrow that he would be cancelling for her; she was positively babbling.

'Bella,' he said gently. He reached across the table, across the pizzas that were covering almost its entire surface, one shirt cuff trailing a little in tomato sauce; he glanced down and grinned as he saw what had happened, not remotely caring about the stain on his shirt as he took her hand. His shirt collar was open now; he had taken off his tie, and Bella did not know where to look.

There was nowhere safe. His skin glowed; they had always joked that Ronaldo had a permatan because of his Portuguese heritage. His face, his hands, his muscled wrists, the strong column of his neck, the tight dark curls of chest hair just visible above the button of his shirt: it was impossible not to wonder what the rest of his body was like. When she dropped her gaze to the hand holding hers, she could see dark hairs twisting around his watch strap, and she wanted to unbutton the cuff of his shirt, push it back, reveal his forearm.

She looked sideways at her wine glass, but even there she could see his reflection, distorted by the swell of the glass, his face stretched and floating against a dark red background. He was everywhere.

And he was saying: 'I haven't seen you in over twenty years. Some of my happiest memories when I was a kid were with you guys. It's all coming back to me, sitting here, looking at you – little Bella! I know we're almost the same age, but back then you were always little Bella to me.'

His smile was beautiful.

'Of course I'm free tomorrow night, you crazy girl!' he said fondly. 'Whatever I had booked, I'd cancel it to see you! This is pretty miraculous – it's like I'm finding my family again, you know? I was an only, so you were like my siblings. And when you guys disappeared, you still had each other, but I didn't have anyone. Ugh, that sounds like I'm playing the world's tiniest violin, but you can see how much this means to me—'

'No, no, I feel the same!' she said, though her heart was sinking at Ronaldo's artless comparison of her to a sibling.

He raised her hand, leant forward across the table, kissed her knuckles. It was her left hand, with the huge diamond engagement ring and her wedding band, but he kissed it anyway, and his eyes met hers as he did so.

That brandy sensation was stronger than ever, as if he had touched a match to the brimming snifter, orange-blue flames dancing on the surface as the alcohol burned. She wanted to reach out and drag off her rings, throw them on the floor of the pizzeria, let them roll away under another table for someone else to take, someone who wanted them.

They did not have sex that night. They managed, somehow, to wait until the next one.

Chapter Eleven

Four days later, much to the astonishment of everyone around her, Bella was still in Chicago. Nita's poor assistant Tal was on the worst of terms with the travel department, who groaned every time they heard her voice on the phone. Because Bella had made the decision to stay on a day-by-day basis. Every morning that she had woken up with Ronaldo next to her, as soon as he had left to go home and get ready for work, she had rolled over, taken her phone from the bedside table, and texted Nita to tell her she needed an extra day in the city for work meetings and to make the arrangements accordingly.

Nita, busy rescheduling every single meeting in every city on her boss's itinerary, had passed the travel element on to Tal, and Tal, by now practically sobbing, rang her contact in Travel with yet another fervent apology to tell them that every single booking they had made for Bella was defunct. The entire complicated line of dominoes that they had painstakingly arranged on end had been triggered to fall, and needed to be picked up one by one and stacked up afresh: flights and hotels, continent by continent.

Never before had Bella put her staff through anything like

this, and the speculation in the London office about what was going on was rampant. But Chicago could only inform them that Bella seemed to feel she had a whole raft of unexpected extra concerns about their ability to push through the revamped points scheme, and that she was insisting on coming into the office for a few hours a day in order to rehash the brief over and over again . . .

Bella, meanwhile, was in such a haze of bliss that she was barely aware of how much trouble she was causing. For the first time in her life she was being utterly selfish, and it felt amazing. After sending the text, she would roll into the slight depression Ronaldo had left in the pillows and the feather mattress topper – a Sachs hotel signature, supremely comfortable. Putting her head where his had been, she would smell his scent, lying in the warmth left by his body, her eyes closed as she replayed everything they had done together the night before and just now, that morning; her body sore, the happiest and most relaxed she had ever been.

Not only had she spent a fortune, literally a fortune – Tal's entire yearly salary – on silk underwear, slips, robes, sexy black cocktail dresses, sky-high heels, facials, make-up, at Bloomingdales in the last few days, she had even taken Robin's advice and gone to MAC for a combined makeover and make-up lesson. She had walked away looking like the best possible version of herself, carrying two bags which were, as Robin had predicted, mostly full of brushes.

In addition, every day Bella had booked a hairdresser through the hotel to come to her suite for a blow-dry. How she wished she had let her hair grow like her twin sister's, so that she had sexy long locks for Ronaldo to tangle his hands in, which she could toss around in passion, which would spill out seductively behind her on the pillow. If she had known she would be meeting him, she would have got the best extensions money could buy.

Her wedding and engagement rings were still on her left hand, however. Every evening, dressed in one of her new slinky negligees, sitting in the dressing room off her bedroom as the hairdresser worked his magic in front of the make-up mirror, she sipped champagne to calm her raging nerves and fought the near-uncontrollable desire to pull them off. Tonight was no exception; her hair was being wound onto rollers, and with nothing to do but sit there and wait for Ronaldo's arrival, she started to twist off the engagement ring, an unscrewing action. It seemed weirdly appropriate, a process of undoing something, opening it up, setting free what had been kept tightly inside.

However, every time she had worked it painfully over the knuckle – she had put on weight since the wedding – she stopped and twisted it back into place. She had been trying not to think about her husband at any point during these last few days, though that had been very hard to do. Spending so much money on sexy underwear and robes which Thomas would consider utterly impractical had, oddly, caused her the most guilt of all. When she was with Ronaldo, she couldn't think of anything but the excitement she felt in his presence; away from him, however, thoughts of Thomas kept flooding in.

They had hardly talked since she had been away, as she had been doing everything she could to avoid her husband. Thomas didn't require daily phone calls when one of them was travelling, so this hadn't been difficult. He had rung and left messages, but Bella had texted instead of ringing back. Thomas seemed very understanding when she explained that, due to the demands of this hugely ambitious project, she was completely exhausted, much too tired to talk.

She knew all too well that she really, *really* needed to start moving. Board that plane to Dallas which had been painstakingly booked and cancelled for days now, complete the rest of her round-the-world tour, get back to London and take up the reins there once more. Every day that she lingered in Chicago was another twenty-four hours subtracted from working on probably the most important project she would ever undertake. The huge task of revamping the Sachs hotels was nothing to this.

But Bella could not bear to tear herself away from Ronaldo. Her sexual obsession with him was overwhelming. She couldn't eat, she could hardly sleep: she lay awake beside him at night listening to him breathe, smelling his sweat, her head spinning, her body still throbbing from sex. She had lost four pounds in five days. It was a teenage crush made real, her hormones raging as strongly as if she were sixteen and in love for the first time.

But a teenager would be in love with the idea, not the reality. While Bella knew, without a shadow of a doubt, that she was head over heels in love with Ronaldo and that she always had been. She had been sure of it from the moment she saw him in the bar, her childhood friend all grown-up, that sweet, happy boy who had been so kind to her when she was small, and who was so wonderful to her now. Beside him, Thomas seemed entirely unreal. Her husband might as well have been one of those life-sized cardboard cut-outs of film stars they displayed in cinemas.

Her phone, in front of her on the dressing table, buzzed, and she grabbed it at once, assuming it was Ronaldo, who she was due to meet in just under an hour; please let him not be telling her he was late at work, or even that he had to cancel! This hadn't happened yet, but obsession makes one paranoid, and she never quite believed that he would show up, night after night, until he did—

'Hi!' she said into the phone.

'Hey! Finally!' responded a male voice which was definitely not Ronaldo. Bella pulled it from her ear, stared at the screen, realized it was not a voice call but a FaceTime one, and screamed at the sight of her smiling husband.

'Everything okay?' he asked, frowning, as she fumbled with the phone, turning the screen so that all he could see was her face; God forbid he saw the silky negligee falling opening at the cleavage, the matching push-up lace bra underneath it.

'Yes!' she said swiftly. 'But I'm just—'

Thomas took in the make-up, the rollers in her hair, the stylist behind her, and his eyes widened in surprise.

'What's going on?' he asked, a hint of disapproval creeping into his voice. 'I thought you were working till you dropped every night?'

'There's a gala dinner with the Mayor's office,' she said, thinking fast. 'I thought I might as well go. If there are any problems with the relaunch, it can't hurt to have the local politicians and press on our side.'

There actually had been some sort of gala two nights ago,

which Robin had suggested she attend, but Bella had said regretfully that she had far too many documents to review that evening, and promptly rushed back to her suite to get ready for Ronaldo.

'You've got so much make-up on!' Thomas commented, staring intently at the screen. 'I barely recognized you!'

Bella was about to make an excuse, explain that there would be a lot of photographers and glad-handing at the gala and that she needed to look polished; but she hesitated for a moment, feeling something shift. Something that told her this was the way she used to behave with him, but no longer needed to.

'Actually, it really isn't that much,' Bella said; she knew it wasn't, having applied it herself. She wanted to look natural for Ronaldo, not plastered in foundation and fake eyelashes that would look as if she were trying too hard and would leave smears on the bedsheets. Above her head, the hairdresser nodded in agreement as he started to remove the heated rollers.

Thomas looked vexed.

'Well, it's more than you usually wear!' he said.

The hairdresser halted momentarily, fingers hovering over the next roller for a second or two before he started to unwind it. Bella, who had been going to defend herself, paused too, and then, as it were, stayed paused by deciding that she didn't need to answer this: it hadn't been a question. Instead, she managed a smile for the camera, and said:

'I think it looks nice. I had a very overdue lesson at MAC over here.'

'Would you like some privacy?' the hairdresser asked

tactfully, putting a second hot roller down on the insulated pad he had placed on the dressing table.

'No, I'm fine, thanks,' Bella said, careful to keep holding the phone at an angle that hid her incriminating outfit.

'I would, actually!' Thomas said, his voice tinny through the speaker. 'I would like a few minutes to talk to my wife.'

The hairdresser met Bella's eyes in the mirror, saw her little nod, and, saying, 'I'll wait in the living room till you call me, shall I?' slipped discreetly from the dressing room.

'I don't have much time—' she started to say to her husband as she wedged the phone carefully on the dressing table at an angle which just showed her face and shoulders.

'I got you a present!' he interrupted, reaching down to his side. 'It's especially for all the travelling you're doing.'

A wave of guilt flooded over Bella. Thomas was always so thoughtful about this kind of thing, bringing home little gadgets to make her life easier when she was on the road: clever charging devices, an inflatable ergonomic neck-rest pillow infinitely better even than the ones in first class for long working flights, a new silk eye mask to replace the one that was getting a little worn. He wanted to make her life easier, make her more comfortable. That was always the phrase: make her comfortable.

He reappeared, holding up a plastic packet, transparent, with a smart design on it that prevented her from seeing what was inside.

'You're always saying you run round so much when you're on planes and having meetings and hate it when your underwear digs into you at the end of a long day,' he said, which was perfectly true. 'So I saw this brand advertised and I ordered you some. Look!'

He pulled open the flap of the packet and extracted something that Bella could not quite believe that she was seeing.

'Wait, are those—' she began.

'Travelling knickers!' he said blithely, looking down at the large beige pants he was holding in both hands. 'Though you could wear them every day if you wanted, not just for travelling! They're' – he read from the packet – '*laser-cut, with no seams, and invisible under clothes. The high waist and low-cut leg ensure full coverage and incredible comfort. With nothing to dig in, and a high Lycra content, they fit you – you don't fit them. You won't even realize you have them on.*'

Bella stared at her husband in silence, vividly conscious of the knickers she was currently wearing: these were the smallest wisp of lace that she felt her figure could get away with, fastened on each hip with a satin ribbon tied in a bow.

'They do look very – comfortable,' she agreed eventually.

Thomas beamed. 'I thought you'd like them! I got them in white, black and beige,' he said. 'Size medium. It's a shame you couldn't take them on this trip. But when you're back you can try them on and see if they work for you.'

'I'm sure they will,' Bella said, staring at the granny knickers her husband had bought her. 'I mean, they look as if they'd work for anyone.'

Carefully, Thomas slid them back into the packet.

'Did you get them from the *Telegraph* catalogue?' she heard herself ask, picturing the wide-banded, underwire-free, lace-panelled 'easy-wear' bras that were advertised in the back of the magazine, modelled on smiling thirty-something blondes but clearly intended for a much older, silver-haired clientele.

'No, a travel magazine on the plane,' he said, putting the packet down. 'It's very clever – they're made with this special fabric which means they dry extra fast. Great for when someone's travelling for a few days and wants to hand-wash their underwear as they go! Of course, that's not an issue for you.'

He smiled, an acknowledgement that a Sachs who almost always stayed in a Sachs hotel would not be billed the extortionate costs that mere mortals had to pay to get their washing done.

'No,' Bella agreed in an oddly flat voice. 'No, it isn't.'

Thomas frowned. 'Is everything okay?' he asked. 'You're very quiet, and you've barely been in touch since you left. I know how hard you're working, but still, that's not like you.'

'I'm just so busy,' she lied. 'Sorry. And I have to go out really soon – this gala—'

'I'll let you go,' her husband said, to her great relief. 'It was just that the knickers came this morning and I wanted to show you them.'

'Of course! Um, thanks!' Bella said rather helplessly.

Once more, Thomas beamed. 'Well, good!' he said happily. 'Good stuff! I hope everything there's going just as you want it.'

'Uh, it is,' Bella confirmed, feeling awful at how very true this was.

'Can't wait to see you back home!' he said.

'In the knickers,' Bella found herself saying flatly.

'Yes! Can't wait! Well, love you, darling.'

'Love you too,' she said, her face contorting into a weird and strained attempt at a smile. She hated lying, and that was exactly what she was doing. Of course married people said they loved each other automatically without feeling a surge of passion every time, but those three words had had not a shred of emotion behind them. She was amazed Thomas hadn't noticed.

He waved before reaching to the screen and clicking off the call. She sagged back in the chair, completely drained, and reached out for her glass of champagne, taking a long sip before calling back the hairdresser to complete the removal of her rollers and the plumping out of her hair into thick, flattering waves. It was an overdone style for the kind of restaurant that Ronaldo took her to, hipster, off-the-beaten-track places where Bella Sachs would not be recognized, partly because the lighting was so dim that even the waiters could barely see her face.

But she wanted to look as beautiful as possible for him, wanted to feel their excitement build as they scooted their chairs closer and closer to each other, held hands under the table, worked themselves up to a state of positive frenzy until they could hold out no longer, threw money on the table to cover the bill and jumped into an Uber to race back to the hotel. Then, of course, they would have to let Ronaldo out a couple of blocks before the Sachs, so that Bella could return demurely alone to the hotel and be seen to go up to her suite alone after her business dinner. Ten minutes later, a tap on the door would signal Ronaldo's arrival.

It was a delightful game: the secrecy, the choice of obscure restaurant for their rendezvous, and the sneaking around adding extra spice to the affair. Bella loved to feel the eager anticipation as she waited for him by the door of the suite, threw it open as soon as she heard his knock, bustled him in quickly so no one saw him in the corridor, and threw herself into his arms as soon as the door closed safely behind him.

She would have been bewildered, shocked, horrified, if she had known about the levels of perversity her sister Charlotte had reached with her lover Lee, the twisted games of rape and dominance they invented, the costumes, the accoutrements, the elaborate set-ups. This was not one of the myriad areas in which Bella had chosen the opposite path from her sister to avoid failing in the inevitable competition. She was, naturally, as vanilla as it was possible to be. All she wanted was sex with the right guy, one with a great body and a great cock that he knew how to use. Nothing complicated, no crazy positions that made you feel as if your hip was being ripped out, or that you were choking to death, or that he was able to see the less alluring parts of you in awkward, unseemly close-up.

She would have been happy having nothing but missionary sex with Ronaldo for the rest of her life, her curvy body a perfect cushion for his hip bones, clinging on to his muscular arms, watching the sweat build in the mat of chest hair which, overnight, had become for her the most erotic sight possible; apart from his face as he sped up, let himself go, the cluster of dark curls at his forehead sweaty too, his movements faster and faster as he roared out and shot deep inside her, burying his cock in her as he collapsed onto her.

She had begged him, the first time, not to brace himself

but to give her his entire weight, and now he knew that was what she wanted, he would lie there, splayed, his legs tangled with hers, his body hair scratching her deliciously. Then they would play another little game, so innocuous that it would have given Charlotte and Lee the dry heaves; he would reluctantly stir, start to slide out, and she would protest, hold on to him, try to keep him inside her as long as possible. He would laugh and kiss her and keep going, her strength no match for his, even if she clung to him like ivy round an oak; he peeled her off eventually, reached down, made sure the condom was still on, started to . . .

'Um, Ms Sachs, could I ask you to sit still?' the hairdresser said. 'I'm so sorry, but I know you have to be out of here ASAP for your gala, and I'm worried I'm going to pull your hair with the tongs.'

Bella had been a million miles away, and simultaneously in the next room, on the huge bed, stark naked. She jumped at the hairdresser's voice, and the poor man winced as he inadvertently did exactly what he had been worrying about, tugging at the lock of hair he was carefully tonging into shape.

'That was my fault!' Bella said quickly, to reassure him. 'Don't worry!'

This was the side issue of being Bella Sachs at a Sachs hotel. Everyone trod on eggshells around you. They all knew who you were, even the chambermaids, and their visible nerves never abated.

'I'm nearly finished,' the hairdresser said nervously. 'It's taken just a *tiny* bit longer than it should have done, because—'

'Because my husband rang!' Bella said. 'You're doing a fantastic job.'

She finished her champagne, gloating at the sight of herself in the mirror. Her hair was glowing, due to a rinse the hairdresser had given her at their first session; it was supposed to bring out the gold in her hair, and it really did work. She would have had highlights done if it hadn't been too obvious. Ronaldo would have seen the difference and realized that she had gone out the day after their first meeting and put streaks in her hair to be prettier for him.

Bella reached up to touch one of the loose waves the hairdresser was working on; it was a two-step process, curlers for volume, then these casual waves, loose and natural, as if she had made barely any effort. Certainly not as if she had paid him five nights in a row to achieve this artless, unstudied effect.

'Do you think longer hair would suit me?' she asked. 'Maybe I could grow this cut out, or even get extensions?'

'Yeah, definitely,' the hairdresser said, smiling in relief that she hadn't snapped at him. 'You have a classic oval face, you can carry off most styles. I'd suggest—'

But just then a buzz sounded: someone was at the main door of the suite.

'Shall I go?' the hairdresser asked. It wasn't his job, but she had tipped him excellently every single night, and after all, she was Bella Sachs.

Bella wasn't expecting anyone. She had a cab booked in twenty minutes to take her to the restaurant Ronaldo had chosen for that evening's date, and no one at the Sachs would disturb their boss and owner unnecessarily. Her heart leapt; the brandy burnt inside her chest again.

'Hold on,' she said, and raced across the bedroom, through the living room and down the hallway, looking into the video screen by the main door to the suite. As she had guessed, it was Ronaldo, his face partly obscured by the huge bunch of flowers he was carrying. He had come here rather than the restaurant, so keen to see her that he couldn't bear to wait a mere forty minutes . . .

She threw open the door with one hand, the other pressed over her lips to warn him not to say a word.

'The cleaner's here!' she hissed as he came in. 'Hang on, I'll get rid of her . . .'

Back the way she had come, into the dressing room, now hissing at the hairdresser to pack up his stuff and sneak out by the bedroom door. In an instant, she had realized that unless she let Ronaldo in first, the hairdresser would see him, a handsome man holding a huge bunch of flowers, waiting further down the corridor, realize that this was no business meeting, and spread the gossip all around the hotel.

'Hey, but your hair isn't finished!' he protested. 'I haven't tonged the right side yet!'

'Leave the tongs – I'll pay for them! Take everything else and go – use that door! It's, uh, an urgent business meeting, I need to get right on it—'

She ran to her wallet on the bedside table, grabbed two hundred-dollar bills, added two more for the tongs, pushed the cash at him. His eyes went comically wide. The blow-dry was billed directly to the hotel, so even with the cost of the tongs, this was a huge tip. She saw him safely out before she sprayed on perfume, shoved her feet into the five-inch stiletto Louboutins she had bought the day before, and then went as fast as she could in the killer heels back to the hallway, where Ronaldo was waiting.

'I still need to finish my hair—' she started, but couldn't get out another word; Ronaldo dropped the gigantic bouquet of roses and foliage onto the hall table and took her in his arms, kissing her so passionately that one heel turned under her and she staggered, grabbing onto him for balance.

'I couldn't sit in a restaurant with you, not even for a couple of hours,' he said against her mouth. 'It's so hard keeping my hands off you, pretending we're just old friends catching up, night after night – it's crazy! So I cancelled the reservation and thought we'd order room service – that okay?'

'It's perfect!' she said deliriously.

He bent down, slid an arm under her thighs and hoisted her into the air, making her squeal with happy surprise.

'Sex first,' he said. 'Then dinner. Which is the right way round – I don't know why we've been doing it wrong up till now.'

'If we've been doing it wrong,' Bella said, clinging to his neck as he carried her through to the bedroom, 'I don't ever want to do it right!'

Chapter Twelve

He dropped her on the huge bed and started to unbutton his jacket. Bella sat up, pulling the negligee from her shoulders to reveal the pale-blue lace underwear, and the sheer hold-up Wolford stockings with a wide top band of pale-blue and white lace. Bella had spent several hundred dollars and a good hour that afternoon assembling the outfit, co-ordinating the colour, and she would have paid triple just to see the look on Ronaldo's face, his eyes darkening as he took in the sight of her.

'Fuck, that's hot,' he said as he dropped his jacket and started on his shirt. 'You're so beautiful, Bella. You look like a pin-up girl.'

'Really?'

Clearly he either hadn't noticed the fact that her hair was half-tonged into waves on one side and straight on the other, or he couldn't care less. She flushed with happiness, and, feeling more confident than she ever had, lay down on her back, legs up in the air, ankles crossed, in the classic pin-up pose.

'Sexy!' He grinned at her.

His shirt followed his jacket, his hands went to his waistband. His bare chest was thickly haired, a mat on his pectorals that narrowed slightly to his trim waist, not the slightest hint of a roll; she actually licked her lips as she watched him unbutton, unzip, push everything down from his big reddened cock, bend over to drag off his black silk socks and then deftly kick them away with the boxers and trousers in one go; he had clearly undressed in front of plenty of women, because he knew exactly how to avoid that awkward moment when a man stood there naked but for his socks, momentarily a figure of fun.

Ronaldo, on the other hand, had no problems with co-ordinating the removal of his clothes in the most effective way possible. He had deftly extracted a condom from his trouser pocket in the process and now, with it in one hand, he smiled at her devilishly, climbed onto the foot of the huge bed and started to crawl towards her, his body golden, the muscles in his arms and back flexing superbly as he moved.

Bella's mouth was open in wonder, and she felt that saliva build again. Her legs weakened, and she let them down, awkwardly, as she wasn't particularly fit, wanting to avoid spiking him with a stiletto heel; he caught her calves, spreading them apart, kneeling between them, then guiding her up to sit. Peeling off the foil wrapper, he threw it aside and handed her the condom.

'Why don't you put it on me?' he suggested with a smile of pure anticipation. And then, when she took it eagerly: 'With your mouth.'

Bella felt the blood rush to her face, was sure she had gone bright red. Ronaldo reached out, traced the O of her parted lips, slid his finger between them.

'Put it on with your hot . . . wet . . . mouth,' he said very deliberately. 'Please, baby. I want to feel it all around me.'

Her face was on fire. She had never done this before, but she was too mortified to tell him so. Still, how hard could it be, as it were? Kneeling up to face him, she put the condom over her mouth, feeling like an idiot. Quickly, she ducked her head and settled her lips over the tip of his cock, which was rigid in anticipation, a steel-centred prong almost vertical against his flat stomach.

She pinched the tip as she went, rolling her lips over her teeth, starting to unroll the rubber downwards, his cock butting against the roof of her mouth as she went. His hands were in her hair, stroking through it, his erection swelling even more in her mouth, loving this tight hot contact.

Bella could barely breathe, but it didn't matter. She would do anything to make him happy. On she went, driving the condom further, Ronaldo caressing her hair, telling her how good it felt, how tight and wet her mouth was, how she was magic, could she feel how much he liked it, how sexy she was with his cock in her mouth . . .

She was scared of choking, but still the condom kept going; she knew he used Magnum XLs. The tip was at the back of her throat now, drenched in saliva, and she was making panting, gurgling sounds, was getting truly worried about gagging. Her eyes were watering, her lips cramping, but she was determined to do what he had asked, and only when his big hands gently guided up her head did she pull her lips back from her teeth again, sobbing for breath, but her eyes glowing at the sight of his satisfied smile.

'You're amazing,' he said, tracing her lips once more, pushing her back onto the pillows. 'That was wonderful.'

'I want to make you happy,' she said, sounding pathetic, feeling pathetic; but it was true, it was all she could think about.

Ronaldo was undoing the satin bows that held her knickers in place, just as she had imagined him doing, like unwrapping a present. He sighed in bliss at the sight of her: bending over, he blew gently between her legs, a soft jet of air that was so erotic she jerked her hips up in delight. Again and again he did it, not touching her, driving her increasingly mad, making her beg and plead for actual contact until finally he sank his mouth onto her and gave her what she wanted, wet lips, driving tongue flicking its point into her. She came almost straight away, worked up beyond endurance, pounding against him, and after he had got her as wet as he could, he rose up, wiped his mouth on his arm and butted his cock between her legs, covering her with his body, starting to fuck her the way she loved.

Bella held onto his arms, watched his handsome face, drinking in everything about him: how he looked, how he felt on her, inside her. This was her ultimate fantasy. She literally could not imagine anything she could want more, no film star, no rock god, just Ronaldo, fucking her in the missionary position so that she could see him working away, watch his pleasure rise and rise. Her eyes were greedy, running up and down his body, taking in everything she could; oh for a mirror on the ceiling so she could see that view, see his hard round buttocks pumping away, the sweat pooling at the base of his spine, the long twists of muscle in his back and shoulders, his hairy thighs between her stockinged ones—

She bounced against the pillows; he was close to coming, his thrusts strong enough now to lift her up momentarily. Her arms splayed wide; she liked to lie there, almost like a human sacrifice, letting him use her, drive into her until he reached transcendence – and there it was, incoherent words spilling from his mouth as the sperm poured from him, his cock juddering inside her. He collapsed onto her, mashing her breasts deliciously against his chest hair. She clung to his shoulders, making sure his full weight was on her, just as she wanted. She could not get enough of him.

His head was nestled in the smooth, soft curve of her neck. Only when, with a gusty sigh, he lifted it and started to press himself up again, did he see her face.

'You're crying!' he said. 'What's wrong, baby? What did I do? I thought it was good for you!'

'It was,' she said, the tears streaming slowly down her cheeks. 'It was wonderful. It was the best thing that's ever happened to me.'

'So why are you *crying*? Women!' he said fondly. 'Look, give me a second, I have to . . .'

His weight came off her, he slid out of her, and that only made her cry harder. Her carefully MAC-brushed face was a blotched mess by the time he had cleaned himself up and returned to the bedside, but she was barely making a sound. Her chest was pumping, her breasts heaving as she cried her heart out in silence, the tears continuing to well up and pour out.

Ronaldo had a handful of tissues in his fist. He climbed

onto the bed, rolled her towards him, took her in his arms, tenderly started to dab her face.

'It was wonderful for me too,' he said, kissing away the tears. 'Watching you put that condom on me with your mouth, Jesus – I don't know how I kept going so long, everything about you just drives me so crazy – but did I hurt you? Is that why you're crying? Little Bella, did I hurt you? You always say you want the weight, but I'm not a small guy—'

'You don't understand,' she sobbed. 'I want it so much! It was amazing! But I have to go! If I don't go I never will, and I have this business thing I need to do; it's the biggest deal ever, I *have* to go . . . oh, why did I have to meet you again now? It's like my heart is breaking!'

'Baby! Stop it!' He held the tissues on her cheeks to soak up the flood of tears. 'I knew you were bound to leave town eventually. I've been trying not to think about it, but it had to happen, didn't it?'

She clung to him, buried her face in his neck now, unable to look at him as she said, 'Do you *want* me to go?'

'No! No, of course I don't, but you were just visiting . . .' He took a long breath. 'I don't know what to say. This has been crazy. Yes, it's only been a few days, but I've known you since I was tiny. There's so much we have together. But—' He hesitated.

'But what?' Bella peeled her wet face off his sweaty skin, most of her eyeliner pencil now transferred to his collarbone. There was only so much even an expensive liner could endure before it gave up the ghost.

'Little Bella,' he said, putting the sodden, foundation-stained tissues on the bedside table. 'You have to go. I understand – you're at the start of a long work trip. But baby, there are planes, and trains, and—'

He tailed off, taking another breath. 'Is it time to talk about the elephant in the room?' he said, pulling a pillow behind him, lying back, still holding her. 'I haven't wanted to push you. But if you want to . . .'

'I was scared you didn't ask because you didn't care,' she said in a rush.

'Oh, *Bella*!' he said, sounding exasperated. 'You can *see* I care! Every night, holding you, loving you, being with you . . .'

The word 'loving' was manna to her soul. She pushed up to look at his expression, grabbing a pillow to rest on, turning onto her front so she could keep seeing his face. She wanted to hold on to everything she could see and smell and touch, to have as many memories as possible to summon up during the long, dreary time when she wouldn't be able to see him.

'I have five months, more or less, ahead of me, of the hardest work I've ever done in my life on this rewards points scheme,' she said. 'And I work really, *really* hard anyway. It's going to be crazy. All I'll be doing is eating, sleeping, and working, and not in that order.'

'I get it,' he said, and his shoulders rose and fell in the universal response to an obvious statement. 'You're a business-woman! I know that. But . . .'

He fell silent, but his dark eyes were fixed firmly on her blue ones, and she knew what he was asking her to say.

'This has been out of time,' he said, seeing her falter. 'Is it going to stay that way?'

'I don't want it to . . . if you don't want it to . . .' she stammered, terrified to show him the extent of her feelings for him in case he didn't reciprocate.

'And your husband?'

What an awful word that seemed in the mouth of her lover. He might as well have called her something dirty and shameful. She flinched, but it was her own guilt to which she was reacting.

'Thomas is—' She forced herself to press on. 'He's been – we've been – it's not been good for a long time. If it ever was. I think we got married for the wrong reasons.'

'You said he was a lot older,' Ronaldo commented, trying to sound neutral.

She nodded fervently. Thomas was in good shape, but to compare him to glorious, thirty-six-year-old Ronaldo, hard-muscled, lean, with a cock ready to fuck her whenever she wanted, would be deeply unfair. Though to compare *anyone* to Ronaldo would be unfair. She couldn't imagine ever wanting another man again.

And what if she didn't have to?

'I have to prioritize,' she said, and she heard her tone become less pathetic immediately, less needy. That was good: this was the kind of woman a man like Ronaldo would want. Not a doormat who lay sobbing on a mattress, but a woman who could run a multinational company, who could put a condom on with her mouth while he told her how amazing it felt.

Bella had started to cry the moment his cock drove into her the first time tonight, because it felt so wonderful, so utterly right, as if, in that moment, she was complete; and because she also knew that the next morning she would be leaving this amazing sex behind. It wasn't all she wanted in life. It couldn't be. Much as she craved Ronaldo, the ambition which had exploded to the surface at her father's challenge to his children was too strong to be denied, and it was going to push her onto that plane to Dallas tomorrow morning.

She had finally received her wake-up call. This handful of days had been, as Ronaldo had said, out of time. But she had always known that she couldn't stay here forever. Apart from any business considerations, that would look so weak! Ronaldo had met her in her business persona with her PR by her side. Little Bella, running the Sachs hotels, he had exclaimed, shaking his head in disbelief at how much time had passed, how his childhood playmate had grown up to run the most important division of the company! What would he think if she babbled that she wanted to give it all up for him? That she would move to Chicago, since he loved it so much? Leave Thomas, forfeit her chance to become CEO of Sachs?

He wouldn't respect her. And she wouldn't respect herself. It was important, when you were being swept away by a man with the force of a tidal wave, to remind yourself that your own self-respect ought to matter even more than his opinion.

'So here's what I have to do,' she said, and she sat up, taking the pillow and holding it across her body for comfort. 'I have to get on a plane tomorrow and spend a few weeks going round the world like some modern version of Phileas Fogg. And then I get back to London and I work my arse to the bone for a few months.'

'Not to the bone, please!' Ronaldo protested. 'I like it just as it is!'

He reached out and stroked her round bottom, which made her beam with pleasure.

'And maybe –' she was looking at the pillow now – 'maybe you could come to London for a few days. I could put you up somewhere. Not a Sachs, of course, they all know me there, but . . .'

'Bella.' He frowned. 'I'm not one of the heirs to the Sachs billions, but I make good money. You don't need to put me up.'

'Does that mean you'll come?'

Her face lit up as if she was ten and he was twelve again, and he had said he would play at forts in the garden with her.

'Yes!' He was laughing. 'Yes, I will!'

'But – you know how you said this was out of time?' she continued. 'It has to stay that way until this project's finished and the rollout goes okay – or doesn't, and I need to do a frantic troubleshoot, which I don't even want to think about! It's so much for me to handle that I just can't deal with anything to do with . . . Thomas,' she said, ducking her head again, embarrassed to speak her husband's name in this room so full of the sounds and scents of the sex she had just had with another man. 'I just *can't*.'

'Bella, I'm not asking you to,' he said earnestly. 'I would never put you under pressure.'

Oh please, put me under pressure! she wanted to scream. *Tell me you're madly in love with me and can't bear the thought of me being married to another man, going home to him, maybe to have sex with him . . .*

Since they hadn't said a word about Thomas this whole time, Ronaldo had no idea how curtailed and restrained her sex life was with her husband. Nor did he know about the challenge her father had set her and her siblings: he wasn't aware of how stratospheric the stakes were with this project of hers. Bella wasn't sure why she hadn't told him. Maybe she didn't want him to see her as so competitive. Or maybe it was the rose-tinted view he had of their childhood, him and the Sachs children, running and laughing and playing together in the glorious gardens of the Maida Vale house? Had she not wanted to destroy those memories by telling him how viciously they were now pitted against each other?

Ronaldo was looking at her with dark eyes full of sincerity, wanting to make sure that she believed his reassurance. She reached out and took his hand.

'So, you'll come to London,' she said, the words filling her with happiness. 'I'll be working like a crazy woman, but I'll carve out some time for us. And when my project's all done . . . we'll see where we are.'

He nodded.

'That sounds good,' he said. 'In fact, it sounds great.'

Suddenly, Bella asked herself: *Why* shouldn't *the CEO of Sachs be based in Chicago? Just because head office has always been in London, that's no reason in itself to keep it there. Remember all the studies showing how dangerous the thinking 'we've always done it that way' can be in business!*

After all, Chicago was a major metropolitan city in one of Sachs's main markets. The more she thought about it, the more reasonable the idea sounded. It would certainly reduce costs: the London office was very expensive to run. Of course, this was just a wild idea, one she wouldn't mention to Ronaldo, not for months. It was bound to freak him out, make him see her as desperate, the kind of person who would throw aside a five-year marriage for someone she had spent a mere five nights with, childhood playmate or not . . .

The expression in Ronaldo's eyes changed. His brows drew together in a frown, and her heart plummeted. Had he changed his mind so fast?

'Do you smell . . . *burning*?' he asked, sitting up.

Bella knew instantly what it was. Her Louboutins had long since been kicked off. She threw herself off the bed, skidding slightly in her stockinged feet, and ran over to the recessed dressing room, partly concealed from the bedroom by a half-wall. The ceramic tongs the hairdresser had left still plugged in, expecting her to come back and finish her hairstyle, were on the heat mat, which couldn't catch fire, but the smell was pungent by now. She pulled out the plug, sagging with relief that Ronaldo had noticed it before anything truly bad happened.

'Everything okay?' he called from the bed. 'You need help?'

'No, I just forgot to switch off my hair tongs when you rang the bell,' she lied, walking back into the bedroom, feeling very sexy in her stockings. 'Didn't you notice that half my hair was done and half wasn't?'

'Baby, I just see *you*,' he said fondly. 'I honestly don't give a shit about your hairdo.'

'Hah! You would if it didn't look nice!' she said, thinking

how funny it was that men genuinely believed that they didn't care about how well a woman had done her hair and make-up.

'Tell you what, let's have a bath,' he suggested. 'In your huge marble tub with the jets that go into all sorts of interesting places. We'll get your hair soaking wet and then you can see exactly how much I mind about how it looks as I soap you all over and sit you on my lap . . .'

Ronaldo swung his legs off the bed, stood up, held out his hand to her, his cock heavy, rosy-tinted, in its thick nest of black hair. She shook her head in disbelief that he was indicating he'd be good to go again so soon after their recent bout. He was like a sex machine.

'And then we can order half the room-service menu,' she said happily, taking his hand. 'We'll be *starving*. I'll tell them I want to test out the food and wine, to explain why there's way more than there should be for just one person. It's my turn to get dinner. You've been paying for everything.'

'Well, okay, you can pay just this once,' he said. 'I demand foie gras, lobster, the works! And very fine wines! In fact, let's crack the minibar and have champagne in the bath.'

As she agreed enthusiastically, he looked down at her with a half-smile.

'You know something crazy?' he said. 'For a second back there when I smelt burning, I thought it might be us – like we actually set the bed on fire! Crazy, right? I'm clearly going to have to try *much* harder next time!'

PART TWO

Chapter Thirteen

Two months later

The bottle-green Aston Martin DB11 barely slowed down as it turned through the gates that opened onto the wide avenue, lined with mature linden trees, that led up to Vanbrugh Manor. Bart whistled tunelessly between his teeth as he shot down the straight drive, which had been designed to make the approach to the majestic, sprawling stately home as impressive to the visitor as possible.

Some landscapers had chosen, centuries ago, to slow down the arrival at country houses in order to build the anticipation, sending carriages on a winding fairy-tale journey that allowed brief glimpses of the mansion through carefully planted, increasingly wide breaks in the foliage, building to a dramatic reveal of the final vista. Vanbrugh Manor's architect, however, had eschewed the magical build-up in favour of a much more direct statement of power. It was impossible to reach the end of the drive and start the loop around the gravelled turning circle without being made vividly aware that its owner, almost certainly, had infinitely more money and status than you did.

This was, of course, exactly why Jeffrey Sachs had selected it from the array of extremely expensive mansions in the Chilterns that an outwardly smooth-mannered but inwardly ecstatic estate agent had shown him and Jade a decade ago. Jade had decided that, to further her very active social climbing, she needed a country house not too far from London in which she could regularly entertain weekend parties of the great and good while building bonds with the Cotswolds country set. She had made it clear to the estate agent that her priority was to find somewhere that would take her guests' breath away, price comparatively unimportant.

The Savile-Row-suited young man had earned a stratospheric bonus at the end of that year, and it was well deserved; he had executed his commission perfectly. Externally, Vanbrugh Manor was a Georgian gem with an excellent historical pedigree, but internally it had been updated to twenty-first-century standards. All the bedrooms were en suite, with bathrooms executed to five-star-hotel quality. There was a screening room, a fully equipped gym, and an array of kitchen gadgets that would enable a chef to produce meals deserving of a Michelin star: industrial ovens, a walk-in freezer, sous-vide machines and a ten-thousand-pound, state-of-the-art ice-cream maker.

None of the older Sachs children had ever been invited here before. Since Jade had only let them in the door of the Warwick Avenue villa for a scant couple of hours now and then, there had been no question of their being permitted to stay at her country home. But the regime change had brought many unexpected consequences, and a couple of weeks ago the four children had been taken aback to receive emails from someone styling himself as the personal assistant to Adrianna Rootare, inviting them for a two-night stay at Vanbrugh.

Or rather, three of the children, plus Samantha. Conway's name had been pointedly excluded from the list of email recipients. Jeffrey was still furious with him for the scandal which had dragged Adrianna's name and Jeffrey's divorce, by association, onto the front pages.

In a swirl of gravel, Bart brought the Aston Martin to a halt at the foot of the entrance steps and jumped out, standing back to take in the sight of his father's country house. The whistle was audible now, and openly appreciative. This wasn't Castle Howard, Woburn Abbey or Alnwick Castle, one of the great British stately homes which were so huge and sprawling that the owners needed their own suite of rooms to which they could retire to enjoy a slightly more private life when they were not hosting dinner parties for fifty people. It did not, for instance, boast a series of state apartments for entertaining royalty, plus its own theatre.

Built on a smaller scale, it was essentially a family home. Still, it had a full-sized ballroom, as well as acres of ornamental gardens, a croquet lawn and tennis courts and a heated swimming pool. And it was a beauty. Even Bart, who regularly stayed at the most lavish private homes in the world, could not help but be impressed by the exquisitely restrained Georgian architecture, elegantly symmetrical with its red brick and stone facings and its high windows.

As the car pulled up the front door swung open, and down the shallow flight of steps came a young man dressed in a simple black two-piece uniform, cut rather like a masseur's.

'Hello!' Bart said cheerfully; having been educated at the best schools and visited aristocratic friends from a young age, he knew that it was considered very middle-class and vulgar to be aloof with the staff. 'I'm Bart Sachs. Here for the weekend.'

'He knows,' said a heavily accented voice from the entrance hall, and Adrianna appeared in the arched doorway. From this angle, her legs, clad in white jeans, seemed to go on forever, helped by the wedge-heeled ankle boots which gave her an extra four inches of height; a dazzled Bart followed them slowly upwards, past the narrow waistline of the jeans, emphasized by the belt, a thin strip of orange patent leather from Hermès. Tucked into the jeans was a matching Hermès orange sweater which clung to every curve of Adrianna's upper body, and in her ears were diamond studs, set in rose gold, that were so comically large they looked like market-stall accessories worn by a character from *EastEnders* or *Coronation Street*.

Jade, wanting very badly to fit in with the Oxfordshire county set, had bought Barbours and Husky hunting jackets and Hunter wellington boots as soon as she became the chatelaine of Vanbrugh Manor, eschewing London chic for the low-key country look. One glance at Adrianna, who oozed glamour from every pore, made it clear why Jeffrey might have decided to trade in a wife who had originally been a very sleek, fashionable art gallery consultant but tried to morph into a hunting/shooting/fishing stereotype which was not at all his taste.

Bart executed a flourishing bow at the sight of his hostess. As deadpan as she had been on their previous encounter, she merely nodded in greeting.

'Everyone else here yet?' Bart asked her, handing his car key to the young man, who got in and drove it around the side of the house, presumably to the garages. At this level of luxury living, it would have been unimaginable to actually see any parked vehicles, so there was no way for him to tell if his sisters had arrived.

'Oh yes,' Adrianna said, unsmiling. 'You are the last person. You are late.'

'I'm sorry!'

He bounded up the steps, and it was proof of Adrianna's extreme powers of self-control that she was able to remain blank-faced at the sight of Bart in motion, golden hair flapping over his face, moving as beautifully as a pedigree show pony. Taking her hand, he kissed it like a courtier.

'I keep wanting to call you milady,' he said. 'Can I call you milady?'

Adrianna surveyed him, those elongated green eyes revealing absolutely nothing about her reaction.

'Yes,' she said eventually.

'A woman of few words! I like that,' he said. 'It's very calming, somehow. Would you know what I meant if I said that this is all rather like an Agatha Christie novel? All the children summoned to the stately home, beautiful new fiancée to greet us, elderly Papa in his library . . . you aren't by any chance expecting a Belgian guest, by the way? Egg-shaped head, big moustache? Or a little old lady in the village who knits a lot?'

'No,' Adrianna said flatly. 'We have not invited Hercule Poirot. And there is no village, so no Miss Marple.'

Bart's huge blue eyes widened still further.

'My favourite is *Death on the Nile*,' she informed him. 'It is very sad, though. I always cry at the end. This is how I learned to speak English. I read all her books and when I did not know a word I would look it up in the dictionary. Come in. It is time for cocktails.'

She turned away from him, her magnificent curls bouncing against her shoulder blades as she led the way inside. Wordlessly, Bart followed her. The wedge heels made her so tall that it was very easy for him to watch her bottom move in the tight white jeans without being obvious about it.

'Bart is here,' she announced as she entered a large and very classically appointed drawing room.

'About bloody time!' Jeffrey barked from the prime position, a huge leather chesterfield at the centre of an arrangement of three matching sofas, the fireplace forming the fourth side of the square. A fire burned in the grate, apple wood sending up a delicate scent, a large, heavy brass club fender with green leather upholstery in front of it. Bart lounged over to prop his buttocks on it in classic dominant male style.

'Hello, Daddy! Hi, everyone! This is quite the pad, I must say,' he said, looking around the panelled room, taking in its excellent proportions, its tall windows overlooking the front of the house.

From the sofas, his two sisters looked at him rather warily over the cocktails they were holding. Thomas, Bella's husband, gave his brother-in-law a nod of greeting, and Bart responded with a grin. Conway had always thought Thomas a dull stick of a man, but Bart found him perfectly pleasant. Mind you, it took a lot for Bart to find anyone unpleasant.

'Samantha here?' he asked.

He was particularly fond of his sister-in-law, who reminded him of one of his favourite teachers at school. Yes, he had had a crush on Mrs Stratford, and no, he wouldn't dream of ever giving Samantha the slightest hint that her brisk, efficient manner and impeccably neat appearance brought him happy flashbacks to moments of self-love in the school showers, picturing Mrs Stratford in uncharacteristically dishevelled and revealing positions. But it always gave him a happy surge of nostalgia to see Samantha's bright, lip-sticked smile and smell her very ladylike Penhaligon's floral perfume.

'She's giving the kids their dinner,' Charlotte informed him, 'with Paul and Posy and Quant. I must say, the nursery arrangements are very nice. And the chef has a spiralizer! Posy and Quant are in heaven.'

'You and Conway married very well on the parenting front, didn't you?' Bart said, grinning, and then pulled a face. 'Oops. Bit tactless under the circs.'

'Conway,' their father announced at top volume, 'is not welcome here this weekend.'

Going a bit deaf, poor old chap, Bart thought, noticing the overloud tone of voice. *You can always tell when they start shouting.*

Adrianna sashayed over to the drinks cabinet by the far wall, a beautiful curving piece of furniture, and started to do complicated things with bottles.

'If you're making drinks, I'd like—' he began, but Adrianna, without turning round, held up one French-manicured hand, her elegant fingertips pressed to her thumb in the universal gesture that signified he should stop talking.

'*Okay* then,' he said *sotto voce*, as Jeffrey continued:

'Bloody outrage. Samantha won't say a word to criticize him, of course. Perfect wife, which makes it all so much worse. Doing a wonderful job with the little ones.'

He shook his head in frustration.

'But there's no point denying it leaves the field wide open for you three!' he added, with the bluntness for which he was well known. 'You must all be thanking your lucky stars, eh?'

Bella, Bart noticed, actually cringed back as if she were trying to hide in one of the button indentations of the chesterfield, looking strangely guilty. *Odd*, he thought.

Charlotte looked their father in the eye and said, 'Frankly, yes. I'm ambitious, Daddy. I'm not going to deny it.'

Jeffrey sighed.

'Such a shame you weren't born a boy,' he said, which made Charlotte's eyebrows shoot up practically to the ceiling.

'I wouldn't have minded being born a girl,' Bart mused. 'But would I ever get out of bed in the morning if I had bosoms? Wouldn't I just lie there happily playing with them? How *do* women get out of bed in the morning, come to think of it?'

Jeffrey laughed at this.

'Damned if I know!' he said, raising his glass to his son.

'What on earth are you drinking, Daddy?' Bart said, looking at the bright-red concoction his father was holding.

'A negroni,' Jeffrey said, sipping some. 'I don't even like Campari. But Adrianna knows what's best.'

'He needs to wake up before dinner,' Adrianna said briskly, appearing by Bart's side as if by magic. 'Or he gets too sleepy before the dessert comes with sugar to wake him up. So he needs a bitter drink.'

She handed Bart a Martini glass garnished with a cocktail stick skewering three small silverskin onions.

'This,' she said, 'is for you.'

'I'm so sorry,' Bart said. 'Not very James Bond of me! But I'm not really a martini drinker.'

To his surprise, everyone else in the room let out a chuckle of amusement. Thomas leant forward.

'Apparently, we drink what we're given,' he informed his brother-in-law gravely.

'I got a French '75,' Bella said. 'Which is very nice, though—'

'With cognac,' Adrianna said. 'Not gin. This is the classic French '75, with cognac. Gin is a variation, but I did not give it. It is not good for you.'

She fixed Bella with a green stare.

'It will make you sad.'

She turned back to Bart, who was still awkwardly holding the glass he didn't want.

'Gin is good for *you*,' she said. 'Nothing can make you sad. And this is a Gibson, very dry, with onions, to balance you, because you are always sweet.'

'Uh, thank you?' Bart said, cautiously feeling his way.

'It is not a compliment,' Adrianna said. 'It is an observation. Drink.'

'She's always right!' Jeffrey said, so fondly that all three of his children present jerked their heads round to look at him in shock; they had never heard that tone from their father before. 'She's the Drink Whisperer! That's what they used to call her at the club, you know.'

'I like to make drinks for people,' Adrianna said calmly. 'I know what they need. Not what they want, but what they need.'

'I must say,' Thomas observed, 'I don't usually drink rum, but—'

'You need spice,' Adrianna said matter-of-factly. 'Much spice.'

Since the attention was entirely on her as she walked over to Jeffrey and took a seat next to him on the central chesterfield, no one noticed Bella flinch at this, not even her husband.

Bart sipped at his Gibson. It tasted better than he expected, but that might be the sheer social pressure; clearly, even if it had been a mix of Jägermeister and crème de menthe, he would have been required to finish it off while saying how much he liked it. Still, it was stimulating, and with Adrianna's sphinx-like gaze on him, it went down surprisingly easily.

'I'm not sure if I'm being hypnotized into finding this quite tolerable,' he said, 'or if I actually like it.'

'Does it matter?' Jeffrey said cheerfully.

'I used to run the bar at Farouche,' Adrianna said, sitting back and crossing her ridiculously long legs. 'I was very strict. That was how I met Jeffrey. He asked for a red wine and I said no, I would not serve him that. I made him a whisky sour.'

Her fiancé patted her knee with great affection.

'And she was right!' he said.

'Of course,' Adrianna said seriously, 'these are cocktails. Separate from food. Wine pairings are different. But this is why I am not a sommelier. It is a separate experience.'

'No side to this girl, eh? This is what I love about her,' Jeffrey said happily. 'Met her in a bar. She doesn't pretend to be anything she isn't.'

Farouche was an exclusive members' club off Old Bond Street, stocked with leggy beauties who were unquestionably available to the hedge funders, playboys and art collectors rich enough to buy old masters from the Pall Mall galleries. Being a bartender, a job that required skill and knowledge, was certainly a step up from cocktail waitress or bar-stool decoration. But Jeffrey was still quite right: Adrianna could easily have chosen to say that she met him at the polo, or a gala, a social engagement at which she was a guest, not an employee. That she had decided not to was impressively honest of her.

'So, Adrianna – and Daddy too –' Charlotte said, 'thank you so much for asking us to stay the weekend! I'm sure I speak for the whole family.'

'Absolutely!' Bart said, raising his glass as Thomas and Bella nodded in unison.

'You're welcome,' Adrianna said. 'After all, you are Jeffrey's family. And it is nice to see the children.'

Anyone less maternal-seeming, Bart thought, would be hard to imagine; but Adrianna seemed genuine, and she certainly hadn't needed to issue the invitation in the first place.

'Are you planning to make any changes to the house?' Charlotte asked, looking around the panelled drawing room, with its very conventional antique furniture, its landscape paintings in heavy gilt frames, its heavy rugs.

'How do you know I haven't?' Adrianna asked, neutral-faced.

Charlotte was equal to this, however.

'Oh, this isn't your style at all!' she said, raising her glass of Sauvignon Blanc to Adrianna. 'You're classic, yes, but entirely contemporary! Actually,' she added thoughtfully, 'you're *very* Sash Woman – you know, my boutique brand? I'd love to see you as part of our advertising – in due course,' she added, glancing at her father, aware of his aversion to any publicity surrounding his engagement. 'Whenever you feel like it. Obviously that's a question for you and Daddy to discuss, but please do at least think about it.'

Bella shot a vicious look across the coffee table at her sister, Bart noticed, as this was unquestionably a successful tactic of Charlotte's. Adrianna was, as might be expected, not reacting beyond a nod of acknowledgement, but Jeffrey was beaming at the compliment to his fiancée.

'We're up for *so* many boutique chain awards, by the way!' Charlotte added nonchalantly. 'It's terribly exciting. And people respond so well to the fact that there's a real family behind this big enterprise. Now you're going to be part of it, I could absolutely see you becoming the face of Sash. You're very aspirational. Are you on Instagram?'

'No,' Adrianna said. 'That is not for me. I am more private as a person.'

'So *are* you going to make changes, darling?' Jeffrey asked her, turning to look up at his beautiful, impassive fiancée. 'I know what women are like! You have to come in and put your own stamp on a place just because the previous woman's done it up her way! God knows Jade did that in London. Stripped out half of the house before she was done.'

Despite the fact that they were both trying to make the best possible impression on their father, neither Bella nor Charlotte could keep their expressions completely neutral at this casual observation. The 'previous woman' who had been supplanted had been their mother, the 'London place' their childhood home, which Christie had spent so much love and care decorating to make a haven for her husband and children, only for it to be ripped up at the whim of the woman who had seduced their father.

Even despite the fact that Jade had now been displaced as unceremoniously as Christie had once been, Jeffrey's airy ability to talk about one woman replacing another was very hard to hear. Thomas reached out to take his wife's hand in sympathy.

Bart's gaze flickered to Adrianna's face, and he saw, to his considerable surprise, that for the first time it was actually registering emotion; even more surprisingly, that emotion was empathy for her fiancé's children. Reaching out to Jeffrey, she patted him firmly on the shoulder to make him stop talking.

'Nothing will be stripped out. There is only one change I would like to make,' she said. 'I want a full wet bar in this room so that I can stock it with everything I want to make my drinks. I need shelves, too, but that may be a problem for the panelling. All the reception rooms have panelling, very beautiful. I will need to get a special carpenter, I think, to make sure it is not damaged.'

Her eyes gleamed.

'I want to collect many vermouths,' she said. 'Right now I am – what is the word – obsessed with vermouths. I think maybe I would like to make my own.'

'We could get you to create a signature cocktail for Sash!' Charlotte said brightly, and Bella's eyes narrowed as Adrianna tilted her head, considering this, then nodded as she said:

'I would like that. Yes. I prefer to be associated with the cocktails, I think. Not just to be a model.'

'I love it!' her fiancé beamed. 'We'll go ahead with this after the wedding, shall we?'

Jeffrey Sachs actually simpered coyly, something none of his children had ever seen, and a sight they could happily have done without ever experiencing.

'Well,' he continued, with the same uncomfortably coquettish expression, 'after the honeymoon, I *should* say.'

As one, Bart, Charlotte and Bella picked up their glasses and took swigs of their drinks, their heads ducked in a synchronized effort to avoid watching their elderly father leer suggestively at a woman who was younger than any of them. Again, Adrianna ignored Jeffrey's comments, expertly directing the conversation back to a subject with which his children would be more comfortable.

'So yes, the house will stay as it is.' She swept one hand in a wide gesture, encompassing the drawing room. 'This is perfect. We are in the countryside, it is a country house. It looks the way it is supposed to be. I know Russians or Arabs buy this kind of house and then put gold everywhere – gold and black marble – but that is not right for England.'

'Oh, I'm sure Charlotte didn't mean that you were going to be so clichéd just because you're from Estonia!' Bella said, managing to land a little snark on her sister; it was Charlotte's turn to narrow her eyes.

Oh dear, Bart thought. *Bad twins!* Due to the common stereotypes about twins being closely bonded, Bart's friends had always assumed that his sisters would be joined at the hip; when he had told them that, actually, they had never had much in common, the reaction had always been surprise. It hadn't helped, of course, that their father had always pitted his children against each other.

Bart sighed. He really did hope that the four of them could settle down and accept whatever decision Jeffrey eventually made about the future of the Sachs Organization. Bart hated a bad atmosphere, and the family wasn't particularly close now; if this struggle for power led to a genuine rift between the siblings, something which had never happened before, it would really be a pity, especially with this extraordinary new stepmother-elect seeming to want to bring the family together.

Personally, Bart was still assuming that Conway would be made CEO, his father's current ire against him not withstanding. In Bart's considered opinion, the scandal would blow over. Samantha and Conway would reconcile, upon which Jeffrey would simmer down and decide that that his firstborn son, the one he had groomed for power by making CFO, would be the natural heir. Jeffrey was an irredeemable sexist who wouldn't be comfortable handing the reins to a woman. Look at what he had just said to Charlotte about it being a shame she hadn't been born a boy!

People tended to think, Bart knew, that he didn't notice much that went on around him. But he did. It was just that he didn't care about most of it.

Now, however, that observation of Jeffrey's, the son thing, gave him food for thought. If Conway genuinely was out of the running, and Jeffrey wouldn't consider one of his daughters for the job, that only left Bart! Did he actually *want* the job?

He was still debating that. But he remembered what he had said to Bella in her office, the day Jeffrey reamed out Conway, his idea of being a peacemaker. *That* would certainly be preferable to the prospect of the twins waging out-and-out war against Conway from the moment he took over as CEO, which he was sure they would . . .

'Hi, everyone! You look very comfortable!'

Paul appeared in the doorway, and as always when Bart saw his brother-in-law, his first thought was: 'Damn, Paul really is bloody handsome.' Paul was the kind of man who, while not exactly pushing a straight male to question his entire sexual orientation, still made you think that being locked up with him as your cellmate, or stranded with him on a desert island, might not actually be a fate worse than death. Since Paul was clearly as heterosexual as they came, that only increased his attraction: there wouldn't be any messy assumptions about blossoming romance, just two guys, taking care of each other's business in a sticky situation . . .

This line of thought amused Bart so much that he realized first that he was grinning, and secondly that someone was looking at him. Hadn't he just observed to himself that people assumed he wandered through life oblivious to his surroundings? Well, they were wrong. He noticed what he needed to. And now he realized that his father's fiancée was staring at him curiously.

He turned his head and met her eyes. Christ, she really was a stunner. Quite enough to stop a man from having momentarily inappropriate thoughts about his male-model brother-in-law! And the weird thing was that, somehow, he had the idea that Adrianna had known exactly what he was thinking, though that was obviously impossible . . . but she was smiling, just a tiny little smile, and those extraordinary eyes were flickering from him to Paul and back again . . .

'How are the kids, darling?' Charlotte asked her husband without getting up from the sofa.

'Oh, very happy,' he said cheerfully. 'They've had their dinner and bath, and now they're all four playing together beautifully.'

'It's a bit earlier than our normal schedule,' Samantha chimed in, following Paul, 'but we're very happy to fit into your hours' – she smiled at Jeffrey and Adrianna – 'and besides, they're *so* enjoying being with their cousins!'

'The playroom is wonderful,' Paul said admiringly. 'So many toys, and really creative ones. It really is a pleasure to walk into a room for kids and not see it entirely full of plastic. A lot of that wood actually looks sustainably produced.'

Boner gone. He kills it every single time, Bart thought, even as he got up to greet his sister-in-law; he always rose to his feet when a woman entered the room. *Paul opens his mouth, bless him, and instantly turns into a total passion-killer. How does Charlotte stand it?*

Probably duct-tapes his mouth shut during sex unless he needs it for a specific task, came the answer. *And reminds herself how fantastic he looks on her Instagram, which is really all she cares about. If one of those kids had had the bad luck to come out ugly she'd have had it adopted.*

Yet again, he had the strange sensation that Adrianna was reading his mind; as he passed the sofa, he shot a swift look at her. Yes, she was still looking at him, and yes, the smile had deepened.

She's a bloody odd woman, he thought uneasily. *I wouldn't be surprised if she were a witch. Do they have witches in Estonia?*

'Sam!' he exclaimed, enfolding his sister-in-law in a friendly hug, then pulling back to hold her by the shoulders and look down at her fondly.

He hadn't seen Samantha since the whole dust-up with Conway. You couldn't tell that she had been through anything more taxing than bad traffic on the way here, perhaps. There might be the faintest sign of strain around her eyes, but that was all. This was what it meant when you came from really solid stock, the old military families; the women just picked themselves up and carried on, whatever had happened.

'You look wonderful,' he said, enjoying her Penhaligon perfume. Bluebells or snowdrops or something British like that, nothing hothouse. Trouble was, of course, Conway had clearly wanted something a damn sight more exotic than wild meadow flowers every so often. 'Lovely to see you! Have you done something new with your hair?'

'Oh Bart, you *are* sweet,' Samantha said, patting his cheek. 'No, I haven't. I haven't changed a thing. But I know you really mean it. Thank you.'

She was a nice brunette with a tidy little figure, just like Mrs Stratford, her dark hair brushed back in wings that fell behind her ears, pale-pink lipstick, competence exuding from every pore. Mrs Stratford would probably have worn this kind of outfit for a smart family dinner, too: a simple navy silk dress with blousy transparent sleeves to show that she wasn't completely dowdy, some kind of arty gold earrings dangling prettily, sensible shoes with low heels, suitable for running round after children.

Marriage material, definitely, Bart thought, smiling at her, though his reaction to Mrs Stratford, back in the day, had been entirely lascivious. If he ever – God forbid – thought about settling down, a woman like Samantha would be the ideal wife. But then, that must have been exactly what Con decided, and he'd turned out not to be able to manage without picking hothouse blooms from time to time, and that hadn't exactly been fair on Samantha, had it?

'I'm glad you like the toys,' Adrianna was saying. 'I rang Harrods and told them to send all the stuff they have that is good for children.'

'It was *so* thoughtful of you!' Paul said very warmly. 'The children had so much fun! We played cooking – there was a little Aga, an espresso maker, even a smoothie maker! All in wood, of course. Really charming and creative. And tomorrow we thought we would make dairy-free coconut milk ice cream in the machine. Your chef has been wonderfully understanding about the children's food intolerances.'

Adrianna smiled inscrutably as she glided towards Samantha, handing her a tumbler in which ice and lemon knocked gently against each other.

'What does Samantha get?' Bart asked curiously.

'Gin and tonic,' Adrianna said with an almost imperceptible shrug.

'Why is that?' Bart persisted.

'Because she drinks gin and tonic,' Adrianna said, as if he were a complete idiot.

'I *do* like gin and tonic!' Samantha agreed. 'Thank you so much!'

'And what about Paul?'

Bart was, he felt, becoming unnecessarily obsessed with the cocktails his father's fiancée was selecting for their guests; but he was unable to stop.

'Paul does not drink,' Adrianna said lightly as she glided back to Jeffrey's side.

'Finish your Negroni,' she told her fiancé, glancing at the gold watch on her wrist, its face entirely studded with diamonds, so bright it was a miracle she could see the hands. 'It's time for dinner.'

She started to help him to his feet. Bart realized, to his surprise, that everyone was acting not only as if Adrianna was the hostess, but almost as if Jeffrey were just her rich attendant boyfriend. Jeffrey had always been in the habit of letting the woman in his life take care of the household, as long as his needs were catered to, of course. Adrianna had taken over so seamlessly that it would be easy for a casual observer to think that all this was hers alone. And Jeffrey, smiling up at her blissfully, seemed more than happy for her to act this way.

As she tucked Jeffrey's hand under her arm, supporting him, Bart retrieved his Martini glass and held it up to her.

'A little toast to our gracious hostess!' he said. 'To Adrianna, who's opened the doors to us at Vanbrugh Manor and made us all feel so very welcome, kids' toys, personalized cocktails and all! I'm sure I speak for all of us when I say that this is a very pleasant change, long overdue. I for one very much look forward to coming to your wedding and being able to toast you again as my new stepmother!'

Jeffrey nodded at Bart in approval as he made his way across the drawing room.

'Nice speech,' he said. 'Adrianna's gone to a lot of trouble to put all of you up.'

'I'm very happy to do it,' his fiancée said, patting his hand. And then, sliding her gaze sideways at her prospective stepson, glancing at the glass in his hand: 'You must eat your cocktail onions. I put them in there for a good reason.'

'That's right, Bart!' Jeffrey guffawed as he went past. 'Listen to your new stepmother – she's the boss around here! Eat your onions!'

Bart ate his onions.

Chapter Fourteen

'What is Bart *playing* at?' Bella fumed, safely back in their bedroom, pulling off her earrings and practically throwing them onto the dressing table. 'He was sucking up to Daddy and Adrianna all through dinner! Does he actually *want* the job? Do you think he does? He said a while ago that he had some crazy idea of being the one who could make the rest of us get on with each other – but he knows nothing about business! He wouldn't last five minutes!'

'Sit down, darling,' Thomas suggested, and when she sank onto the upholstered stool in front of the old-fashioned dressing table with its double-hinged mirror, he stood behind her and started to massage her shoulders.

'Mmn, that's nice,' she said, tilting her head from side to side, then returning immediately to the subject that was obsessing her. 'But what do you think Bart's *doing*?'

'I think he's just being Bart,' Thomas said, meeting her eyes in the mirror, shrugging lightly. 'His usual preternaturally charming self.'

'But does he want the job? Charlotte does! That couldn't be more obvious! I mean, I knew she was prepared to do anything to get it, but—'

Bella bit her lip, remembering her own part in Charlotte's scheming, Nita's discreet approach to the head of security. He had been given the impression that Nita had concerns about her niece's new boyfriend, who seemed much too good to be true, and that she wanted to know if there was anyone who could undertake an unobtrusive investigation into his background and dating habits.

Nita had unabashedly enjoyed the whole process – the subterfuge, the exposure of Conway as being far from the perfect married man image he presented to the world, the advantage it gave her boss – which made Bella think that she was judging her twin too harshly. After all, if her own right-hand woman had jumped at the opportunity to take down the front runner, wasn't Bella being hypocritical if she didn't judge Nita as well?

'Did you hear what Daddy said tonight about it being a shame Charlotte wasn't born a boy?' she demanded instead, as Thomas sank his thumbs into her tight shoulder muscles; she'd been tense throughout dinner, had had to plead a headache to avoid joining the others for coffee and liqueurs afterwards. 'Apart from it being sexist – and so worrying, what if that means neither of us are in the running? – he didn't say to *me* that I should have been born a boy!'

'Charlotte was pushing hard, though,' her husband said. 'Maybe too hard? Saying how ambitious she was, selling her credentials. A bit much for a family evening, I thought. It might not have been meant entirely as a compliment.'

Bella shook her head.

'No, it was definitely a compliment. And I should be selling myself too,' she fretted. 'It's just that – well, Charlotte's stuff is sexier! Being up for *Condé Nast Traveller*'s Best Boutique Hotel Chain – that sounds fantastic! "I'm doing a huge revision and upgrading of our rewards points system so it's state-of-the-art and incorporates major technological advances for our business travellers" – ugh, kill me now! It'll be amazing, but it just doesn't have any oomph. In fact, it puts people to sleep. It's *boring*.'

'It won't be boring when it happens, though,' Thomas said, working doggedly away at her trapezius muscles. 'And the prognosis is great, isn't it? You've had hugely positive reactions everywhere you went!'

Once she had finally embarked on the rest of her round-the-world tour, Bella had indeed found it extremely satisfying, and not just because of the excitement the scheme had generated from her management team, who were very keen to stand out in the crowded and highly competitive hotel market. She worked hard at staying in touch with their international offices, but no matter how many Skype conferences she did, there was simply no substitute for visiting in person. It had been overdue: she needed to do it more regularly.

As soon as she had returned, however, Thomas had become unusually – no, unprecedentedly – attentive. It had taken Bella some time to notice, as she had been in a jet-lagged haze. No matter how many first-class beds you slept in, how many limousines were waiting for you landside to whisk you to the latest luxurious hotel suite, the process of going round the world in a comparatively short amount of time could not fail to take its toll. Add to that a second haze – this one rose-tinted – her memories of Ronaldo, naked and inside her, sitting opposite her at candlelit restaurants, kissing her goodbye that last morning as tears streamed down her face, and it meant that there was simply no room in her mind for her husband.

Travelling a lot for work, Bella had always thought that one of the times you were most grateful to have a partner was, paradoxically, when you were on the road and away from them. That moment when the plane landed, the pilot announced that you could turn your devices off flight mode, and phones started to ping with welcome texts from spouses, partners, family checking that you'd landed safely; to have your phone remain silent was very poignant. Alone in the hotel room, ordering room service, knowing you should go to sleep but with your energy crackling from having come from a different time zone and run a very successful day of meetings, you wanted an affectionate text exchange from a loved one to settle you down for the evening.

Bella had always craved that kind of attention from Thomas. But he had been sporadic about answering texts, and very rarely sent her ones wishing her a smooth flight, or sending love and saying he missed her. Maybe it was silly of her to expect that kind of thing given that they had been married for five years, especially as they both travelled for work so extensively. She had tried to show Thomas what she would like by modelling the behaviour, as the self-help books suggested. She'd texted him when he was abroad, giving him an idea of what she'd like to receive, but if he did respond, it was perfunctory, and the tone was very similar to what he would use to a work colleague.

So when, in Dallas, she had yielded to temptation and texted Ronaldo, only to have a text ping back saying how great it was to hear from her and he hoped she'd had a good flight, finishing with 'xxx', Bella had been near-ecstatic. She had been on tenterhooks for the fifteen minutes it had taken him to get back to her, terrified that she had overreached the boundaries, as they hadn't agreed to be in touch at all. After that, she had tried hard not to act as if they were in a relationship, had told herself she needed to limit herself to just one text every few days – but he hadn't. He had started texting to ask how things were going, where she was, and then she would respond, it would turn into a conversation . . .

Thomas was still massaging her shoulders, but Bella was a thousand miles away, barely feeling what he was doing to her body. Her husband might have been a paid masseur in a spa. Her mind drifted off to her lover, to the gloomy fact that she really couldn't text him all weekend, let alone Skype him – because their texts had swiftly progressed to sexts, and then to increasingly explicit Skype sex sessions . . .

'Shall I go and shake hands with my little blue friend?' Thomas said. Bella practically jumped off the stool in alarm, partly because he seemed to have read her mind, at least enough to know that she was thinking about sex, and partly because he had lowered his head and spoken softly into her ear. Since she had been oblivious to his bending over, suddenly finding him that close had been quite a shock.

'Oh!' she heard herself exclaim, even as Thomas staggered back, rubbing his ear; she had bumped it as she jumped up. 'Sorry!'

She settled down on the stool again, meeting his eyes once more in the mirror.

'I really didn't expect you to say that,' she said feebly. 'I mean, *now*? In someone else's house? After *dinner*?'

'Why not? Let's live a little!'

Thomas, to her intense irritation, now started stroking her shoulders again, but this time sexily.

'You never like to do it unless we're completely alone in the house,' Bella said, still looking at him. 'And you never like to do it after dinner, because you feel too bloated.'

Wow. She had never articulated before so clearly Thomas's very specific requirements for when sex could happen. In a moment she'd be saying 'Viagra' out loud rather than using his preferred euphemism about his little blue friend. While Thomas had no difficulty getting erections, he needed Viagra to sustain them. This was another reason for the Sunday morning sex. It could be scheduled so neatly; he could get up twenty minutes beforehand, pop his pill and then settle comfortably back in bed with his wife, waiting for lift-off. No wonder Ronaldo's spontaneity had swept Bella away. And now, clearly, it had freed her to talk frankly about the limitations of her sex life with her husband.

She held Thomas's gaze, refusing to let him look away, forcing him to hear what she had just said. It felt hugely freeing to actually talk about this, speak the truth, rather than dance around it. She was used to pretending, sparing his feelings, agreeing that she was tired after dinner and just wanted to go to sleep, when really, pre-Ronaldo, she would have loved to have a happy roll around the big bed, fuelled into a pleasantly relaxed randiness by the cocktails and wine they had drunk.

'I thought you might like a bit of, er, poum-poum?' he

said feebly, and Bella wondered why she had ever put up with a husband who preferred to use this term to mean sex. 'You've been travelling, you're so stressed . . . wouldn't it relax you? It usually does!'

'I'm okay, thanks,' she said, standing up. His hands fell away and he stood there looking very hangdog.

'I've been missing you, you know,' he said. 'Even when you're home, you're somewhere else.'

So that was it. He had noticed her distance and was trying to close the gap. How ironic that now she had no need for him sexually, he was sensing that and attempting to fix the problem.

Or was it just that he didn't want her to slip away? If his tactic worked, and she turned back into the loving, affectionate Bella who had always wanted more from him than he could give, he would promptly revert to the old pattern of withholding behaviour, surely! It was shocking how clearly she was seeing things nowadays.

'I'm just working so hard,' she said, going past him and into the bathroom, which was all peach and brass fittings and a claw-footed bath, a wooden gentlemen's caddy against one wall, modern fittings posing as antiques, even a brass pull chain hanging from the toilet cistern. She wanted to have a bath, but she was not going to get naked in front of her husband, not with him in this odd mood. She'd have a quick shower tomorrow. There was no way to make a shower look antique, so it was tucked discreetly away behind a garland-tiled wall to keep the old-fashioned look consistent.

'Is this going to – well, keep going?' Thomas had followed

her in and was standing in the doorway. 'You know, your working this crazily? I never see you any more!'

'Wow, I would have thought you'd *like* that!' she blurted out before she could help herself, angry at his hypocrisy. 'You were always ringing and saying you couldn't make it home for the weekend, when I'd shopped and got food in and made plans for us. I'd have thought you'd be *grateful* I'm not getting in your hair and fussing that you're never home!'

Thomas looked genuinely hurt. For a moment she wanted to take the words back. But though an apology had formed, she could not, would not get it out. Because it was *true*, every word she was saying was *true*, and he would be a liar if he denied it.

'I—' He stuttered to a halt, looking genuinely confused. After a long moment, he tried again. 'Bella, I—'

'It's okay,' she said, suddenly exhausted. The effort of being so honest right to Thomas's face had taken a lot out of her.

She turned away, holding on to the edge of the pedestal sink for support, a chamfered white basin set on top of an Edwardian brass washstand.

'I need some privacy,' she said, using the phrase that Paul, who was very much into teaching his children about their right to bodily autonomy, had trained them to use. It sounded less cute when used by Bella than when it was piped in Posy or Quant's high childish voices, but it still got the job done.

'Okay,' Thomas said, retreating, reaching for the door-knob. 'But we need to talk about this another time, don't we? We've got into a rut, I know. With . . . you-know-what.'

He cleared his throat. 'Poum-poum. I'm actually really glad you raised this. I'll give you time now, but maybe we can go for a walk tomorrow and have a talk about it? The grounds look lovely.'

'Sure. Okay. Yes.'

Bella would have said anything at this stage to get him to leave her alone.

'Great. Okay, I'll let you get on with . . .'

Thomas's voice trailed off as he closed the door. Bella leant forward and pressed her forehead against the mirror, enjoying the cool of the surface. Her eyelids closed. How much she wished that she could Skype Ronaldo right now! It was 11 p.m. UK time, which made it 6 p.m. in Chicago; he might even be home from work and free to relax . . .

The memory of Ronaldo a few nights ago, lying back on his bed, pulling slowly on his big cock while keeping eye contact with her, telling her what to do with her vibrator, made her instantly so sexually charged that she had to turn on the cold tap and splash water in her face. There was no way that she could leave this room and get into bed with her husband, only to toss and turn, consumed with need for her lover.

She cleansed off her make-up, brushed her teeth, went to the loo, preparing to face Thomas again briefly as they changed places. He was in his pyjamas by the time she emerged, and he gave her a hug, enfolding her tightly in his arms, asking her to look up and give him a kiss. She complied with the first, but stood passively while he kissed her, managing a smile for him before he padded off to the bathroom.

And as Bella unzipped her dress and hung it up, as she reached for the pyjamas she herself had brought – no sexy Chicago-purchased lingerie for this weekend away; it was all safely concealed in the expansion pocket of one of her travel suitcases, stacked inside two others in her dressing room at home – a thought struck her. There was one thing she had not confronted Thomas about, and that was his 'little blue friend'.

How was it, she had always wondered, that during their courtship he had never needed Viagra to keep going? He had not precisely been ardent or pressing, but the sex had been perfectly fine, good enough for her to sign up to have it for the rest of her life – before she had met Ronaldo. Almost as soon as they were married, however, their sex life had fallen off a cliff. They had nursed it back, with Thomas gradually revealing his increasingly stringent list of conditions under which it could happen; but it had been Bella who had suggested the Viagra, as when he started to lose his erection halfway through she had found it more and more humiliating.

He had been reluctant, but Bella had put her foot down. She actually thought he was grateful, now, that she had insisted. It gave a structure, added even more routine to the sex, which was what he preferred, while she could relax, knowing that at least he would be able to sustain his erection as long as necessary.

But why did it go wrong after we were married? she found herself wondering. *Was it just that he'd caught me, and he didn't need to make an effort any more? Or is it some sort of weird stereotype, that once a woman's a wife you shouldn't think about her sexually any more, the madonna/whore thing?*

Bella climbed into bed, pulling up the sheet and blankets and coverlet. No duvets here: the bed coverings were all in keeping with the style of the house. The blankets were pleasantly heavy, weighing her down. Thank goodness. That would help her to fall asleep faster. She was used to soothing herself to sleep now with memories of Ronaldo. Romantic ones, rather than sexual. But as she closed her eyes, it wasn't her lover's handsome face that she saw. It was her husband's, having just whispered the words: 'Shall I go and shake hands with my little blue friend?'

If I ever hear Thomas say that again, she thought, *I don't know if I'll be able to stay married to him one minute longer. I honestly don't know how I can stick it out until Daddy makes his decision about which one of us to promote to CEO.*

But I have to! Daddy's so furious with Conway for screwing up his marriage that I can't announce that I'm leaving Thomas – let alone for the housekeeper's son! – and expect to have any chance of getting the top job.

I have to put up with it till then. I have to.

But if he says 'little blue friend' one more time, I think I'll scream my head off.

Chapter Fifteen

'Ready for bed, darling?'

Paul smiled at his wife, who was sitting at the dressing table working her way through her very elaborate skincare routine. At that moment, Charlotte was mixing equal amounts of Vitamin A serum and Vitamin A cream on her palm and smoothing the blended result onto her cleansed and toned face. Beside her was a glass of Evian and a small pile of pills, some for tonight, some ready for the next day: biotin and keratin for strengthening nails and hair, milk thistle for liver function, concentrated vitamins for skin nutrition, cambogia fruit with chromium for metabolic support, plant phytonutrients to protect against free radicals.

'Nearly,' Charlotte said, reaching for the night moisture cream that was the last layer to be applied to her face. 'Just need to take my pills. Have you had yours yet?'

'Yes, of course,' Paul said, and certainly his smooth, moisturized, blemish-free skin was testimonial to his own skincare regime. He had applied body lotion, as he did morning and night, and his long limbs gleamed as he crossed the room and climbed into bed naked. 'Isn't it extraordinary, being here? Under Jeffrey's roof?'

'I can't work out what game Adrianna's playing,' Charlotte said, removing the top of her tube of night cream; she never bought moisturizer in pots, because she believed that when you repeatedly put your fingers into face cream you could add bacteria to it. Besides, the pots let in light, which weakened the active ingredients.

Charlotte was quite willing to admit to a mild form of controlling behaviour, or at least a compulsion to research absolutely everything that entered her life so she could make the best decision possible. She monitored the decor of her Sash hotels on a regular basis so that she could make sure that the decorative pillows, the flower vases, even the books carefully selected for the lounge coffee tables, were arranged exactly as she had prescribed.

'Game?' Paul sat up, propping his back against the upholstered, padded headboard. 'Mmn,' he said in parentheses, relaxing against it. 'This is terribly comfortable.'

'Unhygienic,' Charlotte said briefly, looking at him in the mirror. 'It'd need replacing much too often. Much too expensive.'

'It's always hotels with you,' he said fondly. 'Everything comes back to that.'

'Oh, I couldn't stand a fabric headboard at home, either,' she said, shuddering slightly. 'You put body lotion on, then you get into bed – no matter how many pillows you put behind you, some's bound to get on the material. Or your many and varied hair products! I see those cheap, nasty faux-suede headboards on sale for poor people and I just want to vomit. They'll be greasy in two weeks. You know, the beds with built-in TVs in the base. So vulgar.'

'It's *such* a bad idea to have a television in the bedroom!' Paul said, shaking his head. 'Just terrible for the sleep cycles. And I'm sure it's bad for the energy currents too. All that extra wiring so close to you when you sleep and really need to recharge.'

Charlotte had perfected the skill of keeping her face impassive when Paul came out with his latest new-age, hippy gibberish. She hadn't married him for his brain, after all; she had enough of that for both of them.

'Adrianna's playing a game,' she said, returning to the subject she had raised. 'There's got to be something going on beneath this cosy weekend charade we're all acting out. Is that how she snagged Daddy – by telling him how family-friendly she was?'

She answered her own question, as she was really talking to herself in the mirror.

'No way! No man leaves his wife for that kind of reason!' she continued. 'So why is she bothering with all this? Who wants to get on with her husband's *kids*, for goodness' sake?'

'Maybe she really *is* family-friendly?' Paul suggested. 'I know she's very poised, but she was so thoughtful with the children. Apparently Jade shipped every single one of the boys' things to her new house, so Adrianna made sure she restocked the playroom wonderfully. She even told her secretary to let us know we didn't need to bring anything apart from the kids' cuddle toys if we didn't want to, remember? *Very* considerate!'

Having worked in her night cream, Charlotte embarked on the process of taking her evening pills.

'It's *weird*,' she said between swallows of Evian. 'Because it's so *unnecessary*. Daddy simply doesn't care. Right now, she could do anything and he'd go along with it. He's completely obsessed with her. Why isn't she just making him – I don't know, take her to Paris for the weekend to shop till she drops, or inviting her friends down here, rather than throwing a boring family party?'

'Darling,' Paul said fondly, 'I know you're always planning and thinking and scheming, but honestly in this case I think you're going too far. Adrianna actually seemed to enjoy getting to know all of us, making us cocktails, planning activities for the children tomorrow. Pony grooming and riding! They're so excited it was very hard to get them to sleep!'

'Mmn,' Charlotte said as the plant phytonutrient capsules went down. 'I just don't believe it. I don't understand her, and I really don't like that. It's as if she's sizing us up for something. But what would that be?'

She took her last pills.

'So maybe there isn't an ulterior motive?' Paul suggested. 'Maybe she isn't close to her family, and she wants to bring her future husband's together?'

Charlotte looked at her husband with affection. Considering Adrianna's dazzling good looks and her overt sexuality, other men might have defended her simply because she was so attractive, but Charlotte knew her husband too well to assume that. Paul had been modelling with some of the most beautiful women in the world since he was twenty, and was immune to being swayed by female pulchritude.

'Paul. Darling,' she began.

Charlotte stood up lithely, as befitted a woman with an

extensive exercise and stretching schedule, and walked towards the bed.

'She's a glorified nightclub hostess,' she said. 'All this talk about bartending! You can't tell me Farouche hired her because of her crazy drink-prescribing gimmick. And Daddy certainly isn't licking his lips every time he looks at her because of her bartending skills. It's the classic thing with rich men.'

She pulled back the covers on her side of the bed, briefly observing the sheets and blankets and assessing their quality and cost; as a hotelier, she couldn't help herself.

'The first wife's more or less the same age as they are, like Mummy was,' she explained. 'Then they trade her in for a trophy twenty years younger with some accomplishment they can boast about – gallery girl, lifestyle journalist, beauty PR. Thin, wears black, has an artistic haircut, makes them look intellectual. Then they get bored with that, and they need a lot of help getting it up, so they go for a porn-star lookalike Eastern European model who's built up plenty of technique getting herself out of her home country and into a job where she can meet ageing billionaires. A professional who'll do all the work while he just lies there, because he's scared of putting his back out.'

'Darling, that's your father you're talking about!' Paul said uncomfortably as Charlotte got into bed beside him.

'*Father*,' she said sarcastically. 'He stopped being our *father* that day he moved us out and Jade in! Really, Paul, the way you hover over Posy and Quant – remember how you used to check to make sure their poos were the right colour and texture? You of all people should know he's not a *father*.'

Paul's expression indicated his inability to argue with this. Especially as he did still check his children's poos on a daily basis, but kept it secret from Charlotte because she'd constantly mocked him for doing it.

'Still—' he tried.

'You know that crime novelist I like? Laura Lippman?' she continued. 'There was a really clever line in her latest book. She says that men of a certain age eye up women with big strapping builds, because they know they're getting on and they want nurses who can lug them in and out of wheelchairs. That's exactly Adrianna's appeal! She'll help you get in and out of the bath and then give you a killer blow job.'

Paul winced. He was very sensitive to crude talk. Charlotte was usually more careful around her husband, saving her dirty mouth for her team at work and her lover Lee. But not only had she drunk quite a lot at dinner, she had also indulged afterwards in Vanbrugh Manor's superb selection of digestifs. Adrianna was such a perfect hostess that it had thrown Charlotte off-kilter, causing her to lose her customary self-control.

'Let's fuck,' she said, rolling towards her husband. She knew he didn't like that word. Paul was legendary in the modelling world for being visibly uncomfortable when people swore or made ribald jokes; he was regularly teased for it. But tonight, tipsy, on edge because she couldn't get a handle on Adrianna's behaviour, Charlotte wasn't in the mood to make nice for Paul.

Ignoring his pained expression, she slid on top of him and started kissing him. It wasn't long before he responded. Paul was entirely predictable, which, as far as Charlotte was concerned, was an ideal quality in a husband. Despite his tendency to kiss her tenderly during the act and stare into her eyes in a way that frayed her nerves, they had regular, very satisfying sex. She had trained him not to keep asking if she liked it, thank goodness, but when he went down on her he simply could not break himself of looking up from between her legs, his blue eyes doglike as he stared worshipfully at her face.

She coped by closing her own and just concentrating on her own pleasure. Still, knowing that he was watching her the whole time was fantastically annoying, and she needed to balance it out by, once she had come enough, climbing onto him and assuming the reverse cowgirl position. Paul's need for eye-to-eye contact would have been okay if he'd been doing a hard, sexy, look-at-us-fucking stare, but Paul didn't fuck. He made love. And Charlotte's preference was definitely for the former.

Straddling him, working faster and faster, her hands braced on his lean thighs lightly dappled with dark hair, so unlike Lee's, which were much hairier and more solid with muscle – male models needed to be lean in order to fit into the sample sizes – she had a flash of wistfulness for her lover. It was no coincidence that she had mentioned Adrianna's getting Jeffrey to take her to Paris for the weekend. Charlotte had a rendezvous with Lee there next week, and was counting the days.

Still, sex was sex, and Paul had a great body and a very nice cock, whose curvature actually worked better than Lee's for reverse cowgirl. Charlotte was an extremely practical woman.

A cock in the hand's worth two in the bush, she thought, even as she started to speed up, shuddering with pleasure at the way Paul's dick was butting inside her, hitting the place that made her begin to groan in an animalistic, steady rhythm. *No, that doesn't work at all! A cock in the bush is worth two in the hand – maybe . . .*

And then the thought of two cocks made her imagine Lee here too, kneeling up in front of her so that his cock was butting against her lips, and as she drove herself down on Paul, she was opening her mouth to Lee, sucking eagerly on him, gasping for breath as he filled her completely. This was such a deliciously transgressive fantasy, her husband and her lover, Lee's hands in her hair now, forcing her further onto his cock, Paul pumping his hips up, both of them competing as to who could fuck her harder, the furthest thing possible from making love . . .

The noises she was making were out of body now, completely beyond her control. Charlotte was quite unaware of the presence of her children in the next-door room, or her husband starting to try to shush her. The idea of Lee and Paul, fucking her simultaneously, driving deep inside her, was so powerful that she bucked madly on her husband as if she were riding a mechanical bull. He pushed himself to sit up, realizing that she was not hearing him, worried now about the kids waking up, and the movement, the unexpected switch in angle of his cock inside her, catapulted her into orgasm.

Paul clapped one hand over her mouth, something he would never normally have done, as it was very disrespectful to women; but they were not in their master suite on the top floor of their modern, sound-insulated house, where they could safely make a reasonable amount of noise without disturbing the children. They took priority for him, as always. To Charlotte, however, it was an extra fillip, a rare, delicious touch of the BDSM she enjoyed so much and that Paul would not have dreamed of countenancing.

She sobbed happily against his palm even as she ground down for the last time, feeling his own release shoot out inside her in response, hot and wet. She kept moaning just for the feel of his hand gagging her mouth. As her body relaxed, beginning to go limp, her fingers losing their grip on his thighs, Paul took his hand away and started to whisper apologies that his wife barely noticed.

Because Charlotte was forming a delicious picture for her encounter with Lee in Paris: a threesome with another guy. Could they pick someone up in the hotel bar? Too risky? Yes, much though she loved the idea. But Lee was bound to know someone, considering the circles he ran in . . . God, if he could find someone who looked like Paul, that would be incredibly sexy! She knew that Lee would love this idea, as he loved everything perverse, original, unique. Surely fucking a woman together with a man who looked like her husband had to be unique for Lee?

Paul's arms were wrapped around her now, tenderly embracing her, his chest against her back. He seemed to have finished apologizing and was murmuring endearments and loving words into the back of her neck. He always did this afterwards, and didn't require much response from her, as she could easily pretend that she was too overwhelmed by the continuing wonder of marital sex to be able to speak. She put her hands over his, heard him sigh happily at the connection, and thought: *And when we find that guy who looks like Paul, I'm going to beg him to spank me till I'm red. What a lovely change that'll be – a fantasy husband who's rougher than my lover! God, I can't wait to text Lee and get him to set it up!*

Chapter Sixteen

She was running. Not jogging, but running flat out, practically a sprint, her legs pumping the soft ground, following a narrow track on a grassy lawn, speeding as if the hounds of hell were on her heels, her eyes fixed unwaveringly on the ground ahead. Since the track was uneven and rutted, one false step could see her turning her ankle out here, and it would be a long way to limp back.

The track curved around a high stone boundary wall, and in the distance the long straight drive bordered with lime trees, which led directly to the house, came into view; but it was still far off. If anything, her pace increased as she headed for the avenue, her knees coming up like pistons, her elbows stabbing back. She ran like a superheroine in an action film. The man observing her from his hiding place thought that she looked as if her feet were going to leave the ground entirely, like a plane speeding up for takeoff.

The wall was bending towards the track now, forcing her into a looping circuit towards the ornate entrance gates and the start of the linden avenue. To avoid a knee-wrenching sharp, right-angled turn onto it, she struck out over the grass, which was soggy with dew and recent rain and slowed her down, the muddy terrain catching at the flanges of her trainers. So she hit the tarmacked drive not quite like a bullet being fired from a gun, and as a result, when the man unexpectedly stepped out into her path from behind one of the lime trees, she did not actually mow him down.

She had only a few seconds to react, and she made the most of them. She was going much too fast to stop without injuring herself, but she could fractionally alter her course, and she did that, heading to his side with one hand coming up in a fist, aiming for his throat. Women are often advised, in self-defence, to hit an attacker in the larynx, but the drawback is that they are rarely tall enough to reach it. Adrianna had no such problem, and if her blow had made full contact, she would at the least have completely disabled him, at the worst have knocked him down.

Bart shrieked in fear as he saw her coming for him, fist up like an avenging fury. It was his turn to react instinctively in a matter of seconds, and all he could do was duck down. Luckily for her, he wasn't quite fast enough, and her blow glanced off the side of his head. She had put so much force into it that it would have sent her spinning off-balance, maybe even flying to the ground, if it had not connected.

As it was, she took a few more paces until she could halt, carried on by the speed at which she had been running. She blew on her fingers ruefully, then shook them out as she turned and looked at her stepson-to-be, who was now rising from the crouch into which he had dropped, his expression very wary, holding up his hands in the universal gesture of surrender.

'I'm really sorry!' he said. 'Please don't hurt me any more!'

He rubbed the side of his skull.

'You hit *hard*,' he observed ruefully.

'I would not have hit your head with my fist on purpose,' she said equally ruefully, still shaking her hand. 'That's stupid. A skull is stronger than fingers. I was going for the neck.'

'So I take it you don't like surprises,' Bart said.

'The light is behind you,' she pointed out. 'I could not see your face until I was too close to stop.'

Bart shook back his very distinctive fall of golden hair.

'You couldn't hazard a guess?' he asked politely.

This drew a reluctant smile from Adrianna.

'Okay,' she admitted. 'I don't like surprises.'

They stood looking at each other for a long moment, blue eyes to green, almost the same height. Eventually she said:

'So? Why did you ambush me?'

'I was out jogging too,' Bart explained. 'Or rather, I should say that *I* was out jogging. *You* were running like you were being chased by a serial killer. Do you always do that?'

'Maybe I run like I am a serial killer chasing someone,' she said, deadpan as always.

Bart laughed. Writers have often commented poetically on the beauty of some women's laughs, comparing them to silver bells or bubbling fountains. It is much rarer to see a man's laugh praised in print. But Bart's was wonderful, completely infectious, the best possible indicator of his open, friendly nature; it was a laugh that in crowded bars regularly had people turning to see what the joke was, hoping to join in, wanting to be a part of whatever delightfulness was amusing him so much.

Even Adrianna, with adrenalin still spiking through her and a hand sore from punching him in the side of the head, found herself smiling in response.

'You are a fucking idiot,' she said to compensate for having smiled at him. 'You say you were out jogging, but that's not true. You were hiding behind a tree.'

'I *was* out jogging,' Bart said patiently. 'But then I saw you tearing around the boundary wall like Road Runner – at first I thought you were a cheetah, you were going so fast! – and I thought it would be nice to – well, surprise you. Trust me, that's the last time I do that.'

Balancing adroitly, Adrianna bent her right leg, reached behind her with her right hand and caught the ankle, pushing the foot into the buttock, stretching out her quad.

'And why did you want to stop me?' she asked. 'Out here, far away from the house, where no one can hear what we're saying?'

Bart ambled over to the closest tree, leaning back against its wide trunk.

'If you pull in over here, as it were,' he said, making a beckoning gesture, 'not only will no one be able to hear what we say, they won't be able to see us either.'

It was, indeed, the perfect place to have an entirely private conversation, as on either side of the drive was nothing but grass, stretching out to the wall on one side, blending eventually into an ornamental Italian garden on the other side of the house. There was no cover. Nobody could possibly have approached without being spotted immediately. Even if, in the manner of an actor in a comic spy film, someone had tried to dodge from one linden to another to sneak up on the two of them, the angle at which Bart had positioned himself meant that he would have seen the movement.

Adrianna looked back towards the house while still balancing on one foot, a feat of difficulty that Bart fully appreciated. Then she turned back, lowered her right foot, strolled over towards him, enough so that she was no longer visible from the house, and proceeded to repeat the stretch on the other side.

'So?' she said, a woman of few words.

'I want you to push Daddy to appoint me CEO of Sachs,' Bart said, managing for once to match her conversational style.

'Why should I?'

She was watching him very carefully now, analysing every little movement, every inflection and tone.

He said: 'Okay, for the purposes of this conversation let's assume that Conway's out of the running – Pa certainly seems dead set against him, doesn't he? Well, I don't know if you've noticed, but Charlotte and Bella are both Daddy's girls. They hate him for treating our mother so badly, but they're still desperate for his approval, even if they won't admit it. You may be behaving like the ideal hostess this weekend, but they'll still resent you because you're younger than them, more beautiful than them, and getting married to their father. Perfectly natural, I suppose, when one puts it like that,' he added, shrugging. 'Can't really blame them. But if one of them gets power, I'm betting that they'll do everything they can to screw you over.'

Adrianna lowered her left foot and started to stretch out

her calves against the tree, still with her eyes fixed on his face.

'Especially if you have kids,' he said. 'I know Jade's pushing for her boys to get a degree of voting stock in the company as part of the divorce. It's tied into the family trust, which means that we have a stake in it. Pa's lawyers are negotiating a payoff for the four of us to get us to sign the papers. He's hell-bent on getting that divorce as soon as he can, obviously, so he'll throw money at us to get us to do it.'

Adrianna nodded briefly; she knew all about the divorce negotiations.

'And when *that* happens,' Bart continued, 'it means that there'll be six kids in the trust. Our quarter still has the majority, of course, if we stick together, and I can't imagine any one of us siding with Jade's boys. But if you have children too – which you're bound to do – then the odds start ticking up, don't they? What if you have two, and you insist on them being part of the trust too, and Pa's still infatuated with you so he twists all of our arms until we agree? Then what if your kids team up with Jade's as a voting block? Suddenly the trust looks a lot less . . . trustworthy.'

Adrianna's eyebrows rose as she stretched her triceps, one elbow up, one down, hands clasped behind her back.

'I know,' Bart said rather smugly, correctly interpreting her expression as surprise that he was able to analyse the situation this clearly. 'People think I'm the most awful dimwit, bumbling through life like something out of a P. G. Wodehouse novel. But I'm not a *complete* idiot. I can look ahead and see how things might turn out. And I'm telling you, the girls will be a lot harder on you and your kids than

I'd be. Did you see how Bella went after Jade with that cushion? Whacked the hell out of her! And you should have heard what Charlotte said to her afterwards. Practically flayed her with her tongue. Not pretty at all, let me tell you. Called her kids "brats".'

He pulled a comic grimace.

'Trust me, if one of the twins gets made CEO, they'll never give you a fair shake. Daddy won't be around forever, and to have Charlotte or Bella gunning for you won't be at all comfortable.'

'What if I don't want kids?' Adrianna asked, stretching her other arm now.

Bart burst out laughing.

'Of course you'll have kids!' he said easily. 'Every woman who marries a rich guy has at least one kid. It's her insurance. You get a house, child support, all the good stuff – way juicier in the divorce. I know a friend of Ma's who's pulled off what she calls the Holy Trinity – three by three separate husbands. She's absolutely rolling in it, apparently.'

'So you're saying I'm a gold-digger?' Adrianna said, leaning back against the tree.

'Well,' Bart said, 'to partially quote the song, I don't see you messin' with no broke . . . um, bros.'

Unexpectedly, this was what cracked her up. She started to laugh, the first time Bart had ever seen her yield to a spontaneous emotion. Her beautifully sculpted features softened, her green eyes flashed; she bent over, propping her hands on her thighs, cracking up.

'Your *accent*!' she managed. 'Oh, that was very good!'

'Bit rich,' Bart said sulkily, 'considering you've got one of your own. Okay, so maybe I don't do the best American-rapper accent in the world, but I don't think it warrants out-and-out hysteria.'

'Okay,' Adrianna said finally, standing up and wiping her eyes. 'I am a gold-digger. Okay. I say I don't want kids, you don't believe me. Okay. It doesn't matter. I will not divorce Jeffrey. Maybe you don't believe that either, but it's true. I want to be part of . . . everything. So I am very interested in the question of who becomes the CEO.'

'I don't want kids either,' Bart said, 'by the way. I won't have ones who're battling with yours for part of the trust, or control of the company. But I wouldn't mind being filthy rich and powerful, I must admit. And I'd like to see my siblings settle down and stop looking like they're going to tear each other's throats out. I actually think I could manage that as CEO.'

He looked serious for a moment.

'Just to say, FYI, Con would be quite the opposite. He's a bossy bastard. Giving him supreme power would be a disaster – he'd lord it over me and the girls and drive them insane with rage. Quite genuinely, I don't think he should get the job. We've had one psycho authoritarian running Sachs for decades – we don't need another.'

He grinned.

'It would piss all of them off, I know, because they've always thought I wasn't any good at business. But that would be quite a lot of fun too.'

'Your father is still very angry with Conway,' Adrianna observed. 'Because of me. He thinks that because Conway was having an affair with a prostitute from my country, it makes me look like one too.'

'Oh, I don't think anyone actually said she was a—' Bart started.

'Believe me,' Adrianna said, shaking her head. 'I know that . . . girl. She is definitely a prostitute.'

'Um, fair dos, then,' Bart muttered as she went on:

'If I tell Jeffrey that I am fine, it does not matter to me, he will relax a little about this,' Adrianna continued. 'But if I say that I am very upset – because she *is* a prostitute, so that part is true – Jeffrey will keep being very angry with Conway.'

'And what are you going to do?' Bart asked intently.

She looked straight at him. 'I don't know,' she said softly.

'Pa would much rather hand over the company to a son, not a daughter,' Bart said. 'He's very old-fashioned that way. Did you hear him telling Charlotte she should have been born a guy?'

He was speaking on autopilot, however. His lips were moving, he was making sense, but he could barely hear his own voice, and he doubted that she was fully aware of what he was saying, either. They were staring at each other now in a way that was unmistakable. The air between them was as charged with electricity as if a clap of thunder was about to sound, a storm break overhead.

'What if you get the job and make a terrible mess of it?' she asked, still in that soft voice.

'Then I make a mess and eventually get kicked out,' he said, shrugging. 'It won't be any skin off your nose. You've got nothing to lose by supporting me. Or even just smoothing the way for me. Why not?'

'Why not?' she echoed, and now those two words took on an entirely different meaning.

Bart pushed off the tree and took a couple of steps towards her.

'I'm getting married to your father,' she said, her eyes still fixed on his.

'That's okay,' he said. 'I don't want to marry you.'

'I don't want to marry you either,' Adrianna snapped back. 'You are pointless. A pretty toy for someone. You do nothing useful.'

'Bit harsh,' Bart said.

She snorted a little laugh. '*Bit harsh*,' she repeated. 'I love this English way of talking. If someone stabbed you in the stomach, you would probably say "bit harsh".'

'You know what?' Bart said, taking another step towards her. 'I probably would.'

He shoved his hands into the pocket of his sweatpants and looked from side to side briefly, making sure that no one else was out in the early morning, walking through the dewy grass. Then he leant in to kiss her. Just his mouth, no other contact.

The storm might have broken, a flash of lightning over-head followed directly by a clap of thunder, the heavens opening, rain pouring down; if it had, neither Bart nor Adrianna would have noticed. Their senses were entirely focused on the soft, sweet kiss, surprisingly romantic, their lips meeting tentatively, their breath warm in the cool morning air. Adrianna moved towards him, deepening the contact, and he felt the tip of her tongue touch his, a perfect, intoxicating moment.

He sighed in pleasure, opening his mouth, trying to coax hers further open too. After her exercise, her lips tasted delicately salty. Her hand touched his chest, slid slowly down to his belly button, feeling his abdominal muscles jerk and tauten at the contact, hollowing in as if they wanted to make it even easier for her to keep going.

They kept kissing as her fingers reached the waistband of his tracksuit bottoms, slung low on his hips, her thumb circling his belly button. He wanted her to go lower so badly that his hips jerked towards her, a silent plea; but the next thing Bart knew, he was practically kissing the tree. Adrianna had ducked down between his arms and slipped away. His hands slapped against the wide trunk of the linden tree for balance, the blood rushing from his head to his groin so fast he felt dizzy.

'Fuck,' he said to the tree. 'Fuck, fuck, *fuck*.'

'I'm not going to do anything to put my marriage in trouble,' Adrianna said, stepping back to the tarmacked drive, her voice full of amusement. 'But I will think about what you said about the future, and the CEO job. I am impressed. You surprised me twice this morning.'

Bart knew she didn't mean the kiss; that had come as no surprise to her. He turned his head to watch her as she jogged away, her buttocks high and superbly muscled in the tight exercise leggings, her hips slender as a model's. The ponytail bounced with every step.

She did not look back. He doubted that Adrianna had ever looked back in her life.

'Bloody hell,' he said devoutly to the tree as he peeled himself away from it. He still wasn't sure if he could stand unsupported; he turned round, resting his back against the trunk. His cock stood up like a fully engaged handbrake on a manual-drive car, and just as hard.

Bart looked down at it. Where was he going to go with this thing? He could barely walk; his balls were swollen and aching. Once more he glanced from side to side, making sure that the field was completely clear. The huge entrance gates were closed. In the old days, someone would have lived in the gatehouse, their accommodation free in return for their being available to open and shut the gates at any hour of the day or night.

Nowadays, of course, there was an electronic panel set into one of the pillars, with a code to enter and a buzzer to press if you didn't have it; but this was the main entrance, for the owners and their guests, and Bart, in selecting this location to ambush Adrianna, had known that no one was expected at 8 a.m. on a Sunday morning. Any deliveries would be routed through the back approach road to the servants' entrance.

So as he reached into his sweatpants and, with a groan of anticipation, extracted his swollen cock, he felt very confident that he could take care of his extremely pressing physical need without anyone being the wiser. And it didn't take long. His cock was already moist with pre-cum; one spit into his palm, eyes closed to imagine Adrianna's face, Adrianna's mouth, Adrianna's buttocks, Adrianna's hand sliding over his cock – just a few strokes and he was hissing between his teeth to make sure he didn't shout out loud as the hot sperm started to gush through his fingers, dripping to the ground.

He smiled drowsily, imagining his come sizzling as it hit the cold dewy grass. The orgasm had hit him hard, exploding as if she had reached inside him and dragged it out herself, and he thanked God for the tree trunk behind him. Not only was it safe concealment from the house; without it, he was pretty sure, he would have fallen over when he came. His knees were still buckling.

God, what a woman! He shook his cock as best he could, and then ducked down, grabbed a handful of wet grass and wiped himself off. A couple of blades of grass clung to his damp cock as he stowed it away in his briefs once more and drew in a long, deep breath, shaking his head in disbelief about what had just happened.

Stepping back onto the drive, he couldn't help looking down it for a glimpse of Adrianna, even though, at the speed at which she travelled, he knew that she had to be long gone. And he couldn't help wondering whether she was doing what he had just done, ducking into a downstairs loo as soon as she was back inside the house, pulling her leggings down to her knees, slipping her hand between her legs, strumming herself until she, too, exploded.

Was she thinking of him? Pretending it was his hand making her come? She unquestionably wanted him: he had seen it in her eyes, tasted it on her mouth, he had known it since she had gently teased him on their first night here. He had already pulled on his cock in the shower yesterday, imagining Adrianna coming to his room, sinking to her knees, taking him in her mouth as the water poured down over them and he shot into her mouth, getting her wet inside and out . . .

He had to stop this line of thought right now. It was simply too risky to even contemplate starting an affair with the woman with whom his father was obsessed; she was clearly even more aware of that than he, having much more to lose. Bart's trust fund was beyond his father's control. Adrianna's financial security, however, was entirely in Jeffrey's hands, and she was never going to risk losing that.

Okay, I can't shag her, he said to himself. *And she can't shag me. But we can hang out, get to know each other, can't we? There's something about her I genuinely like, quite apart from the fact that she's insanely sexy.*

Jesus. What am I saying? It's like I want to be friends with a woman. When has that *ever happened to me? But I like talking to her. She makes me laugh. You'd never be bored with her, that's for sure.*

Pa's a bloody lucky guy.

Yes, that was the line to take. She was going to be his father's wife. Absolutely nothing could happen between them that was not appropriate behaviour for a stepmother and stepson. That insane kiss was a one-off; there were plenty of other girls in the world. He knew that better than anyone. When he got back to London he'd go through his phone and line up a bevy of lovelies who were bound to distract him from the image of his stepmother-to-be with her hand on the waistband of his jogging bottoms.

In fact, why wait? He could start right now. He pulled his phone out of his pocket and started to scroll through names. It was a positive roll call of models, actresses, It girls, reality TV stars from *Love in Chelsea*, girls with long hair and longer legs who smiled more in a minute than Adrianna did in a day, and every single one of them would be delighted to hear from him. That was what he needed: some uncomplicated, no-strings fun with cheerful, chatty girls who were thoroughly up for it, and whose antics would banish the image of the glacially poised, laconic goddess who would become Mrs Jeffrey Sachs in a few months' time.

When she did, Bart decided, he would start calling her 'Mummy'. It would be a passion-killer for him, and, if he didn't miss his guess, would annoy her tremendously.

And if Bart was actually looking forward more to seeing Adrianna's reaction after the wedding when he called her 'Mummy' for the first time than to rendezvousing next week with Daphne from *Love in Chelsea*, who was a lithe twenty-five-year-old with a concave stomach, sexy belly-button piercing and a vivid imagination, he did not admit that to himself as he started to saunter down the drive, cheerfully anticipating a shower, a shave and a lavish cooked breakfast.

Chapter Seventeen

'You're back! And *very* sweaty!' Jeffrey said gleefully, taking off his glasses.

He was sitting up in bed, propped up by a pile of pillows, an almost equally large pile of Sunday newspapers beside him, through which he was working his way. The sports sections were discarded on the floor. Jeffrey, as befitted a hotelier, focused on the business and lifestyle sections. Next to him was an iPad on which he was also reading the *New York Times* and *Washington Post*; Jeffrey was far from the stereotype of the pensioner befuddled by modern technology. Before meeting Adrianna he had been quite a prolific tweeter. Now, however, he was on social media much less, as his spare time was mainly spent with his adored fiancée.

He stared at her worshipfully as she crossed the living room of their master suite. She stood just inside the bedroom doorway, her tall, slim body outlined very clearly in the tight-zipped exercise jacket and leggings. In the latest fashion, a series of mesh insets were slashed into the opaque fabric, wrapping snakelike around her legs. It was a very odd look, as only a very specialized fetishist would want to see the back of a woman's knees revealed through black mesh set into exercise tights. Still, if anyone could carry off an eccentric clothing trend it was Adrianna, whose body was perfect for clothes: slim, lean, with strong shoulders and slim hips.

Even the obviously enhanced breasts were in relative proportion to the rest of her, rather than being comedy melons. Adrianna had known that the kind of rich man she wanted to snag, while requiring her to have a bosom, would prefer a look which skewed more towards elegance than vulgarity. Besides, she worked out regularly, and did not want breasts that were big enough to be an encumbrance as she did so.

'Did you run very hard?' Jeffrey asked, his eyes bright as he looked her up and down, taking in with relish the visible dampness at her hairline and her throat.

'Very hard and very fast,' she said. 'I am *very* sweaty.'

'Show me,' he said, leaning forward eagerly.

Walking to the foot of the bed, Adrianna unzipped her lightweight jacket and dropped it on the carpet. Underneath, she was wearing a racerback top which showed off her beautifully sculpted shoulders. Jeffrey licked his lips, watching her reach down to the hem of the top and start to peel it off, wriggling as she worked the built-in bust support over her breasts.

She bunched the top up and let it fall on top of the jacket, trying to minimize as far as possible the contact of moist, sweat-sodden Lycra with the very expensive carpet. Jeffrey was so careless about his possessions that if she had said she didn't want to mess it up by getting it damp and smelly, he would have laughed at her. But Adrianna hated not taking care of the lovely things that now surrounded her. It was disrespectful to their beauty and the price that had been paid for them. She couldn't imagine being able to take them for granted, no matter how much Jeffrey encouraged her to do so.

Because this lavishness and luxury was very new to Adrianna. She might have been wearing a designer cocktail dress when she met Jeffrey – bought on final sale, of course – and working in the extremely sleek and chic surroundings of Farouche. However, like so many young women who knew how to present themselves as glossily as if they lived in Mayfair or St John's Wood or Notting Hill, and who only ever travelled by cab, the truth was that she lived six travel zones away, a journey of two tubes and a bus back to a small rented room in a house that the owner had converted almost back to the days of single-room-occupancy tenements.

As Eastern Europeans surged into London, armed with their excellent English, their polite manners and their willingness to work long hours for less pay than the locals would accept, enterprising landlords had seen the trend and reacted accordingly. Adrianna's landlord had been a Romanian who had realized that all his tenants wanted, at the end of a lengthy shift and a gruelling journey, was to come home and crash. They were saving their money for a mortgage deposit or sending it home; they did not want to spend one extra unnecessary penny on rent.

So he had converted his houses accordingly, keeping a small, basic kitchen, but turning the rest of the rooms into studios, each with a built-in sink. There was one shared bathroom plus an extra toilet. Most of the tenants bought little fridges and portable electric mini hobs, as food left in the kitchen could not be relied on to remain there until its purchaser needed it, and besides, no one ever cleaned the place up.

It was the polar opposite of the apartment blocks for overseas students springing up in the centre of London, with chicly designed individual living pods, cleaned by professionals several times a week, communal kitchens, and bike racks and gyms in the basement. So many young foreigners flooded into the capital every year, with such a disparity in their incomes. Most of the ones from Asia had parents who could afford to send them to university and put them up in custom-built luxury flats situated close to their colleges; the majority of the ones from the Eastern bloc lived in squalor and competed desperately for minimum-wage, long-hour jobs in Costa and Pret A Manger.

Adrianna shivered at the thought of ever going back to that room in the Romanian's house. There had been no way to keep it fully clean, since the house hoover never worked properly and the carpet tiles had stains crusted into them which never came out, no matter how hard she scrubbed. She spent money she couldn't afford on diffusers and plug-ins that could only do so much to counter the smells of her fellow tenants' cooking, let alone some of her fellow tenants. She couldn't trust the expensive clothes she needed to wear for work to the house washing machine, so she sponge-washed them for as long as she could get away with before finally taking them to the dry cleaner.

And when she came back from a run, she would have to strip off her workout gear and wash it straight away, again by hand. There was nowhere to put it, no ventilated laundry hamper in the bathroom which the staff would empty every morning, sorting through the dirty washing, removing the cashmere and wool and silk from the pile and ensuring it went through the most delicate cycle in the Miele machine, washed only with Sicilian-lemon-scented liquid which Jade had imported in bulk from the Parisian manufacturer at thirty-five euros a bottle.

Once you had lived like this, you could never go back to scrubbing your sports bra in a small sink while hoping that it wouldn't rain for a few hours, until your exercise clothes, pegged to the little plastic rack hooked outside your bedroom window, would stop dripping enough, at least, to be brought inside. Adrianna was fully prepared to do whatever it took to ensure that the enterprising Romanian's stained, smelly room receded still further in the rear-view mirror.

She was standing now in her sports bra and leggings, her skin glossy with sweat. Jeffrey licked his lips again.

'Keep going,' he said.

She reached behind her and unclasped the bra. It was a huge relief to take it off, as its straps and band were saturated with moisture from her run. And the same with the leggings: the wide waistband, double fabric, also damp through; that had always been the hardest part for her to dry at home, with the worry that before it eventually did dry it would start to stink of mildew. Yes, there was a launderette, but those big machines ruined Lycra, and she couldn't afford to keep buying exercise clothes, even from Primark . . .

The leggings were peeled down, her thong coming with them. Jeffrey held out his hand eagerly, and she tossed him the thong even as she kicked off her ankle socks; her trainers had been left downstairs in what was apparently, very appropriately, called the 'mud room' in this country. Naked, pushing aside her fastidiousness at leaving her workout clothes on the carpet, she walked around the bed to the head of it. Jeffrey, having thoroughly sniffed the thong with an expression of ecstasy on his face, was eagerly throwing back the coverlet and scooting over to sit on the edge.

Adrianna closed her eyes. His lizard hands caught her hips, pulling her in, and his dry scaly tongue started to lick her, darting into her belly button, tasting the salt sweat there, caught in its whorls and folds.

She could not understand his craving for her sweaty skin; to her, after exercising, it always felt spongy, as if it had soaked up too much liquid. But Jeffrey loved it. And at least he wasn't requiring a reluctant girlfriend to work up a sweat on a regular basis, as she already had a regular exercise routine which she thoroughly enjoyed. Merely sitting in a sauna would not have been good enough; he wanted the specific smell and texture of skin that had been encased in Lycra for a minimum of half an hour as the wearer exercised as hard as she could.

He would lick her all over, from head to toe, and he would end between her legs, sucking and licking and almost snuffling with excitement, no longer like an old greedy lizard but a boar in the forest undergrowth, rooting for acorns and bulbs. Mostly, this was all he required. Afterwards, he would have her lie down, and he would perch as best he could above her like a wizened old elf, satisfying himself over her prone body.

Mercifully for Adrianna, Jeffrey was unable to manage

penetration. His heart was not strong, and his doctor had strongly advised him against using Viagra or Cialis. How many gold-diggers had rued the day when pills for erectile dysfunction were invented! In the old days, when you seduced a wealthy gentleman over seventy into leaving his wife and children for you, pretty much all you needed to do was put on shows for him, play with yourself, possibly get in a friend or two every now and then as an extra treat for him to watch.

But nowadays sugar daddies wanted it all, the full monty. They expected feats of gymnastics even as you tactfully helped them into position, braced yourself to support them as well as yourself, listened to them complain about their creaking hip replacements, and kept a smile of delight on your face as you bounced around on top of them, cursing the inventor of those pills with everything you had. Adrianna knew perfectly well that if her ex-colleagues, not only at the bar but other places she had worked, had met a billionaire whose main requirements were for them to work out as hard as possible and then let themselves be licked from head to toe, they would get down on their knees on this very luxurious carpet and thank God in gratitude with tears running down their faces.

Yes, she had hit the jackpot. The companies with whom she'd held credit cards were less lucky, as they were no longer making a small fortune in interest from her. Those cards were paid off and cancelled. Jeffrey had given her an Amex Black, which had no limit.

Eyes still closed, Adrianna visualized that credit card, as she usually did while Jeffrey's lips closed over first one nipple, then the other, his hands eagerly squeezing her round breasts like a child with a toy that would squeak if you pressed it hard enough. Unfortunately, however, her recent encounter with Bart was still fresh in her mind, and the Amex Black faded, replaced by Bart's face going suddenly serious as he leant in to kiss her.

He was irresponsible, a playboy, feckless, unreliable. If he had walked into Farouche and asked her out, she would never have accepted, because he would have been wanting only an affair. He was not marriage material, and she would not have settled for anything less. But the memory of his soft lips kissing her so sweetly, his flat abs contracting in pleasure as she stroked down them, made her moan despite herself.

'You like that,' her fiancé said into her breasts, his head between them now, his tongue licking up the dampness there, raising them so that he could access the even sweatier undersides. 'You like that, don't you?'

And, thinking of Bart, of Bart naked, kissing her breasts, Adrianna summoned up all her self-control. She could not answer too enthusiastically. Jeffrey did not like any overt eagerness, she had learnt almost immediately. He wanted her aloof, poised at all times, a marble statue come to life, a goddess who had stepped down from Mount Olympus, whose physique he loved to worship.

So she answered almost coldly: 'Yes. It's good,' and went somewhere in her head that was far away, far from this lavish bedroom, this soft carpet beneath her feet, these lizard hands pulling at her, the lizard tongue lapping eagerly at her spongy flesh. A place where she and Bart were naked in a huge bed, lying head to toe, his balls in her mouth, his mouth between her legs, driving each other crazy with desire. When, eventually, Jeffrey pulled her to lie down on the bed, clambered over her, she was still picturing his younger son.

And disconcertingly enough, there was something that helped her with that mental image. As often happened with family members, Jeffrey and Bart smelled unnervingly similar.

Chapter Eighteen

'I just wish we could have some time that wasn't in hotels,' Bella said wistfully into her laptop camera. 'Or on screen. Something more – normal.'

'I know, baby,' Ronaldo said, sighing into his own laptop screen.

He was sitting cross-legged on his hotel bed, his Mac propped in front of him. Bella had not realized previously how much travelling Ronaldo did for work. Ever since she had got back from her round-the-world tour, connecting with him had been a constant dance of time zones and scheduling, finding slots where both of them were awake and alone, which of course meant Thomas being away.

That last was the trickiest condition of all, since Thomas, with basic animal instinct, had sensed his wife's emotional withdrawal and was reacting accordingly. As Bella had realized at Vanbrugh Manor, after the years that she had spent pushing for more closeness from him, they had swapped roles: now she was withholding and he was pursuing. The walk in the grounds he had insisted on taking, so they could talk about their feelings, had been agonizing. He had not even been placated by Bella's telling him that she was wearing the comfort knickers and that they truly did live up to expectations.

During the walk, Thomas had kept asking how she was doing, and, with appropriate sympathetic marital concern, how the rewards points project was going. This had only served to make Bella realize with horror that not only did she not want to have sex with her husband, she had very little interest in talking to him either. She didn't believe a word that came out of his mouth; it was all too obvious that he was only acting like this because she had pulled away from him and he wanted to get her back, not because he cared. As soon as she became sweet, loving, needy Bella again, he would revert to the Thomas who cancelled weekends together at the last minute and thought that buying her oversized underpants would serve as compensation.

Her attention outside of work was entirely focused on Ronaldo; her husband now seemed entirely irrelevant to her existence. Thomas had clearly picked this up, because ever since that weekend, he had been a nightmare. Clingy, needy, puppy-eyed. Thank God she had been able, quite plausibly, to blame the dramatic change to her usual behaviour squarely on her father's challenge to his children and her determination to drive through an extremely ambitious revamp plan with a terrifyingly tight deadline. When Thomas reproached her for being distant, not sufficiently grateful that finally, after several years of marriage, he was ready to give her what she had always wanted, Bella simply answered that the timing was all wrong for her to have any kind of soul-searching conversation.

And when he pushed for more, she flipped the tables and

reproached him in her turn for choosing such a terrible time to finally try to give her what she wanted. She was neither rude nor hostile. She wasn't even angry that it had taken her having a passionate affair outside the marriage for Thomas to act like a dog in the manger and try to court her back.

When he told her that he'd realized how much he'd been missing her when she was away on her long trip, and had had barely any free time to get in touch with him, she smiled at him. It was a nice smile, but a distant one, the kind you gave to the porter at a hotel after he'd brought up your cases. So it was dismissive, too. The smile you gave someone that said: 'Thank you for your help. You can leave now.'

Since that was exactly what she was thinking, she was being entirely honest. As far as she was concerned, Thomas had fulfilled his purpose. He had saved Bella from the humiliation of seeing her twin sister zoom too far away from her in the marriage and baby stakes. Good-looking, eligible, well-mannered, well-regarded at work, he had been a good match. Her father had definitely preferred Thomas to Paul, considering a commodity trader a much more appropriate husband for one of his daughters than a male model.

Well, that credit would be comprehensively lost when she announced – as she daily dreamed of doing – that she was leaving her extremely respectable husband for the man whom Jeffrey Sachs would always see as the housekeeper's son. No amount of selling Ronaldo as a successful, Harvard-educated advertising executive at a top Chicago firm would counter the embarrassment to Jeffrey of having his house-keeper and her husband as in-laws.

Adrianna seemed so keen on family get-togethers! Bella

briefly pictured Maria and Jose turning up at Vanbrugh Manor for a Christmas celebration, and her mind boggled. Could Maria even stay on as Jeffrey's housekeeper? Would Bella have to move to the States to live with Ronaldo to avoid the whole issue?

Bella caught herself up, knowing that her imagination was running riot. She simply couldn't stop the thoughts, the fantasies, the temptation to flash ahead to a future in which Ronaldo was her acknowledged boyfriend, turning to look at her as they sat next to each other, holding hands, dropping a quick kiss on her lips as their eyes met, the way Paul did with Charlotte.

'I so wish I'd visited your place when I was in Chicago,' she said to Ronaldo wistfully. 'I thought if I did, I'd crash after we'd had sex and then I wouldn't be able to drag myself away, and I absolutely couldn't stay out all night without everyone at the hotel noticing . . . but now I really wish I had, because I could picture you there – cooking your dinner, watching TV, having a shower . . .'

In other words, she thought, *the domestic things I want to do with you. Of course I'm loving the hot Skype sessions, the sexy talk, dressing up for you, feeling glamorous and beautiful, and I want to keep that . . . but I want the cosy, homely, cuddling moments too. I want to plan what we have for dinner, take it in turns to cook for each other, argue about which show to stream next.*

I want it all.

'Aww, that's so boring!' Ronaldo said, laughing. 'You want to picture me cooking? Baby, I have a freezer full of bags of chicken fillet slices and a bigger bag of prepped veggies. I dump one each into a pan once a week, stir-fry them up and portion them out in baggies in the freezer so I can eat healthy when I'm not out at restaurants, entertaining clients. My mother would die if she saw me doing that after all the cooking lessons she gave me! But you know, I'm a single guy, that's how we live!'

He had automatically raised his hands to show the size of the bags, and Bella started to giggle.

'Wow,' she said. 'Those look like really big bags of veggies.'

'They *are*,' he said, immediately slipping into the tone she had adopted; he was incredibly fast and intuitive, she had noticed. No wonder he was so successful as an advertising executive, a business that required not only excellent customer relations but a mental suppleness, an ability to read what the client wanted but couldn't quite verbalize, jumping ahead to give them their perfect solution. 'They're *huge* bags. Gigantic. Really hard to get into the freezer.'

'Super-sized,' Bella said. 'Massive.'

'*Enormous. Enormous* bags of veggies.'

'This big?'

She held her hands even wider than his, which caused the lapels of her silk robe to fall open. She had, naturally, dressed up for the video chat in some of her best Bloomies underwear, a plunging, halter-necked sapphire slip which set off the vivid blue of her eyes. She had stopped at a blow-dry bar on the way home, which she knew was crazy. Sooner or later, Ronaldo was going to see what her hair actually looked like without someone deftly pinning in rollers, taking them out again and running their hands through the curls to separate them out, creating a series of cascading tresses which were beginning to look like Charlotte's now that Bella's hair was growing longer. The blow-dry bar's efforts didn't last more than a couple of days, but as long as she looked beautiful for her lover, she didn't care.

She looked at herself in the little window at the top of the screen and saw a glowing, vibrant woman. She was still a plumper version of her sister, but now she was just as stunning in her own way. It was the first time Bella had ever thought that she didn't need to lose weight to be equal to Charlotte as far as their relative attractiveness went. Now, however, she realized that being slim was not an essential requirement. The curves of her full breasts, revealed as the robe slipped open, pushed up by the well-cut slip, which cupped and gently lifted them, were opulently sexual: certainly nothing that her athletically toned sister could offer.

Ronaldo swallowed so audibly that she heard it over the microphone.

'Wow,' he said, his hand going down to stroke his crotch. 'Yeah, I'm not feeling all that jokey any more. Baby, put your hands on your tits for me? Let me see you get your nipples hard, like I'd be doing if I were there right now. Jesus, you're getting me so excited. You're like napalm. You set me on fire.'

When they had started Skyping, Bella had been worried about being self-conscious, acting awkwardly or clumsily, making a fool of herself in front of a man she was obsessed with. But Ronaldo had immediately swept those doubts away without her even having to voice them. He was just so good at this. His dirty talk was world-class.

Holding his eyes with hers, she slid her hands over her

breasts as he wanted, pinching her nipples, letting him see them harden, watching his lips part in a long moan.

'Oh yeah,' he said. 'Yeah, like that. God, you have great tits. So big and round, just perfect.'

'See, I have big bags too!' she said; she was even confident enough to joke now during sex, and he rewarded her by throwing his head back in a laugh.

'Show me,' he said, still laughing. 'Show me those big bags, baby!'

Bella reached back and untied the wide silk ribbon straps of the slip, which were fastened in a bow behind her neck. Letting them fall, she pulled down the top of it, revealing her breasts, cupping them once more in her palms as if she were offering them to him.

'Ah, fuck,' he moaned, starting to unzip his trousers. 'I want to rub oil over them and get you to hold them just like that while I push my dick between them . . . did we do that yet?'

She shook her head.

'Wow, I must have been crazy,' he said, kneeling up, slipping down his trousers and his boxer shorts. Her mouth went dry as she saw his penis springing free, fully erect already: she must really be napalm, burning him up, getting him to this state of excitement just by showing him her breasts. 'Why did I never do that to you? God, I could come right now thinking about it . . . feel my cock sliding between your oiled tits, watching your face, holding out as long as I can before I finally shoot all over them, all over your big tits . . .'

He was pulling on his cock now. He had a hand towel

beside him, which he must have taken from the hotel bathroom, and with the other hand he pulled it in front of him, getting ready for his explosion.

'I hate that you're going to come over a towel and not my tits!' she said, massaging them, running her thumbs in circles over her nipples, more porny than she had ever been with anyone and loving every moment.

'You're going to come first, baby,' he said. 'I can hold out. Get that finger buzzer I sent you and put it on. I want to see you spread your legs and come for me. I want you to pump that ass up and down again and again and call out my name while you do it.'

Her face flushed with excitement that tingled like electricity running through her, Bella scrabbled frantically in the bedside drawer, pulling out the little battery-operated gadget that Ronaldo had FedExed to her in Sydney. It was amazingly effective. She didn't want to know which previous girlfriend had used this same device, where he had learnt that this one, with its subtle ridges, was miraculously designed to deliver just the right pressure where she needed it.

Sliding it onto her finger, she shrugged off the robe and lay back on the bed, hoicking up her nightdress with barely any embarrassment, letting its folds drape over her stomach, so that all the good parts of her – breasts, thighs – were revealed, and the tummy which pooched out was not. Later she would prop herself up on the pillows, but for now she was fully immersed in bringing herself to orgasm, and she would come faster without his eyes on her. She still wasn't as sophisticated as Ronaldo: she couldn't stare directly at her lover while letting her body let go completely, falling apart under his lustful gaze.

His voice, however, spurred her on. He told her how amazing, how beautiful she looked, how delicious it was to see her damp pussy, her legs parted for him, her hips pounding as she came, hear her moans and wails as she let go and thrust herself against the clever little buzzer again and again. He cheered her on, encouraging her to keep going, telling her how hot she looked like this, how he'd been looking forward to seeing her pussy during his long days of work and business travel.

Bella was in a different dimension. Her eyes were closed, her only sensations the touch of her finger between her legs and the sound of Ronaldo's voice. He was incredible. It was the greatest fantasy, a man who could talk dirtily but eloquently, like something from an erotic novel.

'Okay, baby, hold your tits together for me now?' he asked finally. 'Really press them together, good and tight for my big cock. Can you feel it? I'm sliding it up between your tits – fuck, that feels so good, your tits are amazing, so big and round! Oh baby, this is so good. My cock's right between your tits now, you're reaching forward and licking my head, oh yeah, your tongue feels unbelievable, you're so good at that – I'm so close—'

Just then, three things happened at once. Bella scooched back, up on the stack of pillows at the head of the bed, so that she could watch him in turn, moving awkwardly on her elbows, as her hands were still squeezing her breasts tightly together for her lover. Ronaldo started making the unmistakable sounds that meant he was about to come. And downstairs, the front door banged and Thomas's voice could be faintly heard calling, 'Bella? I'm home!'

Then it was all a blur of frenzied activity. Bella jerked up, her face red, her eyes panicked as she dragged her nightdress over her breasts, grabbed for her robe. On-screen, Ronaldo let out a bellow as his cock started to spurt an impressive fountain of come onto the towel.

'Fuck, yeah!' he groaned. 'Fuck, yeah, I'm coming on your tits, your big beautiful tits – Bella, you're amazing, look how you're making me come, I'm shooting so hard for you – I'm covering your tits with come—'

Bella half fell off the bed, so desperate was she to get to the laptop. Then she tripped over the trailing robe and nearly went flying. Only sheer, panicked determination got her across the room; fabric ripped, but she kept going, frantic to slam shut the MacBook and stop the stream of words and come that were pouring simultaneously from her lover. Never had the click of the screen meeting the keyboard been more welcome.

Panting, gasping, she caught sight of herself in the full-length cheval mirror and squeaked in horror. Her face was lobster-red and damp with sweat, her eyes glazed with lust. It could not have been more obvious what she had just been doing. Frantically, thinking fast, she threw herself back onto the mattress again, snatching at the folds of her robe to cover her body, and jamming her hand between her legs, so that when her husband ran enthusiastically up the stairs to find his wife, he opened the bedroom door to see her apparently enjoying a moment of happy self-pleasure.

As the door opened, Bella screamed out of sheer nerves.

Though she knew perfectly well that it was Thomas, it still felt as if the villain of a horror film had suddenly burst in on her, complete with ski mask and chainsaw. Never had Thomas seen her masturbating; they did not have that kind of sex life. If Bella had been in any state to take in his expression, she might have burst out laughing, because he looked thunderstruck: absolutely, comically amazed.

And then his head jerked back as if he had been slapped. He looked wildly around the room, ran across it to the dressing room beyond, could be heard tearing open the wardrobe doors and rifling inside. When he did not find what he was looking for, he tore into the bathroom, the leather soles of his handmade shoes slapping on the tiles, and promptly exited again.

Bella sat up, made sure her nightdress was tied again at the nape of her neck, gathered her robe around her and exclaimed, sounding as surprised as she felt: 'Thomas! What on earth are you *doing*? Why are you even *here*? I thought you were in Berlin!'

Thomas appeared in the doorway, breathing hard. He dropped to his knees and looked under the bed.

'Where is he?' he demanded.

'What do you *mean*?' Bella felt she was on very strong ground. 'Have you gone mad? Who are you talking about?'

'The guy who was here!' Thomas yelled, standing up again and looming over her.

'Oh, for God's sake!'

She waved her right hand at him and realized with horror that the little vibrator on her finger was still buzzing; hastily she turned it off.

'*This* is the guy, okay?' she shouted, pulling off the pink bit of plastic and throwing it on the bed. 'Got it now? I was on my own having a good time, which you've completely bloody ruined. Thanks so much!'

She climbed off the bed and faced him, the mattress between them, both their chests heaving with fury. Too exposed in her nightdress, she belted the robe around her; covering up her cleavage instantly made her feel less vulnerable.

'Got it now?' she repeated, pointing down at the vibrator, since taking an aggressive tack seemed to be working. 'You're acting like a madman! Why are you back here, anyway?'

'I thought I would surprise my wife, who's been asking me for years to come home at weekends!' he said, his eyes darting back and forth, clearly trying to work out if there were anywhere else at all that a man could have concealed himself. But there wasn't. The house was built on clean modern lines, no nooks or crannies or priest holes, and the open bedroom door was flat against the wall; it was clear that no one could have concealed themselves behind it.

Suddenly an idea struck him. He dashed over to the windows and, with a dramatic flourish, dragged open the heavy floor-length curtains to reveal nothing but the fake-Tudor panes beyond.

'There's *no one here*!' Bella yelled. 'Oh my God, I was *having a wank*! What is *wrong* with you?'

Thomas rounded on her, the curtains falling back into place.

'*Really*?' he said accusingly. 'Dressed up like that, with your hair and make-up done? I don't believe you!'

Fuck, Bella thought. This had not occurred to her. Thomas had not become extremely successful in a very competitive industry by being unable to read a situation fast and accurately.

'In fact, I've never seen that – get-up!' he continued, gesturing at the cream silk swathing her. 'I know all your night clothes! It's new, isn't it?'

Bella put her hands on her hips and fired back: 'So what if it is? I got it when I was travelling, because I wanted something to make me feel nice on the road! You're acting like a maniac!'

But just then, Thomas's eyes fired up. He had never stopped looking around the room, as if he could somehow magically conjure up a hidden cupboard in which Bella's lover could be concealed. His stare had passed several times over the MacBook lying sleekly on the dressing table, such a familiar sight that previously he had taken it for granted. Now, however, an idea had clearly occurred to him with blinding force.

Bella saw the idea hit him, and they sprang into action at exactly the same moment, both of them racing to grab the laptop. She was closer, and made it to the dressing table first, dragging it into her hands, pressing it to her chest as she backed away from him towards the door.

'So I was looking at porn!' she screeched at him. 'Is that what you want to hear? *I was looking at porn!*'

'Bullshit!' Thomas yelled, and she flinched, because her mild-mannered, avoidant husband had never shouted swear words at her before. 'That's total bullshit! You were talking to someone – having virtual sex with someone, whatever they call it—'

'Leave me *alone*!' Bella screamed. 'Just leave me alone! I was having a really good time and you've ruined it – I've humiliated myself begging you for sex for years, and finally I'm taking care of myself and not bothering you. You should be *grateful*, instead of badgering me and yelling at me!'

'So it's true? There's someone else?'

Bella hesitated for a moment. She'd wanted to have this conversation after the CEO decision, and that would still be infinitely preferable. Jeffrey had violently turned against Conway for cheating, and Thomas, she felt, was by no means above sabotaging her own chances by telling her father what had been going on.

'So there *is*!' Thomas bellowed, taking her silence for tacit agreement. 'I knew it! You whore!'

'First of all,' Bella snapped furiously, 'whores do it for money! I never get why people use that as an insult to people who're doing it for fun! It's completely the wrong use of the word!'

Thomas's mouth opened and stayed open in shock. Never had Bella corrected him like this, never had she pushed back to this extent. He had expected that she would crumple entirely at his accusation, confess everything, promise never to do it again; he had thought he would have a hold over her for the rest of their lives. Instead, she had taken his insult and used it to correct his vocabulary.

'Who *are* you?' he said in disbelief. 'Where's my sweet, gentle Bella?'

'Fuck your sweet, gentle Bella!' she yelled. 'Which you

hardly ever do, by the way! So, secondly, how dare you throw a huge scene about me watching porn and having a wank when you hardly ever have sex with me? I'm only thirty-four and I *like having sex* and if you're barely going to fuck me yourself, you don't get to complain if I have to take care of myself on a regular basis!'

This was the technique she had seen Charlotte operate to great effect in her own office when Conway had stormed in; push back harder, show no vulnerability, take their energy and use it against them. It had stopped Conway in his tracks, and for a moment she thought that it had also worked on Thomas. He took a deep breath, and something moved behind his eyes. Resignation, Bella thought. Admission of defeat, or at least that Bella was doing nothing but tell the truth. His shoulders sagged, his head bowed a little.

Then he raised it again and looked straight at her, and she saw that his eyes were black.

'Give me the laptop, Bella,' he said with ominous calm.

'No! It's mine, and I won't!'

She sounded like a little child, she realized. But that was what this situation had devolved to. First it had been like a French farce, the husband catching the wife with her on-screen lover: now it was something much more frightening. Thomas knew he had no right to demand to see anything on her computer, and yet he was advancing on her as she backed away . . .

'Stop it! Leave me alone!' she said, even as she edged towards the door.

'Bella. Give me the laptop,' he repeated, still in that eerily calm tone.

Bella had no idea what he would see if he managed to get hold of it: definitely the history of her Skype chats, with only one name on the account she was talking to, clearly a man's. But would he be able to replay what had just happened? Did it record in some way? The mere possibility made sweat spring out on her palms, the laptop slippery in her hands.

She wasn't feeling remotely guilty, however. Thomas deserved this. He had neglected her for a long time, and she had finally found someone who actually wanted her. Big deal.

'I want a divorce,' she blurted out.

Four little words. Five little syllables. But the relief of saying them was immeasurable to Bella. It was more than a weight coming off her shoulders; it was as if a growth had been cut away from her body, leaving her feeling so light she was almost hovering above the ground.

Until Thomas's face darkened with fury and he lunged towards her.

Bella turned and ran faster than she would ever have thought that she could move, her breasts bouncing uncomfortably in the nightdress. She made it to the head of the stairs before her husband caught the back of her robe and dragged her to a halt. It was a brutal jerk, and it scared her badly. Swinging round, the laptop gripped in her hands, she whacked it across his face without even thinking about the damage it could do.

The corner smashed into his nose, and he reared back, grunting in shock. His hands went up to cover it protectively, releasing his grip on her robe. She stared in horror at what she had done, at what was happening between them.

Never had Thomas given her any indication that he had this kind of anger inside him. Never had he laid a hand on her like this.

'I'm sorry!' she said. 'But you shouldn't have grabbed me! Can we—'

Thomas's hands came away from his face. There was no blood, but a bruise already looked as if it was forming across the bridge of his nose, and there was something off with it, something dissonant, as if Bella were viewing him through a distorting lens.

'Fuck you, you bitch,' he said, his voice thick. 'I catch you cheating on me and you *hit* me? I think you broke my nose! How fucking *dare* you!'

'I didn't mean—' Bella babbled, truly frightened now.

Her back was to the newel post at the corner of the balustrade, a heavy dark-wood feature in keeping with the mock-Tudor style of the house. She could have swivelled around it and darted down the stairs, but every instinct was telling her not to run. Her husband, who had so shockingly revealed his lack of self-control, might react once more as a predator animal did when something had defined itself as prey by fleeing rather than standing its ground.

So instead she swallowed hard and said in as strong a voice as she could muster:

'Thomas, come on. You grabbed me, I reacted. Let's take a deep breath, calm down and talk about this like adults.'

It was a very good speech. Her tone was excellent, her words sensible. She thought for a second it had done the trick. And then her husband said slowly, sounding exactly like the child she had just tried to tell him he was not:

'You hurt me. Now I'm going to hurt you.'

She barely recognized him. His eyes were even blacker, the bruise on his crooked nose darkening rapidly, and he was breathing heavily. His hands lifted, formed themselves into open claws, and came straight for her throat.

Afterwards, Bella kept telling herself over and over again that she had never meant to do it. She sat, sobbing, head in her hands to avoid the sight of her husband being loaded onto the stretcher, one of the paramedics putting his arm around her shoulders in consolation, telling her that it would all be okay, getting a foil blanket and putting it round her because she was shivering uncontrollably.

I didn't mean it, ran on a loop inside her head. *I didn't mean it. I had to defend myself, I had to . . .*

All she had done was to shove the laptop towards him in an attempt to keep some distance between them, stop his hands from reaching her neck and starting to squeeze. And because Thomas was lunging towards her, the metal edge hit him squarely in the solar plexus, taking the wind out of him. Bella twisted past him, trying to reach the staircase, all thoughts about not fleeing blotted out now that he had threatened her. If she could make it downstairs, out into the street, she would stand there and yell her head off for help: in the quiet of the Suburb, that would immediately have the neighbours running out to see what was going on.

But she didn't make it. Thomas recovered quickly enough to grab her forearms, the laptop caught awkwardly between them. His breath was hot on her face, his closeness a horrible, twisted parody of the embraces that she had wanted from him so badly and that he had refused to give her. Frustration and anger rushed up in her in a great surge. Thomas was trying to grab her, control her. After the long years that she had yearned for more physicality from him, *this* was what she was getting? *Now* he wanted to put his hands on her?

Fuck you! she thought, and she shoved the laptop at him again, hitting him once more in the solar plexus, so forcefully this time that he doubled up, propelled away from her. They were so close to the top of the staircase that those couple of steps back sent him over the edge. He lost his footing, tripping over his own feet and falling backwards in a contorted ball, banging against the heavily carpeted steps in a series of dull thuds that seemed to go on forever.

Bella stood there, her breath coming fast as she watched her husband's body beat itself again and again into the staircase. Finally, it crashed to the hall floor, resolving itself into a tangle of limbs flung out from his torso at strange angles, and lay entirely still.

She did not move, not yet. She was waiting to see if he showed any signs of getting up, or whether he had been thoroughly knocked out, or worse, by the fall. Her heart was pounding out of her chest. But her strategic brain was turning over, processing what had happened, working out her next necessary move.

After a few minutes in which Thomas remained prone and motionless, Bella took her laptop back into the bedroom, moving slowly because her limbs were trembling, and replaced it on the table. She took off her make-up, pulled back her hair into an elastic, put away her sexy nightwear and changed into a pair of cotton pyjamas. Now she looked like a woman who had been spending the evening quietly at home by herself. Holding on tightly to the wide banister, she walked downstairs very carefully, still shaking with shock; what a comedy of errors it would be if she too ended up in a pile in the hall next to her husband.

Carefully picking her way past Thomas's crumpled body, she headed for the small rolling travel suitcase and leather laptop carrier that were still standing where he had left them, just inside the front door. Unbuckling the latter, she pulled out his own MacBook, her hands wrapped in the sleeves of her pyjama top to conceal her fingerprints. As well as she could with that grip, she bashed it once, twice, three times against the carpeted stair edge, denting and buckling the metal so that it looked as if it had tumbled down the stairs with Thomas, smashing into his nose as it went.

One more thing, and that was the worst of all. Cautiously, Bella pushed at Thomas's body with her foot. Thank God he was lying face down. He didn't move at all: real life, she told herself, was not like horror films. The villain didn't take a catastrophic tumble down a staircase and then jump up a few minutes later, freshly recovered and ready to attack the heroine once again. Kneeling down beside her husband, she took his limp hands and pressed them around the laptop, splaying them wide, so it looked as if he had been holding it during his fall. That would explain any marks or bruising that were not consistent with him hitting against the staircase.

And then, and only then, did she ring for an ambulance.

Chapter Nineteen

'Bell! You poor thing!'

Charlotte tore down the corridor of the hospital, arms outstretched, her clear, ringing, aristocratic tones catching attention, her extreme beauty drawing double takes from even the most hardened of emergency nurses and doctors, especially with the ludicrously handsome Paul following behind her.

Bella looked up from her seat at the approach of her sister and brother-in-law, heads turning behind them to goggle at their sheer gorgeousness. Charlotte dropped to her haunches in front of her twin, pulling her into an awkward embrace.

'I'm so sorry!' Charlotte said against her sister's shoulder. 'I'm so sorry!'

The man sitting on one side of Bella, tapping away on a tablet, cleared his throat, stood up and shifted to an empty row of chairs a little further down the corridor, giving Charlotte his seat. She slipped into it, still hugging her sister, not acknowledging the man in any way, let alone thanking him.

'What *happened*?' she asked, as the woman who had been flanking Bella in the other seat looked up at Paul, gesturing to indicate that he was welcome to take it if he wanted. He shook his head, muttering thanks.

When Bella didn't answer, the woman leant over to Charlotte. She was wearing a simple two-piece dark-blue uniform, a lanyard hanging round her neck.

'I'm Ms Sachs's patient liaison officer,' she said. 'She's in very understandable shock at the moment, and I'm here to—'

'How's Thomas?' Charlotte interrupted impatiently.

'Mr Hargreaves is in surgery,' the patient liaison officer said. 'There's been extensive bleeding and swelling as a result of the head trauma, and he has some broken bones. I'm afraid we can't possibly give a prognosis at this stage—'

'Oh, *Bell*!'

Charlotte snapped her attention back to her twin, cradling Bella's face in her hands now.

'Darling, what *happened*?' she repeated. 'Did you see it? Have they given you anything for the shock? I didn't even know Thomas was home – wasn't he supposed to be away this weekend?'

'Um, I'm really not sure if you should be asking her all these questions when she's not in the best state to . . .' the patient liaison officer began awkwardly.

She wasn't sure, however, of what was correct procedure here. It was unprecedented for a patient liaison officer to be involved in effectively babysitting a patient's wife while the patient was in intensive, long-drawn-out surgery. But her instructions had been to stay with Bella Sachs until she eventually left the hospital, making sure that she had everything she needed.

It was equally unprecedented, in the patient liaison officer's experience, for the wife to have been accompanied to the hospital by someone who her boss had told her was a very high-powered solicitor: this was the man who had just moved his seat, apparently also prepared to stay with his client the entire time she was at the hospital. But then, the officer had never before had to look after a patient's relative who had her name on a whole chain of hotels. She hadn't realized there was an actual family behind the Sachs hotels, like the Hiltons: was there a Marriott family too? Clearly, though, when you were at this stratospheric level, normality bent and expanded to accommodate you.

The patient liaison officer's words stuttered to a halt as Charlotte waved a hand to silence her. Bella had started to speak.

'He came back from Berlin,' Bella told her sister. 'I wasn't expecting him . . . it was so nice to see him . . . he dashed upstairs to surprise me and then he said he'd go downstairs and make us drinks and order some food from Deliveroo. He had his laptop. I always told him not to walk with it open, and he always did! I heard a crash and ran out – he was lying there in the hallway, not moving . . .'

The solicitor, who had been listening intently, his eyes fixed on his client, nodded in approval.

'It was such a shock, it happened so fast!' Bella went on. 'I rang the ambulance, and then I rang Daddy straight after . . . silly, really, ringing Daddy! But I was so scared, and it felt like being a kid again, needing my dad!'

This elicited another nod of approval from the solicitor. Unsurprising, considering that Bella's story had been carefully worked out by him some hours before. Summoned by Jeffrey Sachs, he had arrived at the Hampstead Garden Suburb house very shortly after the paramedics had whisked Thomas off to hospital, thus ensuring that no one from the police could talk to his client before he had consulted with her first.

So by the time the police turned up at the hospital to interview Bella, as was routine in this kind of situation, her story was ready for them in minute detail. The solicitor had asked her a slow, patient, and very careful series of questions, most of which, in fact, were prompts towards the construction of a version of events that would keep Bella as far away from the entire incident as possible. He was an expert at making gentle suggestions couched to end with an interrogation mark.

And once the story had evolved into its final form, the solicitor had impressed on her that it needed no elaboration. She was to keep it simple, to repeat the same series of facts, and if pressed she should say that she was too upset to talk further. The role of Jeffrey's eye-wateringly expensive firm of solicitors, whom he had on permanent retainer, was to avoid any hint of scandal and to minimize any legal misfortune that might occur to him or any member of his family.

Bella knew this perfectly well. It was why, directly after calling 999, she rang her father. Just as she had expected, after expressing due concern for Thomas, he had told her to sit still and wait for a phone call from Greenberg and Clinton. A mere five minutes later it had come, from a soft-spoken man who identified himself as her solicitor and instructed her not to admit anyone else to the house but him; she was under no obligation to talk to the police should they turn up, he had informed her, no matter what they told her. She should not go to the hospital with the ambulance if they offered her a lift; he would take her there himself.

As it turned out, the police had come instead to the hospital, which had provided them with a private room for the short interview. This was no more usual than the assignation of a patient liaison officer to Bella, but everyone knew exactly who Jeffrey Sachs was and what spheres of influence he could summon up if he chose.

It was a poignant fact that for the truly rich, even near-infinite wealth could not entirely protect them from occasional fleeting moments of contact with how the rest of the world lived. You could give birth, or have procedures scheduled, in private hospitals like the Portman or the Wellington, but for A&E visits, let alone brain surgery after a life-threatening fall, you needed the NHS. Still, the NHS was very aware of the need to avoid complaints from one-percenters with connections to the highest levels of government.

'Oh, *Bella*,' Charlotte breathed on hearing her sister's version of events. 'I bet he opened up the bloody laptop to look at Deliveroo and tripped. How awful and stupid, especially when you must have been so happy to see him! I'm sorry it took us so long to see Daddy's call. We were at an opera benefit and had our phones on silent. God, I don't even know what to *say*!'

The patient liaison officer couldn't help thinking that Charlotte did not seem to be exhibiting any symptoms of being tongue-tied.

'Hi, you must be Ms Sachs's sister,' she said, leaning forward. 'I'm Joan. Can I get you a cup of tea or something? Ms Sachs, would you like another one?'

'That would be nice,' Bella said over her shoulder.

'And something to eat!' Charlotte said. 'You must be starving – you haven't had your dinner. Can you bring us the menu?'

The solicitor, although remaining blank-faced as befitted his profession, saved up the sight of Joan's expression so he could imitate it as faithfully as possible to his colleagues the next day at work.

'I'm so sorry, Ms Sachs,' Joan said, almost wringing her hands. 'We don't actually have a menu here! I was going to make you and your sister tea in the nurses' room, which'll be nicer than the vending machine ones . . .'

'Darling, this isn't a private hospital,' Paul murmured to his wife.

'I can see *that*!' Charlotte's gaze was positively blistering as it swept round the corridor, taking in the battered chairs and peeling paint. 'But surely there must be something – a cafe – a bistro—'

'This time of night I'm afraid it's just the vending machines,' Joan said in a tiny voice. 'And there's a McDonald's across the street. I mean, we'd all love the cafe to stay open, obviously, but management—'

'This is *intolerable*! Nothing but *vending machines*?' Charlotte exclaimed. 'Paul, *do* something!'

'I'll get the tea in the meantime, shall I?' Joan said, taking the opportunity to escape the scene. She was briefly detained by Paul, and blushed deeply at his sheer beauty as he apologized for stopping her and asked quietly how long she thought the wait would be before they had any news about Thomas.

'The last we heard was several hours, I'm afraid,' she said, almost unable to look directly at his handsome face, which she recognized from aftershave advertisements. 'They're having to drain off cerebrospinal fluid and that can mean maybe removing a section of the skull—'

Paul waved his hands around frantically, and Joan stopped immediately, recognizing him as one of the class of relatives whose stomach was too delicate for detailed surgical information.

'Would you like a cup of tea as well?' she asked. 'Or a coffee? It won't be what you're used to, of course . . .'

'I'm fine, thank you so much,' Paul answered, with a smile that, though by no means his full wattage, made Joan, once safely in the nurses' break room, fan herself madly for a good few minutes before she could even put the kettle on. She was disappointed, on her return, to see that he was no longer there. Charlotte had sent him home to put together what she called a 'survival kit' for the hospital.

'I found some Darjeeling for you,' Joan said proudly. 'It's really Dr Singh's, but she's in surgery, and I'm sure she wouldn't mind if—'

'Ugh,' Charlotte said, looking at the chipped mugs. But Bella took hers very gratefully.

'Thanks, Joan,' she managed, ducking her head over the cup.

'I put in lots of sugar,' Joan said. 'You always need it, even if you think you don't.'

On hearing this, Charlotte promptly handed her mug back to Joan, who retreated to sit further down the corridor by the solicitor. She offered it to him, but he shook his head politely, so Joan could, in good conscience, treat herself to Darjeeling from a mug, no matter how chipped, instead of vending-machine tea from a polystyrene cup. Charlotte was occupied in compiling a list of things on her phone that she felt Bella needed to sustain herself in these brutal surroundings, which Paul would fill out once he got back home: mineral water, a thermos of good tea, a range of healthy snacks, a cashmere blanket, a pillow, slippers, handwash, hand lotion, a hairbrush, Evian facial spray, eau de toilette, moisturizer . . .

This gave Bella a much-needed respite to explore how she was feeling, now that she had once again recounted her version of events and had it unquestioningly accepted. It was shocking how easy this was proving to be. Blowing on the surface of her tea, Bella realized that she was half believing the solicitor-constructed story herself. It sounded much more plausible than the ridiculously dramatic truth. Even the paramedics who had attended the scene, seeing the laptop lying beside Thomas, had mentioned sympathetically to her how often they dealt nowadays with people who took tumbles looking at their phones or electronic devices.

The solicitor was the only person who knew there was more to the story than Bella was telling. When Thomas had grabbed at Bella's arms, she had had no sense of how hard he was gripping her. She must be stronger than she knew to have made him let go, because on both her forearms the imprints of his fingers and thumb were clearly visible, bruises which would take weeks to fade completely.

And as she had talked to the solicitor, pointing up the staircase, the sleeve of her pyjama top had fallen back a little from one arm, enough to reveal the marks: they had noticed them simultaneously. This was where it became obvious how Greenberg and Clinton earned their huge retainer and mammoth fees for billable hours: even as Bella swiftly covered up her arm again, the solicitor had suggested, without so much as a blink, that she go upstairs and put on something 'warm and comfortable' before going to the hospital. Bella had found a sweater with long sleeves finishing in knitted welts, snug enough that they could not accidentally expose her bruises, and a pair of cashmere lounging trousers.

As she held her mug, she found herself instinctively wrapping her free hand round the other forearm, putting the lightest amount of pressure on the bruises her husband had caused. It barely hurt, but it was a reminder that she had nothing to feel guilty about.

Bella examined her conscience about the fact that her husband was having emergency surgery, and could not find any sensitive point. He had chased her. He had attacked her repeatedly. He had told her he was going to hurt her. Her arms were proof of that. And he would not have stopped there. She was very lucky that she hadn't been seriously injured fighting him off. She hadn't even meant to hurt him, just to get him away from her. Thomas had got exactly what he deserved.

There had been no indication that the police might want

to talk to her again. They hadn't even asked for Thomas's laptop, which the solicitor had told her might be a possibility, in a superbly casual way that was also a tacit enquiry about whether they might find anything on it she might prefer them not to see. Bella had responded instantly that she would be fine with handing over her husband's computer. So far, however, that had not happened, and the two police officers had expressed condolences for her husband's accident in a way that had seemed to make it clear that, short of Bella walking into a police station to make a confession, she would not be hearing from them again.

'You seem so calm, Bell!' Charlotte said, finishing her list for Paul, hitting Send and looking once more at her sister, who could not help noticing that Charlotte had not asked her once what she might like or need. Charlotte knew best. 'Did they give you anything? Do you *want* anything? I could get Paul to bring some of my pills—'

'No, I'm okay,' Bella said, and saw the solicitor shift position. 'I mean, of course, I'm not okay!' she corrected herself quickly. 'But I can't quite connect with anything. I must still be in shock, I think. I didn't even know Thomas was coming home, and then just a few minutes later I was having to ring an ambulance for him!'

The solicitor gave a small nod. That had been one of the points he had made, that Thomas had barely been in the house for ten minutes before falling down the stairs, a fact, he had observed, that would be easily verified by the taxi firm with which his company had their account. Clearly, there had not been time for any kind of fight or even awkwardness to happen, he had said blandly, which was even more corroboration for Bella's version of events.

Not, of course, he had added, that any were needed . . .

'You'll begin to feel the natural emotions of all this sooner or later, when the shock wears off,' Joan said, leaning forward, eager to do her job. 'I'd be more than happy to give you the info on our counselling services—'

'Oh, *do* be quiet!' Charlotte said impatiently to her. 'If Bella needs any counselling, it certainly won't be from someone in this godforsaken place! Do you actually need to be here? I'll wait with my sister. And why are we sitting in the corridor? Isn't there some room we can take her to? Why don't you go away and see if you can find one?'

The solicitor's face went perfectly blank again. Joan, managing not to make a humphing noise, stood up and bustled off, and Bella reached over and took her sister's hand, squeezing it hard, and not just out of gratitude that she had silenced Joan.

'God, Bell, I don't know how to ask this,' her twin said more softly, returning the squeeze, 'but what are they thinking about Thomas? I mean, he's been in the operating theatre for a while, right? Do you have any idea if . . . um . . .'

'It's not good,' Bella answered, her voice oddly flat, which Charlotte attributed to Bella trying womanfully not to break down in public. 'There's brain swelling they need to take down. We don't know anything yet and won't for a while. But Joan's been explaining to me that Thomas rates as a severe brain injury on the Glasgow Coma Scale. She said I have to drastically lower any expectations about how okay he'll be if he survives the surgery.'

This was a direct quote from Joan, who had delivered it with great empathy, quite unaware of the enormous relief it brought to the recipient.

Which means he's very unlikely to be able to tell everyone how he came home and caught me Skyping with my lover and I pushed him down the stairs, Bella thought now. *I'm not a doctor. But when he lay there in the hallway for twenty-five minutes till the ambulance came, barely moving a muscle, I was more and more sure that he wasn't going to wake up on his own. I sat there and watched him and I could hardly even see him breathing. By the time the paramedics got there, it was obvious that he was really badly injured.*

And that I was safe.

'Oh, *darling*,' Charlotte said, putting an arm around her twin's shoulders. She glanced at Bella and saw that her sister's lips were pinched together, defending her emotions: she knew that meant she shouldn't offer any more sympathy for the moment.

'I've left a message for Bart,' she said instead. 'And I talked to Samantha. She sends huge sympathy and love. I've said I'll let her know as soon as we have any news. It looks like Conway might be back with her, by the way. She said they'd both come and visit whenever you want – it sounded like she was talking for them as a couple.'

The sisters exchanged a glance, and in that moment, the solicitor thought, the resemblance between them was positively eerie. It was the absolute similarity of their expressions, even more than their identical features. He could not, of course, know that they had been directly involved in the estrangement between their brother and his wife, and that they were now speculating whether Conway reuniting with Samantha would put him back in the running for the CEO position. If it did, they asked each other silently, would he automatically be once more at the top of their father's list?

'Daddy and Adrianna are coming up to town tomorrow morning,' Charlotte continued. 'They were at Vanbrugh this weekend, but they said of course they want to be in London for you. How things have changed, eh? I wonder what would have happened if he'd still been with Jade! I can only imagine!'

'He was very sweet when I rang him,' Bella said. 'He sent someone from Greenberg and Clinton to look after me.'

She indicated the solicitor. Charlotte acknowledged him with a swift glance.

'Yes, he told me,' she said. 'Very sensible. Everything's okay with that side of things, right?'

'Totally fine,' Bella said, as the solicitor nodded confirmation. 'The police came and took a statement from me, but that's completely standard, apparently.'

'Good,' Charlotte said. 'I mean' – she grimaced – 'it's good to get a line drawn under that, anyway.'

She shifted, moved her arm away, and rolled her shoulders back one after the other, stretching out. When she spoke again, her tone had altered fractionally. Her twin, acutely attuned to every nuance of her sister's voice, sat up a little straighter, wondering what was coming.

'So does this mean that Thomas'll need a lot of looking after?' Charlotte asked, and it was all Bella could do not to show, by the faintest flicker of her expression, that she knew exactly why her twin was asking this seemingly concerned question. Only a few more months remained until Jeffrey was due to crown the new CEO of the Sachs Organization. If Bella's husband required a significant amount of care, that would undeniably sabotage her work on the very ambitious rewards points scheme on which she was counting to make an excellent impression on their father.

Ever since Jeffrey's announcement, Bella had been on the steepest of learning curves, both personal and professional. Now, however, she found herself at the intersection of those two, and it was a considerable shock to hear in her sister's voice Charlotte's sudden shift from supportive twin to work rival.

'I'll just have to wait and see, I suppose,' Bella said, tilting her head a little. Her sister mirrored her gesture, nothing but sympathy in those big blue eyes, no hint of the calculations Charlotte must be making, her assumption that Thomas's head injury might mean that Bella would not be able to put in the work necessary to equal Charlotte's own efforts.

Bella studied her twin sister's face for any hint of triumph, and couldn't find it. Charlotte was really good at this. But then, wasn't Bella also pretty good? She closed her hand once more around her arm, pressing gently on her bruises, reminding herself again why Thomas's welfare was no longer any concern of hers. To her twin, her eyes were limpid, with nothing to indicate how little Bella cared about Thomas's potential recovery.

Is it possible that I could play this game better than Lottie? Bella wondered. *I know her, but she doesn't know me. She thinks I'm her sidekick, the boring one, the plodder.*

Lottie doesn't know me at all. She'd be amazed to find out I was having an affair with Ronaldo, let alone that I was quick and clever and resourceful enough when Thomas fell down the stairs to cover my tracks, swap out the laptops, make sure I rang Daddy to get the best lawyer possible, give the police the story so convincingly that they believed every word.

I think I definitely have the advantage here. Because I know exactly what Charlotte's capable of. But she has no idea about me.

Chapter Twenty

'It's so brave of you going out this evening,' Nita said, shaking her head in sympathy for her boss. Bella, who was having her hair and make-up done, could move neither her head nor her mouth, but she raised her hand and waved it at Nita to show that she appreciated the sympathy.

Behind Nita, a stylist wheeled in a rack of dresses she had picked out for Bella's appearance at the *Style Travel* award ceremony that evening. How things had changed since Bella had sat in that bar with Robin in Chicago, and Robin had so nicely and tactfully pointed out that Bella Sachs could summon any make-up artist or hairdresser she wanted to come to her office! Nita had been delighted to arrange for Bella to be painted and primped, positively rejoicing in the fact that her boss was taking an interest in her appearance. These last weeks had been gruelling: Thomas lying in a coma in the hospital, while Bella bravely threw herself into her work by way of distraction.

Brave, Bella thought, as her lips were outlined and filled in. *That's my new adjective.* Nita had told her all about the upswell of sympathy for her throughout the Sachs

Organization, conversations from the canteen to the board-rooms, the refrain that went:

Bella's so brave considering her husband's in a coma! It's so brave the way she's thrown herself into work! Did you know she barely goes back to their house any more? It's too upsetting for her. I don't blame her – can you imagine using those stairs every day after her husband nearly died falling down them? She's taken over a suite at the Sachs Piccadilly and she's pretty much living there. I don't know if I could carry on with this huge project with my husband lying in a coma! But you know what Bella's like – so conscientious – she doesn't want to let everyone else down. Have you seen her recently? She's lost weight with it all, poor thing, but she's still pushing on. Nita says she's got meetings scheduled from morning to night! It must be so hard for her. She really is so brave.

Bella certainly had lost weight, but it was unrelated to grieving for Thomas. Once the doctors had broken the news to her that Thomas had survived the operation but was, as they had anticipated, in a coma, she was lifted up once more by the sensation which had flooded through her as she told him that she wanted a divorce. Lightness, floating, freedom. It was as if she had been granted the divorce, but without any mess or fuss or division of common property.

All that had shown on her face, however, was a dazed expression, which was perfectly natural under the circum-stances. Her solicitor had driven her back home, and when she walked into the house that she had never liked, full of old-fashioned furniture and noise-muffling carpets, she stood in the hallway, staring at the staircase down which her husband had fallen, wondering what to do next. This was her home, where she had lived for years, and yet she had a very strong urge to turn on her heel, walk out the front door and never come back.

What happened next? What did you do after you had left your husband in a coma and were, frankly, pretty okay with that state of affairs? Was she thirsty? Did she want to eat something? The healthy snacks Paul had brought her from his and Charlotte's larder had been dry as dust and entirely unsatisfying, puffy and nutty and flavoured with algae. She still had bits stuck in her teeth. But she had no desire to go into the kitchen, open the fridge and pull something full-fat from the cheese drawer to cancel out the taste.

Slowly, it dawned on Bella that her dizzyingly light-headed feeling of new-found freedom, of being untethered from an older, old-fashioned husband who was tying her down to a place she didn't want to live – had never, if she were honest, wanted to live – and her lack of appetite were very closely connected. She thought of Thomas's insistence on regularly shopping at the local French delicatessen, the Viennese patisserie, the Italian vinoteca, which he had said they were so lucky to have in the neighbourhood: the cheese and bread, the wine and cake, with which the house was always well stocked.

And she had a blinding flash of revelation: a husband who was avoiding sex with his wife might well fill the house with fattening food so that she would put on weight, feel less happy about her body, press him less often for intimacy . . .

Bella had no desire to be as slim as Charlotte. Apart from anything else, that would be putting herself into direct competition with her sister, and she had enough of that already.

Some basic instinct told her that Charlotte would take Bella weighing the same as her as a full-frontal attack.

No, Bella just wanted to get back to the weight she had been on her wedding day. She had dieted hard to get into her dress, looked lovely in the photographs, been happy with her curves, and thought it was a sensible weight that she could maintain. But that had been before Thomas had started his cheese and patisserie regime, and Bella had promptly put the pounds back on, with a few more to boot.

So that afternoon, very discreetly, Bella moved out to the Sachs Piccadilly and consulted a nutritionist. To the latter she explained, in case anyone thought it odd that she was starting a diet the day after her husband went into a coma, that she was naturally distraught and wanted to make sure she did not fall into bad, comfort-eating habits, but stayed healthy for him during this difficult time. Currently, her breakfasts and most of her dinners were prepared at the Sachs Piccadilly in accordance with her new eating plan, and the nutritionist provided daily lunches at the office, calorie-counted and portion-controlled. Since Bella was in the office every single day, the opportunities for temptation or snacking outside were very few. She knew the five pounds she had already lost were being attributed to grief, which was exactly what she had hoped.

The last thing her solicitor had said to her as he dropped her back home was to advise her to visit Thomas regularly.

'Make sure you're seen at the hospital on a consistent basis,' he had suggested. 'Perhaps you could visit on your way to work, or coming home? Establish a pattern, especially in the beginning. It can't hurt to keep up the best appearance possible, can it? And then, as time goes on . . .'

The solicitor had cleared his throat discreetly, rather than finish his sentence, but they both knew what he meant. The prospects for Thomas recovering from his coma, the doctors had gently explained to Bella after the operation, were very poor. The younger you were when you suffered a brain injury, apparently, the higher your chances; patients under twenty were three times more likely to survive than those over sixty, for instance, and Thomas, at forty-eight, was edging towards the latter odds. It was too early, they had said, to see if Thomas had any motor response or pupillary reaction to light; if he exhibited one or both of those, it would be very encouraging.

But twenty-four hours after the injury, when they had tested for these reactions, the results had been inconclusive, after which there was nothing left but to wait and see.

To be brave.

As advised by the solicitor, Bella had settled into a routine in which a car took her three times a week to the hospital, first thing in the morning. She planned her work around the car trips, took her tablet into Thomas's room, sat there for a respectable length of time, and asked Nita to organize gifts of biscuits and chocolates for Bella to bring, on a regular basis, for the nursing staff, expressing her gratitude for the care they were taking of her husband.

The rest of the time was entirely occupied by work, sleep, and the occasional Skype rendezvous with Ronaldo. And tonight, she was finally going to see him in person! Everyone else assumed that the panoply of grooming Bella was undergoing today – she had already had a mani-pedi that lunchtime – was because of her attendance at the awards ceremony. Only she knew for whose benefit all this effort was being mustered; only she knew that her heart was beating even faster with excitement at the fact that Ronaldo was booked into a room at her hotel and would be sneaking into her suite after the ceremony, than at the prospect of Sachs Hotels winning the Best Chain Experience award earlier that evening.

'I was told your measurements might be a little smaller than the ones I was given,' the stylist said, taking from the rail a black cap-sleeved silk dress embroidered heavily in turquoise, 'so I pulled this one just in case it worked. With your eyes I think this blue would be perfect, and I have some great earring choices in case we go with it . . .'

'I love it!' Nita clapped her hands on seeing the dress. 'And I think it's going to be just right! I'm so happy Bella gets a wonderful night out, looking so lovely – you deserve this, Bella, you really do!'

Bella was genuinely touched to hear the choke in her assistant's voice, realize that she had a lump in her throat. Nita bustled round Bella's chair, which was turned away from the office, facing the windows, to give the hairdresser and make-up artist the advantage of the natural light; she was carrying the dress to show her boss, and Bella's eyes widened in happiness.

It was beautiful. Chic, elegant, classic, with a flattering scooped neckline and a relatively demure hemline. She wasn't trying to look like Charlotte, whose figure could allow her to carry off the most challenging of trends. Bella wasn't the figurehead of a boutique hotel chain; she ran a much larger, much more lucrative company, and looking professional was equally as important as looking attractive.

'It seems light as a feather,' the stylist said, 'but it's fully lined, and has very clever built-in shaping panels ... and I've brought a variety of shapewear too, of course. Which is *totally* standard,' she added quickly. 'I dress size zero ladies who wouldn't go near a red carpet without their Spanx.'

'Oh, thank you,' Bella said, her mouth now lipsticked to perfection. 'Nip me in as much as you can. I'm not a gym bunny – I need all the help I can get.'

'Trust me,' the stylist told her, sounding relieved that this new and potentially highly lucrative client had not taken offence, 'the gym bunnies all wear Spanx too. The ones who give interviews about how much training they do and are always photographed carrying their yoga mats – they're squeezing into their shapewear before big events like everyone else. One of my clients wears two pairs, one over the other!'

The make-up artist and hairdresser nodded in unison.

'So,' Nita said excitedly, waving the dress at Bella as if she were a flag-bearer at a ceremonial event, 'why don't you try it on?'

As she stood up, polished and preened to look the best she had in years, curls bouncing on her shoulders, her skin smooth and glowing not just from the make-up but also the healthier diet she had been eating for the last few weeks, Bella realized that she was dressing up as if she were single and going to a wonderful party where she might possibly meet a wonderful man. And that no one around her seemed to think, for a moment, that this was strange behaviour for a woman whose husband was in a coma.

Yes, she might as well have had the engraved brass nameplate removed from the door to her office suite, replacing it with one that read *Brave Bella*. But practically no one, she thought, had said 'Poor Thomas.' They were concerned for her, how she was reacting to the sudden tragedy; but no one had talked about Thomas as a person, commented on a happy memory they had of him, or mentioned how supportive he had been of Bella.

Looking at her assistant's eager face, it occurred to Bella to speculate whether Nita had actually liked Thomas. In fact, had anyone really liked him? Or had they just tolerated him as her husband?

She had a feeling that, from the general reaction, she knew the answer to those questions already . . .

Chapter Twenty-One

'You look lovely!' Bart said, enfolding Bella in a hug and then stepping back, holding her shoulders, looking her up and down with brotherly appraisal. 'I have to say, Bell, you're being bloody brave.'

'*So* brave,' Charlotte agreed.

'Stiff upper lip,' Conway said, nodding in approval. 'Best way.'

The Sachs family were gathered around a drinks table in the bar, socializing before they moved into the enormous dining room and took their places at one of the best tables, together with a handful of the highest-ranking company executives. Naturally they had purchased several tables for the various divisions of the company, but, for thirty years, the one in the centre of the front row, directly below the stage, had been where Jeffrey held court. He adored awards ceremonies, and was currently surrounded by sycophants and admirers much in the manner of Henry VIII with his entourage.

Adrianna, who had been standing quietly by his side, taking the tiniest of sips from a glass of champagne, glided over to welcome her prospective stepdaughter. She was wearing an ankle-length sequinned dress, extremely form-fitted, which made her figure look even more Barbie-doll than usual, and she moved with the grace of a serpent as she practically slithered towards Bella.

'You look beautiful, Bella,' she said to her very sincerely, placing kisses in the air just above her cheeks. Though she did not touch her shiny lips to Bella's powdered skin, she was close enough that Bella could feel her warm breath, smell her deliciously rich perfume. 'I'm glad to see you looking so well.'

'Thank you,' Bella said, looking up at her father's fiancée. 'I can tell you really mean that.'

Across Adrianna's beautiful face a faint expression of surprise flittered for a moment.

'Of course I mean it,' she said. 'I never say anything I don't mean. How is your husband?'

'There's no news,' Bella said. 'We just have to wait and see.'

Adrianna nodded.

'Perhaps I should wait until you tell me, next time,' she said. 'It's hard for you to keep giving the same answer. But you are good to keep working, coming out to parties, with your hair and make-up nice. You didn't do that yourself.'

This was so clearly a statement, not a question, that Bella didn't even attempt to confirm it.

'You must go on and live your life,' Adrianna continued. 'Your father feels the same as I do.'

It was the oddest feeling, to be mothered by a woman who was several years younger than herself, looked like the winner of a worldwide beauty contest, and had sexually entranced her elderly father into paying a fortune for a divorce so that he could be free to marry her. And yet Bella found herself strangely comforted by it, particularly because it was something that had been lacking in her life for at least ten years.

Because, having battled Jeffrey for her own and her children's rights, brought them up single-handedly after the divorce, and seen them successfully launched into adulthood, Christie had moved to the South of France and declared herself effectively retired from maternal responsibilities. Considering what she had achieved for them, her four children had accepted this and the subsequent toy-boy parade with easy-going understanding, but Bella couldn't help feeling how nice it would have been to have Christie talking to her as Adrianna was doing.

And suddenly she realized she had an impulse to blurt out to Adrianna – who never said something she didn't mean – the question of what *she* had thought of Thomas . . .

'What a lovely new mummy we have, eh?' Bart said affably, interposing himself into the little tête-à-tête. 'Not only is she a raving beauty and a superb hostess, but she actually cares how we're doing! Quite the pleasant change, eh?'

The look that Adrianna gave Bart, Bella thought, could only be described as enigmatic.

'Family,' she said calmly, 'is very important to me.'

'Me too! Here's to ever-closer family ties!' Bart said, clinking his glass of champagne with hers. 'Oh, Bell, you need a drink!'

He gestured at a waiter, who approached immediately

with a tray of filled champagne flutes. Bart had a knack with summoning service staff.

'No news, I suppose?' he said to Bella, who shook her head, understanding that he was trying, tactfully, to ask about Thomas's condition.

'From now on, I think it is best to let her volunteer that,' Adrianna said as Bella took a brimming glass. 'So don't keep asking her.'

'Yes, Mummy!' Bart said irrepressibly. 'Anything you say!'

Adrianna's expression remained entirely unreadable, but her gaze met Bella's for a moment. One elegant eyebrow rose, and Bella was reminded of the way she and Charlotte had used to bond over Bart's latest idiocy when they were children. It felt very familiar, as if Adrianna were a third sister, not the woman who was marrying their father.

'Bella, darling!' Bella's sister-in-law Samantha bustled up to her, giving her an affectionate hug. 'It's so nice to see you looking so well. Excellent job!'

This was a verbal tic of Samantha's, and Bella had heard it enough to realize that it wasn't meant as patronizingly as it sounded. Samantha's air was that of a bright, cheerful head teacher at a private girls' school, doling out support and encouragement for achievements she considered worthy of praise, and 'Excellent job!' was how she praised children and adults alike.

'You've lost weight, haven't you?' Samantha said, casting a swift practised glance at her sister-in-law. 'It suits you. And what a lovely dress!'

There was no side to Samantha; Bella knew this wasn't a dig at how well she was looking while her husband lay in a coma, a sort of merry widow. A coma widow. Samantha's entire ethos was keeping calm and carrying on; during the weekend at Vanbrugh Manor, there had not been the slightest indication in her behaviour that Conway was absent because he had been caught cheating with a sexy Eastern European temptress half his age. He might merely have been on a business trip that sadly prevented him from joining the rest of the family for a delightful break at their father's country home.

'Thanks,' Bella said. Samantha enfolded her in a hug that involved a couple of encouraging pats to the back as they disengaged. 'You look lovely too.'

Samantha was, as always, dressed entirely appropriately, in a long print dress with an asymmetric neckline and pleated skirt. Her face was almost bare of make-up, with no attempt to call attention away from a very horsey mouth by, for instance, using plenty of mascara and liner on her round blue eyes. The Samanthas of this world didn't derive their attractiveness from their physical appearance but from their social status, which was impervious to any change. She could divorce Conway tomorrow and still be the Honourable Samantha.

Bella had no idea why her sister-in-law wasn't doing exactly that. Was it love? Stubbornness? Determination to keep her family together? She was very curious, but she could never put the question to Samantha. Friendly as they were, there was a distinction: they had never been friends. Samantha had her friends already, the people like her with whom she had grown up, gone to school; a closed circle of aristocrats which would never open to any outsiders.

Why don't you ask Adrianna what she thinks? she wondered suddenly. *Look at her, saying so little, watching everyone, observing us so she can dose us with her perfectly chosen cocktails! I bet Adrianna has a pretty good idea about what's going on with Conway and Samantha . . .*

'So,' Bart said casually to Adrianna as Samantha hugged Bella, 'how are things going? Wedding plans smooth as silk, or d'you have any creases to iron out?'

'That is a question a woman asks,' Adrianna responded coolly. 'Do you want to know if I am happy with my dress? Or if the flowers will be just the way I imagined them?'

'No,' Bart said bleakly. 'No, I don't. I was making conversation. I couldn't give a shit about your wedding.'

They stared at each other. The large, crowded ballroom seemed to drop away, the sounds of chattering networkers and chinking drink glasses faint now, heard through fog. It was just the two of them, intently focused on each other, palpable emotions crackling between them. They were standing by one of many small, high drinks tables; Bella and Samantha, on the other side of it, were absorbed in conversation, and there was no one else close enough to overhear. For a little while, they were on their own tiny island.

'Why should you care?' Adrianna said finally. 'There is no reason for it.'

'Not in the least,' Bart said, shrugging. 'I couldn't care less about who you marry.'

There was a long pause.

'You will be there, though?' she asked eventually. 'Your father is expecting you to come.'

'Sure,' he said. 'I always like Venice. Will there be any pretty bridesmaids for me to flirt with?'

'My sisters,' Adrianna said. 'Liilia and Sirje. They are both at least as beautiful as me, maybe more. And they are very . . . friendly girls. More friendly than me. That will be perfect for you.'

'I'm not sure I like friendly girls that much any more,' Bart said. 'Recently, I seem to have become obsessed with cold-hearted, gold-digging bitches.'

Adrianna bit her full lower lip.

'Then you should go for a drink at Farouche,' she snapped. 'The girls there have ice cubes for hearts. Perfect for you.'

'But none of them will make me drink a martini with cocktail onions,' he said.

Another pause. Adrianna, very deliberately, looked away, searching for her fiancé across the ballroom: finding him, she gave him a little wave and blew him a kiss. He beamed back at her.

'I can't stop thinking about you,' Bart blurted out.

'If you are trying to find a way to make me tell your father you should run the company,' she said after a pause, 'I am not impressed.'

'You know it's not about that any more,' he said impatiently. 'Don't pretend. You know I'm telling the truth. And you think about me too. I'm sure of it.'

'Stay away from me,' she said, in a tone as gelid as the hearts of the girls at Farouche. 'You have no choice. Stop thinking about me. You know if your father has any concern about . . . this, I will sacrifice you and feel no guilt at all. I will tell him you have been bothering me, and he will believe me.'

'Oh, I'm sure you won't feel guilty,' Bart said. 'But I know you'll feel *something*. Look at me.'

He made it happen through sheer force of will, staring at her so fixedly that she reluctantly turned back to meet his eyes.

'There,' she said. 'I looked at you. Now leave me alone.'

But even as she spoke, Bart was turning to his sister-in-law, leaning over the table and lavishing on her the ridiculously extravagant compliments that made her blush even as she told him he was being an even sillier boy than usual. Adrianna stood alone, self-assured as always, her expression so blank she might have been a statue of herself. It took her a few moments to realize that, now that Bart was flirting with Samantha, Bella was saying something to her. Adrianna shook her head to clear it and swivelled to an angle that ensured her fiancé's younger son was out of her line of vision.

'Things are crazy at the moment, obviously,' Bella was saying brightly. 'Your wedding, plus the four of us in this battle that Daddy's pitched us into. I was thinking it would be nice for you and me to meet for lunch and get to know each other a bit. You were so busy hosting when we came down to Vanbrugh that we didn't have much time to chat.'

Adrianna's lips curved into a smile.

'I always think that's funny,' she said. 'When you say "came down". Vanbrugh is above London on the map.'

Bella grinned at her.

'I know,' she said. 'It's posh-English speak. You go down to the country and up to town.'

'But you are not posh,' Adrianna said with devastating accuracy.

'No, we're not.' Bella was liking her father's fiancée more and more. 'We're upper middle. Professional, very well off, but not posh. There's a huge difference between us and—'

She nodded at Samantha.

'Because she is Honourable?' Adrianna asked.

'Yes, but it's not only because of the title. She could easily be posh without one. It's about being born into it. You either are or you aren't.'

Adrianna nodded, absorbing this information. 'So, you're asking me to lunch?' she said. 'Is this because you want me to tell your father that you should run the hotel company?'

Bella, who was rationing her champagne in order not to drink too many calories – she had not failed to notice that Adrianna, who ran every morning and was younger than her, also watched her alcohol intake very carefully, presumably to maintain her weight – had just taken a sip. On hearing these words, she promptly spat it back into her glass.

'You're so direct!' she said, when she recovered. 'No, that wasn't what I was thinking.'

'Really?' That eyebrow of Adrianna's rose again. 'You would not be the first of your brothers and sister to try it.'

'Bart,' Bella said instantly. She hadn't heard what Bart and Adrianna had been talking about just now, but it had looked intense. 'And what did you say?'

'He is a stupid boy,' Adrianna said, disdain dripping from her words. 'He should not even run a branch of . . . McDonald's.'

Though relieved that Bart's notorious charm did not seem to have cut any ice with the woman who had their father's ear, Bella, who adored her younger brother, couldn't help but say:

'Oh, he's not that bad. He'd be great at motivating his staff, at least.'

'Maybe I was a bit harsh,' Adrianna said with a brief, twisting smile, the words clearly meaning something more to her than Bella could understand. 'Tell me – what is the word for brothers and sisters? I wanted to use it but I can't think of it.'

'Siblings,' Bella said.

'Yes! Siblings! I hate not to be perfect,' Adrianna unexpectedly admitted. 'It is difficult for me.'

'I have that at work,' Bella confessed. 'I'm a real perfectionist. Which,' she added quickly, 'is *not* me pitching to get you to tell Daddy that I should be CEO.'

'I know,' Adrianna said calmly, allowing herself another small sip of champagne.

'Oh! Okay.'

Bella was an extremely experienced businesswoman. She had been to Harvard Business School, and graduated summa cum laude. Her division of Sachs was extremely well run, and she was known for being a firm and clear-headed negotiator. And yet, her father's fiancée, a twenty-something Estonian with goodness knew what formal education, who had clearly moved to London to meet and snag a rich man, was very disconcerting. Bella simply couldn't read Adrianna.

'Tell you what – let's have lunch *after* Daddy decides,' Bella suggested. 'Then you'll know I'm genuinely interested in what you have to say.'

Adrianna looked at Bella, those angled green eyes much amused.

'You may be the cleverest of all your siblings,' she observed. 'So, what do you want to hear me say?'

'What you think of us, of course!' Bella said, and her eyes were sparkling with amusement. 'I know you have strong opinions on everyone.'

She was intoxicated, and not just from the half-glass of champagne she had drunk after a few weeks of teetotalism. She looked wonderful; her rewards scheme was powering forward ahead of deadline, partly due to her motivational tour of Sachs offices around the world, partly due to her team's superb organizational skills; and she had a rendezvous with her lover booked in for later that evening. Whatever happened with Thomas, whether he woke up from his coma or he didn't, Bella would no longer be tied to him.

'Hah!' Adrianna raised her glass to Bella. 'You are very brave, I think!'

'Everyone's been calling me that since Thomas's accident,' Bella said dryly. 'It's nice to hear it meant in a different way.'

'Mmn,' Adrianna said, her eyelids lowering and lifting. It meant something. Everything Adrianna did meant something. Bella realized that she was looking forward to trying to decode some of her gestures, perhaps over the promised lunch.

'Time to go in to dinner!' Jeffrey announced. Immediately Adrianna was snaking back to his side, the hand not holding the champagne flute slipping discreetly underneath one of his elbows, supporting him even as she made it look as if she were a decorative adjunct to the king, his latest arm-candy consort.

'That woman is a total professional,' Conway muttered to his brother as they fell in behind their father's near-royal procession. 'Worth every penny.'

'I'll say!' Bart agreed cheerfully, though in the same lowered voice. 'I tell you, I need to make sure my jacket's buttoned up the whole time around her at this kind of thing. Just looking at her gives me a stiffie.'

Ever since that encounter in the lime alley at Vanbrugh Manor, Bart had become increasingly obsessed with Adrianna, to the point that, as their recent conversation demonstrated, he was not fully in control of his emotions. With animal cunning, he had realized that the best way to stop people noticing was to hide this in plain sight by joking about it on a regular basis.

'Oh, absolutely,' Conway agreed, huffing out a laugh. 'Me too. Pure sex on legs. Can't blame dear old Pa for spending a king's ransom to have that comforting him in his declining years, can you?'

He dropped Bart a wink.

'I'm putting my time in with the wife and kids now,' he said. 'Made my apologies to Sam, told her it was a moment of madness, never happen again, all that stuff women like to hear. I'm getting back on the straight and narrow with Pa, toeing the line until I take over. Then – not so straight and narrow.' He winked again. 'I want you to be my right-hand man, Bart. I've been thinking about how things will work out after I take the throne. There's a real role for you there if you want it.'

The brothers had pulled aside from the group as the conversation took a professional turn, halting by one of the bar tables. Conway threw an arm around Bart's shoulders in a way that was fraternal but also, between men, signified an assumption of superior status.

'That's very kind of you, Big Bro,' Bart said gravely. 'Good to hear.'

'I know I can rely on you,' Conway said bluffly.

They might not be twins, but the two brothers were very similar, and the sight of them standing together drew many admiring glances. Both so tall and blond, their blue eyes extraordinarily vivid: the two crown princes of the Sachs Organization, each equally handsome in his own way.

'Conway?'

Samantha, who had fallen into polite conversation with one of the Sachs executives who had a seat at the centre table, realized as they reached the dining room that her husband had dropped out of the party. She stopped dead in her tracks, looking back for him, and for a moment her calm demeanour, the centuries of breeding which had trained generations of Honourable Samanthas to keep a politely neutral expression in the most challenging of circumstances, fell away.

It was clear to Bart, looking at his sister-in-law, of whom he was extremely fond, that she was frantic with fear that her husband was hanging back not for a quick word with his brother, but for a woman of the type with whom he had already cheated. A second Adrianna, almost a parody of femininity, with her heavy make-up, cascading hair, figure-hugging dress, and bosoms which owed more to art than to nature. In other words, the opposite of Samantha.

Bart raised a hand and waved vigorously to get Samantha's attention. The relief in her face on spotting him next to Conway, no alluring siren anywhere near the pair of them, was palpably obvious for the split second before her carefully composed facade went up once more.

'She's a really nice woman, Con,' Bart said as they strolled towards where she was waiting in the dining-room doorway.

'I know,' Conway sighed. 'That's the problem.'

'Mmn, that's not really good enough,' Bart said, his tone so unexpectedly serious that his brother shot him a look of frank surprise. 'Not good enough at all. You picked her, you bred with her. She adores you and she's doing a great job bringing up your sprogs. It's stupid to chuck that all away for some Slavic temptress who's more interested in your bulging wallet than anything else.'

'Bloody hell, I never thought I'd hear you lecture me about being faithful!' Conway said rather huffily. 'That's a turn-up for the books!'

'But the thing is, Con, I can, because I've never made any promises to anyone,' Bart pointed out. 'I like Samantha. I don't want to see her get hurt. You've done that once already and it sounds as if you're planning to do it all over again.'

'God knows what's come over you,' Conway muttered. 'Turned into the morality police all of a sudden! Bloody boring, if you ask me.'

Disengaging himself from his brother, Conway joined his wife, putting his arm around her waist, dropping a kiss on her head. Briefly, Bart glimpsed the near-worshipful smile

Samantha gave to her husband, and it was his turn to heave a sigh.

'Damn shame,' he thought as he brought up the rear of the procession. 'She really is a very nice woman.'

Chapter Twenty-Two

'And the winner of Best Boutique Hotel Chain goes to . . . the Sash Collection!' announced Lexy O'Brien, the reality TV star, waving the card on which the winning nominee was written. 'Very classy hotels, I love 'em! Congratulations to Charlotte Sachs, who's looking mint, I must say! Feel free to bung me any freebie stays you have going, won't you?'

Delighted, Charlotte jumped to her feet, Paul deftly pulling back her chair so that she could move seamlessly from the table into the aisle and thence to the nearby steps to the low stage. Lexy was holding the award out to her, cracking one of the bawdy jokes for which she was famous about the shape of it and what uses Charlotte might put it to. An artistically crafted piece of metal and Perspex, it did have an undeniably phallic aspect to the central tower.

'Good girl,' Jeffrey Sachs said in satisfaction as the applause died down and Charlotte gave a short speech about how hard everyone on her team had worked and how excited she was to be taking Sash into more territories, continuing to prove that you could truly deliver a quality boutique experience while still being part of a leading worldwide brand with all the benefits of that organization.

It was not the speech she would have given if her father had not been there, or if she had had the freedom of being CEO and thus able to deliver something much more spontaneous and less robotic. Jeffrey, however, was following along approvingly, mumbling the key words he insisted his employees use about the company in public, nodding as Charlotte rolled them out one after the other. He was very much a top-down manager. Further applause followed as Charlotte swept back down the steps, her wide taffeta skirt caught up in one hand to avoid tripping, the award raised high in the other and a pageant-worthy smile on her face.

'Good girl,' Jeffrey repeated, beaming at Charlotte as she resumed her seat at the table. 'Now let's see how your sister does, eh?'

The Sachs hotels were nominated for Best Worldwide Hotel Chain, but Bella was certain that tonight was not her turn. They had won it two years ago, and it would go to either Hilton or Marriott this year, with her money on the latter. Nita agreed with her. There was nothing to be done about it, nice as it would have been to cruise up to Jeffrey's deadline with an award to match Charlotte's under her belt.

At least they had not wasted precious energy and resources in mounting a big campaign. Nita had organized a stealthy but effective research probe to find out which way the judging was leaning, and after she had concluded that they had no chance of winning, they had let it go and concentrated their energy into the rewards scheme revamp instead. Bella and her team prided themselves on being ruthlessly practical.

Charlotte was already reaching for her phone, snapping

herself with the award, getting Paul to take further shots, uploading them to her social media, her fingers flying over the screen, her smile perpetually photo-ready for the journalists who were gathering around the table to get a quick quote from her for their Twitter feeds.

'Charlotte, is Sash going to be part of the huge Sachs online redo we've been hearing so much about?' one asked eagerly.

'Yes, there's been so much buzz about it already!' a second agreed. 'Are you going to have the same room-scanning abilities and virtual check-in for priority travellers as the Sachs hotels?'

'Plus billing updates on a daily basis on the app?' the first one asked. 'I hear the minibar use is actually going to update in real time, is that right?'

Charlotte's eyes widened and fixed into shape in a way that meant she was absolutely furious but trying hard not to show it.

'Oh, that's going to be rolled out through Sachs first to smooth out all the glitches before we even *consider* applying it to Sash!' she said smoothly. 'We're aware that our guests are looking for a different experience from the ones who visit Sachs, who are a much higher percentage of business travellers. Our clients are—'

'But there's an obvious crossover, isn't there?' asked the first journalist. 'Sachs's business travellers are going to want to use their points when they're holidaying at the Sash hotels, or even staying on business at Sash. Aren't they going to want a full rollout immediately?'

'And what glitches are you anticipating?' The second

journalist, who was faster on the uptake, darted in. 'Any problems with the revamp we should know about?'

Jeffrey, his face like thunder, glared at Charlotte.

'No glitches!' he said bluffly. 'It's going to be smooth as silk! Bella has a top team assembled to drive this through, and I have absolute confidence in her.'

Charlotte hurried to agree with this, the skin around her eyes still fixed into that slightly unnatural, overstretched shape. Jeffrey decreed that Bella and Charlotte pose together for photos, and Bella duly shifted over as Paul jumped up to let her have his chair. Bella could almost smell the fury emanating from Charlotte. Her sister was clearly livid that her moment in the spotlight had been almost immediately eclipsed by questions about the Sachs reward scheme; she was tense as a wire, vibrating with anger, even as she smiled brightly, putting her head next to her twin's, holding up her award for the cameras. The winners would mingle later for longer interviews, once the ceremony was over, but the demands of social media caused a quick flurry around a winner as soon as they left the stage.

'I'm going to the loo,' Charlotte said as soon as the fuss had died down. Standing up, she hugged Paul briefly, and saying over her shoulder, 'Best of luck if I miss yours, Bell! I'm sure you'll win!' she slipped away between the various tables, smiling and nodding at all the people wanting to congratulate her, but not slowing her pace.

Behind her, Bella grimaced momentarily; not only did she know she wasn't going to win, she was quite sure that Charlotte did too. That comment had been a deliberate dig, meant to sink and fester in Bella's flesh as she waited to lose the award for which her division was nominated.

As always happened at awards dinners, the bar area was busy with refugees from the tedium of sitting through the speeches, hard drinkers not content with the wine served at their tables, and journalists updating their various feeds. The world was scarcely waiting to find out who had won all the various categories, but PRs, travel agencies, blogs and the media felt they needed to tweet the results instantly to make themselves seem relevant. The fact that they themselves were pretty much the only consumers of the news didn't worry them in the slightest; it made them look busy and up to date for their bosses, who felt it was crucial to have an active social media presence but had very little idea of what it actually achieved.

They snapped to attention on seeing Charlotte, asking her for a quote and a photo: she called cheerfully that she was heading to the Ladies and would be back soon, making her way with commendable speed, considering her voluminous skirt and high heels, across the spongy hotel carpet and towards the exit on the far side of the bar where the toilets were located. She did not, however, go into the Ladies, but through a second set of double doors, following an obscure path down a corridor and then turning into a small passage that branched off it.

These awards were always held in the same place, a central London exhibition centre, to avoid any competition between rival hotel chains to host the event. A few years ago, when the women's toilets were very busy in the rush after the close of ceremonies, Charlotte had wandered off to look for alternatives, and been very pleased to stumble across a disabled toilet rather oddly situated down this short passage leading to a fire exit.

In subsequent years, she had used it as a brief refuge from the pressure of the awards ceremony: for a few minutes, she could escape entirely from that central table where all eyes were on them, her father assessing each one of his children in turn, whose division was nominated, how they were doing, how much attention they garnered from the assembled press and from their peers. Now, however, as Charlotte cast a brief glance behind her, saw the passage was empty, and tapped quickly on the toilet door, she was about to indulge in a different kind of respite.

Lee pulled open the door and she darted inside, sweeping her huge skirt around her legs so it didn't get caught as he shut and locked it again behind her.

'How much time?' he said, already unzipping his trousers.

'Not much,' she said, dragging up the voluminous skirt, plaid-printed taffeta, its width balanced by a tight black top fitted snugly to her upper body. Under the skirt she wore just hold-ups, no underwear, the outfit selected so that she wouldn't need shapewear on her lower body for the cameras; though her waist was made even slimmer by a elastic cincher which had dug into her all evening, as she grabbed folds of the skirt and pulled them up around her waist, Lee had full, instant access to her crotch.

'I have lube,' he said, taking a small tube from the sink surround and squirting some into his hand, breathing on it to get it even warmer before he worked it between her legs.

'Great! I'm so pissed off I'll definitely need it,' Charlotte said between clenched teeth.

As Bella had sensed, Charlotte was absolutely furious. She had planned this rendezvous with Lee as a delicious treat for herself: a reward if she won, a consolation if she lost. What she had not expected was to win, but to have the triumph whipped away almost immediately because all the bloody press wanted to talk about was Bella's relaunch of her damn loyalty scheme! That wretched thing that would just cause way more trouble than it was worth; that no other hotel chain would touch with a bargepole because it would be so prone to glitches and problems; that Bella had only embarked upon in a desperate, last-ditch attempt to rival her sister for the prize of CEO: *that* was what had stopped the journalists from even offering her congratulations before they dived into asking about whether she was incorporating it in the Sash brand . . .

Lee coated her with the lube, his thumb circling her clit, making sure she was ready before she heard the condom wrapper rip open. She braced herself, knowing he was going to slam into her, that she would barely have time to feel him before he was driving hard inside. He knew exactly what she wanted: a quickie, hard and fast, the contrast between her family dressed up and respectable in the dining room while she was here with her skirt hoicked up around her waist, with her arse bared and him fucking her ruthlessly from behind. The toilet had a rackety old-fashioned extractor fan, which meant that she could make some noise, cry out as his cock drove into her and then keep moaning as her breath synchronized with his strokes.

Her hands were splayed out on the plastic sink surround, her head thrown back. She was watching herself in the mirror, him behind her, pumping hard. He knew better than to touch her hair or her face, to mess up her make-up in any way, because she would have to walk right back to the awards ceremony as if nothing had happened. He held her hips at first, controlling the rhythm, getting it precisely how he wanted it, and then he reached around her body, placing his hands on hers. She looked down at the dark hair on his knuckles and felt the wash of desire that always surged up in her when she saw his hands; it was visceral, absolutely conditioned into her now.

Her mouth was open. Normally she would have wanted his thumb in there so she could suck it, but her lipstick could not be smudged. She could only allow herself the cock inside her, reaming her out, a savage fucking which was exactly what she had told him she wanted a few minutes ago when she sent him a text telling him she was ready to meet, deleting it immediately afterwards.

'You want to come?' Lee panted in her ear.

'I won't – I'm too pissed off – seriously, my fucking sister—' she managed to say.

'Fuck your sister,' he said, and she caught her breath in a laugh and said:

'Yes, fuck my sister! Fuck her, *I'm* the one that won tonight!'

One hand came away from hers, ferreted under her skirt, burrowing under the folds and layers of stiffened fabric, found her clit and positioned his thumb there so he would push her onto it with every stroke.

'You won tonight,' he said in her ear. 'She's sitting there at the table and you're the one who won, the one with her arse in the air getting fucked like a cheap tart – you're the one who's going to come from me fucking you. Let it happen – let go – let that anger work for you, make it a hate fuck—'

Deep inside Charlotte, these words stirred at her core, melting something, sending a surge of moisture over Lee's fingers and thumb.

'There you go! Tell me you hate me!' he encouraged, feeling her reaction.

'I hate you,' she said, bucking back against him, making him groan as she took even more of him inside. 'I hate you, you fucking bastard, I'm going to fucking kill you for doing this to me, I don't even *want* to come—'

She didn't. She hadn't planned this. She had wanted a quick dirty fuck, like he had said, a fantasy of being a tart bending over a sink whose client was too cheap to spend the money for a room. Coming would soften her, make her too relaxed for the battlefield to which she would be returning in just a few minutes.

And yet . . .

'I don't want to come!' she repeated, driving herself down harder, hurting her most sensitive areas, taking huge pleasure in it; this was a wonderfully masochistic moment, fury that her success at the hotel awards had been eclipsed by her sister. 'Fuck you! I won't come, you can't make me . . . I hate you, *I hate you . . . bastard . . .*'

She broke, spasming onto his thumb, her hips pounding a crazy tattoo against the sink, hearing him spit out curses, his hand digging into her frantically as he let go himself, shooting inside her. They were both swearing, a stream of insults and hate words. Charlotte tried to keep her eyes open, to watch the whole scene, to store up yet another memory of their wild sexual encounters for when she was masturbating on her own or having sex with Paul, layering a darker, nastier, much more exciting tinge onto Paul's gentler, slower rhythms.

'Fucking *bastard*!' she practically sobbed, collapsing onto the sink but still keeping enough self-control to make sure she didn't touch it with her face, that her hair was still in its artfully disordered bun on top of her head. Lee was pulling out already, careful to keep his cock away from the folds of her skirt. She moaned in distress as he came out of her, missing him instantly.

But he was right. There was no time to waste. She straightened up, checking her hair, dabbing with a piece of toilet paper to blot the sweat that had formed on her cheekbones. Taking a deep breath, her skirt still bunched around her waist, she stepped over to the toilet for a quick wee. Lee, dragging toilet paper from the roll, wadded some up and handed it to her, then took another handful to clean himself up, wrapping the used condom in it.

'Hope I gave satisfaction, ma'am,' he said, grinning at her.

She stood up and flushed the toilet.

'Keep that sticky cock away from my skirt,' she warned him as she let the folds fall, rearranging them with a few deft, practised flicks of her fingers, the fabric falling neatly back into place.

'Yes, milady!' he said, putting both hands over his penis

and pulling a comic face as she whisked over to the door. 'Hate me still?'

'*So* much,' she said over her shoulder, and she wasn't lying. It was, exactly as she had known it would be, much harder to pull herself together now that she had had an orgasm. She was dizzier, softer, melted, distracted. Swivelling, she turned on the cold tap and ran her wrists underneath it for a moment or two, cooling down. And then it was more than time for her to leave.

'I'll ring you,' she said, unlocking the door.

'Make it soon,' he said.

She threw him a wonderful smile over her shoulder.

'Next time I'm going to make *you* suffer,' she said. 'That's a promise.'

Taking the swiftest of glances down the passage, finding it as empty as ever, she swept out, back to the corridor again, her skirt swirling around her ankles and her heart beating a crazy tattoo which seemed to parallel the movement. She re-entered the dining room as the award for which Bella's Sachs chain was nominated was announced. Marriott was the winner, and as she slipped back into her seat again, politely applauding, she leant across the table to Bella and said: 'It'll be you next year!'

Out of the corner of her eye she saw her father beam approvingly; her statement had been for his benefit. Beside him, Adrianna, that inscrutable creature, glanced at her for a moment, her face as smooth and expressionless as ever.

'Aww, thanks, Lottie!' Bella said, her face open, her smile seeming quite genuine.

It probably is, Charlotte thought. For all her hard-headedness in business, Bella tended to think the best of people in her personal life. She had certainly done so for Thomas, that dry stick of a husband who had acted as if he were decades older than he was. Bella had attributed the best motives to everything he said, seemed to find even his dullest utterances interesting, looked at him as lovingly as if he had actually had a personality worth caring about.

Charlotte had always assumed that Bella must have a major father complex. It could be the only explanation for her picking Thomas, of all people. Charlotte wondered whether Bella had noticed that people had expressed barely any regret for her loss of Thomas. Charlotte had heard this absence multiple times: Sachs employees gushing with sympathy for Bella's situation, but struggling to muster up anything positive to say about Thomas himself beyond a rather feeble observation that she must really miss him and they were so sorry for what she was going through.

And with her husband in a coma, her twin was positively flourishing! Look at Bella now: she must have lost half a stone. Someone had finally told her to get her hair and make-up professionally done for big events, and Charlotte was willing to bet that a stylist, either a private one or a consultant from a Knightsbridge department store, had been involved in picking out that dress for her.

Dowdy, podgy Bella was now looking more and more like a boss. Groomed, sleek, suitable for promotion; not just a drudge who toiled away in the shadows, keeping her head down, working on the boring bread-and-butter side of the company. As Charlotte sat back, reaching for her glass of wine, she took stock of where she stood in the competition with her siblings. Had Conway's reconciliation with Samantha swung Jeffrey back towards the assumption that his older son would be the natural head of the Sachs Organization? Or was he truly ready to promote a woman to head of the company?

If he was, Charlotte would have taken it for granted that she would be the one chosen. But look at all these journalists who had flooded over after her win to ask her, not why she thought she had triumphed tonight, but about whether her hotels would be incorporated in her bloody sister's fantastically exciting new scheme! The ceremony was winding down, some diners already pushing back their chairs, wanting to head for the bar, stretch their legs, circulate and network. And that freed up the journalists and bloggers, a horde of whom were surging over to their table. It was obvious by the direction they were taking that they were almost all heading in Bella's direction – Bella, who had lost that evening, rather than Charlotte, who had won . . .

She glanced over at her father. Suddenly he looked very tired and frail, as if he had expended all his available energy on keeping alert and attentive during the awards. His shoulders drooped, and there were shadows under his eyes and cheekbones that she had not noticed before. His hand reached out for Adrianna's, and it looked like an ancient claw on the white tablecloth, veined and bony, grabbing for his fiancée's elegant, manicured fingers like a predator eager to consume a tender morsel of flesh.

He's old, Charlotte thought with a little shudder of shock. *Daddy's really getting old now.*

It had been less noticeable when Jeffrey was with Jade,

Charlotte realized. Jade's style had been pared-down and unshowy. Her appeal to Jeffrey had been as an intellectual, black-wearing art gallery consultant, with an austere haircut and practically no make-up, dressed in artistically draped Japanese designer creations. She gave him artistic credibility as he made the transition from hotel mogul to art collector and patron and museum gala attendee, a definite ascension of the social ladder to high society. When Jade had decided that she wanted to transition, in her turn, to county lady in Huskies and Barbours and Hunter wellies, she had remained as bare-faced as before, her skin now more weatherbeaten. She was still striking because of her strong bone structure, but she looked her age, late forties.

Jeffrey had the regular pattern of trading in his wives for an entirely different model two decades younger than the last one. But this time the contrast with twenty-something Adrianna was deeply unflattering to him. How much more sensible his friend and contemporary Rupert Murdoch had been when he decided to settle down with the sixty-year-old Jerry Hall, a beautiful woman who, however, was not so eerily smooth, so completely devoid of any visible signs of ageing, that she made him look as if he had one foot in the grave!

Frail as Daddy seems, he'll definitely survive long enough to make his decision about the CEO job, Charlotte thought, watching Adrianna help him to his feet as effectively as she had guided him to lean on her while she accompanied him to the table. *Adrianna'll make sure of that. If necessary, she'll walk him down the aisle to make sure he gets there, even if he drops dead at the altar – after he's said the vows, of course.*

'Bella?' a journalist from *Style Travel* said eagerly, sitting down next to her as chairs cleared, Sachs executives rising to their feet as their boss stood up. 'Can I ask you a few questions about this new scheme you're rolling out? Believe me, it's *all* the industry's talking about!'

Jeffrey's head turned slowly, deliberately. It was like watching an elderly vampire, about to climb into his coffin in the early hours of the morning, scent a fresh blood source and register his interest. Even as Adrianna began to guide him across the room, he looked back at Bella and the *Style Travel* writer, his skin sagging and grey under the unflattering lights of the conference centre dining room, but his eyes bright with renewed interest and calculation.

Fuck, I need to up my game, Charlotte realized with a sinking heart. Everything she had done up till then, all the work she had put in, had clearly not been enough. This evening had been supposed to be her triumph, the culmination of all her scheming and planning. Conway had been exposed as a cheater who made Jeffrey's new relationship look seedy by association; Bart was a joke, Bella a plodder. Charlotte, however, was the award-winning creator of a fantastic industry brand, which had been duly recognized tonight with the award sitting in front of her. She should be the obvious choice for CEO of Sachs, and yet . . .

Charlotte was extremely clear-sighted: there was no mileage in fooling herself. Ever since that day when Jeffrey Sachs had allowed his mistress to throw his first wife and their children out of their home, Charlotte had sworn that she would never allow anyone to blindside her the way her mother had been blindsided. She ran her marriage, her career, her family; on the major decisions in each of those arenas, her opinions were the only ones that counted. Now it was only too obvious that she needed to take the reins of her ambition and drive it as she had never done before.

And it's because of Bella and this bloody points scheme! she thought bitterly. Who saw *that* coming? What if her twin actually pulled it off?

Charlotte looked over at her sister, who was chattering away to *Style Travel* and other journalists who had flocked to take Jeffrey and Adrianna's seats. It was an impromptu press conference, the attention entirely focused on Bella even as Charlotte sat with the huge, eye-catching award in front of her.

Something had to be done. And Charlotte, reaching for her phone, knew exactly what her next move needed to be.

Chapter Twenty-Three

The days after the *Style Travel* awards ceremony passed in a positive whirlwind for Bella. That night, when she returned to her suite at the Sachs Piccadilly, it took only five minutes for Ronaldo to appear; he had flown in from the States that night, landed just a few hours ago, and had been waiting in his room for her text summoning him, sent the moment she walked in the door. Carrying flowers and champagne, beaming from ear to ear at being reunited, he exclaimed with such flattering enthusiasm at the sight of her in her beautiful dress and make-up that she felt as if it had been she who had just won an award, not her twin sister.

For the next three days, her home office, which she had set up in the dining room of the suite, was entirely unused. Bella, who had been working pretty much around the clock, gave herself a much-needed holiday for those evenings. She would have loved to go to the spa with Ronaldo, book couples' massages in the suite, have a cocktail together in the piano bar, but of course that was impossible. She could not even have dinner out with him; although there was nothing odd about her catching up over a meal with a childhood friend when he found himself in London on business, she knew that she would be absolutely incapable of sitting across a table from such a handsome man while maintaining the kind of neutral behaviour that would allow her to get away with this cover story.

And, she thought blissfully, neither would he. His joy in seeing her again was so unabashed, so obvious, that it would be all too clear to the waiters and fellow diners that, as her husband lay in hospital being kept alive by machines, Bella Sachs was out on a date.

What she would do when it was time to reveal her relationship with Ronaldo, she had no idea. How long would it be necessary to wait? The more time that passed, the less likelihood there was of Thomas regaining consciousness. Bella's plan was to consult in due course with a PR team who specialized in maintaining celebrity reputations.

They cost a great deal, of course. This kind of PR was the most expensive, but it would be worth every penny, and she couldn't entrust something of this delicacy to the Sachs in-house press team. The in-house team was very efficient, but reputation management was not their speciality, and frankly the work was above their pay grade. As in all professions, gradations existed based on skill and connections and ability to manipulate the public. Sending out press releases to travel journalists, throwing parties to promote new hotel openings, was on a much lower level than the ability to pull strings behind the scenes, block negative stories, plant positive ones, and spin the facts until they blurred into a dizzy whirl, resolving miraculously into a shape that was as flattering as possible to the client who was paying them.

Unquestionably, this story could be told well and plausibly. Ronaldo, reading in the press about the tragic misfortune that had happened to the husband of his childhood playmate, would contact Bella to offer sympathy and condolences. They would arrange to meet up the next time he was in London or she was in Chicago, and Bella would be greatly comforted by this renewal of their friendship as she mourned her husband. Gradually, as the prognosis for Thomas to make any kind of recovery became increasingly grim, Bella would lean on Ronaldo for support and their relationship would morph into something more intimate.

The PR team would delicately point out how much older Thomas was than Bella, and stress that she and Ronaldo were far more age-appropriate. They would note that it was marvellously egalitarian of Bella to be dating the son of her family's housekeeper, and very generous of her father to have financed Ronaldo's education. The whole story, Bella hoped, would be extremely positive for the Sachs family in the press, if handled correctly.

And, of course, if Jeffrey approved it. This was what made Bella nervous whenever she considered the future. She and Ronaldo had not talked about anything long-term, but how could she not feel excited and positive about what was happening between them? A passionate affair while she was visiting his home town, followed up by sexy Skype sessions, was one thing, but the regular contact ever since, the conversations and texts about work and life and family, the eager plans to meet up again in London, the flowers, the champagne, had moved them into relationship territory, even if they had not had the conversation that officially made them exclusive.

Ronaldo was certainly acting more like a boyfriend than a lover: Bella had kissed enough frogs in her single years to know the difference. They talked about how their days had gone, complained about their work issues and offered each other suggestions on how to fix them. Ronaldo often said wistfully how much he would like to be able to do normal things with Bella on his next visit to London: take a Thames lunch cruise, go out to dinner, walk in Regent's Park, even stroll around the old Little Venice neighbourhood, looking at the houseboats moored along the canal, as they had used to do when they were children.

He was respectful about Bella's situation with Thomas, of course. It was a unique predicament, to have started an affair with a married woman whose husband then fell down a flight of stairs and ended up in a coma. The subject was on hold, however, due to Bella's huge work push. Apart from an occasional polite enquiry about her hospital visits, there was a tacit agreement between the couple not to mention Thomas, not until Bella's revamp of the Sachs hotel tech upgrade and membership scheme had rolled out. Ronaldo had simply said he wanted to support her by following her lead until the enormous work pressure was off her back, for which Bella had been very grateful.

No, it was not Ronaldo she was worried about. It was her father. This would not affect his decision about who would be CEO, as she was certainly not going to tell him until that was settled, but he was still her father, and she couldn't help but be nervous that he would rain down hell on her for this.

Maybe I should talk to Adrianna about it, Bella thought, *over that lunch we agreed to have. She's obviously keen on bringing our family together. She might even sympathize – it's not like she comes from a posh background herself, I imagine. After the honeymoon I'll get Nita and Adrianna's assistant to set up a date.*

Bella wished the wedding hadn't popped into her mind. It brought everything so very close. Her upgrade was due to launch in a mere three weeks! The wedding, to be held at the Sachs flagship hotel on the Grand Canal in Venice, would happen just a fortnight later, with the announcement of the CEO job scheduled for that same weekend. Jeffrey was enjoying toying with his children's nerves by creating drama right up until the last moment.

Bella couldn't help wondering how Adrianna felt about her wedding being so closely tied in with Jeffrey's final decision. It was intended as a declaration of love, a statement that he was abdicating power in order to dedicate his retirement to his beautiful new young wife. But it would mean that his four children would be on edge at best, possibly even at each other's throats, during the entire stay, with its elaborate dinners, boat trips to private islands for al fresco lunches, and the ceremony itself.

Then Bella shrugged. Adrianna wouldn't care a whit, not with her goal so close: the only thing that would matter was getting the ring on her finger. Bella had to give Adrianna great credit for not pretending that she was madly in love with her octogenarian fiancé. There were no cooing displays, no sugary protestations of devotion, no theatrical caresses that would make onlookers cringe with embarrassment.

Adrianna was conducting herself, all things considered, with great dignity. Much more than Jade had shown when she had been ousted from the role of tycoon's wife.

The memory of Jade getting her comeuppance, of the sheer pleasure it had been to hit her loathed stepmother with a bolster so hard she knocked her into an armchair, made Bella smile briefly with pleasure. But then her thoughts slipped, as they so often did nowadays, triggered by her father's upcoming wedding, into picturing her own. Not, of course, the ceremony she had gone through with Thomas, but her dream wedding to the man she was quite sure was the love of her life. Many times already Bella had pictured herself walking down the aisle, Ronaldo waiting for her at the altar, dark and gorgeous, his smile on seeing her flashing white and perfect against his smooth olive skin, his face lighting up as it always did when he clapped eyes on her . . .

'Bella!'

Nita bustled into her boss's office, her eyes so wide that Bella could see the white all around the dark irises, her cheeks flushed and her head wobbling slightly. Nita was normally so composed that Bella instantly knew something very big had happened, and her heartbeat stuttered. As her entire focus was about the relaunch, her instant assumption was that something had gone very badly wrong with the programming. But the next second someone appeared behind Nita, and Bella knew that this emergency was nothing to do with her current project.

'Samantha!' she exclaimed, standing up, taking in the sight of her sister-in-law with a degree of shock. Samantha was as immaculately dressed as always, in a green coat open over a fitted, belted, photoprint dress, her hair and make-up perfect, but she looked as if she had clothed and painted a mannequin of herself. Her face was very white under the foundation and blusher, her movements jerky, her eyes wide and blank.

'Can we get you anything?' Bella said, glancing to Nita for a brief, charged moment and then back to Samantha again. 'Tea? Coffee? Juice? Uh—'

'I'll get some tea sorted out,' Nita said, as Samantha seemed temporarily incapable of speech. 'And biscuits. Tal?' she called. 'Pot of tea, milk and sugar. And use the breakfast blend. Make it strong.'

Nita guided Samantha across Bella's office to the arm-chairs by the window. Samantha, near-catatonic, sank into one of the chairs, her coat still on.

'I'll leave you alone,' Nita said, the reluctance almost audible: she was clearly dying to stay and hear what was coming.

The office door shut quietly and silence fell, a silence which seemed as loud as a symphony orchestra, a palpable presence in the room. Bella's mind was racing with speculation, but she sat quietly without asking questions, sensing that this was the right tack to take. Charlotte would have started chattering away immediately, but Samantha clearly needed to choose her own pace. She could have been in church, or waiting for an interview, sitting there with her hands folded neatly in her lap. In her pretty coat, so ladylike with its covered buttons and angled pockets, and her equally ladylike T-bar shoes, she was the picture of a woman who knew exactly who she was, who had her life completely organized and together. Until you looked at her face.

Her lips, tinted in a pale coral, finally parted.

'He's been doing it forever,' Samantha said. 'Forever.'

Bella's phone rang: not her mobile, but her desk phone. Every call on this line was filtered through Nita, which meant that her assistant had decided that this was important enough to interrupt this moment of family crisis. Muttering an apology, Bella jumped to her feet and went over to the desk to pick up the handset.

'Don't say anything,' Nita's voice came. 'Don't put me on speakerphone! But I've just heard she was up on the twentieth floor before she came down to see you.'

There was no need for Nita to specify further. At the Sachs Organization, 'on the twentieth floor' meant only one thing: Jeffrey's offices.

'I don't know what was said,' Nita continued tensely. 'I'm trying to find out. Just thought you should know.'

'Goodness, Nita,' Bella said smoothly. 'Of course hold my calls! You really didn't need to check.'

She clicked the End Call button and put the handset down on the desk, returning to the armchair.

'So sorry about that,' she said to her sister-in-law. 'We won't be interrupted again.'

'It's fine,' Samantha said blankly. Her hands were still lying in her lap. She did not look as if she had moved a muscle. She was, Bella thought, the zombie version of herself.

'You were saying . . .' Bella prompted gently.

'Conway's been cheating on me since we met,' Samantha said. 'I mean, I suppose that wasn't quite cheating, but it would have been as soon as we were serious, and that

330

happened fairly fast. Maybe he doesn't even see it as cheating? I'm genuinely questioning whether he has any moral compass whatsoever. Can a sociopath even cheat, technically? Does that count? If he doesn't have a conscience, how can he make vows or stand by them? And if he can't, it isn't cheating at all, is it, really?'

It took all Bella's professionalism not to flinch back in horror, or grip the arms of her chair for support. It was as if someone else were speaking through Samantha's lips, a character in a modern psychological drama where people debated abstract concepts by way of conversation. Bella had never heard Samantha talking like this before, and it was frightening.

Her sister-in-law had stopped, and was fixing Bella with a wide-eyed stare of enquiry, clearly requiring an answer.

'I don't know,' Bella said honestly. 'I'm not quite sure I understand.'

'Prostitutes,' Samantha said. 'They call them escorts when they're this expensive, but they're prostitutes, of course. It's just a way for the men to feel better about themselves. If you pick up some poor woman waiting below an underpass, or next to some horrible vacant rat-infested waste ground, and get her to suck you off in the back seat, you probably like that kind of thing. Even *prefer* it to be dirty and sordid and nasty and probably disease-ridden. Or maybe you just can't afford anything more expensive? I really don't know. But I know that dressing up some girl from Eastern Europe in designer clothes and charging hundreds of pounds an hour for her to spread her legs for you is still prostitution, just as much as that poor woman by the underpass with the rats.'

Samantha's clear, cold voice, fluting and aristocratic as ever, was oddly detached, as if she were reciting something in which she had no personal interest. There hadn't been a question at the end of her speech, so Bella kept quiet and eventually Samantha started again.

'Conway's just like his father,' she said. 'I should have known. Mummy always used to say, Look at a man's father, especially if he's the oldest son. But we didn't know about Jeffrey then, did we? We didn't know what a whoremonger he was. We thought he'd done the typical thing – traded in his first wife for some gold-digger in a gallery who caught him in a weak moment and made him feel cultured. That happens all the time with bankers – they make the money and then they want to buy some prestige to go with it. But this new woman! The Russian girl he met in the same club Conway's last one used to work at! Thinking that she's so much better because she worked behind the bar instead of in front of it!'

Samantha was almost spitting now.

'With her *special cocktails*! My God! She might as well have been pulling pints!'

Bella resisted pointed out that Adrianna was in fact Estonian. But an odd feeling was beginning to creep up on her, and it took quite a while for her to identify it: surprisingly, it turned out to be an inexplicably strong urge to defend Adrianna from Samantha's character assassination.

'Like father, like son, the headlines said,' Samantha continued. 'Ugh, if I *ever* thought that about Georgie, I'd kill myself!'

She shuddered as she named her beloved son.

'I did wonder, when the story broke and we were all over the press – which we *hate*, we really do *hate* in my family,' she said, leaning forward, her stare now even more intense. 'Mummy says you should be in the paper three times in your life – your birth announcement, your wedding, and your obituary. Hatched, matched, dispatched. It hasn't exactly been easy for me being in the press so much. But I did it for him because I loved him, and because it was good for the company. That was our children's inheritance, you see.'

A tap came at the door, and Bella called to Nita to come in. She knew it wouldn't be Tal, even though this task was more suited to a subordinate: Nita wouldn't dream of passing up this chance to see what was going on in Bella's office, take in the scene with her beady, highly observant gaze.

Bella was quite right. Nita bustled in, placing the tea tray on the table between the two women.

'Sugar would be good,' she advised, tactfully not looking directly at Samantha as she did so. 'Put plenty in the tea. There's some nice shortbread and butter cookies too.'

Nita's glance at Bella as she whisked out of the room again and shut the door behind her was comprehensive, a brief nod all Bella needed to confirm for her that Nita and Tal were working the phones and email, reaching out to everyone at Sachs who might have information on what had just happened in Jeffrey's office on the twentieth floor, and whether Samantha had chosen to visit Bella directly afterwards, or if she had made any other stops along the way . . .

As Bella poured the tea and added both milk and sugar, two teaspoons each, she was reminded horribly of the sweet Darjeeling the patient liaison officer had made for her as she waited to hear news of Thomas's operation. It had helped, though. Nita was right. Samantha made no objection when Bella handed her the cup, staring down at it as intently as if she had already drunk it and was trying to read her tea leaves.

'Women like me don't leave just because of infidelity,' she said to the milky brown liquid. 'It's not the way I was brought up. We turn a blind eye and remind ourselves that we're the mother of their children. But then, when they're up to something, it's usually with someone else's wife, and it doesn't last that long. They're just letting off steam. And it keeps it in our social set. No messy gossip.'

Bella could only be grateful that she had her cup and saucer in her hands and was blowing to cool down her tea, so that she could keep her head lowered and not meet Samantha's gaze at this point.

'I still don't quite understand,' Bella said to the cup. 'I mean, the problem is that—'

'He's been paying prostitutes huge sums of money for the entire time that we've been together,' Samantha said simply. 'I got someone to go through his emails and bank records. It was terribly expensive, but we can afford it!'

The horribly dry laugh that issued from her throat was painful to hear.

'And of course a lot of Conway's prostitutes were classed as business expenses, too!' she added. 'Under the category of entertaining clients! Very tax-efficient! But believe it or not, his cheating isn't actually the main issue. I'm sure that's quite the surprise, isn't it?'

Bella's head jerked up, and she felt herself unable to control her expression. What could Conway possibly have done

that was worse than a near-constant procession of prostitutes during his marriage? Bella was sadly unsurprised by
this revelation about her older brother. While she wouldn't
go so far as to call him a sociopath, she had always known
that Conway was intensely selfish. If he wanted to have sex
with a lot of strange women, he wouldn't consider his marriage vows any barrier to his desires. Samantha had been
absolutely right about the oldest son taking after his father:
Conway was a chip off the old block.

Still, women like Samantha were supposed to stand by
their husbands at all costs, support them right or wrong,
work behind the scenes and charmingly in public to build
their careers. Samantha had already taken Conway back after
the public scandal. Something truly extraordinary, truly
unpardonable must have happened to drive her self-
possessed, exquisitely ladylike sister-in-law to these lengths—

'Conway's set up an asset protection trust in the Cook
Islands,' Samantha informed her in a flat voice. 'I don't
imagine you know what that is, do you? I didn't. It's terribly
high-level tax-avoidance stuff.'

Bella had worked that out for herself already at the mention of islands. This was very, very bad indeed. No wonder
Samantha had gone for broke with Jeffrey.

'They're in the middle of the South Pacific,' Samantha was
explaining. 'Much further than the Cayman Islands or Ber-
muda! And if you want to sue a trust, you have to fly out and
do it there with their own courts! I checked with some estate
lawyers. They say it's even harder to get money out of there
if it's owed to you than *Switzerland*. So if Conway stows
money in a Cook Islands trust he controls – I know that's

not supposed to happen, but there, apparently, they can set these things up so that the settlor actually runs things. They appoint puppet trustees who do what the settlor wants. Anyway, once it's in, it's impossible for anyone but him to get it out again. And obviously, he's done this because he's planning to divorce me and try not to pay me what he owes.'

Bella had reached this conclusion too.

'You know what this means?' Samantha asked rhetorically. 'He's cheating our *children*! He's taken away money that ought to belong to George and Emily! They deserve to grow up in the best circumstances possible, not be short-changed in any way. And then, imagine if he's hiding that money away because he wants to marry some Russian prostitute and have children with *her* who'll get what George and Emily ought to have, what's *rightfully theirs*—'

Samantha was almost panting in fury now, the skin around her eyes stretched wide like an animal's.

'Drink some tea,' Bella heard herself say. 'Honestly, it really will help.'

Samantha raised the cup to her lips and drank the now-cooling contents almost in one go, very much as a zombie would have done if a zombie had been commanded to finish its tea.

'That's why I went to see your father,' she said, setting the cup and saucer down, so well trained in social niceties that there was barely a chink as the china touched the tray. 'I knew he wouldn't care at all about the trust itself. I'm sure he found all sorts of ways to hide money from your mother and from Jade. But I knew he would hate the idea of Conway being ready to leave me. Of course, Conway was planning to do it after he was appointed CEO! I'm not a fool. He was getting all his ducks in a very neat row, making things look good to his father, as if everything was back to normal. Then he'd have got the job and promptly kicked me out so he could move in some whore, exactly like your father did! But I scuppered that!'

She took a deep breath.

'That tea *was* a good idea,' she said, reaching out for a piece of shortbread. 'I feel better. Now I think about it, I haven't had a bite to eat all day. I couldn't face it.'

Bella took Samantha's empty cup and refilled it.

'I'm very sorry,' she said. 'My brother's a total bastard.'

'He *is*,' Samantha agreed vehemently. 'Which is another reason he shouldn't be running Sachs, in my opinion. I'm not being naive. Of course a business needs a strong boss, and sometimes you can't be overscrupulous about how you go about things! But this company is my children's inheritance. They'll be part of the family trust one day. One of them may even end up running the company. I don't want a sociopath who only thinks of himself and his own interests taking charge of it.'

Bella bit her lip to avoid pointing out that the Sachs Organization had been created and built into a hugely successful entity by Jeffrey, who exactly fitted this profile.

'I know your father wouldn't care about that,' Samantha continued. 'Or the asset protection trust. But he *does* care about my divorcing Conway, and believe me, that's definitely going to happen!'

That awful dry laugh issued from her lips once more.

'I might as well do it before he does it to me, mightn't I?'

she said. 'There's no other reason for him to be hiding his assets! Your father was absolutely furious at Conway trying to pull a fast one. Convincing me to go back to him for a little while, just until he got the CEO job, and then dumping me like – like a piece of used tissue. It wasn't really me he was trying to trick, you see. It was your father. And Jeffrey will never, ever forgive that.'

She picked up her teacup again and started to sip.

'So that's done,' she said. 'I've had my revenge. My family is entirely behind me when it comes to divorcing Conway, I can assure you. No one expects me to somehow try to hang onto him under these circumstances, even if I could. And I need to take very good care of Georgie in particular, make sure he doesn't come too much under Conway's influence. No one must *ever* say "like father, like son" about him.'

'I'm so sorry,' Bella said again, but her brain was racing. This really did sound as if Conway's goose was cooked so thoroughly that it was charred black.

Over the rim of her teacup, Samantha was staring very seriously at Bella.

'As I was leaving, your father asked me who I thought should run Sachs,' she informed Bella. 'And my answer was you.'

Chapter Twenty-Four

Bella was grateful she wasn't holding her own cup of tea; she would probably have dropped it on hearing this statement. Of course, Jeffrey wasn't going to make his decision based on his daughter-in-law's opinion, but still . . .

'There's quite a lot I still have to tell you. You haven't asked me why I hired someone to look into Conway,' Samantha pointed out.

'I suppose I assumed you had suspicions,' Bella said, frowning. 'Because of something he was doing? Or not doing?'

Samantha simply shook her head, still holding Bella's eyes with her own. For the first time that afternoon, she didn't keep talking; she waited, as Bella had been doing, while Bella turned the question over and over in her mind. And came to a single and unpalatable conclusion.

'*Oh*,' she said.

Samantha nodded.

'I was at a charity luncheon a few days ago,' she said. 'And I found myself having a rather odd and unpleasant conversation with a woman I shan't name, but who clearly seemed to feel it was her business to warn me about Conway. Not just him having affairs – there was a hint about his salting money away too. It was done in a way that she could pretend she was talking about another couple, but I'm not a fool. It was clearly aimed at my situation. I found it strange enough that I googled her when I got home. She's on several charity committees with Charlotte. Lots of photos of them together at balls.'

Bella swallowed. This was what she had herself concluded.

'So I don't think Charlotte should profit by what she's done,' Samantha said. 'She must have investigated Conway, to be aware that it would be worth setting me onto him. Her own brother! And now, frankly, I'm wondering how the press found out about that Russian girl from the bar. It's quite a coincidence that the story broke after Jeffrey invited you all over to tell you about this stupid competition of his, isn't it?'

Accustomed as Bella was to keeping her face straight during tricky negotiations, she couldn't help but react to this: instinctively, she cringed in guilt. Very fortunately for her, Samantha took her response as a sign of horror at the idea that her twin sister might have gone to such extreme lengths to disqualify her brother from competing in the race for the job of CEO of Sachs.

'I'm afraid so,' Samantha said. 'I can't prove anything, of course. But if she was prepared to set a friend of hers onto pushing me into hiring a private investigator, why shouldn't she also have passed a story to the tabloids to discredit Conway?'

'I don't know what to say,' Bella muttered, ducking her head. 'I'm so very sorry about my family.'

'You didn't do anything!' Samantha said kindly, which just added to Bella's shame, especially as she knew that she was never going to confess to Samantha about the role she had played in finding a PI to expose Conway's cheating. 'I genuinely think this ridiculous idea of Jeffrey's – setting his children a deadline, pitting you against each other – has brought out the worst in everyone. It's not exactly a surprise to me that Conway and Charlotte are the ones who cracked under pressure. And it's not just about you being a morally better person, Bella. You're clearly very good at your job. I trust you with my children's inheritance. I trust you not to squander it on vanity projects or squirrel money away for yourself in secret trusts.'

She nodded, a short little jerk of her head that seemed to signal that the conversation was over. She finished her second cup of tea, set it down and stood up, smoothing her coat.

'Thank you for the talk,' she said politely. 'And the tea. Your assistant was quite right about the sugar. I feel so much better.'

'You look a *lot* better,' Bella said, jumping to her feet. It was true: Samantha had some colour in her cheeks now, looked more human than walking dead. 'Can I – would it be okay if I gave you a hug?'

'Of course,' Samantha said, stepping round the table and enfolding Bella in an embrace.

'I haven't been perfect,' Bella blurted out to the decorative-buttoned green epaulette on Samantha's shoulder. 'I've done things too. Please don't think I've been perfect, because I haven't.'

Bella couldn't bring herself to confess, but apparently, greedily, she still wanted absolution from the woman she had injured. She told herself that it had been Charlotte's idea, that her sister would have found a private investigator on her own to follow Conway and catch him with his mistress, and that Charlotte had only asked Bella for help so that her twin's hands would be a little dirty too. While this was true, it didn't help much as it should.

'Oh, you're your father's daughter,' Samantha said, disengaging gracefully from the embrace and giving Bella a little pat on the shoulder. 'I don't mean that badly. I don't expect any Sachs to be a plaster saint.'

She smiled faintly.

'We'll keep in touch,' she said, turning towards the door. Bella walked her out, noticing that Tal and Nita were clearly doing make-work in the outer office; they were on tenterhooks for Samantha to exit, eager to see how the talk had gone.

Bella was still flooded with guilt. She hoped devoutly that it did not show on her face as she waved Samantha goodbye and wished her the best. But as Samantha's green coat whisked away down the corridor, Bella froze in place. An instinctive chill of fear ran down her back as she absorbed how far Charlotte had been prepared to go to sabotage Conway's renewed chance at snagging the prize. Charlotte would not have set Samantha on to digging for dirt if she hadn't known that there was plenty to be found. Which meant, as Samantha said, that Charlotte had investigated her brother first.

And if Charlotte was doing that to Conway, why would

she have refrained from digging for dirt with her other siblings?

Like an automaton, Bella turned to go back into her office. Nita was on her feet, obviously champing at the bit to brief Bella on what she had learnt; but Bella needed to process the revelation that had just hit her.

'Give me a few minutes,' she said through numbed lips. 'I'll buzz you when I'm ready.'

Ignoring Nita's visibly disappointed face, Bella closed the door and leant back against it. Her office was quietly but expensively decorated, plush and classic, richly carpeted and wallpapered in dark jewel tones that made her feel calm and comfortable, plaid cushions on the armchairs. It was a safe haven, a place in which Bella could incubate ideas, take brainstorming meetings that would focus on key issues. She retreated here when she needed to mull over something that was bothering her.

Right now, however, it no longer felt like a sanctuary. Bella was not seeing its familiar, reassuring surroundings, but the hallway of her home, Thomas tumbling down the staircase, head over torso over head; she could hear the sounds too, the dull thunking of his flesh and bones against the carpet. There was no way that Charlotte could ever find out that Bella had been involved in Thomas's fall, surely? No one else had been there!

Bella had done nothing wrong: she had been the victim rather than the aggressor. But no one else knew that. No one could testify on her behalf that Thomas had chased her out of the bedroom, put his hands on her, that it had been a sheer accident that she had knocked him down the stairs.

No one had seen her bruises but her solicitor, and his testimony would be awkward, considering he would have to admit that he had tacitly advised her to conceal the marks from the police.

They *could* find out, however, that she had been having an affair. Everything was available online now if you knew how to look for it. They could trace her Skype sessions, check the time she and Ronaldo had been online that evening, make a connection between Thomas's unexpected return home and a scene which might very well have ensued when he caught her on a call to her lover. Then, of course, that near-fatal fall, which had seemed entirely accidental to the investigators, would take on a very different aspect.

Bella and Ronaldo had been extremely discreet, but there would still be CCTV of him visiting her suite in Chicago. If that had been erased by now, the footage from the Sachs Piccadilly would definitely still be in existence. Bella didn't read crime novels. She had no sense of what the police could do, or what information Skype, for instance, might be prepared to give up. But she did know that a search warrant could force her to hand over her laptop.

She would have to get it wiped. She would have to come up with a reason to ask Nita to organize that without it seeming suspicious. Would that be enough? Bella had no idea, but it would at least be a start, surely . . .

It was telling that Bella had no hesitation in assuming that her twin sister might be capable of betraying her to this degree. But only in retrospect would she realize that she had been protecting entirely the wrong area. Like a general convinced the attack would come from one front, she concentrated her forces there, defending that flank with everything she had, while the enemy had focused on an entirely different point of approach.

It would only take another week before the full scale of her misjudgement became all too horrifyingly clear.

Chapter Twenty-Five

SACHS-SENSATIONAL MELTDOWN!

Stranded travellers beg hotlines for help!

CAT-ASTROPHE!

Megastar Catalina gets Sachs-ed
from her hotel booking!

Computer says **NO ROOM AT THE INN**
for preggers Catalina!

OUT FOR THE COUNT!

Billionairess Countess of Rutland melts down as
her ritzy New York reservation turns out to be
at an AIRPORT IN NEW JERSEY!

It was unbelievable. Unprecedented. Truly as catastrophic
as the blaring headlines suggested. For once, the tabloids
were not exaggerating. The front page of the *Sun* was almost
entirely taken up by a photo of rock goddess Catalina, who
had booked the entire top floor of the Sydney Sachs. She was
standing in the centre of the hotel lobby, surrounded by her

entourage, having been told that there was no record of her reservation. The famously gracious and good-tempered star looked uncharacteristically furious, hands on her hips, her signature mane of hair tumbling around her frowning face, her gorgeous husband by her side carrying their adorable, though tired-looking, toddler in his muscular arms. Catalina had recently announced her second pregnancy, and though she was so slim and fit that she was barely showing, the press were making the most of this extra twist to the story of her being denied accommodation.

'What *happened*?' Nita wailed.

It was the first time that Bella had ever seen her assistant yield, even for a moment, to despair. This could partly be attributed to exhaustion: practically no one who worked for Sachs had slept in the last twelve hours, ever since the magnitude of the crisis became clear. Naturally, with the entire relaunch, the IT team had been on double time, ready to iron out any kinks as soon as they were spotted; no matter how much beta testing they had done, how many complicated scenarios they had run to present as many challenges to the new system as possible, Bella had arranged that every employee on the tech side was paid to be on emergency standby, ready to jump into action at ten minutes' notice when needed.

This precaution had been providential when disaster hit. Because it hadn't been the new system that had collapsed so much as the existing one. Somehow, horrendously, the upgrade had corrupted much of what had already been in the system, and every single staff member was working round the clock to try to retrieve what had been lost.

'*Sachs hotels worldwide lose millions as bookings fall off cliff*', announced the *Financial Times*, more soberly than the red-tops but just as accurately. The company had been inundated with cancellations as travel agents, corporations and private travellers fell over themselves to shift future bookings to hotels that could at least, presumably, be counted on not to lose them.

'Can you let me know how the Catalina situation was resolved?' Bella asked the speakerphone: she was on a group call to the Sachs Sydney, her team clustered around the conference table in her office.

'Yes! Thank God we had a quick-thinking night manager!' the Sydney head of operations said. 'Normally, I'm sure someone would have flagged up that day that her reservation wasn't showing on the system any longer. But with all the ramped-up concerns that we had about the new tech coming in – the whole install of the smart monitors on the minibars, and the new key readers – I know we weren't the only ones to have teething problems with those—'

'No, no, this isn't a fault-finding mission,' Bella interrupted; how many times had she had to repeat these words to panicking heads of ops today? 'We're just trying to verify what happened and how soon it got resolved.'

'Almost all of Catalina's party's rooms were *there*!' the Australian-accented voice said quickly. 'They were showing as booked, but they were pretty much still available! That's why the night manager was so smart – she sent someone up to the penthouse floor to make sure. The few people who had checked in on that floor agreed to move so that we could give her all of it. Obviously I comped their stays, plus her team gave them VIP passes to one of the concerts. We made sure we took care of Catalina to the nth degree – she and her team are totally cool now. But the press has been appalling. Once you have those cameras snapping away . . . and there's nothing we could do about that, there's always one pap who sneaks into the lobby . . .'

'I know,' Bella said with ineffable weariness. 'Okay, it sounds like you handled it fine. We'll sort out a bonus for the night manager later on. That was fast work – trust me, not everyone was as quick to physically check whether the rooms were available. You're not the first one to report vanishing reservations, but this is the largest-scale situation we've heard of. Everyone's checking for VIPs whose bookings may have gone missing.'

'A whole *floor* just disappeared!' the head of ops said in disbelief. 'I've never seen anything like that in my life!'

Bella had a sudden vivid image of the entire penthouse of the Sachs Sydney, with its superb view of the Harbour and Opera House, vaporizing into nothingness. Would you take the lift up and then step out into empty space? For a moment she visualized herself surrounded by white clouds, as if she herself were up there, high above the city, looking for the missing thirty-seventh floor, which had somehow come unmoored and floated away . . .

Bella was insanely tired. Her eyes closed: the image of being carried away on a billowing white cloud was so hypnotic that it had made her nod off for a moment. She felt her head bob forward like a heavy weight and that snapped her back to reality. She was terrified that she had made a noise, a snuffle that was the beginning of a snore.

'Bella?' Nita asked nervously. 'Are you okay?'

'I need another diet Red Bull,' Bella muttered. 'No, don't get up. It'll do me good to move, even a little bit.'

The fridge was fully stocked with cans and bottles of water, juice and energy drinks; there were trays of sushi and sandwiches and biscuits on the side tables, fruit and vegetable platters. Tal had tried to think of everything they might need as they holed up here troubleshooting the relaunch. Though the beta testing had gone very well, Bella's team was nothing if not thorough, which had proved a godsend when the extent of the crisis became obvious.

Bella had never drunk a Red Bull before in her life, and she was taken aback by how effective they were. She was on the sugar-free version, which tasted brutally like cough syrup and pencil shavings, but most definitely did what it said on the tin. She could almost feel the wings sprouting between her shoulder blades.

'So we're identifying two major problem areas,' she said, popping the tab and swigging down the cold brown liquid from the can. She leant back against the fridge as the Red Bull trickled down her throat, feeling instantly revivified. 'Missing reservations, mostly VIP ones. And misdirected ones, also VIPs: customers being sent to low-grade hotels rather than top-end ones. Look at what happened to the Countess of Rutland.'

Everyone shuddered. The Countess was extremely beautiful, highly photogenic and American by birth. This last quality meant that, unlike a British aristocrat, who tended to be more restrained and less publicity-friendly, she had had no qualms at all about making the most enormous scene when she found herself, after a transatlantic flight, taken by her waiting limo not to the Sachs Park Avenue but right across town, over the George Washington Bridge and to the Sachs airport hotel in Newark, New Jersey.

Even viewed in the most kindly, flattering light, Newark had never claimed to be renowned for its sophistication and elegance. And the airport Sachs was the most basic offering in the entire hotel collection. There is always an ugly duckling or two in all hotel chains, and the Newark AirSachs was one of the stumpiest, most tattered-feathered ducklings of all.

It did good business and it was clean, but it had been overdue a revamp for a decade, and the photos of it the furious Countess had promptly uploaded to her social media were utterly depressing: brutalist concrete architecture, walls painted the shade of beige which never looks completely clean even when it is, and even more brutally patterned carpet. The Countess's blonde glamour threw the backgrounds into even worse relief by contrast; she had apparently napped in the limo, hence not having noticed how long the ride was taking, and her eyes were bright, her skin glowing and luminous.

'The driver kept insisting that her reservation *was* actually at the AirSachs, which didn't help,' Tal said, reading from the memo that the New York head of operations had sent after the incident. 'The limo was our booking, sent as a courtesy because we're making a big push to snag her as a regular client – our NYC guest relations head of department has been courting her hard. We stocked it with top-end

351

champagne, all her favourite snacks, pillows and a blanket, a goodie bag of Elemis moisturizer and hand lotions . . .'

'Good work,' Bella muttered in parentheses. The Countess was fantastically rich, titled, beautiful, and never off her Instagram: she was a very important influencer. Like many of the hyper-rich, she adored freebies and discounts with a passion, and was very amenable to being spoilt by hotels and restaurants in return for gracing them with her mediagenic presence. 'If that isn't all completely ruined now.'

'But that's the glitch – the booking went through our system, and it didn't occur to the driver that it was weird to be taking her from one airport to another,' Tal continued. 'She got out before she realized where she was and made a huge scene in the car park. Told the driver to take her to Park Avenue, but he said that wasn't the reservation he had in the booking – trust me, we're never using that company again! So she stormed into the hotel and told them to ring Park Avenue and sort it out, and while they were doing that, she started Instagramming. There's a video where she's standing in the car park with the noise of planes landing and taking off, it's really loud . . . plus, other guests recognized her and started taking photos and uploading them to their social media! It's practically gone viral! We could *not* have been more unlucky!'

'That hotel's a shitheap,' Bella said bluntly. 'A total shitheap. Every time the budget rolls around, we choose not to make the AirSachs hotels a priority. And we get away with it because the really ugly ones are located so well for the terminals, we work very hard on having the best shuttle service of all the airport chains, we have high staffing levels and we keep them *spotless*. Much cheaper to do all those things than to redecorate. Honestly, it's barely a three-star, even by airport hotel standards. But we get good ratings on consumer sites because the travellers get a better-than-average breakfast and we keep the prices competitive.'

She looked at the can of energy drink in her hand.

'Wow,' she said. 'That really kicked in. I just lectured all of you about stuff you already knew.'

'Actually,' Tal suggested, 'it made me think that when we do the upgrade for those AirSachs, we could see if the Countess would cut the ribbon on the Newark one? It would be a nice gimmick!'

'I love it,' Bella said, drinking more Red Bull. 'Make a note. We'll give her literally whatever she wants to do it. Wait. What did you just say?'

Tal stammered: 'Uh, the Countess—'

'No! Before that! I cut in on you with that rant about the AirSachs being a shitheap!'

Nita's eyes were wide with shock: Bella never used this kind of language in the workplace, or indeed outside of it. But the combination of her nerves being run ragged by the scale of this disaster and the Red Bull she was mainlining was ripping away the polite facade, revealing a much less ladylike version of Bella.

'Tal was talking about the Countess Instagramming,' a team member said.

'I said it was really unlucky,' Tal said. 'Her, of all people, taken to that, uh, not very nice hotel—'

'You can say shitheap,' Bella said absently. 'I did. Wait! *Unlucky!* That's it! Unlucky!'

She waved the can in the air, her blue eyes blazing.

'*Unlucky!*' she repeated. Some drops of energy drink spilled on the carpet, but no one was going to point that out to their wild-eyed boss.

'Okay!' Bella said, finishing the Red Bull and striding over to the table, crunching the empty can in her hand and chucking it in the bin as she went. 'Two major problem areas. Any other really famous celebs being misdirected to shitheaps?'

'Wayne Burns – the footballer – he and his husband were taken to the conference hotel in DC, in Silver Spring,' another member of the team volunteered. 'Instead of the Sachs on Dupont Circle. And then they were given the worst room in the hotel, right next to the elevator and the entrance to the car park. It's technically a basement – it doesn't even have full windows.'

Everyone shuddered. Despite its pretty name, Silver Spring had been built as a conference centre and office park. There was little in it but huge, brutally functional office buildings, hotels ditto, and chain restaurants. It was hard to see the dapper Burnses enjoying a stay there whose high-lights would be shopping for discount clothes at Men's Wearhouse, followed by a meal at Panera Bread or Red Lob-ster, even with the latter's well-known endless shrimp offer.

'They were super-nice about it, apparently, which made everyone feel so much worse,' he added.

Bella heaved a deep breath.

'So this huge VIP guest relations push, which was going so well, is actually one of the things that's screwed us,' she summarized. 'Because we wanted to give them a totally customized, airport-to-hotel experience and get them loving the Sachs brand even before they *got* to the bloody hotels, and all it took was a change of schedule sent to the limo driver to mess the whole thing up!'

She looked around the table.

'Tal, Nita, stay with me. Everyone else, the priority is to contact our best hotels, the top echelon, and tell their guest relations team to double-check the details of any VIP bookings which have limo pickups they organized. Look for VIPs who are media-worthy. Not just the rich ones, the famous ones. That's our number-one priority for troubleshooting – restoring those VIPs' bookings wherever we can, getting ahead of the curve. You all know your areas. I want reports in two hours.'

There was a bustle of movement, Bella practically shooing the rest of the team out of the room and back to their offices. By the time they had grabbed their tablets and laptops and hurried out, and she turned to look at Nita and Tal, she could already see that Nita, at least, had connected the dots.

'*Unlucky,*' Nita echoed, looking up at her boss.

'Right? What are the chances?'

'The IT people have been saying from the beginning they don't understand why any of our previous reservations were affected,' Nita observed. 'I was so busy telling them to fix this mess I didn't stop to register that as much as I should have. But yes, it makes sense. Everyone anticipated that the major area for potential problems would be when people tried to make new bookings – the 3D room-visualizing, the sliding scale of the reward scheme discounts – but that doesn't seem to be happening.'

'Actually, the new tech seems to be working fine, which is so ironic!' Tal said, looking up from her laptop. 'I just got a report. They're saying it's a moderate success – which, you know, is fantastic in their terms. Fifteen per cent fewer glitches on average than they anticipated, and the new points icons are working really well visually – consumers seem to be finding them very easy to understand. And barely any hitches with the virtual check-ins!'

'So it's not us,' Bella said. 'It's not our team. It's someone from the outside who looked at our upcoming bookings and cherry-picked the ones that would get the most publicity possible. Catalina, the Countess of Rutland, Wayne Burns and his husband. This was designed to make us look as bad as possible.'

'Why not just crash everything? The whole system?' Tal asked. 'I mean, perish the thought—'

'My guess is that would have been too obvious,' Bella said, her brain on Red Bull firing machine-gun fast. 'It would have signalled clearly that we're under cyber-attack. Whereas this just looks like we completely fucked up, which is much more damaging.'

Nita and Tal's gloomy nods confirmed the accuracy of this guess.

'We'll do a thorough inquest afterwards,' Bella said. 'But right now, I want you to assign a handful of people you totally trust to looking for whatever's doing this, root down and dig it out. You get what I'm saying, don't you? Handpick them. Talk about it between the two of you and make sure you agree. Take them off everything else, isolate them so no one else can hear what they're saying, so gossip doesn't spread that we think we've been sabotaged. Find the bug, or the back door to our system, whatever it's called. You two have been working with IT so closely over the last few months—'

'I know *exactly* who to pick,' Nita said, standing up. She glanced at Tal. 'We can compare names quickly, but I'm sure we'll both agree on the core group.'

'I don't need to tell you to be discreet about briefing them,' Bella said. 'The main thing is to get it fixed so we stop these games that someone's playing with us. But it's almost as important that they don't do anything that would stop us tracing it back. I need evidence, if I can get it. Tell them not to do anything that would kill the trail, if there is one.'

She bit her lip.

'I have to go up to the twentieth floor in a few hours to make a report,' she said, something that Nita and Tal, of course, knew perfectly well. 'If there's *anything* I can say to actively demonstrate that we were sabotaged, for God's sake try to give me something. I mean, we're not Big Pharma or an arms manufacturer! We can't possibly be expected to have protected ourselves against a cyber-attack, can we?'

Both Nita and Tal shook their heads vigorously as they hurried from the room. Bella felt a rush of exhaustion sweep over her. The revelation that the partial crash of the Sachs booking systems, the erasure or change of some of the records, had almost certainly been a deliberate act, felt like a physical blow from which she was still recovering. And the effort of controlling herself so that she did not blurt out her suspicions to her team had been extremely hard.

Bella slumped forward, resting the palms of her hands on

the table, the bones of her arms locked, bracing to take some of her weight. She was scared that if she sat down, she would fall fast asleep.

Then she thought: *Well, why* not *go to sleep? There's nothing for me to do. I've given everyone their tasks, and I'll be only sitting around waiting until they're finished . . .*

She remembered Charlotte, the day that Jeffrey had summoned them all to the Maida Vale house; Bella had hunkered down in her office to prep, while Charlotte had rung up the Nicky Clarke salon for an emergency appointment, turning up in Warwick Avenue looking sleek and beautiful and like a million dollars. Bella had felt then that her sister had a distinct advantage. So why not take a leaf out of her book by turning up as fresh and rested as possible at the meeting?

Tal and Nita were not in the outer office, having both gone down to select their crack IT team; they had locked the main door for security. It was unprecedented for the office to be unattended during work hours, but so was the scale of today's events. Nita was so well organized that finding the contact details of the agency through which she booked Bella's hair and make-up was easy enough. By offering to pay double rate for the short notice, Bella secured a booking in an hour and a half for both services.

Then she put a Post-it note on her own door explaining that she was napping, set an alarm on her mobile to wake her in an hour, kicked off her shoes and pushed the two armchairs to face each other. Propping the cushions behind her, she curled up in one chair, stretched her legs onto the other, and closed her eyes. It was a testament to her exhaustion that, despite the energy drink still running through her veins, she passed out almost at once, her head slumping into the plaid pillows, the slow sounds of quiet snoring rumbling around her office.

Her dreams were vivid and tumultuous. Catalina stepped out of one of her videos to berate the Countess of Rutland, who promptly started dancing with her and Wayne Burns. Aeroplanes landed and took off behind them, and Bella was on one of them, walking up the aisle towards the cockpit; she reached out and opened the door and the pilot turned to glance at her. It was Charlotte, the uniform cap with its gold trim perched jauntily on her head, her hair cascading over her shoulders in the most perfect waves that Nicky Clarke's nimble fingers could achieve. She looked at her twin sister over her shoulder and started to laugh; she laughed and laughed even as she turned back to the controls and shoved the nose of the plane down, and Bella tumbled forward as the plane went into a dive, headed to crash into the earth below, the emergency warnings ringing louder and louder . . .

It was her phone alarm ramping up to make sure it was heard. Bella jerked awake, sitting upright, her legs numb, sweat dampening her hairline. She put a hand up and felt her forehead: it too was beaded and clammy. Bella could only be grateful that she had had the foresight to book hair and make-up appointments before her confrontation with her father on the twentieth floor.

The roar of the hairdryer in her ears, the tug of the hair-dresser's big round brush, pulling Bella's head first in one direction and then the other, the tines digging briefly into her skin each time, the slightly acrid smell of hair singeing under the heat of the straightening irons used to smooth the little flyaways at her hairline; it was hypnotic. She could see why Charlotte used this last-minute strategy to get herself meeting-ready. It wasn't just the sensation of the fat, heavy curls bouncing glamorously on your shoulders, the fact that your hair was lifting regally off your scalp rather than hanging there limply; it was the sheer distraction of the noise, the heat, the smell of hair and hairspray, which blocked her from concentrating on anything else. It was the first time in days that she had been awake without worrying about the worst professional crisis she had ever had to firefight.

'There you go!'

The hairdresser set down the styling tongs and extracted a hand mirror from her case, holding it up to show her client the volume she had achieved.

'Lovely,' Bella said, already pushing back her chair.

'You really have great hair,' the young woman said sycophantically. 'It made my job very easy.'

'Thanks! Can you pack up as fast as possible? I'm on a very tight deadline.'

Bella was already walking over to the door of her office. She pulled it open to see Nita, back from her foray into the IT department, practically leaping to her feet, so eager was she to let her boss know what she had found out. Bella told the hairdresser to see Tal for her tip, the last word putting a smile on the young woman's face as she hurried out.

'You've got something, right?' Bella said, swinging round to look at Nita, propping her bottom against her desk, feeling

360

her curls move with satisfying weight around her head. This truly worked, this emergency blow-dry technique: unquestionably, she felt more confident, more in control.

'Oh, Bella,' Nita said, taking a deep breath. 'We've been thinking and thinking about how to tell you! Do you want to sit down?'

Bella shook her head and reached out wordlessly for the tablet Nita was carrying.

'We hired a kid someone knows on a forum,' Nita said, holding it back for a moment. 'A hacker. It took him no time at all. He was able to pinpoint exactly when the bug entered our system, and which computer. It was out of work hours, and the IT team were here almost round the clock, which means it was accessed in the early morning by someone who was able to come in any time without being flagged by security . . .'

Having done what she could to warn her boss about what she was going to see, Nita yielded up the tablet.

'We keep the footage for a month, apparently,' she said. 'Thank goodness.'

Bella felt sick. Nita was telling her that the perpetrator was someone who could enter not only the building itself without being questioned, but any of the departments: someone whose pass gave them access anywhere they wanted to go – apart from the twentieth floor. In other words, one of Bella's three siblings.

The footage showed the IT department in darkness, pierced intermittently by the glow of various tiny LEDs indicating that the machines were quietly running. As Bella watched, a trapezoid of light spilled into the far side of the room, a door opening. Illumination flooded the space as the overhead lights were turned on, and into the frame stepped the last person she had expected to see.

Her brother Bart.

Chapter Twenty-Six

By the time Bella reached Bart's office she had worked up a head of steam powerful enough to fire a cannon. Unlike Bella, Bart staffed his office with young women who were decorative rather than functional, but even an assistant as effective and experienced as Nita could not have stopped Bella from storming across the reception area and into Bart's sanctum. The two slim, glamorous young women wearing earbuds and streaming shows on their iPads – being Bart's assistant was by no means a demanding job – stood no chance at all.

Bart was sitting behind his desk, a half-empty glass of very expensive tequila in front of him, the bottle within easy reach. Even though he had the best version of their mother's wonderfully distinctive eyes, the huge blue irises almost overwhelming the whites, Bella could clearly see that the latter were bloodshot.

'Hello, Bella,' he mumbled wretchedly.

'Drinking away your guilt?' she said sarcastically.

Bart nodded. Bella stared at him, taken aback: she had not anticipated this swift response. He propped his elbows on the desk and rested his forehead in his cupped hands, avoiding her fierce gaze.

'I feel like absolute shit,' he muttered. 'Bell, please believe me. I never meant to do it.'

'How can you not have *meant* it?' she exclaimed, so shrilly that she cringed to hear her own voice. 'How can you *possibly—*'

'Oh, Bell,' Bart sighed on a dying fall. 'You don't really think this was my idea, do you?'

He sat back again and picked up his glass, finishing off the contents.

Bella plopped down in the visitor's chair, suddenly exhausted; she was realizing that the sight of Bart on the CCTV recording had been, although upsetting, also something of a relief. Because, depressing though it was that her brother had conjured up a scheme which would ruin her chances of becoming CEO, maybe even get her fired from the company, she had preferred seeing him in that IT room rather than the person she had been dreading was behind this.

Her twin sister.

'Was it Conway?' she heard herself ask with sheer desperation in her tone. 'Bart, was it—'

'Oh, Bell, I'm so sorry!' Bart sounded on the verge of tears. 'No, you know it wasn't! Con's a bastard, but this isn't his style. You know that, Bell! You know it was Charlotte!'

Bella's head sagged on her neck as it had done earlier in the meeting, her skull too heavy for her to hold up straight. Bart reached for the bottle of Casa Dragones Joven, refilled his glass and pushed it across the desk to her.

'Have a sip,' he said. 'Seriously, just a sip. It'll do you good.'

He laughed without any humour.

'Says the alkie who doesn't have a proper job!' he added bitterly. 'The guy who's boozing in his office because he was stupid enough to get conned by one sister into screwing over the other one!'

Bart was right, however, about the tequila doing Bella good. Just the smell so close to her nostrils was stimulating, the fresh, strong scent of the blue agave plant from which the liquor was extracted. Slowly, Bella picked up the glass and sipped. It roared through her like wildfire, and she sat up straighter in her chair.

'She told me the whole story about Conway,' Bart recounted, taking back the glass and setting to work on it. 'He's been cheating on Samantha and squirrelling away his assets. As if there isn't more than enough money to go round, you know? That's what really got me when Charlotte told me. It's just so bloody *petty*.'

He shook his head in disgust.

'So Charlotte gave me a USB and told me what to do with it. Said that if I put this bug in the system, it would find his money for Samantha,' he continued. 'Sort of like a heat-seeking missile. It'd ferret Con's dirty dealings out and blow them up in everyone's face so he couldn't deny it any more. I promise you, you were never even *mentioned*.'

'Why would that be on the *Sachs* computers?' Bella couldn't help asking. 'Why would Conway mix up his money with the business?'

'Oh, fuck knows!' Bart shook his head again, but this time

in repudiation of his own stupidity. 'Fuck knows! She spun this whole line, though, and it made sense at the time. I promise, Bell, I promise it did. Conway was funnelling money through the company, she said, and this way he wouldn't be able to hide it any more. She gave me a whole list of instructions so I knew what to do once the USB went in.'

Bella, who had watched the footage of Bart repeatedly consulting first a piece of paper and then the computer screen, tapping at the keyboard as painstakingly as a small child taking their first piano lesson, rolled her eyes in impatience. What Samantha had described in the Cook Islands was a private trust, nothing to do with Sachs at all. There was simply no possibility that Conway would have been stupid enough to commingle private funds which he was trying to conceal from his wife and her divorce lawyers with those of the company; it would make no sense.

No sense to anyone but Bart, Bella thought bitterly. *Stupid, innocent Bart, sitting here in his office with zero business knowledge and the inability to believe that one of his siblings could be plotting to destroy the chances of another one becoming CEO . . .*

'I've been nursing this stupid fantasy for a while now,' Bart was saying bitterly. 'You'll laugh your head off when you hear it. I was thinking that if Pa put me in charge, I could bring everyone together. You and Conway and Charlotte, fighting and bickering the way you are, as if we were kids, but worse – I hate it. I actually asked Adrianna if she could suggest to Pa that I take over as – what do they call it in politics?'

'The compromise candidate?' Bella suggested dryly.

Bart gave her a twisted smile.

'The reconciliation candidate, I think I meant,' he said. 'Bringing peace, stopping all the in-fighting. It was ridiculous, wasn't it? I'm completely out of my league with all this business stuff! Everyone else could run rings round me and I wouldn't have the faintest bloody idea! Fuck it, Charlotte already has!'

He gestured around him with the hand that was holding the glass, slopping some tequila onto the desk.

'Look at this office! State of the art – Annika and Lucinda out there, doing bugger all but taking turns polishing each other's nails – what a bloody waste! Why do I even *have* it? What do I need an office for? The PRs run my charity stuff. All I need to do is turn up and run my race or drive my car or make the speech some other bugger wrote for me and flirt with the rich old lady donors. What's the *point* of me? What do I *do* all day? Look how hard you work! You slog your guts out, and now I've ruined it all for you. Oh God, Bell, will you ever be able to forgive me? I wasn't even brave enough to come and face you. I've been hiding out here, getting drunk, just waiting for you to work it out and come and haul me over the coals.'

Bart's penitence was undeniably sincere. Bella had no doubt that he had been tricked by Charlotte into planting the bug which would allow her to reach into the Sachs booking system, let her or her minions cherry-pick reservations to sabotage that would be guaranteed to draw the biggest headlines. But Bella was the injured party, and she had no interest in wasting one drop of energy on commiserating with Bart for his stupidity, let alone coming up with ideas for him to find something meaningful to do with his life.

'Bart,' she said, pushing back her chair and standing up, 'I can see you're having some sort of existential crisis. But I don't have time for it and honestly, I don't care.'

Bart nodded humbly, running a hand through his hair to push it back from his face in a way that was a pale shadow of his usual jaunty, sexy gesture.

He's a lost little boy, his sister thought, looking down at him. *He needs a sensible woman to knock him into shape, give his life some importance, an actual centre. He's never had boundaries. Everyone's just indulged him and spoilt him and never held him accountable for anything he did.*

Well, that changes now. I'm holding him accountable for this.

'I'm going to tell Daddy what happened,' she said quietly. 'What you did.'

'I know,' he said without trying to plead with her, which raised him several points in her estimation.

'And obviously that means what Charlotte did too,' Bella said, a lump of misery in her throat.

Bart nodded.

There was nothing left to say. This seemed to conclude the proceedings; all that was left was her appointment with their father. And yet, Bella found herself hesitating, because of the sheer gravity of what was awaiting her on the twentieth floor: the task of telling her father that two of his children had stabbed a third in the back and taken the main division of the company down with her.

In half an hour's time her father would be confirming that

Bella was the only one of his children fit to be CEO. He would have had no problem with them scheming and plotting and manoeuvring to come out on top; it was, after all, how he had grown his company so fast.

But he would never approve the imperilling of the reputation of the hotel chain he had built from scratch. What Charlotte had done to the brand that bore Jeffrey's name was so extreme that she would never recover from the fallout. All Bella had to do was march upstairs, present her case, and watch her father affirm that, out of all of his four children, she was the only one remotely appropriate to be appointed as CEO.

So why was she still standing in Bart's office, when she should be hurrying to claim her prize?

She reached over the table, took the glass from Bart's hand and sank the rest of the contents. Bella had never drunk tequila neat before. She had always considered it far too dangerous. It was, she decided. Definitely dangerous. And even more effective than Red Bull.

'Okay!' she said again, and turned to go.

'Be gentle,' Bart said quietly behind her. 'Not for us. Me and Charlotte, I mean. But for him.'

And there it was, put into words, the reason that Bella had been hesitating. She heard those words again and again, ringing in her brain, all the way up to her father's eyrie on the twentieth floor. Her increasingly frail-looking, eighty-year-old father, who was about to get the shock of his life.

She heard them even louder as she stepped out and nodded at the receptionist, Tania, a very elegant German woman of a certain age who had worked for Jeffrey for over twenty years. Tania's bearing was so impeccable that she kept her face as neutral as ever as she greeted Bella, showing no sign that she was aware of the scale of the disaster that brought Jeffrey's daughter to his office this afternoon.

Charlotte, who had been sitting on the sofa, jumped up and came forward to intercept her sister. Bella flinched involuntarily, even though she knew that Tania was observing the interaction to report back to their father in due course.

But what did that matter? Bella was in the right. She had truth on her side and backup from Bart, who, riven with guilt about what he had done, would confess everything to their father if necessary. Why should she back down just because her sister was standing in front of her, those huge blue eyes burning into hers, saying insistently:

'Bell. We need to talk. Now.'

'No thank you,' Bella said, pegging her chin high. 'I have an appointment with Daddy and I'm already overdue for it, so—'

'You don't get it,' Charlotte said urgently, pitching her voice low enough so that Tania, across the sprawling office, would not be able to hear. 'You *need* to come with me, Bell. I have stuff you *have* to hear.'

'Charlotte' – since Bella and Charlotte never called each other by their full first names, this was a declaration of war – 'stop it,' Bella said, setting her jaw. 'It won't do you any good. I know exactly what's been going on. I've come straight from talking to Bart and I'm going to tell Daddy everything he said to me—'

Charlotte was fishing in her bag, yet another one of those

hideously expensive, ridiculously flimsy ones that Thomas had despised for being disposable fashion, but so pretty it made Bella long for it to be hanging off her own wrist. From it, Charlotte's hand was emerging, the gigantic phone she used for her social media clasped in her slender fingers.

Charlotte had obviously prepared herself for this. She had assumed that her words would not be enough to convince her twin to come with her for a quiet word before her appointment with their father, had known that she would need to click her phone on and turn the screen towards her sister and show her what looked like a screen shot of something Bella couldn't quite make out, but which had *Skype* at the top of it.

So this was what it meant to have your blood run cold. It was the opposite of the tequila, which had warmed and stirred and fired Bella up to action. Now she was frozen, horrified, her worst nightmare come to life. She made no further attempt to protest as Charlotte took her upper arm and guided her down the corridor, towards the sprawling suite that Jeffrey had installed on this floor: bedrooms, bathrooms, a full kitchen, a sauna, a steam room, put in with the idea that he might regularly stay here overnight rather than undergoing the horrors of a thirty-minute chauffeured journey back to Maida Vale after a long day of work, and, of course, barely ever used.

Charlotte guided her twin into a living room which had been decorated decades ago, all heavy pelmeted furniture and equally thick rugs. It looked preserved in amber, kept immaculate by the cleaners, so dated that it could be hired out as a film or TV location for a 1980s shoot. Only when

Charlotte had closed the door and pulled her sister right across the expanse of carpet, over to the windows, safely away from any eavesdroppers, did she finally say:

'Whatever you wanted to tell Daddy, Bell, forget it. I know *everything*. Do you really want the police to reopen the investigation into what happened to Thomas?'

Chapter Twenty-Seven

There are sights you can never unsee, words you can never unhear. The gloves were off. The truth about Charlotte's character was finally clear to her twin sister. Bella had been aware, of course, that her sister was very self-centred, would put her own interests over those of her twin without a second thought; but she had had no idea of the depths of unscrupulousness to which selfishness and ambition would propel Charlotte.

Now she knew, however, and as the knowledge sank in, she felt, to her surprise, extremely calm. The worst had happened. After having thoroughly sabotaged her sister's professional life, Charlotte was now threatening her with the possibility of criminal charges in her personal one.

So: Charlotte could never be trusted again. Bart was weak and easily entrapped in scheming. Conway was self-obsessed and patronizing, looking down on his sisters for being female. Which meant Bella was on her own. Bella had always been on her own.

What a realization! Bella had never felt so centred in her entire life. And the strange thing was, she thought, gazing at her sister, her living mirror, that Charlotte had never looked so beautiful.

'Blackmail and backstabbing really suit you,' Bella said calmly. 'You're absolutely glowing.'

Charlotte frowned; out of everything her sister might have said, she had not been expecting this. She shook her head as if a fly were buzzing around her.

'Did you hear what I said?' she asked.

'How could I avoid it? You're threatening me! I assume you've been hacking into my computer? You've already done it with Conway's.'

'How do you—' Charlotte began. 'Oh, Samantha. She guessed. I could have been more subtle about that, but I was in a hurry.'

She was dressed in off-white, a fitted dress with gold metal inserts at the neckline which substituted for jewellery. Her hair was parted in the centre and drawn back into a bun at her nape, simple gold studs in her ears. The whole effect was of purity and simplicity, doubtless selected specifically, Bella decided, to make her look as innocent as possible.

'I can't feel guilty about Samantha,' Charlotte said, shrugging. 'Not really. Con would have left her anyway. Look, Bell, I don't want to draw this out or make it harder than it has to be. I just need you not to tell Daddy about what Bart and I did with the Sachs reservations, that's all.'

'"Bart and you"?' Bella echoed. 'That's outrageous! You make it sound as if you were equal conspirators! It's bad enough you dragged poor Bart into this. At least be honest about what you did!'

'Whatever,' Charlotte said simply. 'Really. Whatever. None of this *matters*. Don't you see that? The only thing we're here to talk about is what you go and say to Daddy. I'm not going to completely dump you in the shit without a paddle, okay? That would be stupid of me. You might get tempted to spill the beans, even with me knowing all about your Skype chats – not to mention the timing of the last one. I've got a cover story worked out for you with the whole bookings debacle. We were hacked by a rival and you're tracking it down.'

'Are you serious?' Bella said incredulously. 'How could I possibly trust you to keep my stuff secret after I've lied to protect you?'

Charlotte was ready for this.

'Because you've got the CCTV footage of Bart in the IT department,' she said, and watched her sister register surprise. 'Oh yes, I've got my team too, just like yours. Stupid me, I could have sworn it got wiped every week! I must have missed the protocol being extended to a fortnight. Anyway, that's water under the bridge now. You've got the dirt on Bart. He certainly won't lie for me, and unfortunately everyone will believe him as soon as he starts spilling his story. Bart's totally transparent. You can expose me any time you want – don't you see that?'

Her eyes were wide with sincerity.

'So why not take my help and tell Daddy that story? Don't worry, he won't order an investigation that'd open up the whole can of worms. He's old and tired and on the way out.'

'Stop turning this around! *You're* the one who should be worrying about him doing an investigation!' Bella snapped.

Charlotte's eyes flickered in surprise that her sister was pushing back so hard.

'Exactly!' she said quickly. 'So you wouldn't be risking anything, you see? Tell him that you've found a back door in the system, that someone's been doing this deliberately to mess with us. You can say that all the press you've been getting drove one of our rivals crazy.'

'That's nothing but the truth! It certainly drove *you* crazy!' Bella said bitterly.

'Look, Bell, this isn't going to get us anywhere,' Charlotte said almost gently. 'Daddy pitted us against each other. I didn't create that situation, did I?'

'If he ever finds out what you did—'

'But he *won't*,' Charlotte cut in. 'Because you'll be protecting me as much as I am myself. You don't have a choice. If the police ever find out that you were Skyping with your boyfriend just before Thomas fell downstairs, they'll look at what happened to him in an entirely new light. You're not stupid. You know that perfectly well.'

Bella opened her mouth to ask Charlotte if she would actually do that. Would her sister truly be prepared to send whatever she had to the police? Bella assumed this was the record of her Skype calls, all to the same account, particularly, as Charlotte had said, the damning timing of the last one.

But what would be the point in asking that question? Of course she would say yes, whether she meant to do it or not. Bella wondered if Charlotte knew that it was Ronaldo that

Bella was seeing. There was no hint of it in her manner, and Ronaldo's Skype name and email address were both joking film references, nothing that would signal his identity.

Bella decided that Charlotte could not possibly be aware of it. She would not only have teased Bella about dating Ronaldo, she would unquestionably have used it as extra leverage against her, pointing out that Jeffrey would be livid if the papers screamed that Tragic Coma Husband Bella was actually having an affair with the son of their father's housekeeper.

No, Bella could relax on that score. It was an enormous relief to realize that Charlotte would not be able to play that card against her, at least.

'Let me think this through,' Bella said slowly. 'You've got records of my Skype calls – you've made that clear. Which means you can hold them over my head forever.'

'As you can with that CCTV footage, and what Bart will say!' Charlotte said instantly. 'It's a standoff, don't you see that? You can't tell on me and I can't tell on you. We keep each other safe. Forever.'

Charlotte's use of the word 'safe' provoked a bitter laugh from Bella. She turned away from her sister, staring out of the window, down at the superb vista of the London streets below: even Kingsway, one of London's uglier avenues, looked infinitely more attractive from this lofty height. But even the view below was not a respite from the sight of her twin. Charlotte's white dress and blonde cap of hair were reflected in the glass, as if she were a ghost floating in the air beside Bella.

'*Safe*,' Bella repeated. 'That's funny.'

'Oh, I don't think you had anything to do with Thomas's fall!' Charlotte said. 'Don't misunderstand me! I know how much you cared about him. And I don't blame you for flirting with someone else, or whatever it was. I mean, with the best will in the world, Thomas *was* quite a bit older, and very stuffy. I'm not judging you in any way. It's just that it looks – bad.'

'Whatever,' Bella said in exactly the same tone that her sister had used earlier. In the window she saw Charlotte flinch, as Bella had done when she saw Charlotte in Jeffrey's outer office.

'I think we're done here,' Bella continued, turning away from the windows. 'You've made your position very clear. I'm looking forward to your full support in the meeting with Daddy.'

'*What?*' Charlotte exclaimed. 'I'm not going in there! I just came up here to make sure of talking to you beforehand!'

'*Oh yes you are*,' Bella said, rounding on her. It was her turn to fix her sister with an intense look, forcing her to submit to her will. The twin sisters glared at each other as Bella continued: 'You're going to come in there and have my back, a hundred per cent. You'll say how great the scheme is, how brilliant and successful you're sure it's going to be, how much you're looking forward to rolling it out with Sash in the next year or so. That's really important. You have to say you're going to be incorporating it yourself into the boutiques. And we'll tell him we'll add more cyber-experts to protect us from now on.'

Charlotte's mouth drew into a straight line, which her

twin knew from experience meant she was resisting this with all her might.

'This isn't negotiable, Charlotte,' Bella snapped. 'You've screwed me over. You've attacked me, when I've done nothing to you but keep my head down and get on with my bloody job. And you dragged poor Bart into it, so you'd have an accomplice to shift some of the blame onto, just like you asked me to look for a PI who could find out whether Conway was having an affair. You could have done that on your own, but you wanted to pull in someone else so that you'd never have to take full responsibility. Well, you're coming into Daddy's office and standing by me. I swear, Charlotte, if you don't, I'll tell Daddy everything and let you do your worst.'

Bella did not wait for Charlotte's assent. She had the upper hand and she knew it; she could read the energy between them. Turning on her heel, she strode from the living room, sure that Charlotte would be following.

'Is he ready to see us now, Tania?' she asked as she swept back into the reception area. 'Charlotte will be coming into the meeting with me.'

Tania's eyes flickered from Bella to Charlotte, assessing the situation. Then she stood up, said, 'Give me just a moment, please,' and approached the huge carved door which led to Jeffrey's office, rapping briefly on it before disappearing inside. It was barely a minute before the heavy Gothic oak trefoil-panelled door, which had once separated the vestry from the chancel in an ancient parish church, cracked open again and Jeffrey Sachs could be heard shouting:

'Fine! If she's idiot enough to back up her idiot sister, let them both in!'

Tania emerged, silently holding the door open. It was for Bella to go first, and she did not look back at Charlotte as she walked into the lion's den. She just hoped that, as she followed her in, her sister could not see how badly her legs were shaking with fear.

Chapter Twenty-Eight

It could almost have been a cathedral, this room, with its double-height vaulted, ribbed ceiling and its marble floor. But then, a cathedral would not have antique carpets strewn over the expanse of marble, nor landscape paintings in huge gold frames hanging on the panelled walls. Over the last decade, Jeffrey's eyes had become increasingly weak, and the gigantic candelabra suspended directly above his head was at full wattage to compensate. It was, against stiff competition, the most Gothic item of furniture in the whole room: a wrought-iron, curlicued, elaborate monster, the size of a baby elephant, hanging from a dramatic chain as wide as a man's forearm but also, for extra safety, secured with several finer, more discreet skeins of tension cable radiating out to the corners of the ceiling.

The inspiration for the office had been Jeffrey's image of himself as a Medici prince of commerce. It was a throne room crossed with a judge's bench. Jeffrey was installed behind an enormous Victorian mahogany desk which had been designed to break down into several sections, as it would otherwise not fit through any doorway. His chair and desk were on a low dais so that visitors had to look up to him, and the chair itself was massive, throne-like and carved so elaborately that it needed daily dusting to keep it immaculate.

He said nothing as his daughters filed into the room, but this was only what they had expected. Jeffrey's favourite technique, on summoning an employee to his inner sanctum, was to remain silent to see if they would lose their nerve and start to babble. Bella, however, had been in training with her father for decades longer than the average employee, so she was able to walk across the expanse of flooring and take a seat in one of the high-backed chairs in front of the dais without feeling compelled to break into a stream of apologies and explanations. Out of the corner of her eye, she saw a flash of white as Charlotte seated herself, but Bella never took her eyes off her father.

He looked shrunken and wizened, and she wondered if he realized how unflattering his throne was to him. In his prime, it had seemed like a extension of Jeffrey, making him larger and more dominating, giving him even more authority; now it functioned the opposite way, stressing his mortality. His hands were frail on the wide armrests, his thinning hair accentuated by the pool of light from the chandelier.

'We were hacked,' Bella announced, sitting up confidently. She was happy to hear her voice ring out loud and confident; the room had tricky acoustics. Many Sachs employees had speculated over the years that these had been designed so that Jeffrey's slightest utterances would boom out imposingly while the responses would get lost. That, or his interlocutors would make the mistake of shouting to overcompensate.

'Someone put a bug in our system,' she continued, as

Jeffrey's only response to this piece of information had been to frown deeply and gesture for her to continue, another technique he used to intimidate. 'They've been picking out the most famous guests, the ones who were bound to get a huge amount of publicity if their bookings went horribly wrong, and messing with them in particular. Of course there are a lot of average travellers whose bookings got scrambled too, but it's no coincidence that we've found ourselves losing reservations for Catalina, the Countess of Rutland, Wayne Burns – really high-profile VIPs, names known to gossip readers worldwide. We've isolated and blocked the bug and are hoping to trace it back to whoever was using it. We don't know that yet, but we can absolutely assure you that the problems in the system are over. Can't we?'

Bella looked pointedly at Charlotte, who responded with a nod.

'*What?*' It had taken a while for Bella's information to sink in, but now Jeffrey half rose from his chair, his face flushing deep purple. 'Someone *targeted us*? Someone dared to come against Sachs, against *me*, to make everything I've worked for all these years a public *laughing stock*? That's my name in every story that's plastered over the news stands! They're making *jokes* about my *name*, dammit! I'll . . . I'll . . .'

He subsided back into the chair, pounding the arms with his withered fists, struggling to catch his breath.

'Jeffrey, you promised me you wouldn't get over-excited!' came a low voice, and Bella jumped in shock as Adrianna appeared from behind the huge chair, as usual seeming to move more like a perfectly calibrated, well-oiled machine than an actual flawed human being. She must have been sitting in the shadows at the back of the huge room.

'Here,' she continued, snapping open an ivory pill box on the desk, pouring a glass of water from the insulated silver jug beside it, and handing both to her fiancé. 'This will help.'

Jeffrey Sachs, terror of his company, merciless discarder of two wives who, in his opinion, had passed their sell-by dates, tyrant to his children, took the pill as dutifully as a good little boy obeying his nanny.

'Take a few breaths,' his fiancée instructed, watching him carefully. 'Finish the water.'

Propping her toned buttocks against the arm of the chair, she looked down at Jeffrey's daughters.

'Give him a little while,' she said, and it was not a request but an instruction. 'You understand, I'm sure. I'm concerned for your father's health.'

Naturally, Bella and Charlotte nodded; Bella was expecting silence to fall as they waited for Jeffrey to drink his glass of water, but to her surprise, Adrianna continued: 'So, the company was hacked?'

Bella's eyes snapped wide. She couldn't help looking over at her father. If he said anything, even lifted a hand to indicate that she should not answer until he was ready to speak . . . but he just kept sipping at his water with his thin, beaky lips. Bella's gaze returned to Adrianna, half sitting, half standing, her face as impassive as always, and she realized that Adrianna had expected this, was waiting patiently for Bella to assess the situation and decide to respond to her question.

'Yes, it was,' she eventually answered, and heard Charlotte

shift in her seat, reacting to the fact that Bella had accepted Adrianna's authority to question her.

'We're still processing everything that's happened, of course,' Bella continued smoothly, concerned that the much younger, computer-literate Adrianna might be able to pick holes in her story that Jeffrey would not. 'But the breach has been found, which is the main thing. There won't be any more headlines about guests with missing reservations, or people sent to a three-star hotel rather than five. We're obviously hoping to be able to trace it back and find the source, but the immediate crisis has been resolved.'

'Good, good,' Adrianna said, nodding. 'Jeffrey, you hear that? It is excellent news, and the girls have been very fast in fixing the problem. Who could expect something like this? It is unprecedented. Oh, are the financial details secure? Jeffrey,' she added, 'wanted to be absolutely sure of that.'

'Oh yes, a hundred per cent,' Bella said quickly. 'Those are all encrypted, and no attempt was made to gain access to them. I can completely confirm that.'

'And what about Sash?' Adrianna's green eyes slid sideways to observe Charlotte. 'Since you are here too, Charlotte, Jeffrey was wondering if the boutique chain was affected by this?'

Jeffrey, still sipping his water like a baby bird taking nourishment, nodded in confirmation.

'No, thank goodness,' Charlotte said, her voice clear as a silver bell. 'Obviously the aim was to sabotage Bella and the fantastic job she's been doing. I'm terribly excited to roll out the revamp to the Sash hotels in due course.'

Adrianna stared at Charlotte for a long moment, then

awarded this a little nod. Turning fractionally on the arm of the chair, she looked at her fiancé.

'Better now?' she said, taking the empty glass from him and placing it back on the desk. 'I can leave you if you promise not to get upset again.'

'No, no! Stay!' Jeffrey beamed at her. 'Very good questions! What it is to have a woman with a brain!'

Bella and Charlotte stared straight ahead with impassive expressions.

'Hacked!' Jeffrey repeated, shaking his head, and Adrianna reached out to take his hand. He clasped hers gratefully. 'I had no idea!'

'Neither did I!' Bella assured him. 'It was a wild guess. I was brainstorming with my team, and we started to think about how many high-profile VIPs this had happened to. Not just the really important people, but ones who would be guaranteed to make the headlines. It seemed more suspicious the more we thought about it. Of course, we'd been looking for flaws in our new software, not for bugs from outside! So when I directed a team to search for those instead . . .'

Adrianna was nodding along with this explanation, pressing Jeffrey's hand to signify that she found it acceptable, her gigantic diamond engagement ring flashing out miniature rays of multicoloured light every time she did so.

'We found it pretty fast, thank goodness,' Bella concluded. 'The theory is that the people behind it were assuming we'd react as we did, think it was our own mistake. I mean, it's unheard of to sabotage a hotel chain in this kind of way! You might get hackers threatening to do it, blackmailing us to pay in Bitcoin, but even then they go after the financial side of things, customers' credit card details. Plus, they rarely attack without warning – they give you plenty of notice because they want you to pay up instead. No, only a professional rival would go after our bookings.'

Adrianna looked thoughtful as Jeffrey blurted out:

'Bastards! This would never have happened back in my day! Yes, there'd be dirty tricks, no denying that. We'd bribe, beg, offer whatever stars wanted to stay with us if we needed the publicity. I had to tell heads of security to turn a blind eye to what some film stars wanted – Christ, all sorts of things! Still goes on, of course. But this . . . *this* . . .'

His face began to darken again.

'We're checking everything we can,' Bella said quickly. 'If we can find out who did it, we will.'

'This is because your scheme was so successful!' her father pronounced, much to Bella's delight. She felt her heart surge at the words. 'They're all jealous! I saw that for myself at the awards. Everyone wanting to interview you, talk about the project, say how new and exciting it was. Don't think I didn't take that in!'

He was gaining steam, and Adrianna patted his hand, signalling that he should pace himself.

'It's a tribute!' Jeffrey said loudly. 'Looked at in the right way, it's a bloody tribute! But this press coverage . . . damn it, it's very bad. We have to find out who did this to prove we were deliberately sabotaged, clear our reputation—'

'Just to say, it'll be very, very hard to prove,' Charlotte cut in. 'They'll have hired it out to hackers, there'll be layers of cutouts and false trails to try to stop us tracing it back . . .'

Jeffrey raised his free hand and pointed it at her almost menacingly.

'You stay out of this, young lady!' he ordered. 'This is your sister's achievement that they're trying to ruin! If you can't be helpful, say nothing at all!'

'We will see,' Adrianna chimed in, 'what they can find. It is true that it might be hard to prove. These hackers are very clever, Jeffrey. But I'm sure that if they can prove it, they will. And maybe we can tell the press that we were hacked, to explain the situation?'

Bella stared at her future stepmother, trying and failing to work out what was happening behind that beautiful, sculpted facade, what motivation Adrianna had for the way she was acting.

'Well?' Jeffrey barked. 'Can we put out a statement saying we were hacked? Why not?'

'Why not!' Bella said slowly. 'We don't have to involve the police, after all. They won't investigate unless we file a complaint—'

'No police! I don't want those buggers poking around in our systems!' Jeffrey said, sitting up straighter. 'You know what they're like. Turn around and sell stories to the tabloids the moment they can. The trouble we've had with them in the past! You keep your security as tight as you can, but those bloody coppers still leak like sieves to the papers. I don't want them near Bella's new upgrade thingamawhatsit! If they can get any specs, they'll try to sell them to—' He named some of Sachs's major rivals. 'No. No police.'

Despite her excellent physical self-control, Charlotte sagged infinitesimally in her chair from sheer relief. The gold inset at the neckline of her dress caught a ray of light from the chandelier and then went dull again.

'If that's your decision,' Bella said, doing her best to sound reluctant. They never called Jeffrey 'Daddy' at work, but sometimes it felt impolite not to; this was a sentence that she felt should end with a title, or a 'sir'.

'He has said so,' Adrianna commented, somehow managing not to make this statement sound dismissive. She patted her fiancé's hand.

'So,' she said, 'you have decided. No police, but the press department can say that the company was hacked, correct?'

Jeffrey beamed up at her.

'Very good,' he said. 'You understand that, girls?'

'We can also say that the upgrade's actually working fantastically well,' Bella suggested eagerly. 'The online check-in and automatic room key delivery are going very smoothly, and so far the data from the daily room charge updates and minibar sensors is actually exceeding speed and accuracy targets. We're monitoring client satisfaction and it's extremely positive so far—'

'Excellent!' Adrianna interrupted, but again, in such a way that she seemed to be chiming in with Bella rather than cutting her off. 'This is excellent. It sounds as if everything is proceeding very well, and the hacking is now stopped for good.'

She looked from one sister to the other.

'I am so sorry,' she continued, 'but I am a little tired. Of course I have not at all been working as hard as you two, so I must apologize! But the organization for the wedding is a lot to do.'

'It has to be perfect,' Jeffrey said fondly to her. 'Absolutely perfect. Just as you want it.'

'Barely a month to go!' Bella said brightly. 'Wow, you must be swamped with stuff!'

'*So* much,' Charlotte added, not to be outdone at sucking up to Adrianna. 'No one realizes until they have to do it themselves, do they?'

'As I said,' Adrianna said politely, 'I am not working as hard as you are, not at all. But I am tired just the same and maybe I will rest now, because later on I must go for my run.'

The message of dismissal could not have been clearer. Bella and Charlotte rose from their seats in unison, missing Jeffrey's delighted, eye-brightening reaction to his fiancée mentioning her plans to exercise later, the excited little wriggle of his body.

'Let me walk you out,' Adrianna said.

She kissed the hand of Jeffrey's she was holding, then replaced it on the armrest of the chair among the clusters of sculpted wooden leaves and flowers. Stepping off the dais without looking down, she swung her high heel back to find the steps in the manner of a Vegas showgirl descending a flight of stairs with her plumed head held high. Bella and Charlotte waited for her to lead the way, which she did, swinging open the heavy door very easily; it was clear that as well as practising regular cardio, Adrianna did not neglect her upper body work.

'Come with me for just a moment,' Adrianna said once they were in the outer office. She walked past Tania's desk, giving her a smile and nod of acknowledgement as she went.

'Can I get you a tea or a water, Miss Rootare?' Tania asked, and the sisters exchanged a swift glance to acknowledge the deference in Tania's tone, which was much more noticeable than it had ever been for Jade.

'No thank you, Tania,' Adrianna said politely, sweeping past.

She led the little procession all the way down the central corridor to the far end of the floor. The room which had once been a master bedroom was now, it turned out, a huge and sprawling gym, with machines and pulleys so complicated that they made Bella, who was not a gym rat, blink in shock. Ropes hung from the double ceiling, and from a metal T-bar frame dangled black straps with Velcro loops at their ends. Another metal frame could be spun a hundred and eighty degrees so that the boots fixed to one end would enable the wearer to hang upside down.

A Pilates Cadillac Reformer with immaculate grey leather upholstery stood next to a Gyrotonics machine, all curved wood and strangely positioned pulley wheels. A tyre was propped against one wall, next to a Pilates barrel with a short ladder and a Wondachair, their upholstery matching the grey leather of the Reformer. As well as all this, there was a full complement of hand and free weights, the normal exercise machines one might expect to find in a gym and several that were more arcane, a trampoline and a padded gym floor.

'I like to exercise,' Adrianna said, perhaps unnecessarily.

She walked over to a glass-fronted fridge and pulled out a bottle of green-tinged liquid.

'I will not offer you anything to drink,' she said, 'as you

will not be here long. I know you are very busy, but I want to make one thing very clear and simple for you.'

Uncapping the bottle, she took a long swig of the foul-looking drink, managing not to leave a drop on her lips.

'This story you are telling, both of you, but mainly *you*,' she said, looking at Bella. 'I do not believe it, but I do not care, okay? You have fixed the problem. That I do believe.'

And now her green gaze, almost the exact colour of her health drink, passed on to Charlotte.

'I think that whatever this problem really was, it would not be good for your father to hear about it,' she said. 'His heart is not so good. You understand, he must go ahead with our wedding. It would be a big problem for me if that did not happen. So nothing must worry him before then. I must make that very clear.'

She did not take her eyes off Charlotte.

'This competition he has set you, this saying that only one of you can be the boss and that you must all fight each other, it's stupid,' she said austerely. 'I could not say anything when he started it, but it's stupid, obviously. How do you get the best out of someone in this way? You don't! You bring out the worst. It is clear that is what has happened. So.'

She took another drink from the bottle.

'I can guess what the real story is,' she informed them. 'But I have no interest in bringing it out to the world and giving your father a heart attack. So, we will work together. A new thing for you two, I think.'

Her eyebrows flickered slightly, as if she were trying to register irony.

'I will support this story,' she said, 'the hacking from outside, the rival hotel chain that hates us so much and wants to destroy us. I will make sure that you are not blamed by your father.'

Bella and Charlotte were as hypnotized by Adrianna as Mowgli had been by Kaa in *The Jungle Book*; her eyes were shaped like long ovals rather than round, swirling saucers, but her voice was as smooth, her effect as mesmerizing. In the remake, Kaa had been voiced by Scarlett Johansson, and Adrianna's voice was even huskier and deeper and more seductive than the actress's.

'But from now on,' Adrianna continued, 'if you do anything to upset your father before the wedding, anything at all, I will kill you. I am not exaggerating. I will kill you. You understand this, yes? We understand where we are? I will protect you from being disinhaired – ugh, is that right? Dis-in-hair-it-ed? I hate to get words wrong!'

She looked genuinely cross, stamping one high-heeled foot on the rubber gym floor.

'Disinherited,' Bella volunteered in a tiny, frightened voice.

'Dis-in-her-it-ed. Thank you. I will make sure that does not happen. But if you do *anything* to make your father stressed—'

'We won't!' Charlotte babbled. 'We promise. We won't make any problems with Daddy, or at the wedding.'

Those extraordinary green eyes of Adrianna's flashed fire, no longer a python but an angry dragon.

'*At the wedding?*' she hissed.

'I mean, up to the wedding! At the wedding! The whole time! There won't be any problems!'

Bella had not heard Charlotte this panicked for years, not since she was a little girl. She herself had not been able to scare her into this state, even though she had Charlotte squarely in the frame for the vicious attack on her twin sister's career. But Adrianna was a force of nature, and Charlotte was stammering apologies in a way she had not even done with their father.

Adrianna let Charlotte run all the way down, like a wind-up toy stuttering to a halt, before she said, 'Good. There will be no problems.'

An expression flickered across her face. It was new, and it took Bella some time to identify, as she had never seen Adrianna look dreamy before.

'I am very excited about the wedding,' Adrianna said, her head tilted to one side, her eyes almost soft with anticipation. 'In Venice. I love Venice! Everything will be perfect. The canals, the food, the wine – everything. I went there once when I was a little girl, and I promised to myself that I would get married there, travel in the private motorboats, eat at the best restaurants, all the very best.'

Her eyes narrowed into green slits.

'And *nothing*,' she said, 'nothing in the world will make a problem for my perfect wedding!'

Chapter Twenty-Nine

There is a very expensive company specializing in destination weddings which offers what is called a cloud-bursting service, guaranteeing blue skies on the day in question. A light aircraft takes off at dawn, with a team of highly specialized meteorologists aboard, directing the pilots; the meteorologists' job is to fire mini rockets into any clouds they find, filled with silver iodide crystals that freeze the water droplets.

After a while, the increased weight of the frozen droplets causes them to fall, first as snow, then, melting, as rain. A brief early shower, and then the skies are clear and blue. Since the droplets swell as they freeze, as the clouds break up it looks as if they're exploding, hence the name 'cloud bursting'. It is also known as cloud seeding, because the fine silver particles falling into the clouds are like gigantic handfuls of seeds being sown.

Cloud bursting is often used for commercial purposes. The obvious ones are to improve weather conditions at airports or to lessen hail damage to crops. But it is also employed in the opposite way, to make weather more extreme, specifically for ski resorts that need to be sure of having enough snowfall. It was invented in Soviet Russia to ensure good weather for its huge rallies, and China has taken up the practice for its public holidays, using it to cause heavy rainfall the day before in order to disperse pollution.

Of course, totalitarian countries can make decisions at which democratic ones will baulk. Cloud bursting is by no means cheap.

Music festivals have considered using it, but have been deterred by the cost, as festivals run for several days. The wedding company charges a basic price of £100,000 for the one-off service, more if the location is very remote or the clouds particularly heavy. It was used at the 2008 Beijing Olympics, where money was famously no object, and rumour says it was used before the wedding of Prince Hugo to his bride Chloe, though that will never be confirmed, as the outcry of the British populace at the expense would be full-throated fury.

Adrianna, with her unlimited wedding budget, had seriously considered hiring a cloud-bursting team, but her planner had regretfully had to inform her that the city of Venice had already rejected all previous requests for permits, citing environmental concerns over the repeated use of silver iodide. Fortunately, the weekend of the extended wedding celebrations was sunny and clear. Guests had flown in from all around the world to attend, and were ferried around the city by a fleet of private water taxis, providing the perfect opportunity for the paparazzi to snap photographs of the bridal party and the most socially prominent invitees.

It was not a large wedding, but it was a star-studded one. Jeffrey, with his habitual cunning, had come up with the idea of inviting Catalina, the Earl and Countess of Rutland, and Wayne and Andy Burns. This was ostensibly in order to apologize to them for the whole bookings disaster, but in reality to create positive PR which would cancel out the previous bad headlines, demonstrating that the celebrities affected had forgiven the company.

The pregnant Catalina, who was back home in LA after her tour, had politely declined on the grounds that travelling to Italy would be too disruptive to her growing family. However, the Rutlands and the Burnses had happily accepted the opportunity to celebrate with Jeffrey and his new bride. The Earl, in particular, was a huge football fan and as excited as a small boy to be a guest at the same event as Wayne, one of the acknowledged stars of the contemporary game.

Adrianna and her planner had truly thought of everything. The female guests had been briefed to select outfits in which they would be happy to be photographed stepping in and out of water taxis onto piers by lurking paps who would be crouching down in the gunwales of their own taxis to achieve angles as unflattering as possible. Specific warnings had been issued about short skirts, which offered opportunities to unscrupulous men with long lenses, and spike heels, which might get caught in the boards of the piers.

The newspaper coverage so far had been superb. A magnate of Jeffrey Sachs's status and connections was guaranteed a stream of fawning articles about the beauty of the bride, the elegance of the arrangements and the attractiveness of his family, with the respective ages of the happy couple presented in the simplest factual terms. Online gossip sites, however, were disrupters with no loyalty to Jeffrey, no markers he could call in, and they had happily gone to town on the age difference. The guests, of course, avidly read those sites daily to see coverage of themselves, while pretending to their hosts that they had no idea of their existence.

It was universally agreed that the celebrations so far had been wonderfully organized, and Adrianna was fast becoming a style icon. She and the Countess of Rutland had not only struck up a friendship, they were both aware of how spectacular they looked when photographed together. The two women were tall and statuesque, with superb curves and Amazonian figures; Adrianna was a brunette, the Countess a blonde, which provided an excellent visual contrast, and they were never seen without their hair cascading perfectly around their faces, their make-up flawless and camera-ready.

It helped, too, that their styles were so similar. Both dressed in classic, expertly tailored clothes. The Countess was famous for her white jeans, which showed off every contour of her toned and liposuctioned body. Adrianna had also packed a pair of white jeans, and after a discussion on the first evening, they had coordinated for the next day's lunch, which was to be held on the small island of Torcello.

By the time the various guests arrived at the island, the shot of the two women in their matching jeans standing together in the bow of a water taxi speeding down the Grand Canal – their manes of hair lifted by the breeze, their beautiful faces half covered by huge designer sunglasses, their light sweaters belted smoothly to demonstrate the perfection of their figures – had already gone viral. The paparazzi had followed the convoy of taxis all the way north to Torcello, which lay in the archipelago of the Venetian lagoon, close to the two most famous of the small islands: Burano, known for its lacemakers, and Murano, with its glass-blowing workshops.

The Locanda Cipriani, the restaurant where the lunch was held, had hosted almost every member of the British royal family over the years, and been the location for many celebrity weddings, including that of Princess Alexandra of Greece. Adrianna would have loved to follow in the Princess's footsteps and marry in a location chosen by royalty. Unfortunately for her, however, when you married a hotel tycoon, you did not celebrate your nuptials in someone else's establishment. The ceremony would be held at a privately owned palazzo on the Grand Canal, stunningly grand, though with less of a history of visiting royalty.

Torcello was a tiny island, with only a few dozen permanent residents. Being mostly composed of vegetable plots and the grounds of the Locanda, it was the perfect location for rich hosts who wanted to hold an event in complete seclusion. The lavish gardens which led off the beautiful restaurant were not visible from the water, so that paparazzi in motorboats were unable to capture any shots of the party as they gathered for pre-lunch aperitivi, working up an appetite for the menu of carpaccio, gratin of tagliatelle verdi – one of the signature dishes of the restaurant – semolina gnocchi alla torcellana, grilled scampi and monkfish and John Dory, followed by sorbets and little crepes filled with crème anglaise.

The children ran around the garden, playing hide-and-seek around the pomegranate trees, the American vines that were trained about the gravel walk, the rose bushes and the landscaped shrubberies. Jeffrey's grandchildren George, Emily, Posy and Quant were more or less the same age as their two uncles, Jade's sons Brutus and Roman. However, this kind of age anomaly was so normal in these circles, where rich men traded their wives in for younger versions as casually as other people did leased cars, that no one batted an eyelid.

'It's a shame that Samantha isn't here,' Bella had observed to Bart as they drank their spritzes, the classic Venetian cocktail of white wine, Aperol aperitif and soda water, garnished with a large green olive. 'I didn't realize how much I liked her until she wasn't around any more.'

'Oh, I did,' Bart said gloomily. 'She was the best thing that ever happened to Conway. I can't believe he pissed it away like that.'

'He's scarcely looking unhappy about it, is he?' Bella commented ironically, looking over at their brother, who was flanked by two of the most beautiful women in that entire glamorous gathering, Adrianna's younger sisters Liilia and Sirje. There was a marked family resemblance. Both women had Adrianna's statuesque figure, square shoulders and narrow hips, perfect for wearing clothes. Sirje, the blonde, was the tallest and most toned of the three; Liilia smaller and darker, but their manes of hair were just as lush and voluminous as Adrianna's and the Countess's, and their strong, photogenic features were so like those of their older sister that it was immediately obvious they were related.

Like Adrianna, too, their breasts were so high and round that they owed more to art than to nature. Despite the jutting bosoms, however, Liilia and Sirje were dressed in the most ladylike of fashions, having been strictly supervised by

Adrianna to ensure that her family made the best possible impression in these elevated circles. Their cleavage was not on show, their nails were comparatively short, their shoes were the wedges which upper-class women wore for walking on grass. Their belted silk dresses floated delicately around their curves; no overly fitted, inappropriately sexy clothes which the columnist who wrote about 'Natashas' would have considered typical of the breed.

'They're so stunning,' Bella said wistfully. 'I could look at them all day.'

'Right,' Bart said. 'They're like walking art objects.'

'I'm surprised you're not over there with Conway, chatting them up!' his sister said.

'Ah, well,' Bart said, smiling at her. 'They're a little young for me. Recently I found myself realizing I need a woman, not a girl.'

His eyes drifted over to Adrianna, who was standing with her arm looped through Jeffrey's, her hair pulled back from her face, pinned in a seemingly casual arrangement which showed off the rich highlights in her chestnut hair and the huge emeralds dangling from her earlobes. She might be wearing jeans, but her jewellery made it quite clear that she was marrying a billionaire.

Bella did not notice the direction of Bart's glance, however, as she was reaching up, playfully touching his forehead.

'It's normal temperature! I could have sworn you had a fever!' she said. 'What's come over you?'

'Oh, who knows? Maybe I'm in love with the one woman I can't have,' Bart said, with a smile even sweeter than the first.

'Bart, you do talk a lot of nonsense,' Bella said tolerantly. 'As if there was anyone you couldn't have! You could stroll over there right now and cut Con out with both of those girls!'

'And yet I'm not,' Bart said. He fished the olive out of his glass and took a bite of it. 'Bizarre, isn't it? Maybe I really am coming down with something.'

'Daddy looks very happy,' Bella said, looking in the same direction as Bart was, but mistaking the reason for his stare. 'Pumped up on love. It's amazing, really, that he's so keen to get married over and over again. I mean, he doesn't *need* to marry her. She'd put up with being his mistress for the right salary, surely.'

'Some guys like being married so much they do it again and again,' Bart observed. 'But you're wrong about Adrianna. She rules the roost. He bloody well does need to marry her, if that's what she wants.'

'You're right,' Bella said, vividly flashing back to that encounter in Adrianna's private gym during which she had so thoroughly intimidated Bella and Charlotte. Bella still had no idea why there had been a tyre propped against the wall. 'She has a will of iron, doesn't she?'

Bart nodded.

'Oh, look at Pa's new mama-in-law!' he observed, as Adrianna's stunning mother, also dressed to the nines, perfectly groomed, and looking not a day over forty, appeared from around a hedge, chatting amiably to the Earl of Rutland. 'No secret where the girls get their looks from, eh?'

'No father in the picture?' Bella asked.

'Long gone, apparently,' Bart said. 'But he wouldn't have

contributed to the aesthetics. Estonia's a typical Eastern European country – the men are as ugly as the women are beautiful.'

Bella giggled at the authority with which Bart had pronounced on this.

'I'll take your word for it,' she said. 'You're the expert on the ladies. God, she looks as if she had Adrianna when she was fifteen!'

'Probably did,' Bart said wryly. 'Not an easy life over there, by all accounts.'

'She should really be marrying Daddy, not Adrianna,' Bella observed. 'That'd look a *lot* more appropriate.'

Bart burst out into a laugh raucous enough to draw stares, but the brother and sister were not foolish enough to be having this conversation where anyone could overhear, but were standing safely in the centre of an expanse of lawn.

'Excellent idea!' he said, taking another bite of olive, his perfect white teeth making short work of it. 'If this were a film, or one of those big sexy novels the ladies love to read, that's exactly what would happen at the wedding. Pa would announce that he's realized that Mrs Rootare is the true love of his life, Adrianna would cry and say she's been in love with the best man all this time and fall into the latter's arms. Happy ending all round.'

'Except Daddy doesn't have a best man,' Bella pointed out. 'Just you and Con standing up with him.'

'Oh yes. Well, that puts the kybosh on that scenario,' Bart said, shrugging.

'Bart, talking about the wedding . . .'

'I know.'

Their high spirits dropped like a stone, as did their gazes; both of them stared at the grass in front of them. Jeffrey, with his flair for drama and suspense, had told his adult children that he would be making the announcement about the CEO job during the post-wedding-ceremony formal dinner. It was hanging over their heads like the sword of Damocles, metaphorically ready to behead three of them, leaving only the lucky winner alive.

None of them had an idea about who that would be. Bella had definitely edged ahead now that her rewards scheme upgrade was under way, but had the terrible publicity caused Jeffrey to have doubts about her? Conway was in Jeffrey's very bad books because of the divorce, but what if Jeffrey decided that his elder son and heir presumptive's personal life had nothing to do with his professional one? Charlotte's Sash chain had won another award in the last fortnight, and Bart was wondering whether Adrianna had listened to him and put his case forward to his father, who seemingly could refuse her nothing . . .

'I hate this,' Bella said unexpectedly. 'I really do. Setting us against each other is so horrible. Look at everything that's happened already! And what if it gets even worse when Daddy's made his decision?'

'How are you and Charlotte?' Bart asked, not meeting her eyes.

'Awful,' Bella said flatly. 'How could we not be? I mean, she apologized, but when your sister does something like that to you, you can never see her the same way. And sorry's supposed to mean that you're never going to do it again, while . . .'

She tailed off, not wanting to complete the sentence, but they both knew what Bella was saying. Of course Charlotte would still resort to underhand tactics if she thought she could get away with them. Much as Bart would have loved to be able to defend her, the words would not come.

Bella was surprised to find Bart's hand reaching out for hers.

'It's a shitty, shitty time,' he said, sounding genuinely melancholy. 'Whatever happens tomorrow evening will take a hell of a lot of getting over. Can we promise to have each other's back? Not in a "let's team up against those two bastards" way, but just in solidarity for not – well, not doing stuff we'd be ashamed of in the battle against Charlotte and Con?'

Bella swallowed hard. She was very glad that Bart was not looking at her but straight ahead, towards the main mass of wedding guests, a group clustered around their father and Adrianna, who, in her four-inch wedges, was tall enough to be clearly visible above the crowd.

'Okay,' she muttered, feeling horribly guilty.

Because just that morning, she had received information that would utterly discredit one of her siblings in her father's eyes, and she was planning to use it at the earliest opportunity.

Chapter Thirty

In truly aristocratic circles, a bride does not have adult bridesmaids. They are little girls, ideally no older than twelve, and even if they are strewing petals up and down the aisle, they are never known as flower girls, which is considered a vulgar Americanism. If the bride wants her grown-up sister, for instance, to carry her train, she does not count as a bridesmaid: the correct title is 'maid of honour', or 'matron of honour' if the sister is married, and there can only be one of them.

Adrianna, who wanted to do everything in the best possible style, who would have loved to have been married on the island where Princess Alexandra of Greece had celebrated her nuptials, had been genuinely torn when the wedding planner informed her of this etiquette rule. Her wedding procession started in perfect aristocratic style, with Posy and Emily in frilled dresses and the four little boys making adorable pageboys in equally frilly shirts.

Posy and Quant, by now veterans of Instagram photo and video shoots, were the stars, the first to appear, as they could be relied on to set an example to the other children. Their backs were straight, their expressions appropriately solemn as they carried their silver baskets of white rose petals, scattering handfuls as they went, trailed not only by sighs of appreciation but also glances of veiled envy from parents whose children were neither so beautiful nor had so much composure at such a young age.

Charlotte and Paul looked extremely smug at Posy and Quant's perfect demeanour, and their self-satisfied smiles only deepened when George and Emily, who were not dealing well with their parents' separation, visibly squabbled their way down the aisle, Emily actually kicking her brother at one stage over a dispute about who should throw their petals where. Brutus and Roman, who were being supervised by nannies during the weekend, as naturally their mother was not invited, were no better behaved. Brutus looked understandably angry, Roman bored and sulky. Both dragged their feet in their shiny polished shoes and made only the most cursory efforts to scatter petals while staring pointedly at their father, who seemed barely aware of their presence.

After the children, however, contrary to posh protocol, came Adrianna's sisters. Adrianna had simply been unable to tell Liilia and Sirje that they could not walk down the aisle carrying bouquets: not only would it have broken their hearts, her mother would never have stood for it. Besides, they were so absurdly beautiful, such excellent clothes horses, that it would have been a waste not to include the two of them on aesthetic grounds alone. Their dresses were in a shade of palest blush pink which would have been challenging to most women, but which threw into relief their green eyes and matt white skin; as they processed down the aisle, every man in the ballroom of the palazzo sat up straighter and unconsciously fumbled with his tie. Bearing bouquets of lily of the valley festooned with trailing greenery, Liilia and Sirje looked like Grecian goddesses in their asymmetric, ankle-length dresses, a perfect pair.

And then the bride appeared. There was no train for her sisters to carry. Adrianna had indulged herself with the wedding dress she had dreamed of since watching Cinderella films when she was a little girl: her two models had been the Disney version and the musical *The Slipper and the Rose*, which costumed the heroine for the ball scene in full eighteenth-century style, with a square neckline, beaded stomacher, puffed sleeves and hoop skirt.

The very distinguished designer whom Adrianna had chosen to make her dress had swallowed hard on being informed of her concept, looked at the bride's extreme beauty and perfect figure, considered her unlimited budget, and decided to go ahead with the commission. It was very old-fashioned but, in its way, quite magnificent. Adrianna had sensibly eschewed the over-the-elbow gloves from the Disney version and the glittering silver wig from *The Slipper and the Rose*, as the dress itself was theatrical enough.

The aisle between the two sets of delicate gilt chairs had been made unusually wide to ensure it could accommodate the hoop skirt, which was so huge that only a woman of Adrianna's height and majestic bearing could have carried it off. The dress was made of white silk, the delicate fabric rippling under the soft lighting, the stomacher so heavily decorated with hand-sewn embroidery and pearls that it looked encrusted. More pearls framed the neckline, a triple band of them, as lustrous and gleaming as Adrianna's smooth, pale skin. Woven into her hair, instead of the Disney Cinderella's over-girlish ribbon, was a pearl and diamond tiara, part of a parure with the matching earrings and wide choker, a style suitable only for a woman with her stature and swan-like neck.

Her sisters had caused every male guest to sit up and blink in appreciation of their beauty, but Adrianna was beyond mere sexual appreciation today; she was like a reigning queen, to be revered rather than desired. There was no veil to hide her beautiful face or make her seem demure. It would not have suited the dress in any case, but it was definitely not Adrianna's style. Her expression was wonderfully serene as she processed slowly towards her fiancé. Jeffrey, wearing full morning dress, as were all the male guests, was beaming proudly, a smile that seemed to reach from ear to ear. It was echoed by Adrianna's mother, following her in a pale-blue dress, who looked as blissful as if she herself were about to marry an ageing billionaire; she was proudly wearing a superb set of blue topaz earrings and necklace that had been the groom's gift to his mother-in-law.

The ballroom was exquisitely decorated with flower arrangements which twined around the classical columns reaching up to the double-height ceiling, and huge candelabras were placed around the expanse of marble inlaid floor, the orange-blossom scented candles subtly perfuming the air. The velvet curtains at the high windows which ran along one long side of the ballroom were looped back to show the stunning view of the Grand Canal bathed in late-afternoon sunlight, but the windows were closed to keep out the inevitable noises of vaporetto buses, water taxis and private boats buzzing back and forth on the water. Up in the gilded musicians' gallery, a small chamber orchestra played a tranquil selection of unchallenging classical music.

The ceremony was large yet intimate, sophisticated but family-friendly. Jeffrey's four adult children were present to demonstrate that they approved of their father's new bride, that there was no scandal attached to the swift divorce and remarriage; Adrianna's insistence that his two young sons should also be at the wedding had cost Jeffrey a significant extra outlay to Jade, but it had been worth every penny to Adrianna. Her goal had been to demonstrate respectability and stability. This ceremony made it clear that she was not a homewrecker like Conway's mistress, but a wife who fully intended to take her marriage seriously.

The road to this moment had been a rocky one. The stress of keeping Jeffrey sexually satisfied, while simultaneously making sure he did not drop dead of a heart attack before the wedding, had been very wearing on his fiancée. One would never have seen the exhaustion on Adrianna's face, however, as she executed the slow-motion glide down the aisle which she had been practising for weeks, giving her guests plenty of time to take in her radiant beauty and her extraordinary eighteenth-century-inspired wedding dress. Halting by her husband-to-be, she turned to hand the pearl-and-ribbon-wrapped bouquet she had been carrying to her mother, and reached out to clasp Jeffrey's wizened fingers as the officiator, the Mayor of Venice himself, began the civil ceremony.

Bart, standing by his father's side, never took his eyes off the bride. He was by now utterly infatuated with Adrianna, and not just sexually, though that was of course a considerable factor. The mere thought of her hand on his waistband that day at Vanbrugh, her lips on his, made him swallow hard and swiftly summon up the image of the TV presenter Anneka Rice: while having a happy morning fiddle with himself, years ago, he had idly switched on the television, only to see her holding forth on a cookery show. He had immediately lost his erection. Ever since, the mere thought of her face was his fail-safe strategy for making sure he didn't get a hard-on.

Conway, beside him, was fully occupied in leering at Liilia and Sirje, both of whom were smiling coyly at their sister's newly single, highly eligible stepson as their mother looked on in approval. Then, however, Mrs Rootare's all-seeing gaze moved over to Bart's face, and her lips pinched together in concern and disapproval. Bart's feelings for her unavailable daughter were all too obvious to her mother.

She watched him like a hawk, but Bart behaved impeccably; there was no outcry from him, no attempt to step forward and beg Adrianna to reconsider. He simply stood there and watched her marry his father, her low contralto voice moving smoothly through the responses, his father sounding higher-pitched than her as he piped up excitedly. The Mayor was smiling at him tolerantly, since Jeffrey's delight in snagging his prize was so blatantly obvious. When the ceremony concluded, Adrianna bending towards her husband so that he was able to kiss her over the breadth of the huge, slightly swaying hoop skirt, Bart's heart physically hurt him for the first time in his entire life.

It was as if she had reached into his chest cavity with one

of those beautiful, long-fingered hands and squeezed it hard, stopping the blood flow. He pictured her smiling as she did so, compressing his heart, the same calm, clear smile of absolute triumph and achievement she wore now as she pulled back from Jeffrey. She nodded in thanks at the Mayor. Then her gaze flickered for a moment to Bart, and his heart expanded, flooded with blood once more, because with great shock and excitement he realized that in that second she looked truly, genuinely wistful.

The look vanished immediately. But it was more than he had managed to elicit from her for the entire weekend. He had been staring at her the whole time, trying to get precisely this: something, anything that would have given him the sign he needed, and she had been avoiding him so completely, refusing to meet his eyes, that he had known it was an entirely deliberate strategy. Only now that she was safely married to his father had she permitted herself this swift glance, a sort of release.

Applause broke out, pattering up to the extraordinary frescoed ceiling of the ballroom, as bride and groom processed back down the aisle. Bart stood and watched them go, his hands thrust into the pockets of his grey-and-white-striped trousers. Liilia and Sirje flitted across the carpeted dais to him and Conway, smiling angelically: twin beauties, available where Adrianna was not: younger, more charming, much more willing to please.

But they were not their sister. Bart had spent some time with them that weekend, enough to know that although they were intelligent and confident, they lacked Adrianna's iron will, her sharp wit, her dominating personality. Even as he extended his arm to Sirje, whom he was supposed to escort into the drinks reception that would precede the celebration dinner, his thoughts were entirely on her older sister. His new stepmother.

Conway was already folding Liilia's fingers round his black-jacketed arm, winking at her as they started down the red carpet; Jeffrey and Adrianna had reached the end of it, the guests standing up now, still applauding. Bart looked at his older brother, whose blond head was ducked over Liilia's, saying something that was making her laugh. Sirje fell in beside Bart, her beautiful face upturned to him, probably waiting for him to say what a lovely ceremony it had been, how happy he was for her sister and his father. Adrianna's sisters were much more typically feminine than she was, more pliant, waiting for the man to speak first, ready to be amused by even the weakest joke he might make.

Well, Bart thought, from the look of Conway, that suited him down to the ground. No more Samantha to organize his life for him and be the ideal wife; he seemed to be much keener on an ideal concubine instead. A year ago, if Bart had been asked what kind of woman he would settle down with – if he ever did – he would unquestionably have answered by describing a Liilia or a Sirje type. Now, however, he had developed a taste for stronger meat.

The Mayor was stepping down from the carved lectern, extending his arm to Adrianna's mother with the anticipatory smile of a sixty-five-year-old Italian man who has been assigned the company of a beautiful woman twenty years younger than him as a dinner companion. Mrs Rootare moved towards him, the blue topazes dancing enticingly in her ears, expensive chypre perfume emanating from her warm skin, her thick hair, tinted lighter than her daughter's to disguise the grey, pulled back from her face in a very flattering style.

But even as she placed her hand on the Mayor's arm, she was surveying Bart, her new grandson-in-law, with eyes narrowed in suspicion.

Chapter Thirty-One

Adrianna needed to open both the double doors to her suite to be able to manoeuvre through it in the wide hoop skirt. She was remembering scenes from films like *Gone with the Wind*, wondering how wide those doorways had been; this was something you never considered until you found yourself strapped into a hoop. Rhett Butler hadn't carried Scarlett O'Hara upstairs in this kind of dress, of course. It had been a velvet dressing gown, as she remembered. Much easier. If Scarlett had been wearing a hoop she would have been completely safe from her husband's advances; he'd have swiftly realized it was far too much work to get it off.

Why are you even thinking like this? Adrianna asked herself wryly. *No one will be sweeping you off your feet and carrying you up a staircase for years to come, whatever you wear!*

It was time for her to take off the dress, and frankly, she was more than ready to do so. After the initial excitement of seeing herself as she had always imagined she would look on her wedding day – a princess from a fairy tale, her dress sewn with real jewels – the boning of the corset was cutting into her painfully, and she was longing to be able to walk normally without having to ensure that the four-foot-wide hoop didn't bump into walls, doors and tables.

She hadn't even been able to sit down; she had found out the hard way that women wearing hoop skirts back in the day had only been able to perch on specially made padded stools. And she was very thirsty, as she hadn't drunk anything all morning so that she wouldn't need to go to the toilet once she was strapped into her dress. That too would have been impossible. They would have needed to find her a chamberpot.

Adrianna and Jeffrey had already posed for their pictures downstairs. Now, she would ring the employee of the designer who had made her wedding dress, summoning him to help her out of it and into the equally beautiful one made for the dinner and dancing to follow. This was a cleverly scaled-down copy of the original. It was made of the same material, white silk heavily sewn with pearls, but it was uncorseted, and though the skirt was full and billowing it was not a gigantic, Disney-princess construction which needed a framework to give it shape.

First, though, after being unzipped and unhooked from the wedding dress, after the hoop had been unfastened so that she could step out of it, Adrianna would slip into a dressing gown and have any necessary touch-ups performed to her hair and make-up. She had plenty of time; the drinks reception, with hot and cold flowing canapés, was timed to last at least an hour. It would run until the bride descended the central staircase, making an entrance in her second dress, drawing oohs and aahs of appreciation and signalling that the group would move back into the ballroom, which was currently being set up for the formal dinner.

The dresser, together with the hairdresser and make-up artist, would normally have been waiting in her suite for her, ready to spring into action like a race car crew at a pit stop, changing tyres and doing repairs at lightning-fast speed. However, Adrianna had told them all to wait in their rooms until she called them. She had sensed that directly after the wedding ceremony she would need some solitude to process her emotions.

And as so often, her instincts had been absolutely correct. She was exhausted from keeping up a perfect facade while surrounded by the horde of hugely important guests, and she was also in a considerable amount of shock. She could still not quite believe that she had pulled it off, succeeded in marrying Jeffrey Sachs. During the entire arduous process of meeting, courtship and engagement, she had never allowed herself a single moment of uncertainty that she would achieve her goal. She had sensed that if doubt ever crept in, she would be unable to maintain the self-possession and sangfroid required to enthral Jeffrey to the point that he was prepared to turn his life upside down for her. It had been essential to act as if he needed her more than she did him: somehow, she had managed to convince him that was the truth.

From the moment Jeffrey walked into Farouche, saw her standing behind the bar and goggled in admiration, it had been a long and nail-biting process. As she told him that no, she wouldn't serve him the Shiraz he wanted, but would give him a whisky sour instead, the words had miraculously flowed out of her as if she were a femme fatale in one of the 1940s film noirs that she loved: Lauren Bacall or Rita Hayworth, as cool as ice on the surface but with passion for the right man simmering underneath. Her manner had been perfectly judged, creating a bubble around her which Jeffrey had been desperate to pierce.

It hadn't all been a role. This was her personality, her style, her way of engaging with people; she was highly sexual, but life experience had made her wary, guarded, and she knew that a certain type of man saw her as an irresistible challenge. She had played a game with Jeffrey Sachs, a dance where she took two steps forward and one and a half back, never fully available, always withholding something that he craved, until, dizzy with desire, he had announced that he was leaving Jade, begged her to marry him, and presented her with an engagement ring so enormous and heavily faceted that it looked more like a weapon than a piece of jewellery.

Having brought Jeffrey to this point, she had harried him to speed up his negotiations with Jade to ensure as swift a divorce and remarriage as possible. Her efforts to reunite him with his children, to bring the fractured family together, had been entirely genuine; she had even suggested that Christie be invited to the wedding, and though Christie had declined the invitation, she had done so in a very cordial way, adding a note to say that she hoped to meet Adrianna eventually, and thanking her for inviting Christie's children and grandchildren to Vanbrugh Manor.

Adrianna had had more than one motive for that invitation. She very much disliked the idea of family estrangement, which stemmed from her own father having run off when she was young, leaving her mother to fend for herself with three young daughters. But also, after Jeffrey's ridiculous challenge, setting his children to compete for the job of CEO of Sachs, she had realized it was crucial that she get to know them as well as she could. Adrianna had very strong feelings about the future of the Sachs Organization.

Well, very soon it would be decided. In a few hours, her stupid old King-Lear-acting husband would stand up, clink his wine glass, look around the room filled with guests stuffed with superb food, sipping their coffees, loosening their belts, and make his announcement. Ah well, he would be coming up to the suite to collect her when she was ready to make her second appearance of the day, and then she would have some firm words with him about how to resolve the entire messy situation . . .

There was a bottle of champagne waiting for her in an ice bucket on the monumental porphyry marble table in the window embrasure with the superb view over the Grand Canal. Canapés too, arranged on exquisite fine china plates with gold borders, decorated with the emblem of the ducal family that still owned the palazzo: tiny bites of cherry tomatoes, mozzarella and basil, the classic Venetian cicchetti; arancini balls of fried rice; polenta crostini topped with *baccalà mantecato* – whipped salt cod pureed with cream – black olives with parsley and tiny pieces of red pepper. Adrianna walked over to the table to pour herself a glass of champagne. Picking up the bottle, she promptly put it down again and stuffed a polenta crostino into her mouth, following it in quick succession with two more.

Her eyes closed in sheer bliss. She never ate anything that had been fried or cooked in cream. For other dieters, a very rare treat might have been ice cream, or strawberries dipped in chocolate, or cheesecake. But for Adrianna it was something savoury, like the crostini. Or the arancini, of which she proceeded to have two. She could almost feel herself bloating; even more shockingly than this mini binge, however, was the fact that she didn't give a damn.

This wouldn't last. She was highly vain about her appearance, and knew perfectly well that she could not afford to be one of those wives who snagged the rich man and then let herself go. But despite her clear awareness of the bargain she had entered into with Jeffrey, Adrianna could not summon up even a tiny flicker of guilt that she had just eaten five mouthfuls of very fattening carbs and was now pouring herself a brimming flute of champagne. If she couldn't pig out on her wedding day, when could she?

'Adrianna!' a voice hissed outside the door of the suite.

It wasn't Jeffrey, who had a key card. Nor the dresser, make-up artist or hairdresser, none of whom would dream of imposing themselves on her, let alone hissing her first name so intimately. A hammer pounded at the base of her throat under the weighty pearl and diamond choker, which suddenly felt as if it were strangling her. She reached up, unfastened it, dropped it to the table, where it landed with a heavy clatter. And then, moving as fast as she could in the hoop, which meant a fast series of short, almost dancing steps, she hurried across the suite and opened the door to find Bart standing there.

'What are you *doing*?' she blurted out, and then hated herself for saying something so obvious. She was never obvious.

'Let me in, please!' Bart pleaded.

Her hoop skirt entirely filled the doorway, its circle belling into the corridor. There was no way he could possibly gain access to the suite if she didn't let him in, and doing that would be a terrible idea for all sorts of reasons.

And yet she stepped back without a word. She told herself that it would be better than to keep Bart standing in the corridor beating on the door like a madman, and she was already concocting an excuse for Jeffrey if he came in early and found Bart here. Bart was desperate to be CEO, she would explain: he had tried to grab a last-minute opportunity to beg his father's new wife to put in a good word for him.

I need just one thing of my own, she told herself, the pounding at her throat ever more insistent. *Just one lovely thing before I have to spend the rest of Jeffrey's life with him . . .*

Bart strode in, slamming the door behind him, and advanced on her. It was exactly like the moment in a film that made you sigh with delight, the one you replayed again and again when you were alone, the hero taking the heroine's face in his hands and kissing her passionately. In the film, of course, the heroine's huge hoop skirt would not tilt wildly off balance with the sudden contact of the hero's muscular thighs, making her shriek and grab his arms for balance. Bart mistook this for womanly enthusiasm and kissed her even harder, making her cling to him even more.

She allowed herself to close her eyes and, for just a little while, kiss him back.

His hands were crushing her earrings into the soft skin of her neck, her tiara into her scalp, and she didn't care. In fact, for a shocking few seconds, she no longer saw the extremely expensive jewellery Jeffrey had given her as the spoils of war, or her wages, but as shackles he had put on her, nailed through her earlobes, clamped to her scalp, weighing her down; fetters she needed to tear off so that she could be free—

This image was so opposed to everything she had struggled for that her hands came off his arms in reflex. Instead of holding him close, she was shoving him away, a strong woman who was more than able to send him off balance. She was still, however, incapable of saying a word. The film noir femme fatale who had ensnared Jeffrey Sachs had vanished, and in her place was a pathetic heroine from a romantic comedy, struck dumb by a man's kiss. She writhed in embarrassment.

It was Bart who finally said: 'You taste really good! Did you eat some cheese just now?'

He took a long breath, staring at her, his eyes on a level with hers, their irises so flooded with blue that she felt she was falling into them, tipping over a cliff edge into a deep azure sea.

'I think I might be falling in love with you,' he said simply.

Adrianna gaped at him. She never did this either. She had known that her wedding day would provide many unique experiences, but these were not the ones she had been expecting. In his morning suit, dressed so formally but so dashingly, his blond hair delightfully tousled, he not only acted but looked as if he had stepped out of a romance novel. Of course, this being Bart, who was always perfectly clad, the silk tie was the exact blue of his eyes, the pale-grey waist-coat cut snugly to show off his flat stomach, the trousers tight enough that . . .

No. She dragged her eyes upwards again. But his own were so extraordinary, and fixed on her so imploringly, as if he actually meant the insane words exploding from his mouth, that this barely helped.

'I've been thinking about it all weekend, and I honestly don't think it's because I can't have you, if you see what I mean?' he was saying. 'That would be so obvious, wouldn't it? Man who never settles down falls for his father's new wife because she's forbidden fruit! But it's not that. It's *you*. You're exactly the kind of woman who would suit me. God knows if you feel the same! Why should you? You were quite right when you said I was useless, a pretty toy. I've never really done anything – well, I suppose I've raised loads of money for charity, but that was only doing things I liked doing anyway, so I honestly can't count that—'

Adrianna stepped towards him so fast the big skirt swayed wildly, grabbed his face and kissed him as passion-ately as he had kissed her, her fingers tangling in his blond curls. She had no intention of entering into an affair with him. Cheating on Jeffrey at all, let alone with his son, would simply be too dangerous. There would be enemies, rivals, people surrounding them, employees of Jeffrey's who would be all too willing to run to her husband or the press with wild stories.

Not even the most powerful people in the world were safe from gossip. And being safe was one of Adrianna's greatest priorities in life. It would have been even if her prenup had not contained huge financial penalties for being unfaithful to her husband.

So this was her unexpected goodbye to being this close to a hard young man's body, to feeling strong muscles and smelling the fresh scent of his skin, to showing real desire rather than allowing someone to do what he wanted to her. Then she pushed him away once more. She had never been a risk-taker; this was already much further than she should have gone. Both of them were breathing so quickly, staring at each other so wildly, that if Jeffrey had walked in at that moment, no excuse in the world about Bart wanting the CEO position could possibly have convinced even her doting bridegroom that nothing suspicious was going on between his bride and his son.

'I just want to make you happy! Let me make you happy!' Bart said, and before she had any idea what he was about to do, he had dropped to his knees, pushed up her skirts, lifted the hoop and crawled underneath it. His hands wrapped around her thighs, working their way up. She was not wearing tights or stockings, as the dress was so heavy and hot she hadn't wanted any more layers: she could feel his hot breath on her skin, and her entire body froze as he grabbed her silk underpants and pulled them down.

From across the room, she heard a click, the lock released with the key card. The doorknob turned. Her legs felt like jelly, but she could not move an inch. She had no choice but to stand there as the door swung open and watch as into the room strode her husband, a deep frown on his face, followed, for some inexplicable reason, by her mother.

Chapter Thirty-Two

One swift look down was all she had time for, a frantic check that Bart was fully concealed by the skirt of her dress. No telltale gleam of black shoe sticking out from beneath the hem, no distortion in the shape of the hoop from his body pushing against it. She felt him shift against her legs as she said loudly to warn him, in case under the layers of fabric and metal he had failed to hear the door opening:

'Jeffrey! What's wrong? You look so angry! This is supposed to be the happiest day of our life! And Mummia! What are *you* doing here?'

'It's my damn son!' Jeffrey said furiously, and Adrianna felt Bart, who was still holding her knickers, which he had pulled down to her knees, wobble dangerously at these words.

'He's got the damn bloody cheek to be flirting with Liilia, right under my nose!' Jeffrey continued. 'He's barely even officially separated – he knows I'm livid with him about leaving Samantha – tomcatting around on her right from the beginning, huge bloody scandal in the making – poor woman, she did nothing to deserve that – and now he's practically backing your sister against a wall and sticking his

426

tongue down her throat! Friends of mine are joking to me about it, asking me how I feel about my wife's sister getting off with my son!'

'I don't know what to say,' Adrianna mumbled, which was no more than the truth.

'There's nothing *to* say!' Jeffrey said crossly. 'I just wanted to let you know! I've had a word with him, and the wedding planner's reorganizing the place settings to put her as far from him as possible. I've just tried so hard to protect your name, darling! The scandal with Conway and that girl from the bar where you used to work – bringing you down, dragging you into it – birds of a feather and all that . . .'

'Oh, Jeffrey, you worry too much!' Adrianna cooed, while darting a look at her mother that combined anger and bafflement. 'Please, let me get myself ready to be beautiful for you for the dinner. I'm going slower than I thought. I'm so happy! I've just been standing here taking it all in. I can't believe I'm finally Mrs Sachs!'

Jeffrey's face broke into a smile of pure joy.

'I know!' he crowed blissfully, coming towards her.

Since she could not move, she stretched out her hands to him rather, she thought near-hysterically, like Cate Blanchett in a similarly stiffened, full-skirted dress, playing Elizabeth I greeting Sir Walter Raleigh. It was a gesture designed to welcome a courtier while still keeping him at arm's length, preventing him from coming too disrespectfully close to the reigning monarch, and it worked perfectly. Jeffrey took her hands worshipfully, gazing with fondness at her wedding band.

Adrianna couldn't help glancing down at her left hand,

too, but her gaze was fastened on the gigantic diamond engagement ring; she looked at it multiple times a day, the physical symbol of everything she had gained. Even now, distracted as she was by her husband's son hiding under her skirts, his hands hot and sweaty on her bare thighs, that enormous chunk of carbon was able to give her a rush of satisfaction.

'I can't wait for tonight!' Jeffrey said lecherously.

Adrianna shuddered. Jeffrey was insisting on taking Viagra on his wedding night, overruling his doctors' strict prohibition of its use. He had had to go to a less scrupulous clinic on Harley Street to get it. Adrianna, dreading the prospect, had behaved in a way that she could feel proud of, pointing out nobly that he should listen to his doctors: but he had overruled her. At least when his heart gave out because of the strain, she could honestly say that she had begged him not to take it.

The old goat was counting the hours until he would pop the pill. Ugh! She couldn't bear to let him talk about it any more with her mother and Bart listening in. If she had had the fan to go with her eighteenth-century-inspired dress, she would have tapped her husband's hand with it in flirtatious reproach. Instead she pulled her hands from his and said reprovingly:

'Jeffrey! Mummia is here, *please*! Though I don't know why she's here – I need to get ready!'

The look she gave her mother, as her husband mumbled apologies and turned away, was a clear command to leave. God knew it was stressful enough to be concealing Bart from Jeffrey without her mother barging in here as well.

'You go to entertain your guests, Jeffrey,' Mrs Rootare said to the son-in-law who was thirty-five years older than her. 'Please! I will come straight away. There is just one thing I wanted to say to my little girl now that she is a wife. I will be right behind you.'

'Of course,' Jeffrey said, nodding. 'Of course. A mother with her daughter on her wedding day . . .' He beamed as sentimentally as if Adrianna were a virgin, and her mother about to sit her down for the talk about the facts of life. 'Darling, you'll send someone to get me when you're ready?'

'Of course I will!' Adrianna said, much too loudly, as if he were deaf. But the relief she felt that he was leaving the room was so overwhelming that she had to let it out somehow. 'The dresser from the designer will come to fetch you while they're finishing my hair and make-up, just like we planned – now go, go on, or by the time I'm ready our guests will be completely drunk—'

'Always so practical!' Jeffrey said fondly. 'I love you so much!'

He bustled out of the suite. As he did so, Bart half-pulled, half-shoved Adrianna's silk knickers up her legs again, clumsily pushing them over her buttocks. Adrianna's eyes widened in surprise, and she staggered a little off balance, which she covered as best she could by going on the offensive. Putting her hands on her hips, she glared at her mother and snapped in their native Estonian:

'What the *hell*, Mummia? What are you *doing* up here? Why aren't you downstairs telling Liilia to back the fuck off Conway because it's driving Jeffrey crazy? How difficult is it for her to keep her legs together so that my husband doesn't have a heart attack on our wedding day because she's making out with his son, the little whore?'

Huh, she thought suddenly. *And would that be such a bad thing?*

The ring was on her finger, and, in consideration of Jeffrey's advanced age, there was no requirement in the prenup for their marriage to last for a specific period in order for Adrianna to get her full settlement. She had been so careful up till now taking care of his health, making sure he didn't get over-excited; but now, who cared? Let him work himself into a frenzy over Liilia and Conway if he wanted! It would save her having to pretend she was looking forward to the prospect of him finally fucking her . . .

'So? Who cares if he drops dead?' Mrs Rootare said, echoing her thoughts, and Adrianna was extremely grateful that Bart could not possibly understand a word of Estonian. 'You're married now! And he's not blaming Liilia, is he? Let him make himself crazy so he has a heart attack! Every time his blood pressure goes up it's a good thing, eh? Dirty old bastard! Now, where is that son of his? He came up here, I saw him! He's hiding somewhere, isn't he? Next door, I bet!'

She darted across to open the door that connected the bedroom to the sitting room of the suite, disappearing inside to search for Bart. Adrianna felt a kind of eruption underneath her skirt, a tipping up of the hoop behind her that sent her off balance. She took a step or two forward to avoid falling as the hoop rose precipitously and Bart, like a human tidal wave, surged out from below it and rolled away. After a split second of panic, she realized that she was standing in front of the canopied four-poster bed and that he was heading for concealment underneath it. Thinking fast, she made a big production of calling out to her mother, 'Mummia, what's going on? What are you doing? I need to start getting changed!' while she walked further across the room, swishing her hoop skirt as loudly as possible to cover the sounds that Bart was making as he lifted the valance and wriggled on stomach and elbows under the bed, like a paratrooper on manoeuvres. By the time Mrs Rootare re-entered the bedroom, Bart was safely stowed away and Adrianna was turning around, presenting her back to her mother, saying:

'I really need to wee! I have to get this dress off! Unzip me,' just in case her very acute mother decided to conduct a detailed search of the bedroom as well.

'I saw him sneak away and come upstairs,' Mrs Rootare said, even as she started to unhook the top of the dress. 'And I saw the way he was looking at you, Adrianna. He's a gorgeous boy, and just your type. You always had a weakness for the tall blond ones. But you can't let him anywhere near you! If Jeffrey had any idea!'

'I haven't!' Adrianna lied. 'He knocked on the door, but I sent him away.'

'You have to tell him he can't do that! *I* will tell him,' Mrs Rootare said so firmly that Adrianna couldn't help but smile as she thought of poor Bart being lectured by her dragon of a mother.

'Please do,' she agreed, and she meant it. 'You'll scare him even more than I will.'

The zipper was sliding down, and she gasped at the relief of feeling the boning of the corset loosening its iron pressure into her flesh. She was perfectly happy to suffer to be beautiful, to quote the French expression, but it was a tremendous relief when that suffering relaxed its grip. She reached up ruefully to massage one of the long red dents imprinted in her flesh.

'I will tell him that he is a spoilt boy who is putting you in danger,' Mrs Rootare said grimly. 'That you were not born rich, like him, and you have worked so hard to help your mother and sisters and send money back to us, and he is a selfish, spoilt boy who is putting everything at risk by thinking with his penis!'

'You're right, tell him to stay away from me, Mummia,' Adrianna said, suddenly feeling very weary again. 'He's a spoilt, selfish boy. Useless. A pretty toy.'

Mrs Rootare nodded so vehemently that Adrianna could feel her entire body bobbing up and down with the gesture.

'Stand still,' she said, easing the dress off Adrianna's arms, working the corset down over the hoop, walking in a slow circle around her daughter, protecting the fragile silk, the pearls stitched to it, the heavy embroidery. The wedding dress had cost upwards of £200,000: despite the fact that Adrianna would probably never wear it again, both women were highly respectful of that amount of expenditure.

Finally, Mrs Rootare had the dress puddled in a wide white circle on the carpet at the base of the hoop. Adrianna bent down, lifted the metal cage so that it wouldn't snag on the delicate material, and took several big steps forward, moving well away from the dress before she set the cage down again and started to unfasten it. It opened like the medieval torture device known as the iron maiden: she stepped out with the relief of someone released from confinement.

I looked wonderful, she told herself. *I had my dream wedding as Princess Cinderella. It was everything I ever imagined it would be.*

But for my second wedding, I'm wearing the simplest dress I can possibly find. Maybe just a bikini.

Walking across the bedroom to the ensuite bathroom with its frescoed ceiling was like floating now that the cage was finally unstrapped from her waist. Above her, fat naked cherubs cavorted with curvaceous maidens whose modesty was barely concealed by wisps of gauzy fabric, just like modern starlets looking for tabloid coverage that would raise their price when they sold themselves on yachts during the summer season on the Riviera.

Washing her hands, Adrianna stared at herself briefly in the mirror. The contrast between her head, elaborately adorned with tiara and earrings, make-up and hair still immaculate, and her body, clad just in bra, knickers and soft, flat leather slipper-shoes, seemed symbolic of her life; perfectly controlled on the surface, vulnerable beneath. Her expression remained inscrutable as she reached for the dressing gown hanging on the back of the door and belted it around her waist.

In the bedroom, her mother had lifted the dress and draped it very carefully over the velvet sofa, its skirt spread out so wide that it covered the entire piece of furniture. She was beaming down at it in pure pleasure.

'So much money!' she said happily. 'So much that Jeffrey spent just for your dress! With thousands of real pearls! You have done very well, Adrianna. I am so proud of you.'

Once more, Adrianna looked down at the enormous diamond on her finger for comfort.

'I need to ring my team and get ready for dinner,' she said flatly.

'Of course! I'll get your phone,' her mother said.

But just then, the suite door swung open once more. As before, there was only one person who would walk into the bedroom without knocking first. Jeffrey's face was unhealthily flushed, and he was hunching over, walking slowly, while Charlotte, following him in, looked triumphant, her eyes bright with excitement.

'Jeffrey?' Adrianna exclaimed, looking from him to Charlotte. 'What's *happening*?'

Rather than rushing to support her husband, however, she found herself walking over to the marble table and retrieving the flute of champagne that she had been about to drink when Bart had knocked on the door of the suite. That felt as if it had been hours ago! And now her husband was back yet again with his bitch daughter behind him, the one who had tried to backstab her hardworking sister and nearly taken the company down with her, while her younger brother lay under the bed on which Adrianna would be celebrating her wedding night by letting her husband put his dick in her for the first time . . .

Not even Adrianna could deal with this situation without fortifying herself with alcohol. Picking up the flute, she drank half the contents in one go, then swivelled to face the scene which was under way.

'I needed to talk to Daddy before dinner,' Charlotte said, meeting Adrianna's eyes with a placatory look that signalled that she had obeyed Adrianna's command and not raised anything contentious until the wedding band was on her stepmother's finger. 'It's really important! He's going to make his announcement about who runs Sachs in a couple of hours, and he needs to have all the information possible so he can be sure he's got the right person for the job—'

Jeffrey was stumbling over to the bed: he collapsed on it, more like a bag of bones being unloaded than an old man sitting down.

'What did you *tell* him?' Adrianna asked, walking over to sit down next to her husband. The mattress sagged; she couldn't help wondering how low it went, how much breathing room Bart had beneath it.

'Jeffrey, some champagne?' she asked, handing him the glass, only to be waved away by her husband. His face was greyish now, the colour draining away. He looked like a man who has had a terrible shock and is only slowly adjusting to the new reality, his breathing stertorous. Mrs Rootare, who had no intention of missing this juicy scene, sank quietly into one of the armchairs that flanked the sofa, folding her hands in her lap, face agog.

'Bella's been having an affair with Ronaldo, Maria's son!' Charlotte announced. 'Since before poor Thomas had his accident! Think of the publicity! That's absolutely *not* something we want in the press! She's serious about him, too – it's not just a fling!'

Adrianna never goggled, but then, as she had already acknowledged, it was a day of firsts. She felt as if her eyes were about to pop out of their sockets. Under the bed she heard a movement, faint enough to be unnoticeable by anyone who didn't know there was a six-foot-two man lying beneath it.

'Maria . . . the *housekeeper*?' she asked. 'In Maida Vale?'

'Yes!' Charlotte said. 'Can you *imagine*?'

Adrianna finished the rest of her champagne.

'Well,' she said with her characteristic understatement, 'no wonder Jeffrey is upset.'

'Daddy? Daddy, are you in there? Daddy? Let me in!'

Someone was pounding on the door, calling out: the voice was muffled, but it had to be Bella. Adrianna looked at her mother, shrugging: a clear 'Why not? In for a penny, in for a pound' signal which had Mrs Rootare on her feet, slipping across the room to open the door to Jeffrey's other daughter.

Bella came in like a hurricane, not even thanking Adrianna's mother for opening the door, which was quite unlike her. She stormed across the bedroom, setting a course that brought her to the centre of the room, triangulating the confrontation. Adrianna and Jeffrey were on the bed, Charlotte closer to it, while Bella, to Adrianna's surprise, had taken the most dominant position, controlling the situation: Bella could see everyone, while Charlotte had to shift to look at her sister.

'What's she been telling you?' Bella demanded, her hands on her hips, staring at her father. 'You'd better be careful, Charlotte! *Really* careful! What's she said to you, Daddy? Tell me!'

Jeffrey raised one hand to his throat in a claw, as if he were having trouble breathing. Since he didn't answer straight away, Adrianna said matter-of-factly:

'Charlotte just told us that you are having an affair with Ronaldo, Maria's son.'

'Oh *really*?'

Bella gave Charlotte a death glare.

'Well, if we're putting all our cards on the table,' Bella said, 'here goes!'

My God, Adrianna thought. *She's going to tell Jeffrey that Charlotte sabotaged her upgrade scheme, messed with the VIP bookings? Does she have any proof?*

Adrianna was quite positive that this was the truth of what had happened, and so was Tania, Jeffrey's executive assistant. Adrianna had put a great deal of effort into befriending Tania, and she had been successful. It helped that Tania had loathed Jade, as most people seemed to have done. It was very rare for a younger trophy wife to have an easy transition when she supplanted the previous spouse, but Adrianna's had been surprisingly smooth.

It had also made a difference that she had treated everyone who worked for Jeffrey with the respect that Jade had failed to show. Tania had been particularly struck by the fact that Adrianna had worked as hard to reunite Jeffrey with his first four children as Jade had done to alienate him from them.

Tania was also as opposed as Adrianna to Jeffrey's pitting his children against each other in a death race for the top job. Like Adrianna, she had done her best to dissuade him from setting them this challenge, and failed. For the last six months, Tania had been monitoring developments from her eyrie on the twentieth floor. According to her, Bella's team was on lockdown, not breathing a word to outsiders about what had happened during the hacking incident.

However, Tania, like Nita, had tentacles everywhere. Bella had been seen, before her meeting with her father, hurrying towards her brother's office; casual enquiries of Bart's two 'assistants' had elicited that Bella had been extremely angry with him, and that Bart had been hitting the tequila heavily that day. Putting two and two together, adding in the fact that Charlotte had been waiting to intercept her sister in Jeffrey's office, and that Bart would never have engaged in anything nefarious on his own account, Tania had correctly concluded that Charlotte had organized the sabotage herself, using her younger brother as a pawn. She had passed this conclusion on to Adrianna.

So this was what Adrianna was expecting to hear. But when Bella actually spoke, her words came as such a shock that the gasps in the room were as loud as viewers of a horror film reacting to the sudden appearance of the psycho killer.

'It's true!' she said, her voice trembling. 'I *have* been having an affair with Ronaldo for months now, and I really cared about him. I thought we had a future. Until I found out Charlotte was having an affair with him as well, way before he got together with me! The two of them set me up!'

Chapter Thirty-Three

Jeffrey turned his head wildly from one daughter to the other, identical lovely faces with wildly different expressions. Bella's was agonized: she had won a Pyrrhic victory, in which the winner suffered such heavy losses that they might as well have been defeated themselves. And Charlotte had suddenly gone pale, putting a hand out to steady herself against the back of a nearby chair. Bella's accusation was obviously true.

'They set me up,' Bella repeated, her voice still unsteady. 'They've been seeing each other for over a decade. He staged bumping into me at a bar in Chicago when I was there on business – I checked. Charlotte's assistant rang Robin's office that night – Robin's the Sachs head of PR there – and asked where she'd taken me for drinks, so he'd know where I was. He did a great job, by the way,' she said bitterly to the side of Charlotte's head. 'A truly brilliant job. I believed every word he said. He isn't even in advertising, apparently – that was a lie too. The investigator I hired says he's some sort of freelance travel consultant. He lied about everything.'

Adrianna was shaking her head in disbelief. It sounded too unbelievable to be true: and yet Charlotte's face was clear confirmation of Bella's story. It could easily have been a coincidence that Ronaldo had bumped into Bella and perversely decided that it would be fun to seduce the other twin sister, bag the set. The phone call from Charlotte's office, however, made it clear that she was involved.

'I imagine you did that as a backup in case your plan to sabotage my relaunch of the bookings system didn't work,' Bella continued, still to her sister. 'You were really thorough, weren't you? Yes, Daddy! It was Charlotte who did that! We weren't hacked by anyone! She made me tell you that story. She blackmailed me by saying that she knew I'd been having an affair and that she'd tell the police about it if I didn't go along with her version of events.'

'The *police*?' Adrianna asked, since her husband was still speechless.

'I was Skyping Ronaldo when Thomas came home,' Bella confessed. 'There was a big scene. Thomas grabbed me, I pushed him away and he fell down the stairs and hit his head. It was an accident – or self-defence – he left bruises on me, Daddy's lawyer saw them—'

Adrianna pursed her lips in sympathy.

'But Charlotte said that it would look suspicious,' Bella continued, 'that Thomas had caught me Skyping with another man and fallen downstairs straight afterwards—'

Adrianna nodded, understanding the point. She glanced sideways at her husband, who seemed frozen in place. She put her hand on his; it felt cold to the touch. He was breathing, but still grey, and his gaze was distant, staring at the far wall of the bedroom, unable to look at either of his twin daughters. Obviously, he had been hit terribly hard by the revelation of how far Charlotte had been prepared to go in her attempt to take Bella out of the running.

'Jeffrey?' Adrianna said softly, but he did not respond.

'So you see, Daddy?' Bella concluded. 'Yes, I had an affair with Ronaldo! But so did Charlotte! And, much worse, *she* was the one who sabotaged the systems, lost us all that income and caused such terrible publicity! She's not fit to run the company!'

Bella, Adrianna noticed gratefully, was at least having the decency to keep Bart's name out of this. She jumped: she had forgotten about Bart beneath her, listening to his sisters tear each other apart like this, finding out that the contest Jeffrey had created had caused infinitely more damage than anyone could possibly have expected—

'He's your brother,' Jeffrey said.

Adrianna froze. Did Jeffrey know somehow that Bart was lying directly below where he was sitting? Her brain raced, trying to come up with an explanation that would cover his being stretched out on the floor underneath his father's canopy bed.

'*What?*' Bella said blankly.

'Ronaldo. He's your brother,' Jeffrey repeated in a flat, emotionless voice. 'I had an affair with Maria a long time ago. She only told me the baby was mine after it was born. She knew I would have insisted she get an abortion.'

Charlotte and Bella stared at their father in utter horror. Bella reeled as if she had been slapped in the face, teetering so much on her high heels that Mrs Rootare jumped up and guided her over to the sofa, pulling the wedding dress away to make room for them both. Bella flopped down like a rag doll, her head on Mrs Rootare's shoulder.

'So *that's* why you sent him away to school!' Charlotte said eventually, her knuckles showing white bone through the skin as her hands formed into fists. 'So we wouldn't hang out with him any more! *That's* why he went to Harvard! You must have told the school to make sure he didn't go to a British university.'

'I paid for everything,' Jeffrey said, 'as long as he stayed away. That was the arrangement. He gets a very generous monthly allowance from me as long as he lives in America. Maria wasn't happy about that, but it was the deal.'

'Wait – if you're sending him an allowance, that means he *knows*!' Charlotte gasped. 'He *knows* he's our half-brother?'

Jeffrey nodded.

'His mother insisted on telling him, and I couldn't stop her,' he said. 'Though I tried. I tried very hard.'

'And she's still working for you,' Adrianna commented, her carefully cultivated poise standing her in very good stead. At least she sounded calm, even if her heart rate was through the roof.

'She cares about me,' Jeffrey said, shrugging. 'And she's so good at her job. I'd hate to have to replace her.'

Well, it's a very good thing I didn't marry you for love, his new wife thought, meeting her mother's eyes, exchanging a glance of silent shock at this family of which Adrianna had just become a member.

'I'm going to be sick,' Charlotte choked, clapping her hands to her mouth.

'There!' Adrianna urgently pointed across the bedroom to the bathroom door. 'Over there, the bathroom—'

Charlotte took off running across the room, ominous noises bubbling in her throat. She shot inside the bathroom, in too much of a hurry to shut the door behind her; Adrianna walked over and closed it to silence the explosive noises Charlotte was making. She must have drunk more than usual at the post-wedding reception, probably to give herself Dutch courage for the revelation she was planning to make to her father. It sounded as if she were vomiting up a fountain of champagne and stomach acid.

By contrast, there was absolute silence in the bedroom. In a bizarre parody of good hostess manners, Adrianna poured Bella and her mother glasses of champagne and handed them round, deciding that everyone could do with a pickup. Looking over at Jeffrey, however, she felt he required something stronger. There was a well-stocked bar in the living room, and she returned from it with a snifter of brandy for her husband. He seemed barely aware of her presence, but at least he took the glass.

On hearing the revelation about Ronaldo, Mrs Rootare had drawn Bella into her arms, hugging her for comfort just as she would have done with one of her own daughters. As Adrianna offered the flutes, Mrs Rootare encouraged Bella to sit up and drink a little, murmuring that it would do her good. Bella obeyed, still half leaning against Adrianna's mother, sipping at the champagne.

'How did you find out about him and Charlotte?' Adrianna asked Bella, sitting back down beside her husband. 'You had some suspicion about them?'

'Not of him,' Bella muttered. 'I wanted some ammunition on Charlotte, something she didn't know I had. I got a team of private investigators to follow her everywhere she went. She took a trip on the Eurostar for the day to Paris and met him there. And once they found out about him, they kept digging. They've been involved for years. He must really care about her to have set me up like that. And she must have thought I was such a passive idiot! That I'd let her spy on me, undermine me, and not start spying on her as well!'

She managed a bitter half-smile.

'I can't say it feels very good to have proved her wrong.'

'And . . . you cared for him?' Mrs Rootare asked delicately.

'It broke my heart,' Bella said desolately. 'But at the same time, finding out that it had been a set-up wasn't as much of a surprise as you would think. I realized straight away he'd been too good to be true. He was . . . *perfect.*'

Mrs Rootare put her arm around Bella again.

'Ah, that is not possible,' she said kindly. 'You will know in future. If they seem to be perfect, they are not. Actually, it is a very bad sign. I am sorry, but it's good you learn this now.'

Bella took a long breath. 'He must really hate us. To do something so terrible, for such a long time. He must have been laughing at us all along – how stupid we were, how ignorant.'

No one looked at Jeffrey, who was staring down at his brandy glass.

'This is a very difficult time for you,' Adrianna said, as gently as she could. 'Thomas is still in his coma, and now – *this*! And Charlotte has behaved so badly, your own sister!

You must be very kind to yourself, Bella. You must go slowly, and be kind to yourself.'

'The doctors say I have to get ready to turn off Thomas's life support,' Bella mumbled. 'There's no positive prognosis for him coming out of the coma.'

Adrianna and her mother shook their heads, partly in sympathy, partly in disbelief at the magnitude of what Bella was going through.

'I'm so sorry,' Adrianna said, as Mrs Rootare stroked Bella's arm comfortingly.

'Honestly, I've been expecting it,' Bella admitted. 'It isn't a terrible shock. From the moment I saw him at the bottom of the stairs . . . he looked dead already. I never really thought he would recover from that.'

Mrs Rootare pursed her lips.

'It's better this way,' she said frankly. 'Better than if he wakes up and there are things very wrong with him. You remember Uncle Alek, Adrianna? It was not good. He was drunk and fell downstairs,' she explained to Bella. 'But he did not die, just broke his back and could never walk again. It was very, very bad for everyone. Him most of all.'

Bella nodded.

'I've thought that too,' she said. 'It's a huge relief to hear someone else say it.'

'Life is hard,' Mrs Rootare said simply. 'But we must carry on. Life is for the living. Drink more champagne, smile if you can, put the past behind you. Have only good thoughts and good memories.'

She patted Bella's arm firmly. Clearly, an Estonian woman who had been through the mill herself was exactly the person to lean on when your husband was in a coma and your lover had turned out to be your half-brother. Mrs Rootare's words had a cheering effect; a spark of light came into Bella's eyes, which had been dull as clouded glass before.

Over her head, Mrs Rootare's eyes met her daughter's. Her expression said clearly that this was all very difficult and dramatic, but they had no choice but to move on with the wedding celebrations; there was a roomful of VIP guests downstairs waiting for their dinner. Adrianna gave the slightest of nods in reply.

'Listen to Mummia,' Adrianna said to Bella. 'She talks great sense. Mummia, you will take care of Bella today, won't you? Make sure she is okay?'

'As if she were my own daughter,' Mrs Rootare said, smiling at poor Bella, who managed another half-smile in return.

'Well, this is very sad for everyone,' Adrianna pronounced, taking full control of the conversation. 'It's hard to know what to say in a situation like this. But one thing I must say, and that is that Jeffrey has to give up this idea of announcing tonight who will be CEO. It is too much. I never liked the plan, and now I am putting down my foot.'

She finally turned to look at her husband, who, though sitting upright, seemed almost as comatose as Thomas.

'I will say now what I think,' she continued, 'and then we will talk about it later. *Not* today. This was always stupid and dangerous. Like the play *King Lear*, when he asks all his daughters to say how much they love him! Look what happens at the end! You can see that King Lear was not a good father. If he had been, his two older daughters would not have been so bad when they took power. Jeffrey, you have not been a good father. You ignored your grown-up children for years and you do not know them very well. Drink some brandy. You have had a shock. It is good for shocks.'

Her husband raised the glass to his lips with trembling hands.

'You should have decided yourself which one of the children it should be, not set them against each other like dogs after a bone,' his wife said reprovingly. 'Tania agrees with me.'

Bella's eyebrows shot up at this; invoking Tania demonstrated how sure Adrianna was of her position.

'You know what I think, Jeffrey,' Adrianna was saying. 'We have talked about who should take over from you, and this ...' She cleared her throat. 'This new information changes nothing. It's clear that, when she is ready, Bella should become CEO. When she has dealt with the situation with her husband, taken some time to rest and recover from ... everything. The technological upgrade has been a great success – we can see that already. It's very exciting and brave, what she has done, and it makes good business sense. You think that she is boring, the safe one, but you are wrong. She has taken a big risk and it is working.'

Bella choked on her champagne, but Adrianna carried on; as far as she was concerned, she was simply stating facts with which no one should have any problem.

'Charlotte is not suitable for the job, obviously, not after this. But what she has done was out of desperation, and not typical of her normal way to work in the company. Tania

447

says this and I believe her. She must be watched in future, but I do not think that Charlotte would do things like this if you had not made them all act like – like dogs with a bone. I think also she has been punished by what you have just said. Much more than Bella.'

Everyone glanced briefly towards the closed bathroom door. The palazzo was large, the rooms huge and sprawling; the bathroom was far enough away that nothing could be heard inside. Whether she was still throwing up or not, Charlotte was showing no signs of being ready to emerge.

'So we keep Charlotte, I would advise, but with checks on her,' she said. 'Put her in charge of the design across all the hotels, not just Sachs. Call her design director. She is wonderful at that, and it will make her feel better about not running the whole company. Bella is not good at design. Not at *all*.'

Bella meekly accepted this. It was no more than the truth.

'The Sachs hotels need Charlotte,' Adrianna continued. 'They need to be fresh, chic, smart. Everyone wants that now, not just the guests who stay in boutiques. Everyone wants to feel they are in a boutique!'

Jeffrey had taken some brandy now, and colour was returning to his cheeks as he stared at his bride, nodding slowly.

'Conway is fine as CFO, Tania says,' Adrianna stated. 'I know you are angry with him, Jeffrey, but what he does with his marriage is not to do with his job, in my opinion. Still, he is not – how do you say it, with the hands?'

She waved hers in the air for inspiration.

'Hands-on!' she said triumphantly. 'He is not hands-on

with the hotels, and the CEO should know about them. He should not be CEO. As for Bart—'

She couldn't help glancing at the base of the big canopy bed to see if she spotted any movement, even though she knew she wouldn't; what did she expect? Was Bart going to jump so violently at the mention of his name that the mattress bulged up in the middle, like a slapstick comedy film?

' – as for Bart, there is no point in him having an office in the building with two pretty girls who cost a fortune in salary and do nothing, apart from maybe have sex with him when he's bored,' she continued firmly. 'His charity work is good for the brand. He should do that. Also he should travel around the hotels, around the world, to meet politicians, ministers for tourism, mayors of cities. He should be a travelling ambassador. He is charming, handsome, everyone will love him. But he should not have an office with secretaries! He could not run a public toilet, why should he have an office? Tania's assistant can easily organize this and work with the travel department to make the arrangements.'

Bella's eyebrows were up again at this further indication of how closely her new stepmother and her father's treasured PA were working together. There was the faintest movement of the valance on one side of the bed, but no one apart from Adrianna noticed it.

'And finally, I will have a role in running the company,' Adrianna announced in a tone that brooked no objection. 'Jeffrey has messed up his children with this nonsense. You four cannot be left to make peace after all the fighting. We will decide together, Jeffrey and I, how this will work. I have been in hospitality since I was sixteen and I know about entertaining and how to run a business. I will have plenty of time for this, because Jeffrey will need to rest a lot, now he is retiring. You will be surprised, I think, Jeffrey,' she said, fixing him with a basilisk stare, 'how much you will need to rest once you are retired.'

'It's all been so much to take in,' Jeffrey said, his voice a feeble whisper. 'Such a lot to deal with.'

'I know,' Adrianna agreed.

She refrained from pointing out that almost all of it was entirely his own fault, as, from the look of him, he was perfectly well aware of that already. He was visibly sagging, his face still ashen. She wasn't sure how much of her well-rehearsed pitch he had heard, but the main thing was that she had convinced him to skip making an announcement about the CEO appointment today.

'We have plenty of time,' she said gently. 'We will go on our honeymoon, relax, talk about all of this. You can decide if you agree with everything I have said. We will talk it over as a team. Because now we are married, we are a team.'

She set down her glass.

'And now it's past time for me to get ready for dinner!' she said. 'No announcement to upset anyone, just a lovely dinner, how nice! Mummia, please go to tell the wedding planner that we are running late, at least an hour by now. It will not be a problem for the food – the main courses are already prepared, they are served at room temperature in the Italian style. The pasta will be cooked when we are eating the anti-pasti. No, wait.'

She looked from her stepdaughter to her husband, and decided that the former was in better shape than the latter.

'Bella, can you do that?' she asked. 'Find the wedding planner? It will be good for you to have something to do, I think.'

Bella nodded.

'It will,' she said. 'Keeping busy is always the best thing for me. If you've got anything else I can help with . . .'

'Yes! Please tell Conway – and Bart –' Adrianna added quickly, remembering that Bart was not supposed to have overheard this whole conversation, 'that there will be no announcement at the dinner. Everyone can relax and enjoy themselves. You don't need to tell them my thoughts,' she said with a small smile. 'Let's wait for that. We have plenty of time. Oh, and make sure you are sitting next to Mummia at dinner. Get the planner to reorganize the seating.'

Bella nodded again, standing up.

'This has been – God, I don't know *what* it's been!' she said ruefully. 'I'm still processing everything. But – only good thoughts and good memories. That's great advice.' She smiled at Mrs Rootare. 'And, Adrianna, thank you for recommending me for CEO—'

Adrianna held up her hand, the diamond engagement ring glittering spectacularly.

'You are welcome. It is best for the business. But go *now*, please,' she said, kindly, but firmly. 'Mummia, I want you to take Jeffrey downstairs. He'll be fine now he has had his brandy. Won't you, Jeffrey?'

It was phrased like a question, but it was a command. Obediently, Jeffrey Sachs gave his empty brandy snifter to Mrs Rootare for disposal on the bedside table and let her put one hand under his arm, gently helping him to his feet.

'I'll be there as soon as I can,' Adrianna said. 'I will come down on my own. Jeffrey can wait for me at the bottom of the stairs. It will be less tiring for him.'

Bella hesitated, looking towards the still-closed bathroom door.

'But what about Charlotte?' she asked.

'I will deal with her,' Adrianna said. 'Don't worry. I will make sure she is okay and send her to her room to recover. If she does not come down to dinner, don't go to look for her. I can check on her later if it's necessary. Remember,' she added firmly, 'be nice to *yourself*. It is not your job to take care of her.'

Nodding once again, Bella hurried across the bedroom to open the double doors for her father and Mrs Rootare.

'Adrianna?' she said, looking back at her stepmother. 'Thank you so much for this. We've been tearing each other apart, and it's wonderful to think we might be able to put ourselves back together again, even a bit. Welcome to the family.'

Jeffrey nodded, perking up at this.

'Good girl,' he said to his daughter. 'Well said. She's a treasure.'

'She truly is a treasure,' Mrs Rootare said fondly as she led her new son-in-law out of the suite. 'And very smart too. If you let her, she will make everything better.'

'You know,' Bella agreed, following behind, 'I honestly think she will.'

Chapter Thirty-Four

Adrianna found Charlotte curled in a ball on the bathroom floor, her back to the huge white marble bath, her face the same colour as the marble. She was hugging her knees and staring ahead of her, her eyes blind. Beside her lay her phone, which she had been carrying in one of the pockets of her wide-skirted dress. She turned, hearing Adrianna enter, and slowly focused her gaze as she looked up at her new stepmother.

'I Skyped him just now,' she said. 'And he laughed at me. He said I was stupid not to have guessed – why would Daddy give the housekeeper's son all that money for his education, especially in America, where it costs a fortune? He said the allowance Daddy gives him is nothing compared to what the rest of us have, and it wasn't fair. He wanted a chance to work at Sachs, like us, but Daddy told him it was never going to happen. So he found a way to meet me and got me into bed. For revenge, he said.'

Charlotte retched on saying the last words, but there was clearly nothing left to come up. She must have reached the loo in time, as there was no sign of vomit anywhere. But the room still smelt of it, the sour, acrid smell of alcohol and stomach acid. Adrianna went over to the vanity stand, picked up her lightest, most citrusy perfume, Pucci Vivara, and sprayed it into the air a few times to improve the atmosphere.

'It's over now,' she said calmly. 'Jeffrey is very much to blame. He should have told you when you were adults, and able to hear it. Let the boy join the family a little, not kept him in America like a dirty secret.'

'Lee was hoping that I'd be CEO and give him a job at Sachs,' Charlotte said. 'He told me, just now. He thought we would keep on having a secret affair, and I'd give him a job, and Daddy wouldn't be able to do anything about it. He wanted to work for Sachs as a victory over Daddy sending him away. I thought he cared about me, but he just saw me as his way in. I thought I had my life so perfectly organized. Paul and the children for home, and Lee for sex . . . Oh *God* . . .'

She retched again.

'I told him I was in love with him, and he laughed at me,' she said pitifully.

Adrianna had neither the time nor the inclination to engage in a therapy session with her wayward stepdaughter.

'It's a difficult situation, I agree. But you need to get up now,' she said.

She considered whether to offer Charlotte a glass of water, and decided against it; given the state Charlotte was in, she might well throw it straight up again as soon as she had drunk it. Adrianna's brow furrowed as something occurred to her.

'*Lee?*' she asked, bending over and extending her hands to Charlotte. 'I thought he was called Ronaldo.'

'Lee was my nickname for him when we were little,' Charlotte said, allowing herself to be pulled to her feet. 'We used to play building forts, besieging each other, in the garden, and he was the general a lot . . . we saw a film with General Lee in it, *Gone with the Wind*. I started to call him that, and it stuck. You know how kids' jokes are.'

Adrianna nodded as she walked Charlotte out of the bathroom.

'Go back to your room and drink some water, slowly,' she said. 'Lots of water, but not much at once. Order some plain bread and some yoghurt. Tell them to bring some salt, too. That helps to balance your stomach after you have been sick. Take your time. If you can come and join us, good, but your father and I will understand if you can't. Maybe lie down for a while.'

By the time Adrianna had finished giving these instructions, they had reached the door of the suite. With a light, firm push, she sent Charlotte into the corridor, where she stood aimlessly, as if unsure where to go. But Charlotte was no longer Adrianna's concern. She shut and bolted the door, then she walked over to the connecting door to the living room and bolted that too.

Finally, for the first time that day, no one could intrude on her. She took a deep breath, relishing this, weight pouring off her shoulders.

Shuffling noises indicated that Bart was finally wriggling out from under the bed. The sight was so comical that she burst out into much-needed laughter, tears springing to her eyes as he caterpillared out onto the carpet, fluff clinging to his face and clothes.

'I think you should have a word with the cleaning staff,' he said, brushing a clump of fluff off his waistcoat. 'Clearly they're skimping on vacuuming! Thank God I don't sneeze easily. I had a dust bunny the size of my thumb hanging over my face.'

He sat up cross-legged on the bedside carpet.

'So,' he said, 'my family is utterly and completely fucked up. I don't even know how to deal with what I just heard.'

He shook his handsome head in disbelief.

'Pa had sex with *Maria*? He's always been able to have any woman he wanted, the most beautiful ones on the planet – I mean, look at you! I adore Maria, she's like a second mother to me—'

He pulled a face at his own words.

'Well, isn't *that* ironic, considering what we've just found out from Pa!' he observed, shaking his head. 'Anyway, she's a lovely woman with a heart of gold, but she wasn't exactly a stunner even back in the day. Pa likes them long and leggy, and she's barely five foot tall and rounder than she's high.'

'For some men,' Adrianna observed dryly, leaning back against the bolted door, 'all they need sometimes is a woman who is there.'

Bart laughed, but without any humour to it.

'I'll bow to your superior experience,' he said. 'In fact, I'm bowing generally. You were right about every single thing you just said about all of us, and especially about me. What the hell am I doing, turning up and sitting in my office—'

He put quotation marks around that word with his fingers, mocking himself.

'– drinking myself into a stupor? Of *course* I should be roaming the world in seat 1A on the best airlines available to humanity, charming tourism ministers into coughing up all sorts of concessions to Sachs! It's the perfect job for me! Frankly, if Pa had any sense he'd make *you* CEO.'

A faint smile curved Adrianna's lips.

'I know,' she said. 'But I will be happy to work with Bella. She will do a good job.'

'Will she be okay?' Bart asked. 'That was bloody brutal. I honestly don't know how Charlotte can look either of us in the eye again.'

'Either of you?' Adrianna said. 'I think all three of you.'

Bart considered this.

'Wait,' he said slowly. 'Conway too? You mean—'

'I mean I think someone gave Samantha a push to check into what Conway was up to with other women,' Adrianna told him. 'She would not have done this on her own – she would not like to think about it. Someone told her, and then because of her pride, she would have to find out the truth. And I had never heard of this Cook Islands place, but I was curious about it. It seemed so unlike Conway to go that far, be that sneaky. Conway, who kisses women in Morton's where other people can see! I talked to Tania and she did research that shows that anyone can open this kind of trust in the name of anyone. We think your sister did it so your father would have another reason not to give the job to Conway.'

Bart heaved a deep sigh.

'After what I just heard, I believe it,' he said. 'This is bloody depressing. You must be wondering what the hell's wrong with this family.'

He looked at her hopefully.

'Not too late to get a divorce!' he suggested.

Adrianna broke into another laugh.

'If I were a queen,' she said, 'you would be my – the clown who jumps around with bells, making me laugh – how do you say that?'

'Court jester,' Bart said, kneeling up on the rug and holding out his arms to her. 'Come here and let your court jester finish what he started. It's not exactly usual for the jester to be the queen's secret lover as well, but you're not exactly a conventional woman, are you?'

'I shouldn't,' she said, but she was walking towards him, untying the belt of her dressing gown, letting it fall to the floor, once more feeling like a femme fatale. Bart's bright-blue eyes were hot enough to burn holes in her skin. 'We shouldn't.'

'Just this once,' he said. 'I swear. We have to do this, just once. We *have* to.'

Adrianna halted in front of him; he pulled down her silk knickers once more, closed his mouth around her, warm and wet, his tongue starting to work magic. It felt like paradise. Her eyes shut in absolute bliss, and she realized there was dampness on her lashes. His hands were wrapped around her high buttocks, pulling her close; she opened her eyes again, wanting to look down and see him making her come, tangling her fingers in his thick blond hair, her hips starting to pump against him.

He made a noise like a deep growl in the back of his throat, and she realized that she was actually crying now, with exhaustion and relief and happiness, as she started to come. How on earth had she ended up on her wedding day with both a new husband and a new lover? Her previous resolution never to let Bart close, never to yield to the temptation he presented, had crumbled to dust and ashes. How could she let this happen only once? How could they stop this sheer, transcendent pleasure, now that they had found each other? Lust she could have fought, pushed back, managed to banish. But this, she knew, was not just lust.

I deserve this, she told herself as her hips pounded against his mouth, as she came over and over again, his tongue flickering against her, knowing precisely what she needed and where. *I've worked so hard. I've done so much and come so far. I've brought my husband's family back together, and I'll make him as happy as I can for as long as he's alive. He deserves that, for marrying me and treating me so well.*

He'll never find out about me and Bart, I'll make sure of it. But I can't give this man up. He may be just a pretty toy, but he's my toy, and no one will take him away from me.

Her fingers tightened possessively in Bart's hair as he licked his lips and smiled up at her.

'Your turn,' she said, sliding down to the carpet, pushing him back, unzipping his trousers. 'You'd better come quickly, like I did. I have my wedding dinner to go to.'

He sighed in bliss as she pulled down his boxers and closed her hand around his penis, which was already as stiff as a rod. Meeting his eyes, she blurted out:

'I think I'm falling in love with you too, okay?' and watched his big blue eyes fill up with joy for a long moment before she lowered her head and took him in her mouth.

Chapter Thirty-Five

One year later

'I'm so excited,' Sirje said with a beaming smile as she sat at Adrianna's dressing table, looking at herself in the mirrors from several angles at once. 'It's so kind of you to let us get married here! I feel like I'm in *Four Weddings and a Funeral* – or *Downton Abbey*!'

'I know, darling,' Adrianna said fondly as she pinned on her sister's veil. 'I still feel like I'm in a film sometimes here too. Did you look at the house listing I sent you, the one that's only five miles away? It's not as grand as Vanbrugh, but it's still lovely, and you don't want to have to manage a whole estate anyway. It's too much work for a party girl like you. But you could come down for weekends. It'd be great to have you so close – I'd love that!'

'I don't feel grown-up enough to have a country house yet,' Sirje admitted. 'I want to travel to every single sexy, glamorous place in the world, and so does Conway. He says he wasted so much time with Samantha playing house, when what he really wanted to do was go crazy in Ibiza and

Sardinia and Aspen and Verbier – oh, I have to learn to ski, apparently!'

She pulled a face.

'I don't see why I can't just soak in the hot tub and wait for him to come back from the slopes! But no, he wants me with him.'

'Better that way. Don't leave him alone for any length of time,' Adrianna said with her usual devastating frankness. 'You know what you're getting into – he screwed around on one wife right from the start. You're always going to have to keep an eye on him. He takes after his father – he'll be looking to trade you in after ten to fifteen years.'

'But I have my secret weapon,' Sirje said with a very naughty smile, sliding her hand down to cup what lay between her legs, the penis and balls that were strapped and tucked away so deftly that no one would ever have suspected their existence.

'Sirje, there are other chicks with dicks in the world,' her sister said firmly. 'Look at the one he cheated on Samantha with! I don't know why it didn't occur to me that he'd *love* to meet you, but there was so much going on before my wedding, it went straight out of my head. But seriously, you're not the only gorgeous whore in the world who happens to have a penis, you know?'

'I know, honestly I do,' Sirje said. 'I know what guys are like, Adri. I know Conway's not exactly the faithful type. But then, neither am I! The couple that plays together stays together.'

'Mmn. Not always, in my experience,' Adrianna said wryly. 'Bring in someone else and things can get very

461

messed up very quickly. The stories I heard at Farouche! But you have a great prenup, which is the important thing.'

'And I get extra for promising never to have kids!' Sirje said blissfully. 'I'm the luckiest girl in the world! It's perfect, Adri, really it is. You know I always worried that when I met a guy I was serious about, the kid thing would be an issue. Of course there're all sorts of ways to have them nowadays, but still, I know lots of girls who've been dumped for not being able to have their own. Bastards, eh? They like that we've got our extra bits for fun and games, but then they bitch that we don't have the full package. Like *anyone* has the full package!'

Sirje reached up to adjust a hairgrip that was digging into her scalp.

'But Con says he's done with kids,' she continued. 'He's not that keen on his own, to be honest. I spend more time with them when they're visiting than he does. So I've promised never to push for adoption, buying eggs, anything like that. Not a problem. I'm making just as much from not having them as if I did, and none of the hassle.'

She met her sister's eyes in the mirror.

'Don't worry, Adri,' she said gently. 'It may not last, but who cares! We'll have a ton of fun together, and if he does leave me in ten years' time for a younger model, I'll be a very, very rich ex-wife. I'll probably end up like his mother – go to live in the South of France and work my way through one toy boy after another.'

She grinned.

'I will turn those boys *out*,' she observed. 'After a while with me, there isn't *anything* they won't know how to do!

Oh, you know Christie's asked Mummia to come and stay? We'd better watch out for her with Christie's young men!'

'Oh, why shouldn't she have some fun?' Adrianna said tolerantly. 'God knows, I can afford as many toy boys for her as she wants. She's worked so hard for us all.'

'My operations,' Sirje said, raising her hand to her throat and jawline. 'She was so wonderful. Never a word of anger. She just accepted me as I was and wouldn't let anyone else in the family say a nasty word to me. And now I can pay her back. *I'll* pay for her toy boys, Adri. God, how wonderful to have money to take care of Mummia! Remember when we promised ourselves we'd come to London and make our fortunes and finally Mummia would live like a queen? And now she can! This – ' she gestured around her, encompassing not just the lavish bedroom, but the entire world they were now inhabiting – 'this is crazy. Beyond our wildest dreams.'

'Beyond our wildest dreams,' Adrianna echoed tenderly.

It was a line from a film they had watched when they were young: it had become the sisters' catchphrase, invocation, mission statement. And now it had come true. Having finished her careful pinning, Adrianna draped the front section of the veil over her sister's face.

'You look beautiful,' she said contentedly. 'Even through a net curtain.'

Sirje giggled.

'I look good through a net curtain because I'm wearing as much make-up as a fucking stripper,' she said. 'Conway likes the hooker effect. I literally can't wear too much make-up for him. And he prefers when my hair looks dyed, too! I went to get really subtle streaks done – you know, that balayage thing, with the toning and highlights they paint on by hand? It looked fantastic. But he made me go straight back and get it all done one colour again, like a cheap whore with a packet of dye to cover the grey. He's such a cliché! I don't know how he stayed so long with his nice little country housewife.'

'Hey, I like Samantha very much,' Adrianna said reprovingly. 'She's a lady, which is more than you are, you slut.'

'Trust me, he never wanted a lady,' Sirje said wryly. 'Even if I hadn't had a dick, Liilia wouldn't have lasted long with him. She might look the part, but she's way too much of a good girl for Con. Did I tell you how I snagged him at your wedding? Jeffrey gave him a stern warning to stay away from Liilia, so he started to flirt with me instead, but more discreetly. So I thought, let's just go for it, and we sneaked away and found some shitty storage room and I blew him. It was filthy! I mean, literally,' she clarified. 'The floor was really dirty. Con *loved* it. Liilia was pissed off when I told her, but when she calmed down she did admit that she wouldn't want a guy who expected her to get down on her knees and blow him in storage rooms on a regular basis.'

'Wait, I didn't know that!' Adrianna exclaimed. 'Why did you never tell me?' She shook her head. 'God, my wedding day! By the time I got downstairs and we went in to dinner, I felt as if I'd run a marathon. So much family drama. And Jeffrey was far too exhausted to fuck me that night, so that was a happy ending.'

'Really? I didn't tell you about the blow job? I was sure I did!' Sirje said cheerfully. 'That's why I was late to dinner, didn't you wonder why? I got my dress dirty and I had to go back to my room and wash it and dry it with the hairdryer. It took forever.'

'I wouldn't have noticed if you'd come back in halfway through, riding on an elephant,' Adrianna said, remembering that evening. She had been in a state of intense relaxation after she and Bart had given each other head – which, as it turned out, seemed to have been the theme of the day. It had been the oddest experience, sitting at the top table, knowing how radiant she looked, glowing, and not just from world-class sex. For the first time in her life she was in love, and it showed.

Ironically, it was exactly how a bride should seem on her wedding day. The contrast between her and Jeffrey had been excruciating. Though slowly recovering, he still looked ashen, like his own death mask. She was very aware that their guests were excitedly speculating on what had happened between him and his new bride to turn him from the ecstatic groom of an hour before into an eighty-year-old teetering on the verge of the grave.

Well, she had thought cheerfully, *let them chatter and gossip all they want. God knows, it's nothing I caused. Jeffrey's made a complete mess of his family, and I'll do my best to straighten it out. But right now, I'm going to sit here and work my way through this amazing dinner. For once in my life, I'm not going to count calories.*

It had been a feast. The delicate *baccalà mantecato* on polenta squares, for which she had developed a real taste; the linguine with clams the size of her smallest fingernail, tiny and delicious, dripping with olive oil, garlic and parsley; the cold poached salmon and the *vitello tonnato*. This was finely sliced veal dressed with tuna mayonnaise, something that she had thought sounded appalling before she tried it, and which she had immediately loved.

It was insanely fattening. She was going to allow herself one serving, once a year. She had drunk white wine, first Tocai and then Grechetto, watching the guests with a smile on her face as cool as the alcohol, knowing herself to be entirely secure.

Jeffrey's children were scattered among the tables, kept apart by her carefully worked-out seating plan. Bella had duly spoken to Conway and Bart, informing them that there would be no announcement of the CEO role, while Charlotte, pleading food poisoning, was still in her room; so there was no tension when the after-dinner toasts concluded. Instead, Jeffrey, who had recovered to some degree, stood up and led Adrianna out onto the dance floor as the orchestra struck up a waltz.

The way he looked at his bride as they moved slowly over the tiled floor, Adrianna's strong arm around his waist half carrying his weight, made it clear to everyone present that, no matter what shock he had suffered post-ceremony, Jeffrey Sachs doted on his new young wife. Conway had followed, partnering Sirje, and Bart, very sweetly, had escorted Mrs Rootare to the dance floor. If Adrianna hadn't already known she loved Bart, the awareness would have flooded over her as she saw him waltzing with her mother, smiling down at her with as much admiration as if she were twenty-three-year-old Liilia with her new D-cup breasts and her skin as smooth as silk.

Bart had asked Bella to dance, since she was alone at the

wedding, but Adrianna had seen Bella shake her head, stand up and slip away. That was fine with Adrianna. Bella had kept up appearances by staying for the dinner, which was as much as she could expect in the circumstances.

She wondered whether the twin sisters would ever be able to reconcile. It was something on which even Adrianna could not speculate. She was so close to her two sisters, so loyal to them, as they were to her. She could not imagine ever betraying one of them the way Charlotte had done to Bella, nor how the relationship could possibly recover afterwards.

When, eventually, Bart led Adrianna out onto the dance floor, their bearing was impeccably neutral. No one, not even the most salacious of gossipmongers, would have thought for a moment that Jeffrey's bride and his younger son had just declared their love for each other while engaging in a passionate quickie in the marital bedroom. Bart was very deliberately proving to Adrianna that he could control himself in public, behave with utter decorum, act as the adult she would need him to be if they were to embark on a secret affair. She understood this completely, and her heart was singing at the awareness that he was able to summon up so much maturity for the woman he loved.

Now, standing behind Sirje on her wedding day, Adrianna shook her head in disbelief at the craziness of her own. That day, that bizarre, dramatic, beautiful day! She had ended it lying next to a snoring Jeffrey, but thinking of Bart: his eyes, his mouth, his body, his arms around her on the dance floor, his tongue making her come over and over again in that very room.

They had sworn they would make it work, and they had.

She did not have a single regret about any choice she had made in her life. How many women could say that?

'Oh, Sirje, you look so beautiful!' Mrs Rootare cooed, sweeping into the bedroom. 'So much make-up! But I know that's what Conway likes.'

Liilia was just behind her mother, dressed in the same flowing pale green that Adrianna was wearing, ankle-length, with matching shoulder corsages of white flowers. Their mother, in her smart hat and matching coat dress, was matron of honour, while Adrianna and Liilia would carry Sirje's train up the aisle of the village church. For all Conway and Sirje's taste for the wild party life, they had chosen not a beach wedding in Antibes, followed by an evening party lit by torches, with bare-chested waiters and scantily-clad waitresses bringing cocktails bubbling with dry ice, but the most conventional ceremony imaginable.

They would be compensating for it, however, when they headed off on their honeymoon in Ibiza. Conway, no longer restricted by the lifelong pressure of being his father's perfect son, had already lined up a highly recommended drug dealer and was eagerly looking forward to moving from VIP privé area to extremely discreet sex club to privé again, out of his mind on various substances, his beautiful wife beside him, more make-up on her face than clothes on her body, ready and willing to indulge in any kind of erotic activity that would keep her husband happy and satisfied.

The revelation that his father had made not Conway, the expected heir, CEO but Bella, had acted on him like a huge release. After an initial bout of fury, he had realized how much he would enjoy the freedom of no longer having to pretend to be someone he was not. Following his initial rush of partying, however, Adrianna was relying on Sirje to keep her husband under control. The CFO of Sachs could not be seen to be falling out of clubs, sweat-soaked and gurning, at 6 a.m. There were plenty of private, highly discreet members' only establishments where he and Sirje could let their hair down, and the couple would have to stick to those if they wanted Conway to keep his job.

'Time to go!' Mrs Rootare trilled, beaming from ear to ear. 'Two girls married so well in a year – how lucky I am! It's more than any mother could ever pray for! I don't know which one of you looked more lovely! Everything is ready, the carriages are waiting, it's like a fairy tale – the *carriages*! Pinch me, I must be dreaming! Oh, Sirje, I'm so happy for you! There's just one little thing I need to say—'

'I know, Mummia,' her daughter said, rising gracefully from the stool in front of the dressing table and shaking out her skirts. Her dress was full-skirted, antique white lace over the palest green fabric, but she had, on Adrianna's advice, eschewed a hoop. 'Adrianna's already had the conversation with me. I know what I'm taking on. Don't worry about me. Conway likes to be married – if he didn't, he wouldn't have proposed as soon as the divorce came through. He's like his father that way. He needs someone like me. Someone who likes to have a good time, let her hair down, not a boring housewife. Trust me, I know *exactly* what makes him happy! I'll be fine.'

Liilia permitted herself a little eye roll, for which Adrianna could not blame her. Liilia had unquestionably been the sister on whom Conway's eye had alighted first, and although she could tell herself that she was perfectly happy not to be marrying a man whose idea of a perfect honeymoon was sex, drugs, and orgiastic partying, it still couldn't help but rankle that Sirje had cut her out with an extremely handsome multimillionaire by dropping on her knees in front of him in a filthy kitchen storage room. Sirje's anatomy was a considerable consolation to her younger sister, as it meant that she could tell herself that things could never have worked out between her and Conway in any case, even if Sirje hadn't acted like a massive slut as soon as Liilia's back was turned.

'Good, good,' Mrs Rootare said in relief. 'You are a good sister, Adrianna. Now we just need to find someone for Liilia, and my work will be done!'

'And *you* can head off to Cannes to stay with Christie and see if her current toy boy has any friends!' her oldest daughter said teasingly.

Their mother's cheeks pinkened.

'Yes, Christie has asked me to visit her for a while,' she said with dignity. 'Two elderly ladies, enjoying the sunshine and a glass of wine by the sea at sunset . . .'

Her three daughters burst out laughing.

'Come on, Mummia! The two of you in leopard-skin bikinis, lying out on loungers at a beach bar on the Promenade des Anglais, watching the good-looking young men, more like!' Adrianna said as she and Liilia gathered up Sirje's train.

They had practised the train manoeuvre in advance, so they were able to follow the bride without a hitch as she proceeded graciously from the room and down the curved staircase to the main hall. Most of the wedding guests were waiting at the church, but the bridal party were gathered downstairs; they greeted the veiled bride in her flowing lace dress with flattering gasps and even a pattering of applause.

Samantha was there, naturally, looking after George and Emily, who were reprising their roles as bridesmaid and page-boy at their father's wedding. Samantha's fiancé, the younger son of a baronet, a childhood friend who had swooped in to console her after Conway's betrayal and stayed to propose to her as soon as he decently could, was staunchly by her side, dapper in his uniform of Major in the Horse Guards.

A male presence was not precisely required in this group, but it was what Samantha needed to be able to supervise her children with complete composure while watching a young Estonian woman in hooker make-up, the spitting image of the many Eastern Europeans with whom her husband had cheated on her, sweep off to become the second Mrs Conway Sachs. Even as she set a good example for George and Emily by politely smiling at the bride and telling her how beautiful she looked, Samantha took the dashing Major's hand for reassurance.

Beside Samantha, Charlotte was busying herself with Posy and Quant, ensuring that their outfits were as immaculate as always. She had lost a great deal of weight after the revelation about Ronaldo, or Lee. Painfully skinny, her cheeks so hollow they were almost gaunt, she was wearing too much pale-orange blusher to compensate, an error that she would never have made a year ago.

Charlotte was only too aware that people assumed her air of strain, her unflattering thinness, were due to her twin sister's being promoted over her to the top job at Sachs. It had been considered quite a controversial decision, since Charlotte's Sash chain had won a string of awards in the run-up to the announcement, while Bella's relaunch had seemingly been plagued with IT problems as bad as British Airways', the hacker cover story notwithstanding. At the time there had been a considerable outpouring of sympathy for Charlotte in the industry, but by now the general view was that Charlotte needed to deal with it and move on.

But that was exactly what she couldn't do: 'it', of course, was not what the world supposed. Not her disappointment at work, but the horror of finding out that she had been in a long-term sexual relationship with her half-brother. Ever since she had rushed to the bathroom in her father's suite to void her stomach, Charlotte had been unable to keep down food. She was existing on a regime of smoothies and protein shakes. It was as if Lee had put a curse on her.

Bella had observed that it was worse for Charlotte than for herself, and she had been right, because Lee had been real to Charlotte in a way he had never been to her sister. His courtship of Bella had been fake, but his relationship with Charlotte had been, as far as she had known, brutally honest from the very beginning. She had thought she knew everything about Lee, had accepted him for who he was, and the revelation that he had kept the most important secret of all from her had been a devastating blow.

Although Charlotte had behaved abominably to her siblings, there was one revelation she had spared her sister. Ronaldo/Lee, as Bella's investigator had found out, was not employed by a big Chicago advertising firm, but neither was he a travel consultant. That was merely his cover story. Ronaldo did circumnavigate the world very frequently, his services in high demand, but they were entirely sexual in nature.

When they met as adults and he informed Charlotte that he was a gigolo, she had accepted his job willingly, even eagerly; she had thought she was so sophisticated, so worldly, on a par with him, relishing the game of paying for sex – she, who could have any man she wanted for free. But Lee had always been ahead of her. She knew that now. They had never been equals. His game had been on a much higher level and played with more cruelty than she could ever have imagined. They had not been in touch since that last Skype conversation in her father and Adrianna's bathroom in Venice, but the memory of it was a knife to her gut which she couldn't pull out. It twisted constantly inside her.

'I'm surprised you're so upset!' Lee had said, his smile as smooth as ever, his face as handsome; after throwing up the entire contents of her stomach, she had been so dizzy and hysterical with dehydration, a headache pulsing at her temples, that she had almost expected to see devil horns sprouting from his forehead, his irises now red instead of velvety brown. 'You loved it freaky – isn't this just a bit more of the same?'

'Stop it!'

Charlotte, by the bath, had twisted frantically over the edge, feeling her insides knot tightly once again, but there was nothing left to come up. Behind her, she heard Lee laughing.

'And you loved paying for it!' he said. 'I knew you would!

I knew after that first time in your hotel, when I told you that was a freebie for old times' sake but from now on I'd need to charge. You should have seen your eyes light up! I suppose being a freak runs in the family, eh?'

Charlotte couldn't even cry. She had propped the phone on the sink surround, out of reach; she slumped back against the bath, exhausted, unable to do anything but let his words flow out.

'Seriously, you're the only client that actually loved being a client, you know that?' Lee was saying with great relish. 'You could lay out exactly what you wanted, and I'd have to go along with it if I wanted my money. You got way more of a kick out of paying for it than if we were just having an affair – be honest with yourself, you know it's true!'

It was true. She couldn't deny it. As soon as Lee had told her his profession, she had been thoroughly turned on by the idea, by having the ultimate control. She could specify what she wanted him to do, in what order, how fast, how slow; the words to speak, the games to play. Her imagination had run riot, and she had indulged it to the maximum. Lee had become her vice, her drug, her obsession.

The extra benefit of paying for it, she had quickly discovered, was that you could summon your gigolo whenever you wanted, as long as he didn't have a previous booking. You weren't dependent on a lover, with his own complicated schedule of work and family and leisure; you were dealing with a man whose job was to be completely available, who would fly to London at your expense just to wait in a bathroom in a conference hotel and fuck you over the sink like a cheap whore.

Well, Lee was the whore, not her. But God knew, he wasn't cheap.

'So, little sister, you know who I am now, and you know how to find me,' he said, grinning. 'I'm still available. I've got no problem with it if you don't! And you won't be happy for long with your vanilla sex at home with your doting hubby. Whenever you get bored, ring me, eh? I'll be ready and waiting for your call!'

This was unbearable. Summoning up the energy to lunge across the room, Charlotte grabbed the phone and turned it off. Her body was drenched with sweat. She was revolted by him, but even more so with herself. She collapsed back against the bathtub, dropping the phone next to her on the mat, and curled up in a ball, hugging her knees. Her brain was racing, turning over and over in a nightmare of circular thinking, of memories of everything she and Lee had done together. Memories that she was trying, and failing, to reclassify as disgusting, repulsive.

It hadn't worked. She still wanted Lee as much as ever. And she had confronted a terrible truth that day, one that was still consuming her. From then on, she would be struggling every single day with the temptation to hire his services just one more time . . .

Chapter Thirty-Six

Although the bride and groom had declined to spend the six figures required for the services of a cloud-bursting company, it had fortunately turned out to be unnecessary. The skies that morning were cerulean blue, barely a white wisp to be seen on the horizon, the sun beating down gloriously. By the time the open carriages bearing the bridal party reached the church, everyone was eager to cool off inside its stone walls. Mrs Rootare insisted Sirje pause by the lychgate so that she could lift her veil and dab at her forehead with pre-powdered rice paper tissues, ensuring her daughter was perfect on her big day.

As she preceded her down the aisle, Mrs Rootare's smile was even more beatific than it had been at Adrianna's wedding. *Two down, just one to go!*, she kept repeating happily to herself.

Posy and Quant followed with their flower baskets, having behaved so perfectly at Adrianna's wedding a year ago that they had been the natural choice to lead the petal-strewing procession today. Sadly, they were not the same happy, secure children they had been in Venice. Because ever since then, their mother had been odd, distant, troubled, and no longer the supremely confident being who had given them so much confidence in turn.

It was only too obvious that their father was distressed as he struggled to deal with the overnight change in his wife. Naturally, like everyone else, Paul was under the impression that Charlotte was suffering because she felt rejected by their father. Phrases like 'Electra complex' and 'childhood trauma syndrome' were in regular use in the St John's Wood house as Paul researched diligently on the Internet, desperate for his wife to go into therapy to help her recover from this crisis.

This was, of course, never going to happen. Charlotte was never going to share her story with a therapist. The mere thought of opening that can of worms made her want to punch herself in the stomach with both fists. She had rejected poor Paul's perfectly reasonable suggestion with so much revulsion that it had opened a rift between them. Not only that: without Lee as a much-needed safety valve letting off steam from the faux-perfection of her domestic life, Charlotte was continually cranky and irritable.

With all of this stress at home, her children were no longer the delightful flower-bearers with exquisite posture that they had been in Venice. Posy and Quant's expressions were sulky, their shoulders hunched, and as they shuffled sullenly down the aisle, dragging their feet, they did not scatter the petals but flung them as far away from them as possible, as if they were handfuls of toxic waste.

Bella watched the children slouch into the pew beside their father, dropping their empty baskets noisily to the stone floor. Paul frowned at them, but Charlotte seemed oblivious to Posy and Quant's poor behaviour. Staring straight ahead of her, she looked, as always these days, as if she were being strapped to a rack and slowly pulled apart.

Though Bella knew she could never really trust Charlotte again, the sight of her sister's suffering over the past year had brought her to a calmer place, even some sort of forgiveness. Not knowing the full story, Bella assumed that Charlotte had been genuinely in love with Ronaldo, and had not only had her heart broken but her life upended by the revelation that he was their half-brother. No wonder she had wasted away to skin and bone.

Looking at Charlotte, who was so obviously struggling with the burden of a secret that she couldn't possibly share with her husband, Bella wondered, as she often did, whether Charlotte had confronted her lover about his true identity. The sisters had never talked about it, and never would. But Bella had to admit to a deep curiosity as to what, if anything, had been said between Charlotte and their half-brother. Bella herself had been unable to resist texting Ronaldo, horrified at what he had done, and needing some sort of closure. All she had got in return was a few lines:

Look, the guy you thought you knew never existed. I've been all sorts of men for all sorts of women for years now and I like it like that. Don't get in touch with me any more, little sister. It won't do you any good.

You were really nice to me when we were kids. I'm sorry I did this to you.

Bella had puzzled over these words for weeks, but she had taken his advice not to push for any more answers, and gradually they had faded from the prominence they had once occupied. Especially as she had to focus on making the brutally difficult decision to switch off Thomas's life support.

There had been a particular kind of guilt to the task, because it was, of course, so horribly convenient for her. Mrs Rootare and Christie had both been with Bella at the hospital when she signed the paperwork and stood by Thomas's bed as it happened, and she was more grateful to them than she could say. She had left for the south of France with her mother that evening, staying with her for a couple of weeks, Brice banished from the house so that Christie and Bella could have proper mother–daughter time together. It had been a complete rest cure, as Adrianna had advised: nothing to do but swim, drive along the coast to Nice or Monte Carlo or Juan-les-Pins for leisurely meals, sleep, and then wake up to another day of relaxation.

When Bella was ready, she had returned to London and experienced another cure: the distraction of throwing herself into the complex demands of the CEO position. She had not expected the third and final cure, the man who was currently sitting beside her in the church pew.

On taking over as CEO, Bella had asked Nita to book her in for fundraisers and charity events twice a week so that she could network, feeling she had neglected this aspect of the job before. There was another motive, too: Thomas had kept her fairly isolated since her marriage, so that she did not have close friends to turn to for a social life.

Under normal circumstances, she would have been leaning on her twin sister for comfort and support, but that was out of the question. So making herself dress up every so often, postponing her return to an empty house by having drinks and dinner with a pleasant group of fellow professionals, had done her the world of good.

She had met Santino del'Aquila, the celebrity restaurateur, six months ago at a charity dinner. Santino was a widower himself, bringing up three young boys as a single father. Although his and Bella's circumstances were very different, they had fallen into conversation about their deceased spouses and their experience of grief. The last thing on Bella's mind had been a new relationship, which was one of the reasons why Santino had found himself so attracted to her. After a brief flirtation with a D-lister on the reality show *Celebrity Island Survivor*, he had told the press in interviews that he was ready, after several years of widowhood, to start dating again. Ever since then, women had been throwing themselves at him in droves.

But not Bella. Quite the reverse: it had been Santino who had courted her. The women who had been chasing him had been status-hungry, their goal not just him but the publicity they would attract by being seen on his arm. Dating him would raise their profiles, propelling them higher up the gossip columns. While Bella Sachs, dedicated to her career, infinitely richer than him, needed neither fame nor fortune. What he *could* offer her, he had gradually realized, was a shoulder to cry on after the painful decision she had had to make.

Like so many men, Santino loved to be needed by a woman. And he found, as time passed, that, increasingly, he needed Bella too. They talked about what had worked in their previous marriages, and, even more importantly, what had not. Both of them had married comparatively young; both felt that they had learned so much since then. Each admitted to the other that, much as they had loved their spouses, they might not have picked them again if they met them now.

Because Ilaria, Santino's wife, had been sweet-natured but almost cripplingly shy. Too reserved, too limelight-shunning to be a good match for a very gregarious chef and restaurant owner. With the best will in the world, this had caused increasing friction between them. Bella, though quieter than the exuberant Santino, was entirely comfortable in the world he inhabited, a much better match for him. He realized that a while before Bella did, and, over the course of a few months, as they went to dinner, to the theatre and to concerts, he worked at convincing her that the two of them would make an excellent couple.

From there, it had been another short step to verifying that they were very happily sexually compatible; thence to Santino introducing Bella to his adorable sons and Bella inviting him to her brother's wedding. It was very new, and there were no guarantees in life, but dashingly handsome, family-oriented Santino, with his bronzed skin and strong-boned Sardinian good looks, was making Bella so happy and satisfied that she could not stop sneaking glances at him, squeezing his hand, sneaking kisses whenever she could. He made her feel silly, spontaneous and youthful, and as a CEO with the weight of running a multinational company on her shoulders, that was exactly what she needed.

Sirje and Conway were speaking their vows now, beaming at each other. It was ironic that Conway's children, sitting beside their mother in the front pew, were behaving better than Posy and Quant, who were pinching each other and kicking the pew in front of them.

Santino, an Italian father whose idea of disciplining children was to let them run amok until they crossed an arbitrary line, at which point he would yell furiously at them, smiled at the children much more tolerantly than their own father did. Poor Paul was tense with mortification, hissing reproofs at them which they were deliberately ignoring. In their eyes, their father was a failure. He couldn't make their adored mother the happy person she had been up until a year ago, so why should they listen to him?

Adrianna, sitting next to Bella, noticed Santino's affectionate glance at a pair of sulky, badly behaved children who weren't even his, and was confirmed in her instincts that Bella's boyfriend was husband material. Bella would definitely pop out a couple of children as well as taking on Santino's boys: they had more than enough resources to run a large family while the parents worked.

Thank God things worked out so well for Bella, Adrianna thought. If Thomas were still alive, according to Tania, Bella would have no chance at a family. Tania had described Thomas as an over-controlling father figure who had not wanted his wife to have children, since that would distract her from catering to his every need.

I can't think how Bella could possibly have picked such a selfish older man to marry! Adrianna thought with the ghost of a smile, remembering her husband with affection, but no illusions about who he had been. Jeffrey had needed children to form his dynasty, but he had not engaged with them in any meaningful way. They had merely been game pieces to move around on his chessboard, living carriers of his DNA.

And that emotional neglect of his children had, in his widow's opinion, fatally shortened his life. He had never truly recovered from the revelation that his bastard son had had sex with both of his daughters, something that could never have happened if he had dealt with the situation more honestly, rather than sweeping his son under the carpet like a dirty little secret.

Everyone thought I was going to fuck Jeffrey to death and he'd die happy, Adrianna reflected. *But it was his own family who weakened his heart so that one day, just a few months after we were married, he never woke up.*

She had slipped out of bed at 6 a.m. that morning and gone to the gym, as was her daily routine. She would never know whether her husband had been dead by then, or if he had passed away in his sleep while she was working out. One last lost opportunity for Jeffrey to lick the perspiration off her skin; poor Jeffrey, it had been a hardcore workout with her trainer that morning, and he would have loved to watch her peel off her exercise clothes and offer him her extremely sweaty body to worship.

He had, however, looked serene and peaceful in his last and longest sleep. To Adrianna's surprise, tears of mourning had sprung to her eyes as she looked down at her husband. And then she wasn't surprised at all. Jeffrey had been nothing but wonderful to her. He had done justice to her intelligence in his will, leaving her a fantastically rich woman with a seat on the governing board of the Sachs organization and a significant stake in the business. He had trusted her implicitly, and he had been right to do so.

Tania had agreed to continue as her assistant, though Adrianna had entirely redecorated her husband's office. It wasn't remotely her taste, and besides, it would have been ridiculous for her to sit on a throne when Jeffrey's daughter was now the CEO. Bella had chosen to stay in her own cosy executive suite: her style as the boss of the Sachs Organization would be much more accessible, she had decided, than her father's terrifyingly intimidating management style and near-medieval decor.

So Adrianna had taken down the wall between Tania's exterior office and Jeffrey's throne room, exposed the windows that his Gothic panelling had blocked, and stripped out the chandelier, the dais and the throne. Now the two women shared a modern, beautifully decorated open-plan office full of light and art.

Tania was at the wedding, of course, sitting further back in the church with her wife and sons. But it was Bart, his brother's best man, standing to one side of the altar with his hands folded in front of him, listening respectfully to the end of the wedding ceremony, on whom Adrianna's eyes settled as Conway lifted Sirje's veil to reveal her beautiful face, the groom seeming delighted that his new spouse was made up like a dancer in a nightclub rather than a bride at a daytime ceremony in a village church.

As attuned to Adrianna as she was to him, Bart was instantly aware of her gaze. He met it with his own, a happy, fully contented acknowledgement of their attachment that was a sea change from the wild, partying Bart of a year ago.

They exchanged a smile before Adrianna looked back to Sirje and Conway, and was taken aback to see them kissing passionately.

At least Sirje had the decency to raise her hands and lightly ease Conway away as soon as he tried to prolong it beyond what was suitable, out of respect for his ex-wife and children sitting in one of the front pews. Then, much to Adrianna's approval, Sirje held out her hands to George and Emily. After a swift glance at their mother, who nodded, they went very willingly to hug their father and new step-mother.

The handsome groom and gorgeous bride, flanked by the groom's small children, holding hands in a family chain, were walking down the aisle to sign the register in a niche by the doors; the little village church was too small to have a vestry. Liilia darted out to pick up Sirje's train, and Adrianna let her do it alone. The task didn't require two bridesmaids, and she wanted a moment to herself. The vicar followed, together with Mrs Rootare and Christie, who were the witnesses, a verger bustling ahead to open the church doors.

Sunlight poured in over the flagstones. The wedding guests stood up, stretched their legs, started to head for the door as they chatted happily about how lovely the ceremony had been, how attractive a couple they made, how nice it was that Conway's children were here. In lower tones, they commented that these things could be so difficult, couldn't they? So how lovely it was that everyone was behaving so well . . . Samantha certainly seemed happy, which was wonderful, considering . . .

Gradually, the church emptied out. Bella and Santino,

hand in hand, wandered down the aisle, smiling at each other with the dizzy delight of lovers at a wedding who see their way, perhaps, to the prospect of their own. Charlotte and Paul marshalled Posy and Quant, keeping them separate, as the children were now squabbling, and bustled them out, their faces tired and strained. Bella looked back, hearing the scuffle, and impulsively asked Santino to go on ahead with Paul and the kids so that she could have a word with her sister.

'You look awful,' she said frankly to Charlotte, pulling her aside.

'I know. And *you've* got a lot blunter since you became CEO,' Charlotte said with a skewed attempt at a wry smile.

'I suppose I have,' Bella said, guiding her sister out of the church and down a side path. Just a few steps into the small garden, but enough distance so that no one could hear what they were saying.

'You're right to be like that,' Charlotte observed. 'It was time to get serious, make sure that no one can take advantage of you.'

She gave that awful half-smile again.

'Like me.'

'Lottie, that's exactly what I wanted to say to you. It's time to leave the past behind us,' Bella said. 'We should be drinking champagne and toasting the bride and groom. Having good thoughts and good memories.'

How often had Bella repeated those words of Mrs Rootare's to herself! How often had they helped her! Charlotte looked truly taken aback, not only by the familiar sisterly shortening of her name, but at Bella's words, the philosophy of a tough Eastern European matriarch with no illusions about the shortness of life and the need to plough through it as well as possible.

'Do you actually mean that?' she asked, with more uncertainty than Bella had ever heard from her sister before.

'Yes,' Bella said simply. 'I can't forget what you did, but I can put it behind me.'

'I never thought you'd say that,' Charlotte muttered. 'After everything I did . . .'

'Lottie, look at me. I'm happier than I've ever been,' Bella said. 'Really happy, not the fake trance I was in with . . . him.'

Charlotte nodded very swiftly. Neither sister wanted to say his name.

'And I wouldn't have this if you hadn't . . . done what you did,' Bella continued. 'I would still be with Thomas. That wasn't living. It was just existence. What you did broke me free.'

Charlotte looked dumbstruck. Underneath the pale-orange blusher, her cheeks flushed with a healthier colour.

'You're not just saying that?' she asked. 'To make me feel better?'

'Why would I do *that*?' Bella said, and the words came out sardonically, because that was how she had meant them.

Charlotte's eyes went wide and she nodded slowly.

'Well, yes, good point,' she acknowledged. 'Why would you do that?'

She drew in a long breath.

'You need to pull yourself together now,' Bella said, channelling Mrs Rootare with everything she had. 'Your husband looks like shit and your kids are acting up really badly. You can't afford to lose Paul. He's an amazing man and he looks like you've been putting him through the wars. You need to get on with your life and leave the past behind.'

'You really *have* changed,' Charlotte said, with considerable respect.

'Yes, I have,' Bella agreed. 'And it's partly thanks to you. In the worst way possible, you did me a weird kind of favour. So you can at least stop feeling guilty about me, okay? I wouldn't be with Santino if it weren't for . . . what you did. And I'm happier now than I've ever been in my life.'

It was no more than the truth, and it seemed, to some degree, to have set Charlotte free. Her eyes were brighter; she pulled back her shoulders, standing up straighter.

'Will you come round sometime?' she asked, almost shyly. 'We could have a dinner for you and Santino. It would be nice to get to know him.'

'Maybe,' Bella said. 'Probably. Let's see how we go.'

She had not been planning to do it, but she found herself reaching out and hugging her twin. Charlotte was as stiff as a board for a moment, and then everything yielded, and she fell against Bella, collapsing into her arms. Bella winced at how bony her sister had become.

'You need to eat something,' she said into Charlotte's hair. 'You need to sit down at this big wedding lunch and eat everything they put in front of you.'

'I'll try,' Charlotte said, sounding as if she were on the verge of tears. 'I'll try, Bell. I know I need to.'

'And don't cry! Don't you dare cry! Get it together! Good thoughts and good memories!'

Bella pulled back, looking sternly into her sister's face. Charlotte swallowed hard, putting a finger to each eye in the classic gesture with which women dab away moisture without ruining their make-up.

'Bella? *Cara*, the carriages are waiting!' Santino called from the lychgate.

'We're coming!'

Bella took her twin's arm and they walked down the path to the waiting group. Posy and Quant were by a gravestone, taking turns to kick it: clearly they were malevolently, deliberately scuffing their polished shoes.

'Posy! Quant! What are you *doing*?' their mother shouted, and they both jumped in the air with shock, turning round to see her bearing down on them. 'Someone's *buried* there! Have some respect, both of you! Your behaviour today has been *appalling*. Pull yourselves together right now, or I'm taking you straight home and you won't get any wedding cake!'

Posy looked stunned: Quant burst into tears.

'Oh, stop it,' Charlotte snapped. 'Cut the waterworks, they don't impress me. And listen to your father! He's been trying to keep you two in line all day and you've been completely ignoring him.'

Paul, who had been talking to Santino by the gate, turned on hearing these words, looking as taken aback as the children. Charlotte grabbed her daughter and son and frogmarched them down the rest of the path, taking no notice of Quant's snivelling.

'You have a rest,' she said to her husband. 'I'll take over from here. Sorry I've been a bit MIA, but I'm back now.'

She bustled the children through the gate and to their assigned carriage. Paul's astonished eyes met Bella's, and he mouthed 'Thank you!' at his sister-in-law, correctly associating her with his wife's return to the no-nonsense mother she had been until recently. Bella smiled at him. She had given Charlotte some much-needed relief, but at no cost to herself; all Bella had done was tell the truth, something that had been in short supply in their family.

Bella hadn't made any concessions. She hadn't promised forgiveness she wasn't sure she could give; she had been honest about the fact that she could never forget. Trust would never be taken for granted between the twin sisters. But the air was clear now, and they could both breathe much better.

Mrs Rootare really should teach self-help seminars, Bella thought as she strolled down the church path. *She'd make an absolute fortune.*

Chapter Thirty-Seven

Adrianna and Bart were the last to leave the church, Adrianna hanging back by the altar, watching the congregants leave with the quiet satisfaction of someone who has organized a wedding which has gone off without a single hitch so far. She was completely aware of Bart, however. She knew when he came up behind her, not quite touching her but close enough that she could feel first the heat of his body and then his breath on her neck.

'We need to do this too,' he said.

'Not yet,' she said, still looking ahead. 'We have to wait at least a year. At *least* a year.'

He sighed gloomily.

'I know. But as soon as we can, decently.'

'Decently,' she agreed. 'It's much sooner than we could have hoped.'

'I know,' he said. 'Poor old Pa. It was hard watching him at the end. I felt bad, because of course I wanted to be with you, so my motives were messy, but he went downhill very fast. He never got over . . . you know. Couldn't see either one of the girls without looking as if he was going to have a heart attack.'

Adrianna nodded. She had been curious as to whether Ronaldo was mentioned in Jeffrey's will; he hadn't been, though a generous sum had been settled on Maria, who had promptly retired, much to Adrianna's relief. Adrianna had made discreet enquiries of the solicitor and discovered that the trust fund Jeffrey had drawn up for Ronaldo would continue for life. Normally she would have considered it her duty to do something more for her husband's illegitimate and unacknowledged son – the solicitor had suggested a lump sum payment in return for a confidentiality agreement – but under the circumstances, it had been an easy decision to let that one go.

'It was a release for Jeffrey, I agree,' she said. 'But we still have to be respectful, for the family's sake. For the reputation of the business, too.'

'I'm just sick of all the sneaking around,' Bart said, sounding as sulky as a ten-year-old. 'It was fun at first, but it got boring much faster than I thought it would.'

'Listen to you!' she said, a smile in her voice. 'Always keen on something when you can't have it!'

'That's not fair,' Bart said reproachfully. 'I have you a *lot*, and I still want you.'

She allowed herself a little laugh. There was no one left in the small village church but them; it had quickly emptied out. Charming as it was, it had no pretensions to grandeur. The carriages and a small fleet of cars were waiting to take the inner circle of guests to Vanbrugh Manor for a lunchtime reception, then back to their hotels to rest and change clothes. After a break of a few hours, several hundred guests would descend on Vanbrugh for early evening drinks, dinner and dancing till dawn.

The house, like the church, would not accommodate such a large party. But Adrianna had hired, not a marquee, which for the truly rich was now passé, but a giant glass greenhouse at a six-figure cost. It had been installed on the Great Lawn yesterday, and was entirely weatherproof, with blossoming trees in enormous pots wheeled in to give the interior the appearance of an orchard in full flower. Even the rented portaloos were so top-of-the-range that they had carpeted floors and their own dressing rooms, with porcelain sinks, full-length mirrors and oak fittings.

'It's going to be a wonderful party,' Bart said, his hand lightly touching the back of his stepmother's waist, where no one could see. 'You've done a superb job.'

'Ugh! If I get married again. *If*,' she said to the open doors, 'I don't want any fuss and I don't want to waste any more money. The toilets alone are costing me nearly seven thousand pounds! I want to elope to a beach somewhere in a bikini, with a flower in my hair.'

'Duly noted,' Bart said. 'A warm beach, right? I mean, not Iceland. Bit cold for the bikini. You'd have to wear it with wellies.'

'Maybe we could hire the Blue Lagoon,' she said. 'Have it to ourselves, and then send the priest and the witnesses away and have a lovely swim afterwards.'

'Sounds fantastic,' he agreed. 'I'll get my team right on it.'

'Your *team*?' she said as derisively as he had known she would. 'You don't have a *team*! You don't have anyone, not since I sacked those models of yours who used to do their nails all day!'

'Only when they weren't blowing me,' Bart said. 'Which, to be fair, was an essential part of their job. I made that very clear during the initial round of interviews.'

She snorted.

'Oh well,' she said. 'Now I do it for you for free. Just one of my many cost-efficient savings for the company.'

She started to walk towards the doors, and he came up beside her, side by side, his shoulder brushing hers.

'I like walking next to you,' he said casually. 'In step, like proper partners. Shoulder to shoulder against the world. Spartan warriors in pairs.'

'You're ridiculous,' she said. 'And we're not partners. You will have to sign a huge prenup before we get married, promising not to get a penny from me if things go wrong.'

'Please!' Bart held up his hands. 'You run things! I'm very happy for you to wear the trousers! But you know that.'

They emerged into the sunshine, blinking at the bright light. Bart reached for the sunglasses tucked into his jacket pocket. Liilia was arranging Sirje's train in the first carriage; Posy and Quant were being shepherded into the second one by their mother. Adrianna, who noticed everything, raised her eyebrows. So finally Charlotte was bothering with her own children, rather than leaving everything to Paul. Posy and Quant looked considerably more subdued than they had been earlier, while Paul was actually laughing as he joined his wife.

Something had clearly altered for the better. Adrianna determined to find out what it had been; she liked to know everything that went on around her. Meanwhile, Bella, being helped chivalrously into the third carriage by Santino, gestured to Adrianna to take her assigned place with them.

'How do you feel about walking back to the house with me?' Bart proposed. 'Lovely day for a stroll down the village lanes, arm in arm, shoulder to shoulder . . . you're fine in those shoes, right?'

Since Jeffrey's death, Adrianna had taken to wearing flats. After years of wearing the spike heels without which a certain type of man would not be interested in her, she was relishing being able to run around easily rather than pick her way along while pretending that she loved being handicapped by five-inch stilettos.

'Yes,' she said with her usual efficiency, waving at Bella to go on without her.

The first carriage was pulling away, hooves clip-clopping on the cobbled road. Bella waved back and took her seat, watching her brother and stepmother standing together as the driver shook the reins for the horses to start moving. The look in Bella's eyes had been there for a month or so; it acknowledged her dawning realization that Adrianna and Bart had quietly, discreetly, become a couple. Bella, it was clear, was amused by the fact that Adrianna was entranced by the man she had described a year ago as a charmer not fit to run a public toilet.

But who cares! Not everyone needs to be able to run things! Adrianna thought. *I can do that well enough for both of us! And besides, this way our egos don't clash.*

'You don't need to rush back, do you?' Bart was saying.

'Oh no,' she assured him. 'Everything's ready for us at

Vanbrugh. They don't need me to be back there running things. That would be poor management. You wouldn't know, of course,' she added with a superior air, 'but good management is to empower your staff so they can run things on their own. Besides, I've been sitting still too much today, getting my hair and make-up done – it would be great to stretch my legs.'

'Please don't!' Bart said. 'They're quite long enough. I'm glad you've stopped wearing heels. They made me feel emasculated.'

Adrianna burst out laughing, such a full-throated, happy laugh that the rest of the guests looked back to see what the joke was.

'I'd *love* to see what would actually make you feel emasculated,' she said, placing one hand on his arm and catching up the hem of her ankle-length dress with the other so that her legs could move freely, her long strides matching Bart's.

'Oh God,' Bart said. 'You're going to take that as a challenge, aren't you?'

It was the first week in June. Rambling roses rioted everywhere, and the honeysuckle trained over trellises on top of the low stone walls bordering the cottages was still rich and fragrant. As they passed through the village, the hedgerows that lined the road back to Vanbrugh Manor were as green as grass, bumblebees swarming in the meadows beyond. The limousines began to slide past them, very slowly, their speed constrained by the horse-drawn carriages leading the procession.

The road stretched out before the two of them. Summer was on its way, and the skies were blue as the waters off

Gozo. The good weather wouldn't last, of course. It never did. But for stepson and stepmother, almost the same height, walking in perfect sync, strolling back to a wonderful party, able to be an acknowledged couple much sooner than they could have imagined, this day felt as if it could last forever. As if they were cloud bursters themselves, and could reach up to every cloud in the sky, exploding them one by one with just the touch of a finger.

Acknowledgements

Huge thanks to:

The amazing double team of my editor Wayne Brookes and Amanda Preston, whom I trust so much that, when thrashing out a *very* important plot point, I pretty much sat back and let them fight it out – and doing edits, it was so clear they'd reached the right decision! I am so lucky to have them on my side.

All the lovely people at Pan Macmillan, who are doing such a fantastic job with my books – Jeremy Trevathan, Alex Saunders, Stuart Dwyer and James Annal, thanks so much for everything you do to support me.

Ed PR did a particularly cracking job with my last book, *Killer Affair* – really looking forward to working with them on this one!

Dan Evans at Plan 9 does such a superb job with my website and business cards that you should all use him for yours.

Darling Matt B, my reading twin, as always, for all his help, support and loans of Eleanor Burford/Philippa Carr/Jean Plaidy/Kathleen Kellow/Anna Percival/Elbur Ford books!

The gorgeous team of McKenna Jordan and John Kwiatkowski, and everyone at Murder By The Book, for bringing my smut to Texas.

Cornelia Read, for the best placement *ever* of one of my books! She knows where! Plus Alafair Burke, McKenna again, and Sarah Weinman for being the best gay piano bar companions I could imagine . . .

I've been wanting to use Katherine Walsh's story of getting her hair done before an emergency meeting ever since she told it to me years ago, and finally I have.

Michael Devine again, for knowing about Imperial London yellow stocks. Mine of knowledge!

Nicole Belskis for checking my French and finding Anne-Charlotte Le Diot to give me 'les bijoux de famille' for 'family jewels'.

Ellen Clair Lamb for naming Posy and Quant.

Hannah Haq for suggesting hemp milk.

Joe Beck and Angie Kinsey for services to troll-fighting.

Michael Coggin-Carr for confirming that General Lee is mentioned in *Gone with the Wind*.

Alice Taylor for 'Basingstoke' as a great safe word.

Laura Lippman for giving me Casa Dragones Joven as one of the best tequilas available to humanity. And, together with Greg Herren, for being such great friends and mutual venting partners!

Chloe Saxby, because she is my Bad Twin and because she was the inspiration for the scene where Charlotte is appalled by not having a menu in an NHS hospital.

I couldn't have written this book without the Rebecca Chance fanfriends on Facebook and Twitter cheering me up with delightful banter! The list has got too long to put here now, but I'm so grateful to all of you for making social media such a pleasure and a delightful distraction.

The Board and the FLs of FB, the best work colleagues I could imagine.

And Countess Luann. Who is never uncool.

Mile High
by
Rebecca Chance

First class can be murder . . .

Pure Air's new LuxeLiner is flying from London to LA – on
its inaugural journey – with a first-class cabin packed with
A-list celebrities. As the feuding crew compete to impress
their famous passengers, the handsome pilot tries to win the
attention of a pretty young stewardess.

    But one VIP singer is battling something seriously sinis-
ter: watching her every step is a very determined stalker,
someone who will go to any lengths to get the star to satisfy
their desires. At thirty thousand feet there is nowhere to run,
and nowhere to hide . . .

Killer Diamonds

by
Rebecca Chance

They're to die for . . .

When Oscar-winning beauty Vivienne Winter decides to auction her multimillion-dollar jewellery collection for charity, there's no shortage of people eager to buy a piece of her incredible history.

Young, ambitious Christine Smith is a jewellery expert working for a centuries-old auction house. She's desperate to secure the sale of Vivienne Winter's gem collection, set to be the biggest auction since Elizabeth Taylor's. However, meeting the Hollywood star is just the first hurdle Christine has to jump.

Vivienne's spoilt and sexy playboy grandson, Angel, is the heir to her fortune. The anger and resentment he feels towards his grandmother for selling what he believes to be his inheritance sets in motion a series of events with deadly consequences. Angel is totally unscrupulous, and family secrets cut sharper than diamonds . . .

Killer Affair
by
Rebecca Chance

A shocking betrayal deserves a wicked revenge . . .

Stunning, charismatic Lexy O'Brien is the reigning queen of
British reality TV. Her life in front of the camera is planned
and manipulated as successfully as any military assault.

But success breeds jealousy. When you're on top, the only
way is down – and there's always someone standing by to
give you a shove . . .

Dowdy Caroline Evans, a part-time blogger and writer of
erotic fiction, is brought in to chronicle Lexy's life. Being
taken under Lexy's wing is a dream come true for Caroline.
But sampling the star's lifestyle is like tasting the most
addictive of drugs, and it's not long before she's craving what
she can't possibly have – or can she?

As Caroline and Lexy's lives and loves become increasingly entwined, it's only a matter of time before the hidden
rivalry becomes a powder keg waiting to explode . . .

extracts reading groups
competitions books new
discounts extracts
competitions extracts
books new discounts
events extracts reading groups
extracts books events
new titles reading groups
interviews
books events extracts
discounts
new books events
events new

extracts events reading groups
competitions books extracts new